ANG LARAWAN

From Stage to Screen

Anvil Publishing

Ang Larawan From Stage to Screen

Copyright © 2017
Culturtain Musicat Productions Inc.

All rights reserved. No part of this book may be reproduced in any form or by any means without the written permission of the copyright owner and the publisher.

Published and exclusively distributed by
ANVIL PUBLISHING, INC.
7th Floor Quad Alpha Centrum
125 Pioneer Street, Mandaluyong City
1550 Philippines
Trunk Lines: (+632) 477-4752, 477-4755 to 57
Sales and Marketing: sales@anvilpublishing.com
Fax No.: (+632) 747-1622
www.anvilpublishing.com

Book design by Clara Gallardo and Benjor Catindig (cover),
             Benjor Catindig, and Micah Castañeda (inside pages)
Cover photo by Jojit Lorenzo

www.anglarawan.com

ISBN 978-621-420-229-4

Printed in the Philippines

10 9 8 7 6 5 4 3 2 1

TABLE OF CONTENTS

Foreword by Bienvenido Lumbera	5
Introduction by Lourd de Veyra	6
A Portrait of the Artist as Filipino	15
Last Conversation with a Master Director	172
Folio: *Ang Larawan, The Musical*	177
Libretto of *Ang Larawan, The Musical*	185
Afterword	278
Folio: *Ang Larawan, The Movie*	281
Screenplay of *Ang Larawan, The Movie*	289
Learning Guide for *Ang Larawan, The Movie*	364
Acknowledgments	366

FOREWORD

SI NICK JOAQUIN AT ANG UGNAY SA NAKARAAN NG KASALUKUYAN

May tungkulin ang artista sa kasalukuyan, ayon kay Nick Joaquin. Kailangang pasanin niya ang nakaraan upang mabigyan ng kabuluhan ang kasalukuyan. Nangangahulugan ito na ang kulturang nabuo noon ay dapat tangkilikin bilang pamana, na makagagabay sa bayan tungo sa hinaharap. Kinakatawan ni Tony ang henerasyong umaayon sa bagong kultura na dala ng mga mananakop na Amerikano. Pansinin na ang takbo ng buhay niya ay nakabatay sa madaliang pagsunggab sa bawat pagkakataon na makaaahon sa kaniya sa kahirapan. Kuwarta ang nagtatakda ng kaniyang mga hangarin sa loob ng pamamahay ng mga Marasigan: para sa kaniya ang pinta ni Don Lorenzo ay nangangahulugan ng komisyong kaniyang makukuha kung ang likha ng don ay mapagbili. Para sa magkapatid na Candida at Paula, ang pamana ng kanilang ama ay kailangang maangkin at handa silang magpakahirap upang iyon ay manatiling kanila. Subalit ang pista ng La Naval na tila nakalutas sa kanilang problema ay pansamantalang solusyon lamang. Lumabas ng silid si Don Lorenzo Marasigan upang maging bahagi ng pagbati sa Birhen ng La Naval. Malinaw na ang masayang pagtitipon ng mga labi ng kahapon ay pansamantalang resolusyon ng dula. Ang digmaang Pasipiko ay deux ex makinang inimbento ni Joaquin upang patingkarin pang lalo ang malumbay na kapalaran ng kaniyang magkapatid na tauhan. Sa pagsiklab ng digmaan tila nalutas ang problema nina Candida at Paula. Pero ang katotohanan ay binuksan lamang ni Joaquin ang isang bagong panahon ng pakikibaka ng mga Filipino sa paghahanap ng kulturang gagabay sa kanilang paglalakbay bilang bayang naggigiit sa identidad nito bilang malayang sambayanan. Kapansin-pansin na hindi ilustradong pintor na galing sa panahon ng Rebolusyon 1898 ang lilikha ng bagong Retrato del Artista kundi isang karaniwang peryodista-artista ang pumapasan sa kultura ng kahapon sa paglikha ng bagong Larawan. Narito ang buod ng huling pangungusap sa dula ni Joaquin: *To remember and to sing, that is my vocation.*

Bienvenido Lumbera
National Artist for Literature

INTRODUCTION

YOU AND NICK AGAINST THE WORLD: A PORTRAIT OF "PORTRAIT" IN THREE PORTRAITS (Or 25 Reasons Why You Must Read *A Portrait of the Artist as Filipino*—No. 23 Will Make You Cry, I Think)

1. To things we hold most dear we ascribe nicknames. So it is lovingly referrred to as "Portrait" the way we abbreviate the *Noli* and the *Fili*. Thankfully I have yet to hear of anyone reducing it to what would sound like—at least to Filipino ears—a rather inelegant acronym, or someone about to cough out a swear word: APOTAAF.

2. Nick Joaquin's *A Portrait of the Artist as Filipino*, which was first serialized in *Women's Weekly Magazine* in 1952, is one of Philippine literature's enduring works. By the time of its publication, Joaquin, at only age 33, was already a literary rockstar. Says the biography penned by his nephew, prior to *Portrait*, Nick Joaquin had never written a play and it was only upon the prompting of his sister-in-law Sarah. Not bad for a first-timer. Kinda like Orson Welles, who makes his first film and, oh, look, it just happened to become the most influential movie of all time.

3. You could run a finger across the words "Portrait of the Artist as Filipino" and get a thick dusty clump on your fingertip. Aging spinsters? Bedridden painters (bedridden *and invisible*, depending on which version you watched)? They're not usually cast as lead characters unless they're stabbing each other to death or are actually winged superheroines in mild-mannered disguise. Perhaps for the Millennials of today, it would be interesting to ask: what is the significance of *Portrait* to their manic-click-and-share lives? How would it fit into their instant-gratification, five-thousand-frames-per-minute-140-character- attention span, this generation for whom any online video over three minutes is usually an epic and anything over two pages on the computer screen is Proust's *In Search of Lost Time*? How does it stand in the age of dissonance, memes, fake news, and covfefe? Apart from Instagram fodder for students in the National Museum re-enacting the tableaux of dead gladiators, what else is the significance of the Spoliarium— unless given a new reading to reflect the escalating iconographies of tokhang?

4. The setting: October 1941 two months before the Pearl Harbor attack, the winds of war already howling in this part of the planet. In the crumbling Marasigan home in Intramuros, two sisters are at war with immediate domestic concerns like unsettled electricity, gas, medical bills, etc. with no one answering their ads for Spanish and piano lessons. On a symbolic level, they are also at war with the present and its values that the house's inhabitants find abrasively alienating.

Their brother Manolo and sister Pepang want to sell the house and divide the furniture amongst themselves. The centerpiece of the decaying house is a painting by their father Don Lorenzo, a famous artist and former revolutionary. The painting already has a potential buyer. With such a temptingly huge price tag, the sale could be Candida and Paula's ticket out of creeping destitution and dream jaunts to Spain, France, and Italy.

5. In today's psycho-sphere rattled by clickbait articles, terrorism, social-media porn, and extra-judicial killings, *Portrait* stands out like a glaring anachronism. You might accuse it of living, to use the words of a cynical character here, in "the dead world of the past," peppered by passing references here are of antiquarian provenance: ancient Latin chants by Franciscans (*"Dies irae, dies illa,"* anyone?), lines by Keats, "Vereda Tropical," Kolynos dental cream. There's some screaming, yes, but no bitchslapping involved (bitchslapping, along with hairpulling, face-scratching, eye-gouging, back-to-the-wall emotional breakdowns being usual requisites in Pinoy dramas). There's also very little physical movement happening. No fireworks of limbs and expletives, unless your idea of pyrotechnics is the La Naval.

6. Thus the question: Is the *Portrait* not future-proof?

7. *Portrait* is one of the major works that cement Joaquin's reputation as Great Venerator of Our Hispanic past. "To accuse the Spanish, over and over again, of having brought us all sorts of things, mostly evil, among which we can usually remember nothing valuable "except, perhaps," religion and national unity, is equivalent to saying of a not very model mother that she has given her child nothing *except* life."

A recurring notion throughout *Portrait* is that the past is perpetual paradise, a lost Eden, a more innocent, genteel time of tertullas, piano lessons, fluency in Spanish, religious parades, etc. La Naval? I mean, seriously, who gets turned on by the second Sunday of October except theology nerds in UST? (*"Why sure! A commemoration of Catholic triumph over the Dutch armada in 1646 through the intercession of the Blessed Virgin Mary? Bring out the beer!"*) Nick Joaquin, by the way, wrote a glittering tribute to La Naval de Manila in 1943.

8. But how is it "dead?" Can anything in this crazy post-post-postmodern cultural universe be actually dead? Hollywood still actively ransacks ancient Greek and Roman myths for their superhero series and fastfood toys. Technically, the Liberation of Manila was just a little over 72 years ago, and Nick Joaquin's play is only 62 years old. For some perspective, *Superman* the comicbook first appeared 79 years ago. And all three things—the Liberation, Superman, and *Portrait*—are still literally younger than Juan Ponce Enrile. At 93 years old, Enrile is still living and breathing, occasionally seen on social media justifying Duterte's Martial Law in his white tennis shorts.

9. The past, Joaquin argues, "can become 'usable' only if we be willing to enter into its spirit and carry there a reasonably hospitable mind. As long as we regard it with hatred, contempt and indignation, so long will it remain hateful and closed to us. Like a mirror (to borrow Aldous Huxley's image of the Future), it will meet us with spears if we advance toward it with spears. And as long as we remain estranged from it, so long will we remain a garish and uncouth and upstart people, without graces because without background."

10. *Portrait* is about three people fighting off the world—at least the world of mahjong, jai alai, horse races, crass commercialism, advertising and Hollywood, a world that is increasingly hostile to their fragile and dwindling sphere of dignity and grace. Against a generation, described using a reference to Eliot's "Hollow Men" as "behaving as the wind behaves."

The war—by "sword and fire—may have killed Candida, Paula, and Don Lorenzo but what the play affirms is that the war did not extinguish the values they cherished. In the end it is not the melancholic past we mourn but the tragic, vulgar present.

But it is precisely the "deadness" of this world where the play draws its defiant fist. *Contra Mundum*—literally "against the world"—is a refrain heard in the second act, and in the closing part repeated with heroic, almost talismanic affirmation by Candida and Paula. It is, in essence, the play's battlecry—a raging against the tides of time. While Joaquin calls in an "elegy," *Portrait* actually ends on a hopeful note: the antagonistic characters (most of them family) finally driven out the house, the Marasigans are finally at peace, watching with friends and guests the La Naval Procession outside the window below. Life goes on.

11. But you can still enjoy *Portrait* even without having to wrestle with the terrifying Angels of History and Literature. Not everything written by National

Artists has to go under the scalpel of Lit Crit 101. Read *Portrait* for sheer pleasure. In his 1951 essay on the Rizal novels, Joaquin pointed out that our trembling veneration for Rizal's books—as sacred tomes meant for profound genuflection and unlocking deep-seated truths—are the same things that keep us from appreciating them as literary works, if not simply as enjoyably well-written stories. After decades of stagings, critical deconstructions, and multimedia adaptations, it might seem ironic that Joaquin's play may have taken on the same intimidating veneer.

12. But for the language. My goodness, the intoxicating language. There's Bitoy Camacho as a somewhat Sophoclean expressionistic narrator. The force of his intro alone is vintage Joaquin—a breathless recitation of Manila's byzantine incarnations and inhabitants, sweeping through the arrabals of remembrance, through ancient Biblical locations to Rome, from mystics and merchants to harlots. Manila in this oration sounds like purely magical realist city (Note: *One Hundred Years of Solitude*, itself a book inhabited by magicians and whores, was not to be published until 1967).

It's a rather lengthy intro, but it's seductively Joaquinesque prose and you shouldn't really mind, unless you're a stage director or a filmmaker and producer shackled by a strict running time. And to this concern, Avellana, both for the stage renditions of 1956 and onward as well as the '65 film, had done some major surgical facelifts. *Portrait* as printed in the 2017 Penguin Classics edition of *The Woman Who had Two Navels and Tales of the Tropical Gothic* runs to approximately 132 pages. *Portrait* the play was first staged in 1955 by the Barangay Theater Guild led by Lamberto Avellana and wife Daisy Hontiveros (who also played Candida). As originally written, the play would have lasted four hours, so the Avellanas with Joaquin's permission, trimmed it to two hours and a half.

In the service of cinema, the literally invisible elements of the play—the painting and Don Lorenzo—appear in Avellana's movie. "The most potent elements in a work of art are, often, its silences," argued Susan Sontag. But time is when you really can't argue with the filmmaker.

13. *Portrait* has often been accused by critics as being a "drama of ideas," substituting "statement for dramatization," a philosophical treatise on the tension between past and present disguised in the habiliments of theater. Someone also said that it seems it was truly meant to be read rather than staged.

14. But on the issue of prolixity, I would anytime gladly dive into Nick Joaquin, a writer incapable of a vapid sentence. Study his rhythm, the sublime choreography of words, the tension between rhapsodic fusillade and short bursts. From this they can only benefit, young readers and writers of today weaned on "listicles" and other social-media formats that demand graceless brevity, the generation of today for whom reading a long-form magazine article is already a Proustian feat.

15. Read it for the magnificent one-liners: *"How can you write about Art and not bring in the slums of Tondo?"* Pete's lengthy diatribe against the old and bitter Revolutionaries *("Bacause they were not big enough after all to handle the Future")*. There are the convos on debates on art and compromise, boiling with wit and sarcasm:

"Art should be socially significant; Art has a function…"

BITOY: *Like making people brush their teeth?*

PETE: *Like making people brush their teeth.*

BITOY: *Then Don Lorenzo is a highly successful artist.*

PETE: *He ought to go and work for Kolynos Toothpaste.*

CORA: *As I always say, the real artists of our time are the advertising men.*

BITOY: *Michaelangelo plus Shakespeare equals a Kolynos ad.*

16. This is not to say that *Portrait* does not make for great drama. Read it for the scenes, many of which have become the stuff of ikon: quasi-seduction by hot chocolate, for instance, when the smooth devil Tony Javier sips from the flabbergasted Paula's cup—a gesture that scandalized her sister Candida, as if he showed up wearing only a condom and a 666 tattoo on his forehead. Imagine how Candida would react to today's tequila body shots.

17. Read it for the moments of black-comic relief: an earnest Candida applying to the local health department as rat-catcher and distraught when they laughed and threatened to throw her into the nuthouse. (This alone could be the plot for a quasi-absurdist one-act play.) Actually, Candida would have been gainfully employed in Mumbai, India with a salary of somewhere near 15,000 rupees a month (around P19,000).

18. Joaquin's play has also been translated into Filipino a number of times, by Alfred Yuson and Franklin Osorio, Bienvenido Lumbera, to name a few. Yet it is testament to *Portrait's* immensity that it persists not just in translations but also in incarnations in other genres. In 1997, based on the Joaquin masterpiece Rolando Tinio wrote and directed the musical *Ang Larawan* starring Celeste Legaspi and Zsa Zsa Padilla, with Ryan Cayabyab setting the Tinio libretto to music. In 2017, Culturtain Musicat Productions, the same producers behind *Ang Larawan*, takes their opus to the big screen, this time with Rachel Alejandro and Joanna Ampil, with Loy Arcenas directing.

19. Of course, every translation becomes a different creation—a completely fresh protoplasm. But the libretto for *Ang Larawan*, the musical and the screenplay for the movie aren't just a matter of linguistic transference.

You may ask what exactly is the point of publishing a screenplay or a libretto for that matter? And by what standards exactly? Fidelity to the original source material? But they're entirely different animals altogether. Also, this question: how does one evaluate a libretto and a musical? Wouldn't that be like judging cake-baking competition based on the recipes alone? The world of opera, for instance, brims with librettos that have some of the goofiest, the most contrived stories, plots, and characters. Yet nobody complains when the music of Handel or Mozart begins, the point being the music always seems superior to the drama. However, it is to the great fortune of Philippine literature and theater that Rolando Tinio's translated adapation is a masterpiece on its own. And to further count our blessings, Ryan Cayabyab's music is equally brilliant (*Ang Larawan, The Musical* is available on Youtube for everyone to enjoy. Thank you, Girlie Rodis).

20. Tinio's Tagalog text is wonderfully colloquial, conversational, lean and muscular, distills the natural efflorescence of Joaquin's dialogue into robust one-liners with an unimpeachable poetic ear. Consider this duet by the sisters, with the simple power of near-monosyllables.

"Bakit natin hinangad
Na ritrato'y maibenta
Para magkapera't makasali
Sa mundo ng walang kuwenta?
Bakit tayo naiinggit
Sa mundo ng ordinaryo?

Bakit ba naloka't naisipang
Buhay natin ay kalbaryo?
Kung ang tao sa ngayon,
Nasa isip puro pera
At hindi na uso'ng poesia,
Di na baleng magkagera!"

Tinio's text is deliberately terse and sinewy, its short choppy lines meant for musical appropriation but never fractures the spirit of Joaquin's original. For instance, this line by Candida from the original source: *"Well, they are not going to make us do it. You and I are going to stay right here. We were born here and we will die here."*

Tinio divides it, with a kind of stoic cadence, and allots the first part to the other sister:

PAULA
Hindi nila tayo mapipilit. Basta't dito tayong dalawa.

CANDIDA
Dito tayo ipinanganak, dito tayo mamamatay.

21. A screenplay is a filmmaker's roadmap. And to this end, *Ang Larawan* the movie's responsibilities are manifold: how to navigate Joaquin's narrative and at the same time, Tinio's text and Cayabyab's music. It's a different challenge faced by Lamberto Avellana's 1964 opus. Naturally, *Ang Larawan* the 2017 film appears to us as youthful and vibrant placed side by side with Avellana's. Of course, there is something about the black-and-white patina that instantly transports us to another time, or, if you wish, reminiscent of the Italian neorealist visual palette. Both Tinio's musical and Avellana's film are draped in the original's Gothic penumbra.

22. The two films adopt different strategies for Bitoy Camacho's opening narration. The '65 Avellana compresses it into a masterful montage with a voiceover and jumps right into a nightclub scene where Tony Javier plays piano as tropical dancers sashay onstage. This short dance interlude dissolves into a dimly lit scene in the back of a calesa where he slithers with a pretty dancer. As they sneak into the old house, two old sisters peek from the window. This the first time we see Candida and Paula, bathed in shadows, illumined only by a solitary candle. Also, just the first few minutes into the film Avellana actually shows the painting. Not too long after, we also see Don Lorenzo who even has speaking lines.

Ang Larawan the Movie director Loy Arcenas prefers the painting invisible, as in Tinio's musical and renders the opening monologue into a seductive tango, establishing the film's mood and tone. Before introducing us to Candida and Paula, Arcenas's camera first takes us to a short rendezvous with some supporting characters, with a little inside joke thrown in involving Ricky Davao.

23. The end of Sequence 17, where the sisters embrace each other sobbing is a masterful shot, easily one of the most striking images in *Ang Larawan* the 2017 movie. And, as in the original Joaquin, it is among the most memorable, a thespic tour-de-force: All of a sudden the lights are out and the sisters are gripped not by the darkness but by the fear of unpaid electric bills, and the potential humiliation in the eyes of neighbors—until they remember that the blackout was part of a wartime drill. Candida's descent into fits of half-laughing half-sobbing is a supreme challenge to any actor. Truly, there are things a script doesn't fully provide, that ultimately, everything remains subject to directorial fiat. Note, in the screenplay, how the dialogue sizzles but followed by a rather unremarkable scene description.

CANDIDA
[Patuloy na tatawa.] May black-out ngayon. Nagpapraktis ng black-out! Naghahanda para sa giyera. At akala natin… Natatakot tayong magsara ng bintana! Natatakot tayong matanaw ng kapitbahay! 'Di ba isang pares tayong tonta at kalahati?! Isang pares na tonta! Naku, Paula! Nakatatawa! Nakatatawa! Nakatatawa!

[Patuloy na tatawa si CANDIDA hanggang sa mapahagulgol. Lalapitan siya ni PAULA at yayakapin ito.]

PAULA
Candida, Candida…

CANDIDA
Hindi ko na kaya! Hindi ko na kaya!

[Mapapasalampak si Candida sa sahig dahil sa panlulumo.]

24. Think of this book as a bag of goodies, a bundle of possibilities: The original play, the libretto for the musical and the screenplay for the latest movie version. It will prove to be of great value, to the student not just of translation but also of adaptations in other genres. Both libretto and screenplay are precious since they are carved out of the same exquisite stone. Treat it as a map, or a guide for comparative studies, for the prospects are endless—and *Portrait* is a gift that keeps on giving. A full-on rock-and-roll operetta? Why not? How about a jazz musical from the point of view of a more drunken and disillusioned Tony Javier? Or a backstory of why the senator Don Perico had compromised his ideals? Or a play focusing on the most intriguing character of them all—the narrator Bitoy Camacho himself —and why he thinks his childhood a lie? Or, as mentioned earlier, Candida as professional rat-catcher?

A spoof? Why not? In 1993, Nonon Padilla wrote and directed his take on Joaquin's masterpiece: *Portrait of the Filipino as Artist* (note the reversal of "artist" and "Filipino," a sequel of sorts set in the Martial Law era when Candida and Paula are now Forbes Parks residents traumatized by pesky reporters. Not at all sacrilegious in the right hands—remember, the first prerequisite of parody is love.

25. Why, in Nick's words, cast "a pious eye for the past?" So what if it isn't "hip?" That is exactly the spirit of *contra mundum*. In the words of pop balladeer Lionel Richie, why would anyone want to be hip? Hip is now. Why be *now* when you can be *forever*? That this play is outdated and anachronistic is precisely the point it rages against, a big fat middle finger to that exact notion. Its timelessness is its subversion. Rhapsodized the 17th century German romantic writer Jean-Paul Richter: *"Memory is the paradise from which we cannot be expelled."*

The past—the classical past, especially—is not an old man croaking for a bit of recognition. It is a majestic, mountainous cloud hovering above the fate of all men at all times. The more we are immersed in the discourse, the more we appreciate the vitality of the ancient.

T.S. Eliot wrote: "Every great writer is always writing about his times, even when he seems to be writing about something else…" To paraphrase another Eliot quote: Someone said that the dead writers are remote from us because we know so much more than they did. Precisely, and they are that which we know. And because of them, we have Google. The past is the shoulder of giants on which we modern pygmies stand.

Lourd de Veyra

A Portrait of the Artist as Filipino

(An Elegy in Three Scenes)

by
Nick Joaquin
National Artist for Literature

How but in custom and in the ceremony
Are innocence and beauty born? —YEATS

THE SCENES—
FIRST SCENE: The sala of Marasigan house in Intramuros. An afternoon towards the beginning of October, 1941.
SECOND SCENE: The same. A week later. Late in the morning.
THIRD SCENE: The same. Two days later. Afternoon of the second Sunday of October.

THE PEOPLE—
CANDIDA and PAULA MARASIGAN,
spinster daughters of Don Lorenzo
PEPANG, their elder married sister
MANOLO, their eldest brother
BITOY CAMACHO, a friend of the family
TONY JAVIER, a lodger at the Marasigan house
PETE, a Sunday Magazine editor
EDDIE, a writer
CORA, a news photographer
SUSAN and VIOLET, vaudeville artists
DON PERICO, a Senator
DOÑA LOLENG, his wife
PATSY, their daughter
ELSA MONTES and CHARLIE DACANAY, friend of Doña Loleng

Friends of the Marasigans:
DON ALVARO and DOÑA UPENG, his wife
DON PEPE
DON MIGUEL and DOÑA IRENE, his wife
A WATCHMAN
A DETECTIVE
TWO POLICEMEN

THE FIRST SCENE
The curtains open a second curtain depicting the ruin of Intramuros in the moonlight. The sides of the stage are in shadow. BITOY CAMACHO is standing at far left. He begins to speak unseen, just a voice in the dark.

BITOY: Intramuros! The old Manila. The original Manila. The Noble and Ever Loyal City…To the early conquistadores she was anew Tyre and Sidon; to the early missionaries she was a new Rome. Within this walls was gathered the wealth of the Orient—silk from China; spices from Java; gold and ivory and precious stones from India. And within these walls the Champions of Christ assembled to conquer the Orient for the Cross. Through these old streets once crowded a marvelous multitude—viceroys and archbishops; mystics and merchants; pagan sorcerers and Christian martyrs; nuns and harlots and elegant marquesas; English pirates, Chinese mandarins, Portuguese traitors,

Dutch spies, Moro sultans, and Yankee clipper captains. For three centuries this medieval town was a Babylon in its commerce and a New Jerusalem in its faith...

New look: this is all that's left of it now. Weeds and rubble and scrap iron. A piece of wall, a fragment of stairway—and over there, the smashed gothic façade of old Sto. Domingo... *Quomodo desolata es, Civitas Dei! (From this point, light slowly grows about Bitoy.)*

I stand here in the moonlight and I look down this desolate street. Not so long ago, people were dying here—a horrible death—by sword and fire—their screams drowned out by the shriller screaming of the guns. Only silence now. Only silence, and the moonlight, and the tall grass thickening everywhere...

This is the great Calle Real—the main street of the city, the main street of the land, the main street of our history. I don't think there is any town in the Philippines that does not have—or that did not use to have—its own Calle Real. Well, this is the mother street of them all. Through this street the viceroys made their formal entry into the city. Along this street, amidst a glory of banners, the Seal of the King was borne in parade whenever letters arrived from the royal hand. Down this street marched the great annual procession of the city. And on this street the principal families had their townhouses—splendid ancient structures with red-tile roofs and wrought-iron balconies and fountains playing in the interior patios.

When I was a little boy, some of those old houses were still standing—but, oh, they had come down in the world! No longer splendid, no longer the seats of the mighty; abandoned and forgotten; they stood decaying all along this street; dreaming of past glories; growing ever more dark and dingy and dilapidated with the years; turning into slum-tenements at last—a dozen families crowded into each of the old rooms; garbage piled all over the patios; and washlines dangling between the sagging balconies...

Intramuros was dying, Intramuros was decaying even before the war. The jungle had returned—the modern jungle, the slum-jungle—just as merciless and effective as the real thing—demolishing man's moment of history and devouring his monuments. The noble and ever loyal City had become just another jungle of slums. And that is how most of us remember the imperial city of our fathers!

But there was one house on this street that never became a slum; that resisted the jungle, and resisted it to the very end; fighting stubbornly to keep itself intact, to keep itself individual. It finally took a global war to destroy that house and the three people who fought for it. Though they were destroyed, they were never conquered. They died with their house, and they died with their city—and maybe it's just as well they did. They could never have survived the destruction of the old Manila...

Their house stood on this corner of Calle Real. This piece of wall, this heap of broken stones are all that's left of it now—the house of Don Lorenzo Marasigan. Here is stood—and here it had been standing for generations. Oh, from the outside, you would have thought it just another slum-tenement. It looked like all the other old houses on this street—the roof black with moss, the rusty balconies sagging, the cracked walls unpainted... But enter—push open the old massive gates—and you find a clean bare passageway, you see a clean bright patio. No garbage anywhere, no washlines. And when you walk up the polished stairway, when you enter the gleaming sala, you step into another world—a world "where all's accustomed, ceremonious..."

(The lights go on inside the stage. Through the transparent curtain, the sala of the Marasigan house becomes visible.)

It wasn't merely the seashells lining the stairway, or the baroque furniture, or the old portraits hanging on the walls, or the family albums stacked on the shelves. The very atmosphere of the house suggested another Age—an Age of lamplight and gaslight, of harps and whiskers and fine carriages; an Age of manners and melodrama, of Religion and Revolution.

(The "Intramuros Curtain" begins to open, revealing the set proper.)

It is gone now—that house—the house of Don Lorenzo el magnifico. Nothing remains of it now save a piece of wall and a heap of broken stones. But this is how it looked before it perished—and I'm sure it looked just like this a hundred years ago. It never changed, it never altered. I had known it since I was a little boy—and it always looked like this. All the time I was growing up, the city was growing up too, the city was changing fast all around me. I could never be sure of anything or any place staying the way I remembered it. This was the one thing I was always sure of—this house. This was the one place I could always come back to, and find unchanged. Oh, older, yes—and darker, and more silent. But still, just the same; just the way I remembered it when I was a little boy and my father took me here with him on Friday evenings.

(The sala now stands fully revealed. It is a large room, clean and polished, but—like the furniture—dismally shows its age. The paint has darkened and is peeling off the walls. The windowpanes are broken. The doorways are not quite square anymore. The baroque elegance has tarnished.

Rear wall opens out, through French windows, into sagging balconies that overhang the street. At center, against the wall between the balconies, is a large sofa. Ordinarily grouped with this sofa are two rocking chairs, a round table, and two straight chairs. Right now, the table and the straight chairs have been moved in front of the balcony at right, its windows having been closed. The table is set for merienda. Through the open windows of the other balcony, late afternoon sunlight streams into the room, and you get a glimpse of the untidy tenements across the street.

At left side of the room, downstage, is a portion of the bannisters and the head of the stairway, facing toward rear. In the middle of the left wall is a closed door. Against back wall, facing stairway, stands an old-fashioned combination hatrack and umbrella-stand with mirror.

At right side of the room, downstage, against the walls is a whatnot filled with seashells, figurines, family albums, magazines and books. In the middle of the right wall is a large open doorway framed with curtains. Next to it, against right wall, stands an upright piano.

Embroidered cushions decorate the chairs. Pedestals bearing potted plants flank the balconies and the doorway at right. On the walls above the sofa, the piano, and the whatnot, are enlarged family photographs in ornate frames. A chandelier hangs from the ceiling. The painting entitled "A PORTRAIT OF THE ARTIST AS FILIPINO" is supposed to be hanging in the center of the invisible "fourth wall" between stage and audience. "Left" and "Right" in all the stage directions are according to the view from the audience.

Bitoy Camacho steps into the room.)

I remember coming here one day early in October back in 1941—just two months before the war broke out. 1941! Remember that year? It was the year of Hitler for the people in Europe—but for us over here, it was the year of the Conga and the Bogie-woogie, the year of the practice black-outs, the year of the Bare Midriff. Oh, we were all sure that the war was coming our way pretty soon—but we were just as sure that it would happen to us. When we said: "Keep 'em flying!" and "Business as usual!" our voices were brave and gay, our hearts were untroubled. And because we felt so safe, because we felt so confident, we deliberately tried to scare ourselves. Remember all those grewsome rumors we kept spreading? We enjoyed shivering as we told them, and we enjoyed shivering as we listened. It was all just a thrilling game. We were sophisticated children playing at rape and murder, and half-wishing it was all true.

(He places himself at stairlanding, as though he had just come up the stairs.)

That October afternoon, I had come here with my head buzzing with rumors. Out there in the street, people were stopping each other to exchange interpretations of the latest headlines. In the restaurants and barber shops, military experts were fighting the war in Europe. And in all the houses in all the streets, radios were screaming out the latest bulletins. I felt excited—and I felt very pleased with myself for feeling excited. It proved how involved I was in my times; and how concerned, how nobly concerned I was with the human condition. So I came up those stairs and I paused here on the landing and I looked at this room that I hadn't seen again since my boyhood—and, suddenly all the people and all the headlines and all the radios stopped screaming in my ears. I stood here—and the whole world had become silent. It was astonishing—and it was also highly unpleasant. The silence of this room was like an insult, like a slap in the face. I felt suddenly ashamed of all that noble excitement. I had been enjoying so much. But my next feeling was of bitter resentment. I resented this room. I hated those old chairs for standing there so calmly. I wanted to walk right down again, to leave this house, to run back to the street—back to the screaming people and headlines and radios. But I didn't. I couldn't. The silence had me helpless. And after a while I stopped feeling outraged, I began to smile at myself. For the first time in a long, long time I could hear myself thinking, I could feel myself feeling and breathing and living and remembering. I was conscious of myself as a separate person with a separate, secret life of my own. This old room grew young again, and familiar. The silence whispered with memories... Outside, the world was hurrying gaily towards destruction. In here, life went on as usual; unaltered; everything in its proper place; everything just the same today as yesterday, or last year, or a hundred years ago...

(A pause, while Bitoy stands smiling at the room. Enter CANDIDA MARASIGAN at right, bearing a chocolate-pot on tray. Seeing Bitoy, she stops in the doorway and stares at him inquiringly. Candida is forty-two, and is dressed in the style of twenties. Her uncut hair, already greying, is coiled up and knotted in the old manner. Her body is straight, firm and spare. Not conventionally pretty, she can, however, when among friends, grow radiant with girlish charm and innocence. When among strangers, she is apt, from shyness, to assume the severe forbidding expression of the crabbed old maid. She is looking very severely now at the grinning young man on the stairway.)

BITOY: Hello, Candida.

(He waits, smiling, but as her face remains severe he walks towards her.)

Candida, surely you know me?

(Approaches, her face quickens with recognition, and she advances to meet him.)

CANDIDA: But of course, of course! You are Bitoy, the son of the old Camacho! And shame on you, Bitoy Camacho—shame, shame on you for forgetting your old friends!

(They have met at center of stage.)

BITOY: I have never forgotten my old friends, Candida.

CANDIDA: Then why have you never—

(She speaks this with emphatic gesture that cause chocolate to splash from pot. Bitoy backs away. She laughs.)

Oh, excuse me, Bitoy!

BITOY: Here, let me take that.

(He takes tray and places it on table. Her eyes follow him. He turns around and, smiling, submits to her gaze.)
Well?

CANDIDA *(approaching him)*: So thin, Bitoy? And so many lines on your face already? You cannot be more than twenty.

BITOY: I am twenty-five.

CANDIDA: Twenty-five! Imagine that!

(She moves away, downstage.)

And the last time we saw you, you were just a small boy in short pants and a sailor blouse...

BITOY: And the last time I saw you, Candida!

CANDIDA *(whirling around passionately)*: No! No!

BITOY *(startled)*: Huh?

CANDIDA *(laughing)*: Oh Bitoy, when you begin to get as old as I am, it hurts!

BITOY: What?

CANDIDA: To be told how much one has changed.

BITOY: You have not changed, Candida!

CANDIDA: Oh yes, I have—oh yes, I have! The last time you saw me, Bitoy,

(She says this with all the gestures of a lively belle.)

I was a very grown-up young lady, a very proud young lady—with rings on my fingers and a ribbon in my hair and the stars in my eyes! Oh, I was so full of vanity, so full of vivacity! I was so sure that any moment at all someone very wonderful would arrive to take me away! I was waiting, do you know, waiting for my Principe de Asturias!

BITOY: And he has not come yet—your Principe de Asturias?

CANDIDA: Alas, he has not come at all! And none of our old friends come anymore...

BITOY: Not even on Friday evenings?

CANDIDA: Not even on Friday evenings. No more "tertulias" on Friday, Bitoy. We have given them up. The old people are dying off; and the young people— you young people, Bitoy—do not care to come.

(She turns her face towards doorway at right and raises her voice.)

Paula! Paula!

(Offstage, Paula is heard answering: "Coming!" Candida approaches Bitoy and takes both his hands in hers.)

Bitoy, how sweet of you to remember us. You make me feel very happy. You bring back memories of such happy days.

BITOY: Yes, I know. You bring them back to me, too—all those Friday evenings I spent here with my father.

CANDIDA *(releasing his hand)*: But how it is you remember? You were only a child.

BITOY: But I do, I do! Oh, those "tertulias"—how I remember them all! On Saturdays nights, there was the tertulia at the Monson house in Binondo; on Monday nights, at the Botica of Doctor Moreta in Quiapo; on Wednesday nights, at the bookshop of Don Aristeo on Carriedo; and on Friday nights— listen, Candida. On Fridays, do you know, I still wake up sometimes, even now, thinking: Today is Friday; the tertulia will be at the Marasigan house in Intramuros; and Father and I will be going...

(He pauses as PAULA appears in doorway, carrying a platter of biscuits. Paula is forty, also slightly gray-haired already, and also wearing a funny old dress. She is smarter than Candida, and looks more delicate, more timid; like Candida, she is ambiguous—the bleakest of old maids, you would call her, until she smiles, when you discover, astonished, a humorous girl—still fresh, still charming—lurking under the gray hair.)

CANDIDA: Well, Paula—do you see who has come to visit us after all these years?

PAULA *(as she hurries to table and sets down the platter)*: Why, Bitoy! Bitoy Camacho!

(She goes to Bitoy and gives him both her hands.)

Holy Virgin, how he has grown! Can this be our baby, Candida?

BITOY: In the short pants and the sailor blouse?

CANDIDA: He still fondly remembers our old Friday tertulias.

PAULA: Oh, you were a big nuisance in those days, Bitoy! I was always having to wipe your nose or to take you out to the small room. Why did your father always bring you along?

BITOY: Because I howled if he tried to leave me behind!

PAULA *(throwing back her head)*: Oh, those old Friday nights! How we talked and talked!

(She begins to move gaily over the room as though a crowded "tertulia" were in progress, chattering to imaginary visitors and fanning herself with an imaginary fan.)

More brandy, Don Pepe? Some more brandy Don Isidro? Doña Upeng, come here by the window, it is cooler! What, Don Alvaro—you have not read the new poem by Dario? But, my good man, in the latest issue of the "Blanco y Negro," of course! Doña Irene, we are talking about the divine Ruben! You have read his latest offering?

"Tuvo razon tu abuela con su cabello cano,
muy mas que tu con rizos en que se enrosca el dia..."

Aie, Don Pepe, Don Pepe—tell me, do you not consider that poem an absolute miracle? Oh, look everybody—here comes Don Aristeo at last! Welcome to our house, noble soldier! Candida, find him a seat somewhere!

CANDIDA *(acting up, too)*: Over here, Don Aristeo, over here! And may I ask my dear sir, why you failed us last Friday? Paula, some brandy for Don Aristeo!

PAULA *(offering imaginary glass)*: I forbid you talk politics tonight! Must we hear about nothing else these days except this eternal Don Q?

CANDIDA: Oh, listen everybody! Don Alvaro is telling us just where Don Q was, during the Revolution!

PAULA: Oh yes, Doña Irene, we went all to the performances—but we consider this zarzuela company inferior to the one we had last year.

CANDIDA: And next month, the Italian singers are arriving! Alas for us girls! The men will all be lined up again on the stage door!

PAULA: More brandy, Don Miguel? Some more brandy, Don Pepe? Doña Irene, would you prefer to sit here by the piano? Oh, go on, go on, Don Alvaro! And you say that General Aguinaldo was actually preparing his army for a last assault?

BITOY (*in voice of ten year-old*): Tita Paula, Tita Paula—I wanna go to the small room!

PAULA: Hush, hush, you little savage! And just look at your nose!

CANDIDA: And how many times have we told you not to call us both Tita!

PAULA: You will call us Paula and Candida.

CANDIDA: Just Paula and Candida—understand?

PAULA: Jesus, we are not old maids yet!

CANDIDA: No, no—we are not old maids yet! We are young, we are pretty, we are delightful! Oh, listen, Doña Upeng—last night we went to a ball, and we danced and danced and danced til morning!

(*She dances around the room.*)

PAULA: Papa said we were the prettiest girls in all the gathering!

CANDIDA: Oh yes, Doña Irene—our papa accompanied us—and he was the most distinguished gentlemen present!

BITOY (*still the ten-year old; gesturing excitedly towards doorway*): And here he comes! Here he comes!

CANDIDA (*whirling around*): Oh, here you are at last, papa! (*Raising her voice excitedly*) Don Miguel, here is papa! Here is papa, Doña Upeng!

PAULA (*joyously excited, too*): Here is papa! Don Alvaro! Doña Irene, here is papa!

(*The sisters gesture towards front of stage as they say: "Here is papa!"*)

CANDIDA: Hush, hush, everybody! Papa wants to say something!

(The sisters stand side by side, directly facing audience, their faces lifted, their hands clasped to their breasts, and their bodies at attention, as though they were listening to their father speaking. Then, clapping their hands, they cry out in joyous adoration "Oh, papa, papa! They hold a pose a moment longer. The PORTRAIT is hanging on the wall right in front of them; and as they become aware of it, the raptures fades from their faces, their bodies droop, their hands fall to their sides. The game is ended; the make-believe is over. They stand silent, bleakly staring up—two shabby old maids in a shabby old house. Bitoy is watching them from upstage. Becoming aware of their fixed stare, he lifts his eyes and sees the PORTRAIT for the first time. Staring, he comes forward and stands behind the sisters, his face between the staring faces.)

BITOY: Is that it?

CANDIDA (*expressionless*): Yes.

BITOY: When did your father paint it?

PAULA: About a year ago.

BITOY (*after a staring pause*): What a strange, strange picture!

CANDIDA: Do you know what he calls it?

BITOY: Yes.

CANDIDA: "RETRATO DEL ARTISTA COMO FILIPINO."

BITOY: Yes, I know. "A Portrait of the Artist as Filipino." But why, why? The scene is not Filipino…What did your father mean?

(He holds up a hand towards PORTRAIT.)

A young man carrying an old man on his back…and behind them, a burning city…

PAULA: The old man is our father.

BITOY: Yes, I recognize his face…

CANDIDA: And the young man is our father also—our father when he was young.

BITOY (*excitedly*): Why, yes, yes!

PAULA: And the burning city—

BITOY: The burning city is Troy.

PAULA: Well, you know all about it.

BITOY (*smiling*): Yes, I know all about it. Aeneas carrying his father Anchises out of Troy. And your father has painted himself both as Aeneas and as Anchises.

CANDIDA: He has painted himself as he is now—and as he used to be—in the past.

BITOY: The effect is rather frightening…

CANDIDA: Oh, do you feel it, too?

BITOY: I feel as if I were seeing double.

CANDIDA: I sometimes feel as if that figures up there were a monster—a man with two heads.

BITOY: Yes. "That strange monster, the Artist…" But how marvelously your father has caught that clear, pure classic simplicity! What flowing lines, what luminous colors, what a calm and spacious atmosphere! One can almost feel the sun shining and the seawinds blowing! Space, light, cleanliness, beauty, grace—and suddenly, there in the foreground, those frightening faces, those darkly smiling faces—like faces in a mirror…And behind them, in the distance, the burning towers of Troy…My God, this is magnificent! This is a masterpiece!

(*He pauses and his rapturous face becomes troubled.*)

But why does your father call it "A Portrait of the Artist as Filipino"?

PAULA: Well—it is a portrait of himself after all.

CANDIDA: A double portrait, in fact.

PAULA: And he is an artist and a Filipino.

BITOY: Yes, yes—but, then, why paint himself as Aeneas? Why paint himself against the Trojan War?

PAULA (*shrugging*): We do not know.

CANDIDA: He had not tell us.

BITOY: Do you know, a visiting Frenchman has written an enthusiastic article about this picture.

CANDIDA: Oh yes—he was very nice, that Frenchman. He said he had long been an admirer of my father. He was thoroughly acquainted with my father's work. He had seen them in Madrid and Barcelona. And he promised himself—

(She pauses. Bitoy has taken out a notebook and is jotting down what she is saying. She and Paula exchange glances.)

BITOY *(looking up expectantly)*: Yes? He promised himself what?

CANDIDA *(dryly continuing)*: Well, he promised that if he ever found himself here in the Philippines he would try to locate father. So, he came here, and he saw father. And he saw this new painting, and then he published that article. As I said, he was a very nice man—but we are sorry now he ever came.

BITOY *(looking up)*: Sorry?

CANDIDA: Tell me something, Bitoy—are you a newspaper reporter?

BITOY *(after a moment's hesitation)*: Yes. Yes, I am.

CANDIDA *(smiling)*: And that is why you have come to visit us after all these years!

(Still smiling, she walks away. Bitoy looks blankly after her. She goes to table and begins to beat the chocolate. Bitoy turns to Paula.)

BITOY: Paula, what is the matter! What have I done?

PAULA: Oh, nothing, Bitoy. Only, when people come here now, it is not to visit us, but to see this picture.

BITOY: Well, you ought to be glad, you ought to be proud! People thought your father died long time ago! Now, after all these years of silence and obscurity, everybody is talking about him. The whole country is agog to discover that Don Lorenzo Marasigan, one of the greatest painters of the Philippines and the friend and rival of Juan Luna, is not only alive but has actually painted another masterpiece in his old age!

PAULA *(gently)*: My father painted this picture only for us—for Candida and myself. He gave it to us as a present; and for a whole year it has hung here in peace. Then that Frenchman came and saw it and wrote about it. And since then we have had no peace. No day passes but we must face a reporter from the newspapers or a photographer from the magazines or a group of students from the universities. And we—*(laying a hand on his shoulder)*—we do not like it, Bitoy.

(She turns away and goes to table where she begins to prepare her father's merienda on a tray. Meanwhile, Bitoy stands where she has left him, staring at PORTRAIT. Then he pockets his notebook and goes towards table.)

BITOY: Forgive me, Candida. Forgive me, Paula.

(Paula goes on arranging tray; Candida goes on beating chocolate.)

Well. . .I suppose I ought to go away.

CANDIDA *(not looking up)*: No; stay and have some merienda. Paula, get another cup.

BITOY *(as Paula goes to doorway)*: Please do not bother, Paula. I really must be going.

PAULA *(pausing)*: Oh, Bitoy!

BITOY: There are some people waiting for me.

CANDIDA *(pouring chocolate into cup)*: Sit down, Bitoy, and no more nonsense.

BITOY: These people are waiting just around the corner, Candida, and they will be coming here in a moment.

CANDIDA *(looking up)*: More people from the newspapers?

BITOY: Yes.

CANDIDA: Friends of yours?

BITOY: Well, all work for the same company.

CANDIDA: I see. And because you are a friend of the family, they have sent you ahead to prepare the way—is that it?

BITOY: Exactly.

CANDIDA *(laughing)*: Well! You are a scoundrel, Bitoy Camacho!

BITOY: But I will go right down and tell them not to come anymore.

CANDIDA: Oh, why not? *(She shrugs.)* Let them come.

PAULA: After all, we have to accustom ourselves, you know.

BITOY: But I do not want them to come.

PAULA: I thought you wanted us to be glad about people coming.

BITOY: No.

PAULA: Then what do you want?

BITOY *(after a pause: parodying again a small boy's voice)*: Oh Tita Paula, I wanna go to the small room!

(They all laugh. Bitoy draws himself up and, one arm akimbo, begins to pace the floor, twirling an imaginary moustache. His gruff voice now parodies a gentleman of the old school.)

Caramba! These young people nowadays, they are so terrible, no? Hombre, when I was young, in the days before the Revolution—Señorita, if you will be so gracious, a little more of your excellent brandy.

CANDIDA *(offering him a cup of chocolate on saucer)*: With a thousand pleasures, Don Benito!

PAULA *(waving imaginary fan)*: Oh, please, Don Benito—please tell us about your student days in Paris!

BITOY *(rolling his eyes at the ceiling)*: Ah, Paris! Paris in the old days!

CANDIDA: Doña Irene, come quick! Doña Upeng, hurry over here! Don Benitois going to tell us about his love affairs with those Parisian cocottes!

PAULA: Where they thrilling? Were they passionate? Were they shameless? Ah, speak no more—speak no more! My head whirls, my heart pounds! I shall swoon, I shall swoon!

(She claps one hand to her brow, the other to her heart, then waltzes out of the room. Candida and Bitoy burst into laughter. Candida resumes beating chocolate.)

BITOY *(approaching able)*: I really am very sorry, Candida.

CANDIDA: Oh, sit down, Bitoy, and drink your chocolate.

BITOY *(sitting down)*: Have people really been annoying you?

CANDIDA: Well, you know how it is—reporters, photographers, people wanting to talk to father—and they are offended when he refuses to see them.
(She looks up towards PORTRAIT.)

And you know what, Bitoy? That picture affects people in a very strange way.

BITOY: How do you mean?

CANDIDA: It makes them angry.

BITOY *(also looking towards PORTRAIT)*: It is rather enigmatic, you know.

CANDIDA: Well, we explain—we explain to everybody. We tell them: this is Aeneas, and this is his father Anchises. But they just look blankly to us. And then they ask: Who is Aeneas? Was he a Filipino? *(She laughs.)* There were some people here the other day—some kind of civic society—and they were shocked to learn that we had had this painting for the whole year without anybody knowing about it, until that Frenchman came along. They were furious with Paula and me for not telling everybody sooner. One of them—a small man with big eyes—he pointed a finger right in my face and he said to me in a very solemn voice: "Miss Marasigan, I shall urge the government to confiscate this painting right away! You and your sister are unworthy to possess it!"

BITOY *(joining in her laughter)*: I begin to see what you and Paula have had to suffer.

(Paula enters with extra cup.)

CANDIDA: Oh, Paula and I do not mind really. It is father we want to spare.

(She picks up tray and gives it to Paula.)

Here, Paula. And tell father that the son of his old friend Camacho has come to visit him.

(Exit Paula with tray.)

BITOY: And how is he—your father—*(gazing towards PORTRAIT)*—Don Lorenzo El Magnifico?

CANDIDA *(pouring a cup for herself)*: Oh, quite well.

BITOY: Is he too weak now to leave his room?

CANDIDA: Oh no.

BITOY: But something is the matter with him?

CANDIDA *(evasively)*: He had an accident.

BITOY: When?

CANDIDA: About a year ago.

BITOY: When he painted that picture?

CANDIDA: A short time after he finished painting it.

BITOY: What happened?

CANDIDA: We do not quite know. We did not see it happen, and it happened at night. We think he must have been walking in his sleep. And he…he fell from the balcony of his room into the courtyard below.

BITOY *(rising)*: Oh, my God! Did he break anything?

CANDIDA: No—thank God!

BITOY: And how is he now?

CANDIDA: He can move about—but he prefers to stay in bed. Do you know, Bitoy—he has not once come out of his room for a whole year.

(She suddenly presses her knuckles to her forehead.)

Oh, we blame ourselves for what happened!

BITOY: But why should you? It was an accident.

CANDIDA *(after a pause)*: Yes…yes it was an accident.

(She picks up chocolate pot again and pours a cup for Paula. Bitoy watches her in silence. Paula appears joyously in doorway.)

PAULA: Come, Bitoy! Hurry! Papa is delighted! He begs you to come at once!

BITOY *(walking to doorway)*: Thank you, Paula.

CANDIDA: Bitoy—

(He stops and looks at her.)

You will be very careful, Bitoy? Remember: you are not a reporter, you are a friend. You have not come to interview him or take his photograph. You have come to visit him.

BITOY: Yes, Candida.

(Exit Paula and Bitoy. Candida sits down and begins to eat. The day's mail is stacked on the table. She opens and glances through the letters as she eats. Paula comes back.)

PAULA *(sitting down and sipping her chocolate)*: Father was really delighted. He even got out of bed to shake hands with Bitoy. And they were talking very gaily when I left them. Oh, father is really getting better, Candida! Do you not think so? *(Candida does not answer. She has propped an elbow on the table and is staring at a letter, her head leaning on her hand. Paula leans sideways to look at letter.)* More bills, Candida?

CANDIDA *(picking up and dropping one by one the letters she has opened)*: The water bill. The gas bill. The doctor's bill. And this—*(waving the letter she's holding)*—this is the light bill. Listen. *(She reads.)* "We again warn you that unless these accounts are immediately settled, we shall be obliged to discontinue all further service." And this is the third warning they have sent.

PAULA: Have you told Manolo?

CANDIDA: I called up Manolo, I called up Pepang—and they said: Oh yes, yes—they would send the money right away. They have been saying that all this month, but they never send the money.

PAULA *(bitterly)*: Our dear brother and sister!

CANDIDA: Our dear brother and sister are determined that we give up this house.

PAULA: Well, they are not going to make us do it. You and I are going to stay right here. We were born here and we will die here!

CANDIDA: But what if they continue not to send us money? What if they flatly refuse to support us any longer? All the bills...

PAULA *(pensively)*: There must be something we can do!

CANDIDA *(leaning towards Paula)*: Listen, I have some new ideas.

PAULA *(not paying attention)*: But what we can do? We are two useless old maids...

CANDIDA *(rising and looking about)*: Where is that newspaper?

PAULA: Oh, I lie awake night after night wondering how we can make money, money, money!

CANDIDA *(who has found newspaper and is standing by the table searching through the pages)*: Ah, here it is. Now listen, Paula. Listen to this. It says here—

(She stops. Below, in the street, a car is heard stopping, The sisters listen; then glance to each other. Candida sighs, folds newspaper, places it on table, and sits down. Paula pours her more chocolate. Footsteps are heard on the stairway. The sisters pick up their cups and sip their chocolate. Enter TONY JAVIER, carrying books and his coat in one hand. He glances towards the sisters, pushes the hat off his brow, and calls out: "Good afternoon, ladies!" Then he opens the closed door at left and flings his coat, hat and books inside. He pulls the door shut again and, smiling confidently, walks into the sala. Tony is about twenty-seven, very masculine, and sardonic. His shirt and tie are blissfully resplendent; his charm, however, is more subtle—and he knows it.)

TONY: Ah-ha, merienda!

CANDIDA *(very old-maidish)*: Will you some chocolate, Mr. Javier?

TONY: Tsk, tsk. That's bad business, ladies. Remember, I'm just paying for room without board.

CANDIDA *(severely)*: Mr. Javier, anybody who lives under our roof is welcome to our table.

TONY: But are good manners good business?

CANDIDA: Mr. Javier, will you have some chocolate?

TONY *(picking up a biscuit and popping it into his mouth)*: Yes, thank you!

(He sees Bitoy's cup.) Oh, you had a visitor!

CANDIDA: An old friend of ours. Paula, get another cup.

TONY: Oh, what for?

(As Paula rises, he reaches across the table and presses a hand on her shoulder. She starts and looks at him, not angry but wondering. He slowly withdraws his hand, their eyes interlocked.)

Please do not bother, Miss Paula. I can use this cup. I'm not particular.

CANDIDA *(grimly)*: Paula, get another cup.

TONY: Or perhaps you would like to offer me your cup, Miss Paula?

PAULA *(her eyes still innocently fascinated)*: My cup?

TONY *(picking up Paula's cup)*: Do you still want this chocolate?

PAULA *(shaking her head)*: No.

TONY: Then, may I have it?

CANDIDA *(rising)*: Mr. Javier, I ask you to put down that cup at once!

TONY *(ignoring Candida)*: Thank you, Miss Paula.

(He lifts the cup above his head.)

To a better business!

(Then he throws his head back and slowly, deliberately drinks the chocolate, the sisters staring at his throat in horror and fascination. Then he sets the cup down and smacks his lips.)

CANDIDA *(coming to life)*: Mr. Javier, it is outrageous—

TONY: *(picking up and gobbling another biscuit)*: Oh no—it was delicious!

CANDIDA: It is useless to treat you with decency!

TONY *(bowing)*: Permit me to remove my indecent person from your sight.

(He walks towards his room. The sisters exchange glances. He stops and looks back.)

Oh—and thanks a lot for the merienda!

CANDIDA: Mr. Javier, will you please come back here? There is something we have to ask you.

TONY *(walking back)*: Okay, shoot.

PAULA *(quickly picking up chocolate pot)*: I must take this out to the kitchen.

CANDIDA: Put that down, Paula. You will stay right here.

TONY: Well, what is it? Come on, hurry up. I haven't got much time. I'd like to lie down a moment before I go out again.

(He yawns and stretches his arms; his brows darken with momentary irritation.)

God—but am I tired! I never get any sleep! I never get any sleep at all!

(He goes to table and pick up another biscuit.)

Studying all day, working all night! Ambition—hah! Everybody has it!

(Nibbling the biscuit, he goes to a rocking chair and flops down.)

Look at me—a cheap little vaudeville piano player. Not a pianist—oh no, no—certainly not a pianist! Hey, you know what's the difference between a pianist and a piano player? I can tell you. A pianist is uh—a pianist is—well—highbrow stuff. Oh, you know. He had professors to teach him; he went to the right academies; and he gives concerts for the high society dames. Culture—that's a pianist! While a piano player—oh, that's me! Nobody ever taught me how to play. I taught myself—and I know I stink!

(He rises and thrusts his hands into his pockets.)

A cheap little vaudeville piano player. Three shows a day in a stinking third-class theatre. The audience spit on your neck and the piano rattles like an old can. And you never know how long the job will last…

(A pause, while he stares at the floor. Then he sighs deeply and shrugs.)

So what do I do? So I get ambitious! So I tell myself I'm not going to be just a piano player all my life. No, siree! I'm gonna be a lawyer—big, rich, crooked lawyer! So I'm going to school—yes, siree! Go to school all day, play the piano all night. What a life! Oh well, it used to be worse…

(He suddenly turns to the sisters.)

Do you, ladies, have any idea what kind of a life I've had?

CANDIDA: We are not interested in your private life.

TONY *(looking her in the eye)*: Oh no?

(Her eyes falter; she looks away. He smiles.)

God! You ladies ought to be—

CANDIDA *(interrupting)*: Mr. Javier, when we allowed you to rent a room in our house, it was with the condition that you would permit no gambling, no drinking, and no women in your room.

TONY: So what now?

CANDIDA: You have broken our rules.

TONY: But I don't do my gambling here.

CANDIDA: I was not referring to gambling.

TONY: Well, I bring home a beer now and then.

CANDIDA: Nor to drinking either.

TONY *(his eyes widening)*: Oh, you mean—

(Grinning, he traces a women's form in the air with his hands.)

CANDIDA *(not smiling)*: Yes!

TONY: But when?

CANDIDA: Last night, Mr. Javier, my sister and I heard you arriving with a woman.

TONY: Holy cow, were you still awake when I arrived last night?

CANDIDA: We happened to be still awake.

TONY *(bashfully dropping his eyes)*: Were you… waiting up for me?

CANDIDA: Mr. Javier, did you or did not bring a woman here last night?

TONY *(wide eyed)*: My dear ladies, you must have been dreaming! That was a wonderful, wonderful dream you had last night—and I sure hate to spoil your fun. So, you ladies dream about me, eh?

CANDIDA: No, we were not dreaming—and yes, you had a woman with you!

TONY: Yes, you were dreaming—and no, I did not have a woman with me!

CANDIDA: How can you have the nerve to lie! I distinctly heard a woman laughing—and so, I told my sister to get up and look out the window. Go on, Paula—tell him. You may have been—! I thought you said you were sure you saw one!

PAULA: Only because you said you were sure you heard one! But it was so dark really—and all I could see was something white. It may have been a woman's dress—or it may have been a man's shirt…

TONY: It was a man's shirt! And the man inside the shirt was—uh—oh yes, he was the drummer in our band! And he came along with me last night because I had some of his music in my room. So he came up; and I gave him his music; and then he went away. And that's all there is to it!

CANDIDA: Are you telling us the truth?

TONY *(putting up his hand)*: The whole truth and nothing but the truth.

CANDIDA: I wonder!

PAULA: Oh Candida, if we have falsely accused Mr. Javier, the least we can do now is to apologize for having hurt his feelings?

TONY *(instantly pitying himself)*: Oh no—why apologize to me? I'm just an animal! Animals have no feelings! It is useless to treat them with decency!

CANDIDA *(stiffy)*: Mr. Javier, if we have made a mistake, we are sorry—and we apologize.

TONY *(Ignoring her; laying on the misery)*: Just a pile of trash…rotten trash. Not worthy even to be stepped on—too sickening, too repulsive…just something the garbage collector ought to take away quick so I don't pollute the air for nice people!

CANDIDA: Mr. Javier, this is not funny at all!

TONY: You bet it's not funny!

(He stands scowling at her. Bitoy appears in doorway, carrying tray. Tony's expression changes into surprise.)

Why, hello there, guy!

BITOY: Hi, Tony! Paula, where do I put this?

PAULA *(approaching)*: Give it to me.

(She takes tray and exits.)

BITOY *(walking in)*: Well, well, Tony!

TONY: Hi, guy.

CANDIDA: Do you two know each other?

BITOY: We used to work together.

TONY: At the piers.

BITOY *(making face)*: The most horrible memory of my life!

TONY: Not of mine! What are you doing here, guy?

BITOY: What are you doing here?

TONY: I live here.

BITOY: No!

TONY: Yes! See that room over there? It's mine. For fifteen pesos a month.

BITOY: Candida, are you taking in boarders?

CANDIDA: Oh, you know how poor we are! Paula and I—we thought we would try running a boarding house. But Mr. Javier is our first—and so far— our only customer.

(Off stage, Paula is heard shouting "Candida! Candida!" Candida raises her voice.)

Yes? What is it, Paula?

(Paula appears in doorway, still carrying tray.)

PAULA: Oh Candida, a rat! A rat in the kitchen!

CANDIDA: *(with a shake of the head):* Oh Paula, Paula!

PAULA *(pleadingly):* And such a big, big rat, Candida!

CANDIDA: All right. I am coming. *(To Bitoy and Tony.)* Excuse me.

   (Exit Paula and Candida.)

TONY *(contemptuously)*: A pair of crazy dames!

BITOY *(rather stiffly)*: They are old friends of my family, Tony.

TONY *(carelessly)*: Well, you better stay away from them. They're man-hungry.

BITOY *(smiling in spite of himself)*: Why, have they been trying to eat you up?

TONY: Ah, they're crazy. If I just look at them, they start shivering. When I talk to them, they get a fever. And if I touch them—

BITOY: So, you make love to them!

TONY: Me? Make love to them? Pah! *(He spits.)* I'd sooner make love to the Jones Bridge! Nah—it's them that's crazy, not me.

BITOY: It must be the poverty…I didn't know they had become so poor…

TONY: Poor? They're desperate!

BITOY: But they still have a married brother and a married sister.

TONY: The brother and sister have been paying all the expenses—but it looks like they don't want anymore. They want to sell this house and put the old man in a hospital.

BITOY: And what becomes of Paula and Candida?

TONY: Candida goes to live with the brother, Paula goes to live with the sister.

BITOY: Oh, poor Candida! Poor Paula! They won't like that.

TONY: You bet they don't like it! That's why they're desperate. They've been trying all sorts of crazy schemes—like trying to run a boarding house—hah! Who wants to live in a house like this? Oh, Intramuros is full of students looking for a place to sleep in. They wouldn't feel at home here.

BITOY: You seem very much at home anyway.

TONY: Oh, I like it here. I'm educating myself, you know. Paula and Candida, they've been wanting to throw me out—but they don't dare. They need the money too much. Besides, they like having me around. Oh, they're crazy. Why, they could have some big money if only—

(He stops and look towards PORTRAIT.)

BITOY: If only what?

TONY *(coming downstage):* See this painting? Well, I know an American who's willing to pay two thousand dollars for it. Dollars, mind you—not pesos.

BITOY *(coming downstage, too)*: And Paula and Candida refuse to sell?

TONY: They absolutely refuse to sell. Just think of it—two grand! Oh, I've been trying and trying to make them sell—

BITOY: You, Tony?

TONY: Sure—me. This American, he hired me to put over the deal, see?

BITOY: And no dice.

TONY: Those dames are crazy!

BITOY: Maybe they love this picture too much.

TONY: Love it? They hate it!

BITOY: How do you know?

TONY: Oh, I just do. And hate it myself!

BITOY: Oh Lord—but why?

TONY: *(staring at PORTRAIT):* The damn thing's always looking at me, always down at me. Every time I come into this house; every time I come up those stairs. Looking at me, looking down at me. And if I turn around and face it—then it smiles, damn it! And if I go into my room and close the door, I can still feel it through the door, and through the walls—looking at me, smiling at me! Oh, I hate those eyes, I hate that smile, I hate the whole damn thing!

BITOY: Oh come, come, Tony! It's only a picture. It won't eat you up.

TONY: Who does he think he is? Who the hell does he think he is?

BITOY: Are you referring to the painting or the painter?

TONY: You were in his room just now, weren't you?

BITOY: Are you speaking of Don Lorenzo?

TONY: Yes, yes! This Don Lorenzo Marasigan—this great Don Lorenzo who has so much damn pride in his head and nothing at all in his pockets. He had you in his room, didn't he? He talked to you, didn't he?

BITOY: He was very friendly.

TONY: I've been living here for months and he hasn't once asked me to his room!

BITOY: But he doesn't know you, Tony.

TONY: He doesn't want to know me! He thinks it's shameful I should be living here! He feels ashamed because his house has become a flop-house! And why should he feel ashamed, I'd like to know! What is he anyway, I'd like to know!

BITOY: Well, among other things, he's a scholar, an artist, and a patriot.

TONY: So he's a great man. So he's a great painter. So he fought in the Revolution. And so what? And what's that old Revolution of his to me? I went hungry and I got kicked about just the same in spite of that old Revolution he's so damn proud of! I don't owe him any thanks! And what the hell he is now? Just a beggar! That's what he is now—just a miserable old beggar! And he has the nerve to look down on me!

BITOY: How do you know he does?

TONY: Oh, I know. I've talked to him. I forced my way into his room once.

BITOY: And he threw you out?

TONY: Oh no, no! He was very courteous, very polite. I went there to tell him about this American wanting to buy this painting for two grand—and he listened very courteously, he listened very politely. And he said he was very sorry but it was none of his business. He said: "The picture belongs to my daughters it does not belong to me. If anyone wants to buy it, they will have to talk to my daughters." And then he asked me to excuse him, he said he wanted to take a nap—and I found myself on my way out. Oh, he threw me out all right— but very courteously, very politely—the damn beggar—but he's going to pay for it! Oh, I'll make him pay for it!

BITOY: Aren't you being rather silly, Tony?

TONY *(grinning at PORTRAIT):* And I know just where it will hurt him!

BITOY: What has the old man done to you?

TONY: Won't his damn heart break when his loving daughters sell off this picture!

BITOY: Oh, is that why you're so eager to make them sell?

TONY: Besides, this American has promised to pay me a very handsome commission, you know!

(Enter Candida and Paula. Tony turns away from the PORTRAIT.)

Well, did you ladies catch the rat?

PAULA *(proudly):* Oh, of course! My sister never fails!

(She and Candida begin to clear the table.)

TONY: She is the champion rat-catcher, eh?

CANDIDA *(modestly):* Oh no—just an expert.

BITOY: Candida has been the official rat-catcher of the family since she was a little girl.

PAULA: Oh, even at night—even in the middle of the night—if any of us heard a squeak, we would cry out: "Candida, a rat! Come, Candida—a rat!" And Candida always woke up. She would come; we would hear her prowling about, peering here, peering there; and then we would hear a sudden dash, a brief struggle, a faint squeak—and nothing more—only Candida sleepily walking back to her bed. She always got her rat!

BITOY: How do you do it, Candida?

CANDIDA: Oh, I just seem to have a talent for it.

TONY *(thoughtfully)*: Yes—but I am planning to—well—develop it, you know—to develop it for more general commercial purposes.

(Tony and Bitoy exchange blank looks.)

After all, what is the point in having talent if you cannot use it to make money?

TONY: What, indeed?

BITOY: Speaking of money, Tony here tells me there is an American who wanted to buy this new painting of your father's.

TONY: And he still wants to buy it.

CANDIDA: We have told Mr. Javier again and again: the picture is not for sale.

TONY: Two thousand dollars! That's not chicken feed.

PAULA: We are sorry, Mr. Javier. Our father painted that picture very especially for us. We will never sell it.

(Sound of knocking downstairs.)

CANDIDA: Who can that be?

BITOY: I think I know.

CANDIDA: Your friends?

BITOY: Shall I tell them to go away?

CANDIDA: You donkey! Tell them to come up.

(Bitoy goes head of stairway. Tony wanders over to the piano, opens it, and runs his fingers over the keys, standing up.)

BITOY *(at stairway)*: Hi folks—come on up.

(ENTER PETE, EDDIE, AND CORA. Pete looks rather rumpled and disheveled. Eddie is immaculate, very much the man-about-town. Cora wears slacks, looks bored and is carrying a flash-bulb camera. Pete, Eddie, and Cora are in their middle thirties. Bitoy turns to the sisters.)

Candida, Paula—these are the people I told you about.

(To the visitors.)

Miss Candida and Miss Paula Marasigan, daughters of Don Lorenzo.

(Chorus of "Hello's" and "Good Afternoon's" from the visitors.)

CANDIDA *(coming forward)*: Won't you sit down? Bitoy tell us you have all come to see our painting.

EDDIE: And to see the great painter, too, Miss Marasigan—if possible.

BITOY: It's quite impossible right now, Eddie. Don Lorenzo is taking a nap. He asked me to convey his greetings and apologies.

CANDIDA: You must excuse my father. He is getting old—and you know how old people are. They just want to sleep and sleep and not to be disturbed.

(She glances towards table.)
We were just having merienda. Would any of you care for some chocolate?

(Chorus of "No, thank you's" from the visitors.)

Then, will you please excuse us? The painting is right over there. Bitoy, you will show it to them?

(She smiles and nods at visitors and goes back to table. Bitoy, Pete, and Eddie move downstage and stand before the PORTRAIT. Paula and Candida pick up their trays and go out the room. Cora parks her camera on the sofa and walks over the piano where Tony, oblivious of the visitors, has been idly picking out a tune, still standing. The tune is "Vereda Tropical.")

CORA: Hi, Tony.

TONY *(looking around)*: Hi, Cora.

CORA *(glancing round the room)*: It is where you live now?

TONY: Very elegant, don't you think?

CORA *(fetching out her cigarettes)*: It looks rather tired to me. Can I smoke here—or would that old bozo *(nodding towards photograph over piano)* drop down from the wall.

TONY *(sitting down on stool; his back against piano)*: Oh, he's an old friend of mine. Here, give me one too.

(They light cigarettes. Cora sits down on the chair beside Tony, facing audience.)

CORA *(leaning sideways towards Tony and gesturing with her head towards the group in front of PORTRAIT)*: The Intelligentsia. Speechless with ecstasy.

(She raises her voice and mockingly declaims:)

"Then felt I like some watcher in the skies
When a new planet swims into his ken...
Silent, upon a peak in Darien—"
(After a pause) Well, speak up, boys, Say something. Or should I send out for some aspirin?

TONY: What do you think of that picture, Cora?

CORA: Don't ask me. I'm allergic to classical stuff. Hey, Pete!

PETE: Yes, Cora?

CORA: Well, what do you say, Pete? Is it Art—or is it baloney?

PETE: Oh, it's Art all right—but I feel like brushing my teeth.

CORA: Oh, good! Hooray for Art!

BITOY: How do you like it, Eddie?

EDDIE: I don't like it at all.

PETE: Well, what do you think of it?

EDDIE: My thoughts are unprintable.

CORA: Oh Eddie, I'm just dying to read them!

EDDIE: Ready, Cora?

CORA *(fetching out pencil and notebook)*: I'm all yours, sweetheart.

EDDIE: Now, let me see...What do we say first?

BITOY: We? You're writing this feature article, Eddie—not us.

EDDIE: But what the devil can anybody say about this picture?

CORA: I'm waiting, genius.

TONY: Just say it ought to be in a garbage can, guy.

CORA: Oh, Tony—don't you like it either?

TONY: I love it! It's worth two thousand dollars to me!

CORA: Hear that, Eddie? Now you can say that a member of the proletariat—you are a member of the proletariat, aren't you, Tony?

TONY: What's that?

CORA: Oh yes, you are. Hey, fellows—this is Tony Javier, a darned good piano player. He and I grew up among the slums of Tondo. And there you are, Eddie! You can bring in the slums of Tondo just like that.

EDDIE: Oh no—no again!

PETE: How can you write about Art and not bring in the slums of Tondo?

BITOY: And the Ivory Tower.

CORA: And the proletariat. Like Tony here. And if he says the picture's worth two thousand dollars to him—

EDDIE: I don't care what he says. This picture's not worth two cents to me. I don't understand all this fuss about it. I don't think it's worth writing about at all. Oh, why did I ever learn to write!

CORA: Darling, who said you ever did?

EDDIE: Come on, Pete—help me out.

PETE: It's easy as pie, Eddie. Just be angry with this picture; just pile on the social consciousness.

EDDIE: I'm sick of writing about social consciousness!

CORA: And besides, it's not fashionable anymore.

PETE: You could begin with a punchline: "If it's not Proletarian, it's not Art."

EDDIE: Sure…let me see…something like this: "As I always say, Art is not autonomous, Art should not stand aloof from mundane affairs; Art should be socially significant; Art has a function…"

BITOY: Like making people brush their teeth?

PETE: Like making people brush their teeth.

BITOY: Then Don Lorenzo is a highly successful artist.

PETE: He ought to go and work for Kolynos Toothpaste.

CORA: As I always say, the real artists of our time are the advertising men.

BITOY: Michelangelo plus Shakespeare equals a Kolynos ad.

PETE: My dear boy, compared to the functional perfection of a Kolynos ad, Michelangelo and Shakespeare were amateurs.

CORA: Shut up, Pete. Go on, Eddie. "Art has a function." Now what?

PETE: Now he must emphasize the contrast between the wealth of artistic material lying all about us and the poverty of the local artist's imagination.

CORA: Oh Christ—must I hear that again!

PETE: Cora, Cora—imagine being a critic and failing to say that!

BITOY (*in mock-oratorical manner*): Outside are the slums of Tondo—and the battlefields of China—

PETE (*same manner*): And what does the artist do?

CORA (*same manner*): He dreams about Aeneas—

BITOY: He dreams about the Trojan War—

PETE: The most hackneyed theme in all Art!

BITOY: And he celebrates with exaggerated defiance values from which all content has vanished!

CORA: He looks back with nostalgic longing to the more perfect world of the Past!

PETE: And he paints this atrocious picture—the sickly product of a decadent imagination!

CORA: Of a decadent bourgeois imagination, Pete.

PETE: Of a decadent bourgeois imagination, Cora!

EDDIE: Will you idiots stop fooling around and let me think!

PETE: But we're not fooling, Eddie, and you don't have to think! Your article could practically write itself. Just compare this *(waving toward PORTRAIT)* piece of tripe with proletarian art as whole. Proletarian Art—so clean, so wholesome, so vigorous, in spite of the vileness and misery with which it deals, because it is revolutionary, because it is realistic, because it is dynamic—the vanguard of human progress, the expression of forces which can have but one—one—only! inevitable outcome!

CORA: Paradise!

BITOY: Heaven itself!

PETE: No tyrants, no capitalists, no social classes—

BITOY: No halitosis and no B.O.!

CORA: Freedom from Kolynos! Freedom from Life Buoy!

PETE: And there you are, Eddie—you've got a fighting article!

EDDIE: Oh, I don't know, I don't know...

PETE: What's wrong with it?

EDDIE: Well, as Cora says—it's old hat; it's going out of fashion.

BITOY: How can loving your fellowman ever go out of fashion?

PETE: My dear boy, you must distinguish between doing a thing and writing about it. We are all writers here; and it is our privilege to write about things, like loving one's fellowman, or like organizing the proletariat. But the kind of writing we do—alas!—can go out of fashion. Look at Eddie here. He says he is sick of social consciousness. Or does it?

EDDIE: Oh, no, no. How I love the lower classes!

CORA: If only they would use Kolynos—

BITOY: And take a bath everyday—

PETE: And wear a necktie and coat like Eddie here—

EDDIE: And be able to discourse on Marxism and Trotskyism like Pete here—

CORA: Boys, boys—no bickering.

EDDIE: Cora—

CORA: Yes, darling?

EDDIE: Shut up.

CORA: That's what I like about Eddie. He knows how to deal with common people. And if you love the common people so much, Eddie, we've got lots and lots of them right where we work. They're down among the machines, and they're there every day—right in the same building with us. They're small and they smell of sweat and they live on fish. I'm surprised at you fellows. Here's the proletariat right under your noses, day in and day out, but I never see you fellows going down to organize them—or to fraternize with them. As a matter of fact, I have noticed that you actually avoid going down to them. You always try to send somebody else to deal with them. Now why? Don't they speak the same language—or are you afraid?

PETE: Cora, Cora, you misjudge us. What you take for fear is not fear at all— merely awe and reverence.

BITOY: Besides, it's so much easier to love the proletariat from a distance.

PETE: A very safe distance.

CORA: From the smell of sweat and fish.

EDDIE: And that's what all our social consciousness amounts to. Just yap-yap-yap from a safe iterary distance. Just the yap-yap-yap of a literary fashion...

CORA: In other words—

CORA and BITOY *(together)*: Just yap-yap-yap.

CORA: Period.

EDDIE: Remember when all the world was divided between the Boobs and the Bright Young People? We were the Bright Young People, and the Boobs were all those little hicks and Babbits who weren't reading Mr. Sinclair Lewis and Mr. Mencken and the beautiful Mr. Cabell.

CORA: And then, suddenly, those little hicks became the Proletariat.

PETE: Yes—and everybody else were just horrid bourgeois and reactionaries.

EDDIE: And of course we were the Champions of the Proletariat, we were the Spearhead of Progress, we were the Revolution! Didn't we know all about cartels and strikes and dialectics!

CORA: And if we never did go to fight in Spain—well, we did go to those Writers' Congress in New York.

EDDIE: And now we've divided the world into Fascists and Men of Good Will.

PETE: Ourselves being the Men of Good Will.

CORA: And Pink is no longer the fashionable color. We're now wearing the patriotic red-white-and-blue. It's no longer smart to be a fellow traveler. We've all become Fourth-of-July orators.

EDDIE: One thing you can say for us anyway—when it comes to literary fashions, we're always right out in front—

PETE: Always right out in the field—

CORA: Behaving as the wind behaves.

BITOY: I wonder what the fashion will be tomorrow?

CORA: I hope it won't be loving those so polite and so heroic Japanese, the champions of Oriental dignity.

BITOY: Oh, impossible!

CORA: Because the marine will keep 'em flying?

BITOY: Because our fashions are always made in America—and imagine the comrades in America starting a fashion to love the Japs! Oh, there's going to be a war, fellows—there's going to be a war! And alas for Culture, alas for Art!

EDDIE: To hell with Culture! To hell with Art! I hope the war breaks out tomorrow!

PETE: I hope it breaks out tonight!

EDDIE: A really big, bloody, blasting war that blows up everything!

PETE: The bigger the better!

CORA: You fellows make me laugh.

PETE: Eddie, we make her laugh!

EDDIE *(in falsetto)*: We're Pollyanna, the Glad Girl!

PETE and EDDIE *(joining hands and prancing about)*: We are the happy, happy boys, who bid your lonely heart rejoice!

CORA *(dryly)*: Ha-ha-ha.

EDDIE: There, we made her laugh again!

CORA: Oh, you fellows are funny all right. Praying for a war—just so you won't have to face up to that picture.

PETE: Eddie, don't we want to face up to this picture?

CORA: No, you're afraid.

EDDIE *(in earnest)*: To hell with that picture! With a big war about to blow us up any moment, who wants to bother about pictures? The times we live in are too tremendous to waste on the pretty visions of poets and artists! Over in Europe, young men are dying by the thousands at this very moment! The future of Democracy and of the human race itself is in peril! And you want us to stand here and wrestle with one little painting by one little man! Think of what's happening right now in England! Think of what' happening right now in China! *(He pauses.)*

CORA: Go on.

EDDIE: Go on what?

CORA: Go on piling up more reasons for not looking at that picture. Go on justifying yourself for running away from it.

PETE: Now, wait a minute. Why should we be afraid of this picture?

CORA: Because it is a work of art—and it makes us all feel very bogus and very impotent.

PETE: It doesn't make me feel anything of the sort!

CORA: Oh no?

(A pause, during which they all look towards PORTRAIT.)

PETE: No...No, it doesn't make me feel anything of the sort! Who is this Don Lorenzo that should I should be afraid to face his portrait?

CORA: He is the creator, and we are the counterfeiters. He is the Angel of Judgement come out of the Past.

PETE: Well, I'm the Present—and I refuse to be judged by the Past! It is the Past rather that has to be judged by me! If there's anything wrong with me, then the Past had something to do with it! Afraid? Who's afraid? I stand here and face you, Don Lorenzo, and I ask you: What were you and what did you do that you should have the right to judge me?

BITOY: Pete, Pete— he did what he could! He wrote, he painted, he organized, he fought in the Revolution.

PETE: And so what? How about afterwards? Did he have the guts to go on fighting? Did he even go on painting? All his best work was done before the Revolution. What has he produced since then? Just this one picture—and he painted this only recently. How about all the time between? What was he doing during all those years?

(He looks around at his listeners; no one answers; and he smiles.)

You see? But Bitoy here will tell us. Bitoy knows.

BITOY: What do you mean, Pete?

PETE: Go on—tell us about their gatherings—the gatherings of these old men, these old veterans, these relics of the glorious Past! You know; you were there. What do you call those gatherings?

BITOY: Tertulias.

PETE: Yes, the Tertulias! And what did they do there? What did these old men do?

BITOY: Well, they...they talked.

PETE: About what? But don't tell me. I can guess. They talked about the Past. They talked about their student days in Manila and in Madrid and in Paris. They talked about the old feuds and bickerings among the patriots. And, of course—in tones of hushed adoration—they talked about their General!

BITOY: Yes—but they also talked about poetry and art and the theatre, and about politics, and about religion.

PETE: Oh, I can almost see them—those pitiful old men—gathered in this room and consoling each other; drinking chocolate and fighting over and over again the Battle of Balintawak and the Battle of San Juan and the Battle of Tirad Pass! They had to feel important—so, they reminded each other how brave they used to be. They had been thrust aside and forgotten—so, they hated the Present. They thought it rude and vulgar and on its way to damnation. Isn't that right, Bitoy?

BITOY: No—not much.

PETE: And that's how the Revolution ended! That's how the Revolution ended! Groups of embittered, envious old men gathering in dusty bookshops and bankrupt drugstores and broken-down tenements like this one! Just look around this room—what does it proclaim? Failure! Defeat! Poverty! Nostalgia! And here they would gather—those bitter old men—to sigh over the Past, to curse the Present, and to execrate the men in power! But what had happened to these old warriors? During the Revolution, they were the big ones, they were the men in power. Why did they lose that power? Why were they thrust aside and forgotten? Because they were not big enough after all to handle the Future! Because they tried to stop the clock! Oh, it's always the same story: the revolutionaries of today, the reactionaries of tomorrow! And so new men arose—new men displaced them—younger and bolder men who were not afraid to be rude and vulgar and damned! Can you name a single top figure of the Revolution who managed to remain on top in the age that followed? No; they were all swept away! Oh, maybe it's just as well that Rizal and Bonifacio and Mabini died young! Who knows? They may only have swelled the ranks of the old and the obsolete; they may only have rotted away in obscurity and resentment; they may only have frittered their lives away going from one tertulia to another, to drink chocolate and to regret. Like Don Lorenzo here. Yes, like this great Don Lorenzo! Look at him! He has been eating his heart away in obscurity and resentment. He wants to comfort his pride, to justify his failure—so, what does he do? So, he paints himself as a hero—as THE hero, in fact—as Aeneas! There he stands—in classic raiment, in a classic pose, and with the noble classic landscape behind him. He has removed himself completely from his native land—because his native land has discarded him. He has placed himself entirely above the rude and vulgar Present—because the Present refuses to recognize his importance. What a pitiful picture! Oh, what a pitiful, pitiful picture! A Portrait of the Artist as Obsolete!

(A silence. They are all staring at PORTRAIT. Unnoticed, SUSAN and VIOLET come up the stairs and pause on the landing, surprised at the mutely staring people in the sala. They glance at each other and giggle behind their hands. Susan and Violet are "old girls," plumplish, cute-mannered, and thickly painted. They are wearing tight-fitting sleeveless frocks; and they are both quite tipsy.)

VIOLET *(leaning forward, cupping her mouth with a hand)*: Yoo-hoo!

(Everybody in the sala gives a nervous start. Susan and Vilolet giggle wildly.)

CORA *(tartly)*: Who are you?

TONY *(rising)*: Holy cow!

SUSAN *(ignoring Tony)*: Excuse us for intruding.

VIOLET: Don't you people know us?

SUSAN: I'm Susan.

VIOLET: And I'm Violet.

SUSAN: We're artists.

VIOLET: At the Parisian Theater. You know, *(wiggling her torso)* vaudeville!

PETE *(hurrying towards them)*: But of course, we know you! Certainly we know you! Susan and Violet, the brightest stars of the Manila stage! Why, girls—I'm one of your most avid admirers! I never miss a show!

(More giggles from Susan and Violet.)

And what a break! What a God-given break! Come in, girls—come right in! Cora, you're your camera.

CORA *(rising)*: What are you up to now?

PETE: I said, get your camera.

(Cora goes for camera.)

VIOLET: Goodness, do you want to take pictures of us?

SUSAN: Are you people from newspapers?

PETE: We're from the "Daily Scream"—and we're going to put you girls right on the cover of our Sunday magazine.

SUSAN (*suspiciously*): Why?

PETE: Because you are great and honest artists.

SUSAN: Quit your kidding, mister.

PETE: Don't you want your picture taken?

VIOLET: Oh, but now! We look terrible now!

PETE: You look wonderful.

VIOLET (*giggling*): Frankly, mister—we're groggy.

SUSAN: I'm not. I feel just fine.

VIOLET: We met a couple of sailors down the street. We just said to them, we just said: "Keep 'em flying, boys!" And you know what? They took us off with them and bought us all the drinks we could hold!

SUSAN: Oh, they were nice. Real gentlemen.

TONY (*approaching at last; grimly*): What are you two doing up here?

VIOLET: Hi, Tony.

SUSAN: We just wanted to see where you live.

TONY: Okay, you've seen it. Now, scram!

SUSAN: Now, look here, Tony—don't you talk to me that way! We'll stay as long as we like!

PETE: Of course you're going to stay. Come on, Tony—be a pal. We want to take their pictures.

VIOLET: Can you beat it! The man is serious!

PETE: You bet I'm serious! Come over here, girls.

VIOLET *(giggling; hurriedly fixing herself up)*: Oh, but we look awful, really! Fine cover girls we'll make!

SUSAN *(following sullenly)*: I hope this ain't a gag or something.

CORA: What girlish optimism!

PETE *(posing girls in front of PORTRAIT; their backs to audience)*: Now, just stand right there. Ready, Cora?

CORA: I hope you know what you're doing.

BITOY: Pete, lay off, for God's sake!

EDDIE: Oh, leave him alone. He's just putting Don Lorenzo in his place.

PETE: Yeah—among his fellow artists. I'll teach him to act superior. Now look, girls. *(Pointing up to PORTRAIT)* See that picture?

VIOLET *(looking up)*: Hmm, very pretty.

SUSAN: What are those two guys doing? Playing leap frog?

PETE: The young man is carrying the old man on his back. They're evacuating from a war, see?

VIOLET: What happened to their automobile?

EDDIE: Oh, it got commandeered by the army.

SUSAN *(still staring up)*: What horrible eyes!

PETE: You mean, the old man?

SUSAN *(nervously adjusting a shoulder strap)*: He makes me feel naked, he gives me the creeps—

(Both girls are staring fixedly at PORTRAIT.)

PETE: *(backing away from camera range)*: Hold it, girls! No, no—don't look at the camera—look up at the picture! That's right. Get it, Cora!

(Cora flashes picture.)

And there we are—all nice and pretty. Will you really put us on your magazine cover?

PETE: Absolutely! And with the fanciest title I can think of. What would you suggest, Eddie?

EDDIE: How about "A Portrait of One Dead Artist and Two Live Ones"?

CORA: Corny.

PETE: Yeah, I want something with more snap to it.

CORA: Why not try a four-letter word?

SUSAN *(who's still standing in same place, staring up at PORTRAIT):* He really has got horrible eyes!

VIOLET: You can beat it! She's fascinated with that old bird! Hey, Susan—he won't eat you up!

SUSAN *(her eyes never leaving PORTRAIT):* He looks like my father...

EDDIE: Your father must be a very distinguished man.

SUSAN *(impatiently):* Oh, I don't mean they look alike! I mean they look at me in the same way—

EDDIE: Your father must be a very refined man.

SUSAN: Oh yes—very refined. That's why I left home. Whenever I did something bad, he never said anything. He just looked at me *(nodding at PORTRAIT)* like that old guy up there. Oh, damn him! He gave me the creeps!

PETE: Why, you haven't been doing anything wrong, have you?

SUSAN: No, I haven't. And even if I have, what right has he to look at me like that? He's not my father!

EDDIE: Nobody says he is.

SUSAN *(suddenly screaming):* Then why the hell is he looking at me like that!

TONY *(approaching):* Now look, Susan—you're dead drunk. And we've got a show in an hour. You go home—*(He lays a hand on her arm.)*

SUSAN: I'll go home when I damn please! And take your hands off me!

TONY: What's eating you anyway?

SUSAN: A lot you care!

TONY: Oh, it's something I did, is it?

SUSAN: Where were you last night? Where did you go after the show?

TONY: I had a headache. So I came straight home.

SUSAN: You never bothered to tell me, did you? You didn't even remember we had a date, did you?

TONY: Sorry. I forgot. But I had such a splitting headache—

SUSAN: Don't make me laugh!

TONY: Now listen, Susan—the show goes on in an hour. You've got to sober up. Violet, you take her home and give her a bath.

VIOLET: I'll do nothing of the sort. We came here together to rehearse.

TONY: Rehearse what?

VIOLET *(singing and wiggling)*: "A-tisket, a-tisket, a brown and yellow basket—" It's the new number we do. We were supposed to rehearse it last night after the show but we couldn't find you anywhere.

SUSAN: He had a head-ache, Violet. Hah!

TONY *(striding fiercely towards piano)*: Okay, okay—so let's rehearse!

VIOLET: You won't mind, boys, will you?

EDDIE: We'll be delighted!

VIOLET: Come on, Susan.

(They go to piano where Tony is already seated and rattling off the opening flourish. Standing side by side, just behind Tony, they go into the "A-tiskte, a-tisket" number with all the appropriate motions. The girls being—uh—plastered, their performance is spirited, of course, but hardly melodious. The newspaper folk listen a moment; then resume their talk, being obliged to raise their voices.)

CORA: Enjoying yourself, Pete?

PETE: I'm thrilled!

EDDIE: So am I! Hooray for boogie-woogie!

BITOY *(grimly)*: I hope the war breaks out tomorrow!

CORA: I hope it breaks out tonight!

PETE: Look around you, fellows! Think of it! This room—those—chairs—that classic painting—those pictures on the walls—

CORA: They ought to drop down from the walls!

PETE: But they don't! They can't!

EDDIE: Their helpless! They're dead!

PETE: Hooray!

CORA *(sarcastic)*: But we're alive—hooray! We can do as we please!

BITOY: Like playing boogie-woogie here!

PETE: Exactly! Oh, think of it! The boogie—woogie—in this room—in this house—in this Temple of the Past—where the bitter old men gathered to recall the old days! Oh, look around you! Savor it fully!

BITOY: What? The outrage?

EDDIE: And there's your title, Pete! "The Boogie-Woogie Invades a Temple of the Past"!

CORA: It's an invasion all right! Are we the barbarians?

BITOY: No, we're Nero—with his fiddle!

(Candida and Paula have appeared in doorway and are looking rather dazedly round the room.)

PETE: And there you are, Miss Marasigan and Miss Marasigan!

(Candida and Paula come downstage.)

We're speechless with admiration for your father's painting!

CANDIDA: What did you say?

PETE *(shouting)*: I said, we admire your father's painting! We love it, we adore it, we are delirious about it! Could we borrow it for a few weeks?

CANDIDA: What was that?

BITOY: Oh, cut it out, Pete!

EDDIE: But that's what we came for!

CORA: Then, dammit, let's shelve the whole idea!

PETE: Will you people shut up and let me handle this!

CANDIDA: But what are you saying? What is all this?

PAULA: Please! Just what do you want of us?

PETE: We want you to lend us this painting!

CANDIDA: What!

PAULA: Lend you our painting!

EDDIE: For a worthy cause!

CANDIDA: What will you do with it?

PETE: We are putting on an Art Show—a benefit Art Show!

EDDIE: We belong to the G.U.D.M.!

PAULA: What is that?

PETE: The Global Union of Democratic Men—and we are putting on this show to raise funds!

EDDIE: Funds to help Democratic cause all over the world!

PETE: We need this painting, Miss Marasigan!

EDDIE: You must lend it to us!

PAULA: We are sorry but we cannot do it!

CANDIDA: It is impossible!

PETE: Only for a few weeks!

BITOY: You heard what they said!

EDDIE: But why impossible?

PETE: They can do it—only they won't!

CORA: After all, the picture is their property!

PETE: If it's a Work of Art, it belongs to the people!

EDDIE: It belongs to the whole world!

CANDIDA: No, no—no! The picture belongs to us! It must never leave our house!

PETE (*thundering*): Miss Marasigan, your father fought for freedom, he fought for democracy! He is an old man now and can fight no more in the battlefields—but it is merely right and fitting that this picture of his should go forth in his place—to fight for freedom, to fight for democracy—in this dark hour when all over the world freedom and democracy are in peril! He himself would wish it so! Miss Marasigan, it is your duty to lend us this picture for the cause! It is your duty to help in the struggle to preserve this way of life we all enjoy! This life of happiness, peace, and dignity!

(*Susan and Violet have reached the climax of their number and are now really yelling at the tops of their voices. So is Pete.*)

Think Miss Marasigan—think of what's going on right now all over the world! Young men dying by the thousands! Women and children shattered into pieces! Entire cities wiped out as bombs rain down from the skies! Death, hunger, murder, and pestilence—and power-mad dictators wallowing in the blood and humanity! This is no time for selfishness! This is no time for private sentiments! We are all involved, we are all in danger! The bell tolls for all mankind! And it is your duty to send this picture to fight! It is your duty to help the Cause of your father! It is your duty—

CANDIDA (*clapping her hands to her ears and screaming*): Oh stop, stop, STOP!

(*The group at piano breaks off abruptly. There is a moment of startled silence. Candida recovers herself.*)

I...I am sorry. Please excuse me.

VIOLET: Can you beat it! They're hysterical! What's the matter? Don't you people like our singing?

TONY (*rising*): Okay, girls—go home.

SUSAN: Wait a minute! Just what did we do?

TONY: I said, go home.

VIOLET: But why? Oh, are those your landladies, Tony? Well, why not introduce us?

SUSAN (*ambling forward; an arm akimbo*): He's ashamed of us, Violet. He thinks we don't look like decent. He thinks we're drunk.

TONY (*hurrying after her and grabbing her arm*): I told you to get out of here!

SUSAN (*wrenching her arm loose*): I'll go when I damn please! I've got as much right to stay here as anybody else! You think I don't know what kind of a house this is? Oh, I found last night, dearie! I saw and that Shanghai woman—

VIOLET (*raising a fist*): SHUT UP! Shut up or, by God, I'll bring that woman in here!

(*She turns to the sisters.*) Now, is that the kind of a house you run?

(*She turns to PORTRAIT.*) And is that the kind of a house you run?

TONY (*grabbing her arm and dragging her off*): You're getting out of here if I have to throw you out!

SUSAN (*screaming and struggling*): Let me go! Let me go! Let me—AOUH!
(*He has slapped her hard across the mouth. She cowers away, holding her mouth.*)

TONY: Now get out! GET OUT OF HERE!

VIOLET (*taking the sobbing Susan in her arms*): Okay, big boy— keep your shirt on! We're going. Come on, Susan.

(She leads the sobbing Susan away. At stairway, she pauses and looks back.)

Hitting a woman when she's drunk—pah!

(Tony waits until they have gone down the stairs; then he strides off to his room, slamming the door behind him.)

BITOY: Fellows, I think we had better go.

PETE: Miss Marasigan, about that matter—

CANDIDA *(quietly)*: It is quite impossible. We cannot lend you the picture. We are sorry.

PETE: Well...*(He shrugs.)* Well, thanks just the same—and thanks for letting us come. And good afternoon.

(Chorus of "Thank you's" and "Good afternoon's" from the others as they move to stairway, Candida and Paula accompanying them. Exeunt Pete, Eddie and Cora. Bitoy lingers behind on the landing.)

CANDIDA: Well, Bitoy—you said your friends were coming just to see the picture.

PAULA: You said nothing about their wanting to borrow it.

BITOY: I'm sorry.

CANDIDA: Did they really like the picture?

BITOY: No—I don't think so.

CANDIDA: Which is just what we thought. Nobody ever likes the picture.

BITOY *(gazing towards PORTRAIT)*: I do.

PAULA: But you are an old friend. Other people are not so kind. They say that picture is beautiful but they do not find it enchanting.

BITOY: Why should they? Art is not magic. Its purpose is not to enchant—but to disenchant!

PAULA: Jesus!

CANDIDA: How impressive you sound!

BITOY: May I come again?

PAULA *(smiling)*: Do you enjoy being disenchanted?

BITOY: No—but I need to be.

CANDIDA: Come whenever you like, Bitoy. We are always at home.

BITOY: Thank you—and goodbye till then.

CANDIDA AND PAULA: Goodbye, Bitoy.

> *(Exit Bitoy. Paula and Candida leave stairway and begin moving back the chairs and table to their proper place at center with the sofa. From this point, twilight starts and the stage dims very gradually.)*

PAULA *(as they shift the furniture)*: What we are going to do, Candida?

CANDIDA: About what?

PAULA *(nodding towards Tony's door)*: About him.

CANDIDA: We must order him to leave this house.

PAULA: Yes—certainly!

CANDIDA: Bring a woman here—

PAULA: And then lying about it!

CANDIDA: Oh, we have been too lenient!

PAULA: Well, we needed the money.

CANDIDA: He can take his money somewhere else—and at once! He shall leave this house immediately!

> *(Tony's door opens and he comes out, wearing his coat and carrying his hat. He now looks gentle and rather wistful. The sisters stiffen and assume their coldest expressions. Candida raps on the table.)*

Mr. Javier, please come over here. We have something to say to you.

TONY *(approaching; guiltily fingering his hat)*: Yes, I know. And there's something I would like to say to you, too.

CANDIDA: There is nothing you can say that would interest us!

TONY: Look, if a man asked you to save his soul—would you refuse?

CANDIDA: What nonsense!

PAULA: Why should any man ask us to save his soul?

CANDIDA: Who are we—God?

TONY: You are good, both of you.

CANDIDA: We have had enough of your flatteries, Mr. Javier—

PAULA: Both of us!

CANDIDA: And your lies!

TONY: Then you refuse?

PAULA: We refuse to be flattered and deceived over and over again!

TONY: But look here—I'm not flattering you, I'm not deceiving you! Oh, please believe me! This is my salvation! This is the one place in the world where I've wanted to be good, where I've tried to be good! Yes, you smile—you don't believe me. Oh, I deserve that all right! I know I'm bad, I know I'm wicked—but that's just the point! I know what I am. Isn't that the beginning of salvation?

CANDIDA: That you recognize your wickedness?

TONY: And feel very ashamed of it.

PAULA: Then why do you continue? Why do you do these things?

TONY *(with a shrug):* The habits of a lifetime.

PAULA: And you do them here, in this house that you call your salvation!

TONY: Oh, I get so disgusted sometimes!

CANDIDA: With our house?

TONY: With myself.

PAULA: You get disgusted with yourself—but it is our house you defile!

TONY: Yes. . .Remember the first time I came here? Oh, I was in a beautiful condition! I had just lost my job and I had been thrown out of the filthy flophouse where I was staying because of a fight. So I came here. I had seen the sign at the door and I thought this was just another Intramuros flophouse. But as I came up those stairs I suddenly felt as if I was coming home at last. Everything looks so clean, everything was so quiet. This was the home I never had; the home that nobody ever gave me. Oh, I was drunk—I had been drunk for a week—and I felt so ashamed of myself standing here in my dirty shoes and my dirty clothes that—you know what I did? I spat on the floor! Now, do you understand?

CANDIDA (*coldly*): No.

TONY: Of course not! How could you? You were born in this house, you grew up in this house! Do you know where I was born? Do you know where I grew up? Listen: when you were going off to your fine convent school in your fine clean clothes, I was wandering about in the streets—a little child dressed in rags, always dirty, always hungry. And you know where I found my food? In garbage cans!

PAULA (*sinking weakly into a chair*): Oh no!

TONY: Oh yes! And do you know what it's like to go begging in the streets when you're still just a baby? Do you know what it's like to have your own brute of a father driving you out to beg? Can you even imagine that kind of a childhood?

CANDIDA (*sinking down too, on the sofa*): We know you have had a hard life—

TONY: You know nothing!

(*A pause, while he scowls at the memory. Then the scowl fades into a bravado smile.*)

Oh, I'm not crying over anything! I never cry! I haven't had a hard time, really. I've always been strong and tough, and I'm clever, and I learn fast. Besides, I'm very good-looking, you know, and I've got a lot of charm. Heck, I don't care if that sounds vain—it's the truth! Ever since I was a kid, people have been fascinated with me—they pick me up and give me the breaks. Nice people, too—people with class. Well, just to be completely honest, I'll admit that when they get to know me they drop me quicker than a hot brick! But what the heck—somebody else always comes along and picks me up again. I'm irresistible! All I have to do is smile and look sort of pathetic—you know:

very young, very brave, and very broke. They always fall for that. Oh, I've been using my charm to get me places—it sure has got me far! Before I was twenty, I had been to America.

PAULA *(in admiration):* To America!

TONY *(his chest swelling):* San Francisco, Los Angeles, Chicago, New Orleans, Mexico City, Havana, and New York!

PAULA: But how wonderful!

CANDIDA *(quite impressed Herself):* How did you do it?

TONY: Oh, an old American couple picked me up and took me along; they were nuts about me. They said I looked like the Infant Samuel.

CANDIDA: Did you have a nice time?

TONY: Wow, the time of my Life! Until they dropped me. And then—oh, Jesus!—did I have to slave! But I didn't mind. It was all part of my education. I was educating myself; I was running away from home. I've been running away from home, you know, all my life—as far away as I can get. But even America wasn't far enough, *(He glances wistfully around the room)* No fooling— this house was the farthest I've got away from my childhood… this house and the piano—any piano..

(The wistfulness darkens again into a scowl.)

But of course you ladies would say that I never left home!

As far as you're concerned, I'm still vermin, I'm still trash, I'm still the Tondo slums!

(He whirls around at PORTRAIT.)

See how your father looks at me! And you wonder why I do the things I do here!

CANDIDA: To spite us?

TONY: And to spite this house—and everything in it!

CANDIDA: And you say this house is your salvation!

PAULA: But do you like it or do you hate it? You change so suddenly from one moment to another. How can we know when to believe you? How can we know you are serious?

TONY *(suddenly griming again)*: How can you? I never know myself!

CANDIDA: Oh Paula, this is all just the same as usual. He is only making fun of us!

TONY: Oh no—honest, I'm not!

CANDIDA: Were you serious when you asked us to save your soul?

TONY *(clapping a hand to his brow)*: Oh Lord, did I ask you to do that?

(The sisters smile helplessly.)

PAULA: You certainly did!

TONY *(bending down)*: And will you?

CANDIDA: Are you serious?

TONY *(throwing his hands up)*: Maybe I am and maybe I'm not. Oh, the hell with this! Does it matter anyway? Look, just tell me what answers will please you and I will give you that answer.

CANDIDA: Is that your sincerity?

TONY: I'm a poor man—I can't afford sincerity. I have to suit my moods to the moods of my batters. That's one of the very first things I learned—and now I'm an expert. Oh, it's not hard. Nothing I feel ever goes deep enough to make me cry anyway. So, I'll change my moods and I'll change my colors if it's to my advantage and if it gets me what I want. That's my sincerity! So, come on—tell me; do you want me to be serious or do you want me to be funny?

CANDIDA: Oh, you are impossible!

TONY: Then you won't save my soul?

CANDIDA: It is too late.

TONY *(glancing at his watch)*: Oh Lord—yes! And I'll be late for the show! I must rush!

(He claps his hat on and runs to stairway where he suddenly stops and turn around.)

Oh, I forgot—you ladies had something to say to me. *(He shrugs and looks pathetic.)* Well, you might as well say it now.

(The sisters look at him, then to each other, and then down at their hands. There is a moment's silence.)

CANDIDA *(looking up, but not towards Tony)*: We merely wanted to say, Mr. Javier, that…that we do not accept the testimony of intoxicated persons.

TONY *(gravely)*: I see. *(A pause.)* And is that all?

CANDIDA *(now looking towards him)*: That is all, Mr. Javier.

PAULA: Good night, Mr. Javier.

TONY *(grinning and lifting his hat high above his head)*: Good night, ladies. Good night, sweet ladies. Good night, good night!

(He puts his hat on with a swagger and runs down the stairs. The sisters burst into laughter.)

PAULA: Oh, he is funny, is he not?

CANDIDA: It would have been unjust to ask him to leave on such doubtful.

PAULA: And besides, we need the money.

CANDIDA *(rising)*: Oh, money, money, money! We must act, Paula—we must act at once. And I know just what we can do. *(She picks up newspaper.)*

PAULA: Your new plans?

CANDIDA: Yes. Listen to this. "Fifty centavos for every rat caught." Now, I wonder where this Bureau of Health and Science is. I shall go there and offer them my services. And, Paula—

PAULA: Yes?

CANDIDA: You will give lessons!

PAULA *(horrified)*: Lessons!

CANDIDA: Lessons on the piano, lessons in Spanish. We will put up—

PAULA *(rising)*: Oh no, no!

CANDIDA: Now Paula, remember—we must be bold, we must become women of the world. Did you see that newspaper girl? And she is younger than we are. We must show Manolo and Pepang that we can support ourselves, that we do not need their money.

PAULA: But lessons for whom—girls?

CANDIDA: Girls for the piano, and some men for Spanish. So many of these young students are eager to learn the language nowadays. And men have more money, you know.

PAULA: They would only laugh at me.

CANDIDA: Nonsense! Be bold! Drink a little wine before you face them. Talk in a loud voice. If they become fresh, call a policeman. We could arrange to have a policeman nearby during the first days.

PAULA: You will not be here, Candida?

CANDIDA: I shall be working at this—*(glancing at newspaper)* this Bureau of Health and Science. If they are so eager to pay fifty centavos for one rat, how will they pay somebody who is willing to catch as many rats as they want. And you know how well I do it. Oh Paula, imagine being paid to do something you enjoy! They will be amazed to see what an expert I am—and my work will be extended. I shall be appointed to clear the entire city of rats. Of course, then, I would hardly have time to do the actual catching anymore. I shall be just a kind of director—with a desk, a map, and a staff of workers. . .

PAULA *(giggling)*: And they will all be calling you Miss Marasigan!

CANDIDA: And I shall make them all wear uniforms. *(She turns wistful.)* Still, from time to time, I should want to do some of the actual catching myself—but only in the more difficult cases, of course...

PAULA: And how much will you earn?

CANDIDA: I must consult Manolo on what salary to ask. Oh, they have a sea of money rolling about in the government!

PAULA: Yes indeed. Just look at the newspapers—always talking of those people who made millions!

CANDIDA: Oh, I have it all planned out. We will make money, Paula—we will make money! And we will show Manolo and Pepang that we can keep up this house with our own efforts.

PAULA *(rapturously)*: And they will not be able to turn us out here anymore! We will not be afraid anymore!

(She sinks down on the rocking chair.)

CANDIDA *(sitting down at the piano)*: We shall stay here till we die! You and I and papa. Yes—and papa! He will get well, he will come out of his room, we will be happy again—just the three of us. It will be like the old days again...

(She begins to play, very softly, the waltz from the "Merry Widow.")

PAULA *(leaning back, and rocking the chair to the music)*: The old days...Yes, how happy we were—just the three of us—you and I and papa. In the mornings, we went to church, the three of us together. Then, after breakfast, you went off to market; I stayed here to clean the house, while papa read the newspapers. When you came back from the market, we would all go down to the patio to take the sun—papa in his rocking chair, smoking his pipe, and you and I walking round and round the fountain, arm in arm, reciting poems or singing, while all about us the pigeons whirled. Then papa would fall asleep in his chair, and we would go up and do the cooking. After lunch, the siesta; and after the siesta, the merienda. Then papa would go out for his afternoon stroll, and you and I would do the washing and the ironing. After the supper, the Rosary—and then we played the piano for papa or he read to us from Calderon. If visitors dropped in, we played "Tres-siete." Remember how we would get so excited over the game that we would play on and on till past midnight? Oh, you were a shameless cheater, Candida—and what a riot when you and papa played against each other!

(She sits still, smiling. Then she rises, humming the waltz, and begins to dance around the room, holding her skirts in her hands. As the music ends, she whirls and slowly sinks down to the floor. There is a moment of silence—Candida at the piano, her face lifted; Paula on the floor, her smiling face lifted too, her hands folded on her lap. The room is dim but not dark, the forms of the sisters and of the furniture and the squares of the balconies being clearly discernible.)

CANDIDA: Can we bring back those days again?

PAULA *(lost in thought)*: Huh?

CANDIDA: Wake up, Paula!

PAULA: What days?

CANDIDA: Those days before...before father had his accident—before he painted that picture.

PAULA: Oh Candida, we were happy enough then—and we did not know it! We destroyed the happiness we had...Oh, why did we do it, Candida, why did we do it!

CANDIDA: Hush, hush, Paula—what is done is done. Go and turn on the light.

PAULA (*rising and going to the switch, which is supposed to be on the left corner of the "fourth wall"*): Oh, why we do it! Why did father have that accident! Why did he ever paint that picture!

CANDIDA: All this unpleasantness will pass, Paula. We will be happy again. All we need is money—money and security. We will be at peace again—the three of us...Father will forgive us for what we did. And we will be all together again, we will be happy together again—the three of us...

PAULA (*in voice of alarm*): Candida, there is no light!

CANDIDA (*looking around*): What! Try again!

PAULA: I have turned this switch a dozen times. There is no light!

CANDIDA (*rising quickly*): Try the switch on the stairway—I will try this one in the corridor.

(*Paula goes to stair-landing: Candida steps just inside the doorway at right. After a moment, she comes in again and looks at Paula across the room.*)

No light either on the stairs?

PAULA: None! How about in the corridor?

CANDIDA: None also. And I saw no light in father's room.

PAULA: Oh Candida, they have cut off our light!

CANDIDA: Sh-h-h!

(The sisters fearfully come to center of stage where they huddle together.)

PAULA *(whispering)*: Shall we call up the company?

CANDIDA: It would be useless...

PAULA: Then call up Manolo, call up Pepang! Tell them what was happened to us! They must send us money right away! Oh, how could they do this to us! How could they possibly allow us to suffer this horrible, horrible, humiliation!

CANDIDA *(bitterly)*: And how shall I call them up, Paula? Am I to go down and borrow the telephone at the corner drugstore?

PAULA: But that is where we always telephone—

CANDIDA: But how, how can I go down to the street now! Think, Paula— everybody who lives on this street knows by now that we have no light, that the company has cut off our light!

PAULA *(in mounting horror)*: Oh Candida. . .oh Candida!

(Trembling, they glace behind them at the open balcony.)

CANDIDA: Go and shut those windows.

PAULA *(shivering)*: Oh no, no! They would see me! The neighbors, Candida— They will be all gathered at their windows, watching our house, pointing at our house—the only house without light in the whole street! Oh, Candida— they are all at the window, pointing and laughing and jeering!

CANDIDA: Yes—I just can imagine what they are saying. Oh, this is the chance they have long been waiting for! Yes—they will be all there watching—and "Look, look!" they will be saying, "Look at those two old maids, those two proud señoras, who are so delicate, who have such grand manners, who hold their heads so high—and look, look: they cannot even pay their light bill!"

PAULA *(covering her face)*: Oh, this is dreadful, dreadful! How can we ever show our faces again in the street!

CANDIDA: We must close the windows.

PAULA: No, Candida! They will see us!

CANDIDA: But perhaps no one has noticed yet that we have no light. . .

(She catiously tiptoes towards balcony, keeping herself out of street range. As she closes the windows, she notices something odd in the street and peers out. Then, boldly, she steps right out onto the balcony and looks up and down the street. She turns around joyously and steps back into the room.)

CANDIDA: Paula, there is no light anywhere!

PAULA: No light?

CANDIDA *(with exultant relief)*: All the houses are dark! All, all of them!

PAULA: What happened?

CANDIDA: Oh, come and look! There is total darkness all over the city!

PAULA *(approaching balcony)*: Why, yes, yes! There is no light anywhere! *(Clapping her hands in gratitude.)* Oh, merciful, merciful God!

CANDIDA *(suddenly bursting into laughter as she moves downstage)*: But what fools we are! What ignorant fools we are!

PAULA *(following)*: What was happened?

CANDIDA *(laughing uncontrollably)*: Nothing has happened! Nothing has happened at all! Oh Paula, Paula—we must read the newspapers with more interest! It was in all newspapers! Didn't you read it? Tonight, Paula—tonight is the night of the blackout—of the practice blackout! All the lights have been turned off!

PAULA: Why?

CANDIDA: It is a part of all their preparations—they are preparing for war!

PAULA *(sighing with relief)*: Oh, is that all?

CANDIDA *(laughing hysterically)*: And we thought. . .oh Paula, we thought. . .we thought our light had been cut off!

PAULA: Oh, thank God, thank God, thank God!

CANDIDA: And how frightened we were, Paula! We were almost trembling!

PAULA: *(beginning to laugh, too)*: And we were afraid to close the windows! We were afraid to go down to the street!

CANDIDA *(gasping with laughter)*: And we. . .we were afraid that we could never... never show our. . .our faces again in the. . . in the street! Oh Paula—how funny! How funny we are!

(She goes off into another wild peal of laughter that ends in sudden sobs. She buries her face in her hands.)

PAULA *(alarmed; approaching)*: Candida, Candida!

CANDIDA *(wracked with sobs)*: I can bear no more! I can bear no more!

PAULA: Candida, the neighbors will hear you!

CANDIDA *(holding out her hands before her face)*: All the humiliations, Paula. . . All the humiliations we have suffered, Paula. . .all the bitter, bitter humiliations we have suffered!

PAULA *(taking her sister in her arms)*: Hush, Candida! Compose yourself!

CANDIDA *(breaking away and standing with clenched fists before PORTRAIT)*: And there he stands! There he stands laughing at us! Oh, there he stands mocking, mocking our agony! Oh God, God, God, God!

(She sinks sobbing to the floor.)

PAULA *(kneeling down and taking her sister again in her arms)*: Please, Candida! Please, please, Candida!

(Candida is still sobbing wildly while Paula holds her tight and strokes her hair whispering "Candida, Candida," as THE CURTAIN FALLS)

As in preceding Scene, the curtains open on the "Intramuros Curtain," BITOY CAMACHO is standing at far left, in light.

BITOY: After my father died—he died when I was about fifteen—I stopped going to the Marasigan house. I had no more time for tertulias. I had to leave school and go to work. My childhood had been spent in the tranquil innocence of the 1920s: I grew up during the hard, hard 1930s, when everybody seemed to have become poor and shabby and disillusioned and ill-tempered. I drifted from one job to another—boot lack, newsboy, baker's apprentice, waiter, pier laborer. Sometimes I felt I had never been clean, never been happy; my childhood seemed incredible—something that had happened to somebody else. When I see the windows of the Marasigan house all lighted up, and I would hear them up there, talking and laughing—Don Lorenzo, Candida, Paula, and their little crowd of shabby old folk.

(The girls go on the stage; through the curtain, the sala becomes visible.)

I would stand out here in the street—tired and dirty and hungry and sleepy—and I would think of the days when father and I went there together—me, in my pretty sailor suit and my nice white shoes. But I never felt any desire to go up there again; I despised all those people—and anyway I was too dirty. I would walk on down the street, without looking back.

(The "Intramuros Curtain" opens, revealing the Marasigan sala daylight.)

I had said goodbye to that house, goodbye to that world—the world of Don Lorenzo, the world of my father. I was bitter against it; it had deceived me. I told myself that Don Lorenzo and my father had taught me nothing but lies. My childhood was a lie; the 1920s were a lie; beauty and faith and courtesy and honor and innocence were all just lies.

(ENTER PEPANG MARASIGAN from the doorway at right. She goes to table at center where her bag is. She opens bag, takes out her cigarettes and lights one.)

The truth was fear—always fear—fear of the boss, of the landlord, of the police, of being late, of being sick, of losing one's job. The truth was no shoes, no money, no smoking, no loitering, no vacancy, no trespassing, and beware of the dog.

(Pepang glances round the room, her eyes stopping at PORTRAIT. Looking at it, she comes forward and stands before it, with a half-wisful, half-mocking smile.)

When the 1940s came along, I had become a finished product of my Age. I accepted it completely, and I believe in it. It was a hard world but it was the truth—and I wanted nothing but the truth.

(ENTER MANOLO MARASIGAN from the doorway at right. He glances towards Pepang as he goes to table and helps himself to her cigarettes. Having lighted one, he comes forward too, and stands beside her, gazing up at PORTRAIT.)

I had rejected the past and I believed in no future—only the present tense was practical. That was the way I thought—until that October afternoon—that afternoon I first went back to the Marasigan house, the afternoon I first saw that strange painting. I had gone there seeking nothing, remembering nothing, deaf to everything except the current catchwords and slogans. But when I left the house, the world outside seemed to be muffled—seemed to have receded far away enough for me to see it as a whole. I was no longer imprisoned within it; I had been released; I stood outside—and there was someone standing beside me. After all the years of bitter separation, I had found my father again.

(The light dies out on Bitoy; he exits. Pepang and Manolo continue a moment longer to stare at PORTRAIT in silence. Pepang and Manolo have inherited their father's good looks; but in Pepang, those fine features have grown hard; in Manolo, they have gone flabby. She looks ambitious, he looks dissipated; she is cynical, he is shifty-eyed. They are both very stylish, and becoming too stout.)

PEPANG: The hero of our childhood, Manolo.

MANOLO: Oh, he was more than that to us.

PEPANG: Only children are capable of such love.

MANOLO: He was our God the father.

PEPANG: And the earth, the sky, the moon, the sun, the stars, and the whole universe to us!

MANOLO: The most wonderful thing that can happen to any child is to have a genius for his father. Oh, the most wonderful thing really!

PEPANG: And the most cruel!

MANOLO: Yes.

PEPANG: Having to break one's childhood here—to spurn one's childhood god…

MANOLO: Oh Pepang, we all have to grow up!

PEPANG: Growing up is cruel. The young have no pity.

MANOLO: But look at Mr. Aeneas up there. He's carrying his old father on his back. He's carrying his father forward with him, along with all the family idols.

PEPANG: But you and I are not Aeneas…Manolo, is that what father meant?

MANOLO *(scowling)*: He always did have a sardonic sense of humor!

PEPANG: And now he has only himself to carry himself…

MANOLO *(testily):* Oh, stop it, Pepang! We haven't abandoned him to die, have we? That's one of father's old tricks—getting everybody to feel sorry for him.

PEPANG *(smiling):* Yes. Poor father! *(She turns away.)*

MANOLO: Oh, he is still the same old hero up there—still all the old god!

PEPANG: And nobody to worship him anymore. *(She sits down on saofa.)*

MANOLO: He still has got Paula and Candida, hasn't he? *(He turns away, too.)* And where can they be—those two? Haven't they shown up yet?

PEPANG: They've probably gone to market.

MANOLO: They got crazier every day.

PEPANG: We must talk to them, we must make them listen. Now, remember you promised to be firm. Where's the senator?

MANOLO: Still in father's room. And they're still talking away!

PEPANG *(glancing at her watch):* That makes two hours of the good old days.

MANOLO: Oh, it's regular reunion of the old boys in there.

PEPANG: With the senator around, we can make Candida and Paula listen to us. You know how they look up him.

MANOLO: Because he's a senator?

PEPANG: Because he is a poet.

MANOLO: Was, Pepang—was! He stopped being a poet a long time ago.

PEPENG: Oh, but they still remember him the way he used to be—when he was still coming here to recite his verses—before he went into politics.

MANOLO: And forgot all about us—the old snob!

PEPANG: And besides, he is their godfather, you know.

MANOLO: Well, if the senator can persuade them to leave this house—

PEPANG: If anybody can do it, he can. And I've made a bargain with him. He says the government is very anxious to acquire that painting. I promised to help him persuade Candida and Paula to sell it if he will help us persuade them to leave this house.

MANOLO: I've got a buyer for the house.

PEPANG: I told you—I already have a buyer.

MANOLO: Now look—you leave all that business to me. After all I'm the eldest son in this family.

MANOLO: Poor father! He ought to hear you!

PEPANG: We all have to grow up, you know.

MANOLO *(looking around):* How about the furniture?

PEPANG *(rising):* Well, let me see...I'll take that chandelier; I need it for my front hall. And I'll take the marble table in the study. You can have all the furniture here in the sala, Manolo—except the piano. I' take that. And I'll take the dining room set. We can divide the plate and the silver.

MANOLO *(sarcastic):* Oh, what for? Why not just take everything, Pepang?

PEPANG: Thank you. Maybe I will.

MANOLO *(raising his voice):* Sure! Take everything! Take the floors and the stairs and take the walls and take the roof—

PEPANG: Shh! The senator will hear you!

MANOLO *(lowering his voice):* ...and take the whole damned house! I'll cram it down your throat for you!

(Through the ensuing scene, they speak savagely but in controlled voices.)

PEPANG: Are we going to fight over a few old chairs?

MANOLO: Excuse me—but you have already given me the few old chairs. Do I still have to fight for them? You have taken everything else!

PEPANG: You know that my Mila is getting married next year—and she will need furniture.

MANOLO: If your Mila is getting married next year, my Roddie is getting married this year—and he's going to have furniture! I shall take all the furniture here in the sala, and all the furniture in the dining room, and all the furniture in three of the bedrooms, besides all the books and cabinets in the study, the big mirror downstairs, and the matrimonial bed!

PEPANG: Don't be funny!

MANOLO: I don't see you laughing!

PEPANG: I shall take the matrimonial bed for my Mila!

MANOLO: Okay, let's see you take it! Let's see you move anything out of this house without my permission!

PEPANG: And why should I ask permission? Who has been paying to keep up this house for the last ten years, I'd like to know!

MANOLO: Okay, who? Are you going to tell me I don't pay my share?

PEPANG: Yes—when you remember!

MANOLO: Now listen—just because I forget to send money now and then—

PEPANG: Forget! I have to call you up and call you up, month after month, before I can squeeze any money out of you! Pay your share! You are the eldest son—this is your duty, not mine! But if I had left you alone to do it, father would have starved to death by now! And do you think it has been easy for me? Month after month I have to ask my husband for money to support my father and sisters. Do you think I enjoy that? Do you think I don't shrink with shame when he demands why it is not you who are supporting them?

MANOLO: Oh, so he asks that, eh?

PEPANG: You never have any money to send here—but, oh, you have plenty of money to throw away at the races or to lavish on your queridas!

MANOLO: Well, you can tell that husband of yours—

PEPANG *(whispering; glancing towards stairway):* Shut up!

MANOLO: Or, no—I shall tell him myself—

PEPANG: Shut up! I tell you, they're coming!

(Manolo sulkily throws himself into a chair. Pepang sits down on the sofa. Paula comes slowly up the stairs, carrying an umbrella and a basket full of the marketing. She looks rather bleak; but on seeing her brother and sister, hurries to them—having deposited her umbrella at stand—with a show of animation.)

PAULA: Oh, are you two here?

MANOLO *(affectionately)*: Hello there, Paulita.

PAULA *(approaching Pepang)*: Have you been waiting long?

PEPANG: Only two hours.

PAULA: I walked all the way from Quiapo. *(She kisses Pepang on the cheek.)*

PEPANG: Well, how are you, baby? You look rather haggard.

PAULA: Oh Pepang, they cut off our light a week ago! We thought at first it was only the blackout—but we found out afterwards that it really had been cut off!

MANOLO: *(after a pause during which he and Pepang look down at the floor)*: Yes, but you have light again now, haven't you? I went over the company and fixed it up as soon as you called me. You have light again, no? Everything is all right now?

PAULA *(bitterly)*: Yes—everything is just fine!

(Manolo and Pepang unwillingly glance at each other.)

MANOLO: We are sorry it happened, Paula.

PEPANG: And where is Candida?

PAULA *(evasively)*: She…she went somewhere.

PEPANG *(firmly)*: Where did she go?

PAULA: She is looking for a job.

MANOLO: Good God—where?

PAULA *(rather proudly)*: At the Bureau of Health and Science.

PEPANG: What did she think she is—a scientist?

PAULA: Why not? They published an advertisement, she has gone to answer it.

PEPANG: You two girls are becoming—oh, I don't know what! All these are crazy ideas! And what are all those signs you have placed down there at the door? "Rooms For Rent." "Expert Lesson in the piano." "Expert Lesson in Spanish." Who is giving all those "expert lessons"?

PAULA (*timidly*): I am...I mean, I want to—I am willing—but...

MANOLO: But you have no pupils yet.

PAULA (*miserably*): No—not one! Nobody has even come to inquire. And we have had those signs for a week!

(*She feels herself at point of tears and quickly moves away, towards doorway.*)

I must take this basket out to the kitchen.

PEPANG: Paula—

PAULA (*stopping but not turning around*): Yes, Pepang?

PEPANG: Don Perico is here.

PAULA: Oh? Where?

PEPANG: In father's room.

PAULA: He has come to visit father?

PEPANG: And to talk to you and Candida.

PAULA: About what?

PEPANG: Well, he feels that being your godfather, and Candida's godfather too, he has a right to advise you two girls about your future.

(*She waits; but Paula says nothing.*)

Paula, Did you hear me?

PAULA: Yes, Pepang—but I must put these things away first. Excuse me.
(*She goes out.*)

MANOLO (*rising moodily*): Oh, the hell with it!

PEPANG: There you go again, Manolo!

MANOLO: But if they want so desperately to stay here!—

PEPANG: But how can they stay here? Do be sensible! We simply can't afford to keep up this house any longer!

MANOLO: Oh, can't we?

PEPANG *(grimly)*: Whether we can or not, I don't want to! This house gets on my nerves!

MANOLO: Yes—it gets on my nerve too...

PEPANG: And I refuse to be sentimental over it anymore. It will have to be sold. And you will take Candida to live with you; I will take Paula.

MANOLO: So you can have someone to look after your house while you go off and play mahjong with your society friends!

PEPANG: And so your wife can have somebody to look after your house while she goes off to her clubs and committees!

MANOLO: Poor Candida! Poor Paula!

PEPANG: After all, we have been supporting them all these years. The least they can do is to be useful to us. And it's about time they learned to be of some use. They're certainly old enough!

MANOLO: They're too old to change.

PEPANG: Oh, nonsense. The trouble with them is this house, this house! They're buried alive here. It will do them good to be pulled out of here. We are really doing it only for their own good.

MANOLO: And besides, good servants are so hard to get nowadays.

PEPANG: And they will learn to be happy, they will learn to live.

MANOLO: They are happy enough here, they have their own way of life.

PEPANG: What way of life? Hiding from the world in this old house; turning over the family albums; chattering over childhood memories; worshipping at father's feet...is that your idea of life, Manolo?

(She picks up her compact, snaps it open and begins to do her mouth.)

MANOLO: Well, what's yours—playing mahjong?

PEPANG: Now look here—don't you want Candida to live with you?

MANOLO: I suppose you want to take her too?

PEPANG: My dear, your wife would never forgive me! Her need is greater than mine. She thinks her clubs and committees are more important than my mahjong.

MANOLO: Will you stop bringing my wife into this conversation!

PEPANG: Oh, is this a conversation?

MANOLO: And all those foolish things you females do!

PEPANG: At least we females always know what we do with our time—

MANOLO: Here comes Don Perico.

PEPANG *(putting away her compact):* But you men just sit around and groan at your watches.

(Enter Don Perico.)

PERICO: Pepang, has my wife arrived?

PEPANG: Is she coming here, Don Perico?

PERICO: I told her to pick me up here at ten o'clock. *(He pulls out his watch.)* It is almost eleven now. *(He groans.)*

MANOLO: Senator, the women always know what they do with their time.

PERICO: I never know what they are doing, most of the time. And I have to be at Malacañan at one o'clock. The president is expecting me at lunch. We have to discuss the present emergency. Oh, I hardly have time now even to eat!

PEPANG: Then come and sit down a moment, Don Perico. Paula has arrived. Manolo, do go and call her.

(Exit Manolo.)

And how do you find our father, Don Perico?

PERICO (*sitting beside her on the sofa*): He has gone to sleep now. (*He pauses, frowning. Don Perico is in his early seventies, a big man with silver hair, handsome and still vigorous; dressed with expensive good taste; and gleaming with success, self-confidence, and that charming democratic friendliness with which the very rich and powerful delight to astonish their inferiors. Right now, however, his frown of concern is sincere; his complacency has been shaken.*) Pepang, what has happened to him?

PEPANG: What do you mean, Don Perico?

PERICO: Oh, I should have come to visit him before!

PEPANG: He has changed very much?

PERICO: No—no, I would not say so. He still is the same Lorenzo I remember—very humorous, very charming. And how he can talk! Oh, no one can talk like your father, Pepang. Conversation is one of the lost arts—but your father is still a genius at it.

PEPANG: Yes, father was in fine form today—so gay, so amusing.

PERICO: And yet—something was missing...

PEPANG: But you must remember that he is not a young man anymore.

PERICO: About this accident that he had—it was nothing serious?

PEPANG: Oh, it was serious enough—God knows! Imagine a man of his age falling from that balcony in his room!

PERICO: And this happened a year ago?

PEPANG: Right after he finished painting that picture.

PERICO: But he suffered no serious injuries?

PEPANG: We called in the best doctors to examine him.

PERICO: Then why does he stay in bed?

PEPANG: We have long been urging him to come out of his room.

PERICO: Pepang, what has happened to him?

PEPANG: Just what did you notice, Don Perico?

PERICO: He seems to have no will to live.

(Pepang is silent, staring at him. Enter Paula and Manolo.)

PAULA *(approaching)*: Good morning, *ninong*. How are you?

PERICO *(rising)*: Is this Paula? *(She kisses his hand.)* Caramba, Paula—I hardly know you! You were only a little girl the last time I saw you.

PAULA: Yes, ninong—it is a long time since we have had the pleasure of your company.

PERICO: Oh Paula, Paula, you must forgive me. We people in the government— we cannot call our lives our own. Our days, hours, even our minutes—all, all belong to the nation!

PAULA: Let me congratulate you on your victory in the last elections.

PERICO: Thank you. As a senator, I find myself in a very good position to help you, Paula.

PAULA: Thank you, ninong—but we need no help.

PEPANG *(rising)*: Now, Paula—listen first!

PERICO: I have been told that your father has refused to apply for the pension to which he is entitled.

PAULA: My father will not accept any pension from the government.

PERICO: Of course, no one can force him to do so—and it is only a trifling sum anyway. But listen, Paula—you do desire your father's welfare, no?

PAULA: He will never take the money.

PERICO: No—and I quite respect his reasons, even while I deplore them. But he has served his country unselfishly; it is merely just that his country should not forget him in his old age.

PAULA: Ah, but his country has a poor memory!

PERICO: A poor memory—how true! We are always too excited over the latest headlines and the newest fashions. But now there is this painting. . .*(He moves toward the PORTRAIT, and the others follow.)* Yes, there is this painting. . .Thank God, there is this painting. . .The whole country is talking about it. We can no longer afford to ignore your father. He has forced us all to remember him.

MANOLO: Do you think this is a great painting, senator?

PERICO: My boy, it would be impossible for me to judge this picture objectively. It is too much a part of myself. Any opinion of mine would be merely affectionate and sentimental—for this is a picture of the world of my youth, a beautifully accurate picture. Oh, I am amused when I hear these young critics accusing your father of escaping into the dead world of the past! And I pity these young critics! When we were their age, our minds were not so parochial. The past was not dead for us—certainly not the classical past. We were at home in the world of the hexameter and the Ablative Absolute; it was not closed world to us—nor an exotic one; it was our intellectual and spiritual atmosphere. We had Homer and Virgil in our bones—as well as St. Augustine and Aquinas, Dante and Cervantes, Lord Byron and Victor Hugo. Aeneas and Bonaparte were equally real to us, and equally contemporary. It was as natural for Jose Rizal to give his novel a Latin title as for Juan Luna to paint gladiators. Oh, you should have heard us—with our Latin tags and our classical allusions and our scholastic terminology—

PEPANG: Oh, we did, we did!

MANOLO: Remember, senator—we had the privilege of growing up in this house.

PEPANG: Father brought us up on the classics.

MANOLO: He tried to, anyway.

PEPANG: Not very successfully.

MANOLO: But, oh, the tears I shed over those Latin declensions!

PAULA: Pepang, our Latin slang, when we were children— remember?

PEPANG *(laughing)*: *Soror mea carissima,* give me a piece of your *cibus*!

PAULA: Nolo, nolo—*quia tu es* my inimical today and *per omnia saecula*!

PEPANG: *Avida*!

PAULA: *Pessima!*

MANOLO: *Peter mi, Peter mi—veni statim! Ecce, feminae pugnantes! (They all laugh).*

PEPANG: And remember all those uproarious games he would play with us?

PAULA: With the blankets!

PEPANG: Yes—we would take the blanket and dress ourselves up in togas. And father would be Jupiter, the king of the gods—and we children would be ancient Greeks and Romans—

MANOLO: And poor mother—how she would groan over her soiled blankets!

PAULA: But father would only laugh at her! He called her the Cassandra of the Kitchen!

PEPANG: Oh, that old laugh of father's!

MANOLO: Like a roll of thunder!

PEPANG: And however angry you were with him, when he laughed at you, you simply could not go on being angry!

PAULA: Remember how poor mother would end up by simply laughing helplessly?

MANOLO: Because father would be sitting here—on an old box—very stern and solemn—Jupiter, the king of the gods!

PEPANG: Oh, father was magnificent at games like that! And you know why? Because he was not stooping down to play with us children. He shared our seriousness. When he played Jupiter, you could almost see the lightnings round his head. You forgot that his toga was only a blanket and his throne only an old box, and his crown only a bunch of old paper flowers...You forgot that it was all only a game—you really felt yourself on Mount Olympus...Oh, how many times have we all sat here wide-eyed, listening to him—and when we looked around, it was not this room that we saw—not those chairs, nor those balconies, nor that shabby street outside. What we saw was a space of blue waters, a white sail, and oars gleaming in the sunshine...

PERICO: Yes, that is your father, all right. Oh, he was a magus. You all know what we called him at school: Lorenzo el Magnifico. There was something lordly about him, even as a boy—an air of elegance and extravagance, though he was poorer than most of us—and a marvellous vitality. He was like—but what need is there to describe him? Look—that is your father up there—that radiant young man! That is the young Lorenzo, the true Lorenzo, the Magnifico. Not that bony, shivering, naked old man is he carrying on his back!

(A silence, during which they all look at PORTRAIT. Unnoticed, Candida comes up the stairs. She glances disconsolately toward the group in front of PORTRAIT; goes to the hatrack to leave her umbrella; and remains there, her head bowed, her back to the audience. Meanwhile, Don Perico, who has been frowning at PORTRAIT, turns resolutely towards Paula.)

PERICO: Paula, your father tells me that this picture belongs to you and your sister. Now listen—would the two of you be willing to make a patriotic sacrifice?

(He waits; but Paula is silent. Upstage, Candida turns her face around.)

Because if you were to be patriotic enough to give this picture, to donate this picture to the government—the government might, as a token of gratitude, be willing to set aside a fund—a fund to be administered by your sister and yourself—a fund sufficient to maintain your father and yourselves while he and you are alive. Your father would then have no objection to the money; it would not be offered to him but to you and your sister as a—well—as a kind of reward for your generosity. Paula, I am in a position to arrange all this. I ask you to have confidence in me. I ask you to be generous: give this picture to your country; give this picture to your people.

(Paula is still silent, her head bowed. Upstage, Candida has turned around.)

Oh Paula, you would be making a noble and unselfish and heroic sacrifice. As you know, our country possesses not a single painting by your father. His great works are all abroad—in the museums of Spain and Italy. That is why the government is so anxious to acquire this picture. Surely, his own land is entitled to one of his masterpieces?

PEPANG *(after a pause)*: Well, what do you say, Paula?

MANALO: But of course, senator, Paula and Candida will want to discuss this first between themselves. They will want to think it over.

CANDIDA *(coming forward)*: We have no need to discuss it, we have no need to think it over!

PEPANG: Candida!

PERICO: Oh, is this Candida? How are you my child? Do you remember me?

CANDIDA: I remember you, Don Perico, and I am very sorry—but you are only wasting your time. You can go back and tell your government that this picture is not to be had. Paula and I will never part with it!

PEPANG: Candida, be silent and listen!

CANDIDA: I have heard all I need to hear! *(She turns quickly towards doorway.)*

PERICO: Candida, wait! *(She pauses.)* Come here, my child. Are you angry with your old godfather?

CANDIDA *(turning around):* You are the last person in the world who should want to take this picture from us!

MANOLO: Don Perico merely wants to help our father, Candida.

PERICO: I understand how you two girls feel about this picture. Your father has painted it for you as a last momento—and of course you find the thought of parting with it very painful. But if you really love your father, you will not think of yourselves—you will think of his welfare. Now listen, Paula; listen, Candida: I am not a doctor but I can see that there is something wrong with your father.

(Paula and Candida glance at each other.)

Oh, I ought to know; I have known him all his life. We grew up together, we went to school together, we went to Europe together, and we fought side by side in the Revolution. I have not seen him for a long time—and blame myself; yes, I blame myself! I should have come to visit him before. But, as you all know, our roads parted a long time ago. I went my own way—and he.... stayed here. When I saw him again this morning I thought at first that he had not changed at all: he still seemed the embodiment of grace and charm and intelligence. But we had been too close once, he and I; we had been too intimate once for me not to notice that—well—that there was something wrong. I could see it and I could feel it. And I know it. There is something wrong with your father.

CANDIDA *(dully):* Yes.

PERICO: He is sick.

PAULA AND CANDIDA: Oh no!

PERICO: I think he is. Very sick. And anyway, I agree with Pepang and Manolo: this old house is not the place for him. He needs light and fresh air and coolness and quiet. He should be under medical care; he ought to be placed in a hospital—some good private nursing home. Now, that will be rather expensive; and I understand that your father... uh—that he has—well—that he has lost his money. But if you accept this offer of the government, Paula and Candida, you will have the means with which to take care of your father as he should be taken care of.

CANDIDA: He is not sick! Oh, you do not know, you do not know!

PAULA: There is no hospital that can cure him!

PEPANG: What do you mean, Paula?

CANDIDA: We mean that we cannot accept the offer.

PEPANG: Are you two out of your senses? Do you value this painting more than your father's life?

PAULA: Father is not sick. He wants to stay here.

CANDIDA: And we shall stay here with him.

MANOLO: But even if he is not sick, you cannot stay here, you should not stay here! Don't you know that a war may break out any day now? And Intramuros is the most dangerous place in the city! Oh, tell them senator—tell them!

CANDIDA *(smiling; approaching):* Yes, senator—tell us. What are we to do? Are we to abandon this house? Are we to abandon this house as you abandoned poetry? Go on, senator—tell us. Who could advise us better than you? I promise that we will do whatever you say. Do you agree, Paula?

PAULA: We will do whatever you think is best, *ninong*. I promise

CANDIDA: There, we have both promised! Our lives are in your hands, senator. Think carefully, think very carefully! Oh, but what need have you to think? You made a similar decision yourself a long time ago. You yourself abandoned the house when you abandoned poetry, when you abandoned our poor dying world of the past! Did you ever regret your decision, senator? But what a foolish question! One has only to look at you now. You are rich, you are successful, you are important—

MANOLO: Candida, be silent!

CANDIDA: I must talk. Someone must talk, no? The senator does not answer.

PERICO *(dully)*: Candida, Paula—I have no right to advise you—

CANDIDA: But why not?

PAULA: We listened to your poetry once; we will listen to you now.

CANDIDA: Surely, a senator has more authority than a poet?

PERICO: I ask you to think in terms of reality not in terms of poetry.

PAULA: Oh, poetry is not real?

PERICO: Poetry will save you from the bombs.

CANDIDA: No—only politics can save us.

PERICO: Candida, Paula—I feel in my bones what you feel for this house; but this is no time for poetic attitudes! If the war should catch you in this house, what would you do? You are two helpless women. And what would happen to your father?

PAULA *(smiling; looking up at PORTRAIT)*: Like Aeneas there, we would carry him on our backs!

PERICO: Yours is classic piety—the piety indeed of Aeneas! But it is a piety that belongs to Art, not to life! It looks sublime in that picture up there; it would only look ridiculous in the real world!

CANDIDA: The sublime is always ridiculous to the world, senator.

PERICO: Then the world is right.

PAULA: You did not always think so.

CANDIDA: And how fiercely you used to stand against it! In what beautiful words you used to pour out your scorn of its laws, your anger against its cruelty, your contempt for its malice.

PERICO: Poetry was the passing madness of my youth, a plaything of my childhood.

PAULA: But when you became a man you put away the things of a child.

PERICO: No man has a right to stand apart from the world as though he were a god.

CANDIDA: Then, what do you advise, senator? Shall we surrender—as you did?

PERICO *(after a staring pause):* Why are you so bitter against me? What have I done? I saw my destiny and I followed it. I have no need to be ashamed of what I did! My whole life has been spent in the service of my country; that is more than your father can say for himself! Yes, I have grown rich, I am successful—is that a crime? What would you have wanted me to do? To go on scribbling pretty verses while my family starved? To bury myself alive as your father has buried himself alive? And what can he show for all those lost years? Nothing except this one picture? Look at yourselves, Paula and Candida—look at yourselves, and then tell me if this one picture is enough to justify what we had done to you! Oh, it is not against me that you are so bitter! It is not against me, I know! For what have I done to you?

CANDIDA: Nothing, senator. But what have you done to yourself?

PERICO *(recovering himself; embarrassed):* I should not have said those things—

CANDIDA: You had to say them. I suppose you have long been wanting to say them?

PERICO: No, Candida—no! I do not resent your father, I admire him. He is a very happy man.

CANDIDA: Because he did what he has done?

PERICO: Because he always knew what he was doing.

CANDIDA: And you don't know what you were doing?

PERICO: Oh Candida, life is not so simple as it is in Art! We do not choose consciously, we do not choose deliberately—as we like to think we do. Our lives are shaped, our decisions are made by forces outside ourselves—by the world in which we live, by the people we love, by the events and fashions of our times—and by many many other things we are hardly conscious of. Believe me: I never actually said to myself, "I do not wish to be a poet anymore because I will only starve. I shall become a politician because I want to get rich." I never said that! I went into politics with the best of intentions—and certainly with no intention of "abandoning poetry." Oh, I dreamed of bringing the radiance of poetry into the murk of politics—and I continued to think of myself as a poet a long, long time after I had ceased to be one, whether in practice or in spirit. I did not know what was happening to me—until it had happened. I thought I was boldly shaping my life according to the ideas of my youth—but my life was being shaped for me all the time—without my knowing it. Too often, one is only an innocent bystander at one's own fate...

CANDIDA *(approaching):* Forgive me, *ninong. (She kisses his hand.)*

PERICO: It is you who must forgive me, Candida—if I have bitterly disappointed you. *(He shrugs.)* But I could not help it—and I cannot help you. I look back on my life and I have no regrets because I know that I would have been unable to live it differently. There is nothing I could have changed. You can choose to go along with the current—or you can choose to stay on the bank—but those who try to stop the current are hurled away and destroyed. I chose to go along with the current; your father chose to stay in the bank—and neither of us can say of the other that he did wrong. Oh, I may dream wistfully now and then of the fine pale poet I used to be—but, believe me, I feel no remorse for that poet. I did not kill him—he was found bound to die.

(He pauses, smiling, and looks at his hands. When he speaks again, his voice is tender, and rather sad.)

To feel that driving urge, that imperious necessity to write poetry, poet needs an audience; he must be conscious of an audience—not only of a present audience but of a permanent one, an eternal one, an audience of all the succeeding generations. He must feel that his poems will generate new poets. Well, poetry withered away for the writers of my time because we knew that we had come to a dead end, we have come to a blind alley. We could go on writing if we liked—but we would be writing only for ourselves—and our poems would die with us, our poems would die barren. They were written in a dying tongue; our sons spoke another language—but it was literally true of my time and of the present. My generation spoke European, the present generation speaks American. Who among the young writers now can read my poems? My poems may as well be written in Babylonian! And who among the writers of my time can say that his poems have generated new poets? No one—no, not even poor Pepe Rizal! The fathers of the young poets of today are from across the sea. They are not our sons; they are foreigners to us, and we do not even exist for them. And if I had gone on being a poet, what would I be now? A very unhappy old mam, a very bitter old man—a failure and a burden—and with no respect for himself. The choice before me was between poetry and self-respect; I had to choose between Europe and America; and I chose—no, I did not choose at all. I simply went along with the current. *Quomodo cantabo caticum Domini in terra aliena?*

(He shrugs, and looks up at PORTRAIT.)

Look at your father up there. He has realized the tragedy of his generation. He, too, has been unable to sing. He, too, finds himself stranded in a foreign land. He, too, must carry himself to his own grave because there is no succeeding generation to carry him forward. His art will die with him. It is written in a dead language; it is written in Babylonian…And we all end alike—all of us old men from the last century—we all end the same. The rich and the poor, the failures and the successes, those who moved forward and those who stayed behind—our fate is the same! All, all of us must carry our own dead selves to our common grave…We have begotten no sons; we are a lost generation!

Caray, who would have thought we would end dismally? Oh, we began so confidently, we began so gaily! When we were young it was morning all over the world, it was the Springtime of Freedom! And was there ever a group of young men as noisy and brilliant and boisterous as our own? Your father, and the Luna brothers, and Pepe Rizal, and Lopez Jaena, and Del Pilar—alas for all those young men! And alas for all the places where we were young together! Madrid under the Queen Regent; the Paris of the Third Republic; Rome at the end of the century; and Manila—Manila before the Revolution—*la Manila de Nuestrus amores*! Oh, they talk a lot of solemn nonsense now about the Revolution—we were not solemn! The spirit of those days was one of the boyish fun, of boyish mischief! Just imagine us—with our top hats and swagger sticks and mustachios—and imagine the secret meetings in the dead of the night; the skull on the table; the dreadful oaths; the whispers and flickering candlelight; and the signing of our names in our own blood! Oh, we were all hopeless romantics. And the Revolution was a wild melodrama in the style of Galdos! And I drank it all up—all the color and the excitement and the romance! I was a poet then; the world existed only that I might put it to music! Even the Revolution was happening only to make any verse more vivid and my rhymes more audacious! I was a poet then—

(From the stairway comes the noise of feet, and of feminine mirth and chatter.)

MANOLO: Here comes your womenfolk, senator.

PERICO *(the smile fading from his lips):* But I was hungry and I traded my birthright—

(Enter DOÑA LOLENG, PATSY, ELSA MONTES, AND CHARLIE DACANAY.)

LOLENG: Who is hungry? Hola, Manolo! And Pepang too! My dear, if I had known you were here, we would have come sooner. And are these Candida and Paula? Jesus, what big girls you are now! And how delighted I am to see you again! Your mother was one of my dearest friends. May she rest in peace, poor woman! You remember me?

PAULA AND CANDIDA: Yes, Doña Loleng.

LOLENG: This is my dauther Patsy. She is my youngest. And this is Elsa Montes—the Elsa Montes. You have heard all about her of course. She is the girl who brought the Conga to Manila. And this is Charlie Dacanay. Oh, Mr. Dacanay is not anybody in particular—just somebody who keeps following us around, all the time. Oh, Pepang, we were all over at Kikay Valero's charity mahjong, you know—and, my dear, you will never believe how much I lost! Oh, I am rabid! But do tell me, Paula and Candida, how is your dear papa?

PAULA: He is quite well, Doña Loleng. Thank you.

CANDIDA: He is having a nap just now.

LOLENG: But how unfortunate for me! I would like to see Lorenzo again. Oh, your father was the great hero of my girlhood! He must let me come and see him sometime.

PAULA: We will tell him, Doña Loleng.

LOLENG: And what were you saying, Perico?

PERICO: I was saying, my dear, that I was hungry—

LOLENG: You must forgive me! I forgot we were to pick you up. Charlie you brute, I told you to remind me!

PAULA: What can we offer you, *ninong*? What would you like?

PERICO: A mess of pottage.

LOLENG: What on earth is that?

PERICO: Just an old joke. So please do not bother, Paula. I really desire nothing.

LOLENG *(moving forward):* And is this the painting everybody is talking about?

PERICO: Would you like to look at it, my dear?

LOLENG: We all want to look at it. Come, come—all of you. Study this work of art and be uplifted.

(Don Perico steps away from front of PORTRAIT to give place to his wife and her comnpanions. Dressed and bejeweled in the grand style, Doña Loleng is, at fifty, still statuesque and stunning—no wrinkles, no grey hair, no baggy flesh—the eyes languid, the nose patrician, the mouth rapacious. Her daughter Patsy is eighteen, pretty, but sullen-looking. Elsa Montes is a sophisticated forty, and strenuously "chi-chi." Charlie Dacanay is around twenty-five, a typical antebellum glamour-boy, rather the worse of wear. All these people stand a moment in silence, looking up at PORTRAIT—Doña Loleng, sadly smiling; Patsy, sulky; Elsa, interested; and Charlie, vacant. The senator watches them ironically, standing at left side of stage. Pepang and Manolo are just behind the newcomers. Candida and Paula have quietly left the room.)

LOLENG *(smiling at PORTRAIT):* The young Lorenzo... the great hero of my girlhood...

PERICO: And what does he say to you my dear?

LOLENG: He says... He says that I am an old woman...

CHARLIE: Doña Loleng, I protest!

LOLENG: Be silent, Charlie! Who asked for your consolations?

ELSA: I'm wondering myself.

PERICO: Our Charlie was only trying to be gallant, my dear.

CHARLIE: Senator, you and I belong to the days when knighthood was in flower!

PATSY: Oh, shut up, Charlie! You know how mommy loves to go around telling everybody she's an old woman.

MANOLO: Anybody as beautiful as your mother, Patsy, can afford to tell the truth. The truth can do her no harm. She is above reproach.

PERICO: Being Caesar's wife.

LOLENG: Thank you, Manalo. Thank you, Perico. You are both too kind.

CHARLIE: Now wait a minute—how about me!

PEPANG: Poor Charlie! Nobody wants his consolation!

ELSA: He could try me—but I'm not an old woman yet, am I?

LOLENG: Certainly not, Elsa—whatever people may think.

ELSA *(sweetly)*: You mean whatever you may try to make them think, darling!

PATSY: Oh, she is a wonderful mindreader! Talk to her about bicycles, and tomorrow she'll be telling everybody you've been having an affair with the postman!

LOLENG: Patsy—

PATSY *(wide-eyed)*: Oh mommy, did I say something wrong?

LOLENG *(studying her fingernails)*: You ought not to play mahjong. You do not have the cold blood for it. You get nervous.

PATSY: Oh, I'm not nervous. I'm just hysterical. Charlie darling, do give me a cigarette.

CHARLIE *(fetching out his case)*: At your service, mademoiselle!

LOLENG *(shaking her head)*:   Uh-uh, Charlie!

CHARLIE *(lightly slapping Patsy's hand as she reaches for cigarette)*: Sorry, mademoiselle—but the *mamang*, she says no.

PATSY *(her hair flying as she whirls around)*: But, mommy, I must have a smoke!

LOLENG *(languorously)*: Perico, will you tell your daughter that she cannot smoke in public? She will not listen to me.

PERICO: Charlie, remember to send me a bill for cigarettes my family consumes.

CHARLIE: The smokes are on the house, senator. May I offer you one?

PERICO: No, Charlie. Thank you very much.

CHARLIE *(putting cigarette in his own mouth and offering the case around):* Well, does anybody else want one? No—not you, Patsy! Elsa?

ELSA *(taking cigarette):* Oh yes—yes indeed!

LOLENG *(as Charlie lights his and Elsa's cigarette):* Elsa has been saying nothing but "Oh yes—yes indeedy!" since she came back from New York. She must have had plenty of practice over there.

ELSA: Did you say something, darling?

LOLENG: Do the women in New York say "Oh yes—yes indeedy" all the time?

ELSA: I really couldn't say. I never had time to go out with the women.

CHARLIE: I'll bet!

PEPANG: You must give us your opinion of this picture, Elsa darling. Having been to New York, you must have been frightfully cultured.

ELSA: Oh, the picture is swellegant! It's delovely! And what's more, it's very inspiring!

PERICO *(who can't believe his ears):* My dear Elsa, did you say—inspiring?

LOLENG: Such as what?

ELSA *(moving close and gesturing at PORTRAIT with her cigarette):* Such as a divine idea for an evening gown—a really eye-stopping evening gown—just like that absolutely stupendous costume that young man up there is wearing—see? The same cut, the same draping, and the same shade of white—no, it's not white really—more like old ivory...

(Pepang, Doña Loleng and Patsy have also gathered closer in front of PORTRAIT.)

And with those marvelous designs on the borders! Haven't you noticed them? Pepang, you must ask your father to give me the sketch of those designs!

MANOLO: And you said, senator, that this picture is written in Babylonian! The woman seemed to understand it perfectly.

CHARLIE *(starring at PORTRAIT):* I don't understand that picture!

MANOLO: Just listen to the women, Charlie, and get wise.

ELSA *(with gestures):* Just imagine those designs in gold embroidery—up here in the bodice—

PERICO: Yes, women can turn Art into Reality.

ELSA: And all around the hemline.

MANOLO: And the sublime into the ridiculous.

ELSA: And just look at the cute belt he's wearing!

PERICO: Naturally. They are the enemies of the Absolute.

ELSA: Will you look at that gorgeous, gorgeous belt! A sort of golden rope with little black figures hanging all around it—oh, it's different, I tell you! It's divine!

PERICO: Divine is absolutely the right word!

MANOLO: The Lares and Penates, senator.

ELSA: Imagine yourself dancing the conga in a gown like that—

CHARLIE: What did you say those little black figures are?

MANOLO: They are the gods of his father.

ELSA: Your skirt's flying—

CHARLIE: Then why is he wearing them around his belt?

ELSA: And those ornaments around the belt would go click-click-click—

PERICO: So the women cannot steal them, Charlie.

ELSA: And you whirled and whirled!

MANOLO: The hell they can't!

PEPANG: And what material would you use for the gown?

ELSA: Let me see…

CHARLIE: Who are those two guys anyway?

MANOLO: They are fellows named Aeneas and his old father Anchises.

ELSA: Some kind of rayon velvet, I think.

CHARLIE: Who the heck are they?

PERICO: They are the Artist and his Conscience

LOLENG: A silk taffeta would do better.

CHARLIE *(grinning at PORTRAIT)*: I don't think they like me much...

PEPANG: Or yellow silk organdie.

CHARLIE: As a matter-of-fact, they don't like me at all!

PATSY: Oh Elsa, imagine a gown like that in white cotton tulle!

MANALO: Well, Charlie—that shouldn't be a new experience for you.

ELSA *(looking around)*: Charlie, lend me your fountain-pen, will you—and a piece of paper.

(Charlie, who's still staring fascinated at PORTRAIT, does not hear her.)

MANOLO: As a matter-of-fact, all of us don't really like one another very much.

LOLENG *(looking around)*: But hurry up, hurry up, idiot!

CHARLIE *(blankly)*: Huh?

LOLENG: Pero, que animal!

ELSA: Your fountain-pen, Charlie, and a piece of paper.

CHARLIE: Oh, sorry girls. Here.

(He gives Elsa his fountain pen and pocket notebook.)

MANALO: No, we don't like one another at all. I wonder why we all keep hanging together.

PERICO: So we won't hang separately.

ELSA *(pondering PORTRAIT; fountain pen poised over notebook):* What I want is that clear classic effect—

MANOLO: Besides, we enjoy tormenting each other.

ELSA: A marble make-up—

PERICO: And being tormented by each other.

ELSA: The arms and one shoulder bare—

CHARLIE: I suppose you mean I enjoy being tormented?

ELSA: No jewels at all—

PERICO: Yes, Charlie—and I sympathize with you very much—

ELSA: And a Greek hairdo.

PERICO: But I cannot help you.

PATSY: And sandals, Elsa?

PERICO: You were born to be a victim—

ELSA: Sandals, of course—

PERICO: You were born to be eaten up.

ELSA: Just like those ones he's wearing. You see his red-and-black sandals? Dramatic is the word for them! Oh, I've got the whole ensemble complete in my mind. Wait—

(She begins to sketch rapidly, glancing repeatedly at PORTRAIT, her companions watching intently and paying no attention to the men's talk.)

CHARLIE: Well, well, well! And I thought I was doing the eating up! I was beginning to feel really bad about it, senator. Oh, I've got a conscience too—like that guy up there—a conscience riding on my back. I can feel its hot breath down my neck.

PERICO: That, Charlie, is not your conscience. It is merely the air, the weather, the climate of our times—the uneasiness of a guilty world.

MANOLO: Oh, we all feel that hot breath down our necks, Charlie, and it makes us all fell very nervous. Maybe that's why we're so damned nasty to each other. We're like vicious brats waiting to be punished and taking it out on each other.

PERICO: Or like the residents in hell, Manolo.

MANOLO: Exactly, senator!

ELSA *(showing her sketch):* There, you see my idea? And girls, just think of the color scheme!

CHARLIE: Okay, but who started this hell anyway, senator? Remember: I just came along and found it open for business!

LOLENG: I see your idea, Elsa, and I could use it myself...

PERICO: I know that it can always use anyone who just comes along and "finds it open for business," Charlie.

PATSY: I could use a gown like that on New Year's Eve...

CHARLIE: I could use a drink!

LOLENG: Oh, Patsy! You—in a Greek gown?

PERICO: The drinks are on the house, Charlie. I can help you that much.

PATSY: Oh, mommy wants me to stay just a naked little baby!

CHARLIE: I wish I had stayed just a naked little brat!

MANOLO: Oh, you did!

PERICO: And you will still be one when the last trumpet blows.

LOLENG: The style of this picture is much too severe for you, darling.

MANOLO: This picture is entirely too severe for us. We're not heroes—just naked little brats!

LOLENG: Pepang, may I send my dressmaker here to see this picture?

PEPANG: But of course, Doña Loleng.

PERICO: But can the dressmaker cover up our nakedness when the trumpets blow?

ELSA: Now wait a minute—who first thought this idea anyway?

PEPANG: Darling, my father first thought up this idea and anybody who wants to copy him is perfectly free to come here and do so.

LOLENG *(beginning to speak while Pepang is still speaking):* And surely, my dear Elsa, my dressmaker can come here if she wants to without having to borrow from the lights of your talent?

PATSY *(beginning to speak while her mother is still speaking):* Oh, mommy thinks this style too severe for me but she's quite sure she can put on some wooden shoes and look like Helen of Troy!

ELSA *(beginning to speak while Patsy is still speaking):* Now, don't think I'm sore when as a matter-of-fact I'm extremely flattered, but don't you see how risky a costume like this would be for certain age groups?

(The next three speeches are spoken simultaneously while Elsa is still speaking.)

MANOLO: Will you girls stop bickering over a costume in which, believe me, you would all look equally implausible and extremely uncomfortable anyway!

CHARLIE: Whoever printed that picture had a fine sense of humor all right but did he have to go and hang his damn painting around my neck!

PERICO:
"Dies irae, dies illa,
Solvet saeclum in favillla,
Teste David cum Sybilla.
Cuanto tremor est futurus—"

(The blast of an air raid siren suddenly fills stage, drowning out their voices. They all jump, startled. Then realizing what it is, they listen with bored annoyance as the siren goes on steadily screaming. Paula and Candida appear running in doorway. Through following scene, the speakers have to shout to be heard.)

PAULA *(as Candida runs to the balcony):* What is it? Oh, what is it!

PERICO: The Trumpets of the Apocalypse!

PAULA: Is it War?

PERICO: It is the Day of Wrath!

MANOLO: It is only the air raid?

PAULA: Are we having an air raid?

PEPANG: Of course not! We are only pretending there is an air raid!

PAULA: Why?

PEPANG: So we can practice what we are to do! This is an air raid practice!

MANOLO: A sort of rehearsal!

CANDIDA *(at balcony)*: Oh, come, Paula! Come and look! Everybody has stopped moving! All the people, and all the vehicles!

(Paula runs to balcony. After a moment, the siren stops.)

CHARLIE: Practice blackouts, practice air raids, practice evacuations! I'm sick of all this practicing! When do we get the real thing? I wish the darned war would break out!

PATSY: Shut up, Charlie! How can you be so horrid!

PEPANG: Oh, Patsy there's nothing to be afraid of! The war will be over almost as soon as it starts!

ELSA: Those poor Japs! They'll never know what hit them!

PEPANG: And the sooner that it starts—

PATSY: But not before New Year's Eve! Not before the big ball on New Year's! I want to wear my new evening gown and really make sensation!

LOLENG: Darling we are going to have the usual ball on New Year's Eve, war or no war!

PEPANG: You know what they say: Business as usual!

ELSA *(flashing the V-sign)*: And keep 'em flying!

LOLENG: Perico, the Manila Hotel will stay open for business, no—even if a war breaks out?

PERICO: My dear, we will all stay for business! We will always stay open for business! We are indestructible!

ELSA: That's the spirit, senator! Keep 'em flying!

PERICO *(beating his breast):* This was a spirit, Elsa—but, alas, it can fly no longer!

ELSA *(startled):* Huh?

PERICO: It has lost its wings!

ELSA: Who?

PERICO: However, it has learned to crawl on the ground—oh, very fast!

ELSA: Loleng—

PERICO: And you know what? It now prefers a gutter below to the stars above!

LOLENG *(approaching):* What do you mean, Perico?

PERICO: I mean, my dear, that we are beyond all change, beyond all hope. Therefore, we have nothing to fear. The earth will quake—but we will hardly notice. We will be too busy playing mahjong and talking about whose husband is sleeping with whose wife.

LOLENG: Do you know what you are saying!

PERICO: And the earthquake will affect us in no way at all. Oh, one of your teacups may be broken, my dear; and your mahjong table may lose a leg; and your dressmaker may be late for a fitting. But do not worry. After the earthquake, you will buy a new cup, you will order a new table, and your dressmaker will arrive at last. And we will go on as before.

LOLENG: Pepang, what have your people been doing to him?

PERICO: My dear, what can anybody do to a corpse?

LOLENG: A corpse!

PERICO: Yes, I have just discovered something very funny, my dear. I have been dead for the past thirty years, and I did not know it.

LOLENG *(after a pause):* Oh, my poor Perico! I see, I see!

(She comes closer and places her hands on his shoulder.)

Oh, why did I let you come here! I should have known this would happen!

PERCIO: Do you know what has happened?

LOLENG: This house, Perico—this dreadful old house! It always has this effect on you! Now do you see why I always refused to let you come back here?

PERICO: Yes, my dear—I see.

LOLENG: Patsy, get your father's hat. We are taking him home at once—and I shall put him to bed right away.

PEPANG: Is he ill?

LOLENG: He has had a slight attack of poetry.

PEPANG *(amused):* Mother of God!

LOLENG: Oh, there is no cause for alarm. I am used to this; I know what to do. Some aspirin, some hot soup, a good night's rest—and tomorrow he will wake up this ordinary self again.

PERICO: Of course I will, my dear.

LOLENG: Of course you will, man! You always do—remember? And you always laugh at yourself afterwards, and at all the things you said and did.

PERICO: Poetry is powerless before aspirin.

PERICO: And tomorrow I will wake up my ordinary self again—healthy, wealthy, debonaire, fastidious, elegant, cool-headed, cool-blooded, confident, capable, callous, and contented!

LOLENG: Regret is ridiculous in a man of your position.

PERICO: Tomorrow I shall be thoroughly ashamed of myself for having been so ridiculous.

LOLENG: And for having been felt sorry for yourself.

PERICO: And for having been sorry for myself.

LOLENG: Believe me, Perico—you could no more have endured poverty than I could. We were both born for the expensive things in life. Imagine yourself without your gold studs. And diamond pins, without your private tailor, without your imported wines. There is nothing of the ascetic in you, my dear Perico!

PERICO: No, my dear—I quite agree. But every now and then, a man tries to assuage his conscience by weeping over what he might have been.

LOLENG *(contemptuously):* You men never know what you want!

PERICO: You have been very patient to me, my dear.

LOLENG: Oh, I knew I was marrying trouble when I married a poet! But I was determined to make you…what you are now.

PERICO: She is absolutely right! Everything that I am, I owe to my darling wife!

PATSY *(offering hat):* Here, mommy.

LOLENG *(taking hat):* All right. Now go on down to the car, all of you.

PEPANG: But listen—you people cannot go now. You will have to wait until the siren sounds again. Nobody can move about in the streets during the alert.

LOLENG: Oh, we can. We have the senator with us, you know.

(She puts the hat on his head, arranges his tie, and straightens his coat lapels, while her companions take their leave and go downstairs. Then, having given his coat a final brush, she steps back and surveys him.)

There, you look presentable again! Now say goodbye to everybody.

PERICO: Goodbye, everybody.

LOLENG *(taking him by the arm):* Now come along. Pepang, do forgive us for hurrying away like this. And remember to give my regards to your papa.

PERICO *(suddenly struggling as his wife leads him away):* Wait, wait a minute! Where are Paula and Candida?

PAULA and CANDIDA: Here we are.

PERICO *(waving with his free hand)*: Paula! Candida! Stand with your father! Stand with Lorenzo—*contra mundum*!

LOLENG *(laughing and dragging him off)*: Come along, come along, señor poeta! You have been delirious enough for one day. Bye-bye, all of you!

(Exit Doña Loleng with her senator.)

MANOLO *(sinking into a chair)*: Poor Don Perico!

PEPANG: The old double-crosser!

CANDIDA *(smiling)*: We promised to do whatever he said, Pepang—and we will keep our promise.

PAULA *(parodying Don Perico)*: We will stand with father—*contra mundum*!

PEPANG *(tartly)*: You can stand with him against anything you please—but not here, not in the house!

CANDIDA: This house shall be our fortress!

PEPANG: Candida, I have a headache. Please do not make it worse.

PAULA: Perhaps you too would like an aspirin, Pepang?

PEPANG: What I would like is a little sense from the two of you! Have you no eyes, have you no feelings? Do you not see what a burden this house is for me and Manolo? Do you not see how unfair it is to our families to spend so much money here—money we ought to be spending on our homes? Do you not know what I have to fight with my husband, month after month, to get the money to support you and this house?

CANDIDA: We are not asking you nor your husband nor Manolo to support us any longer!

PAULA: We will take care of ourselves!

PEPANG: And what will you do? Take in boarders? Give "expert lessons" in Spanish? Give "expert lessons" on the piano? How very, very funny! Just look at yourselves! Are you the kind of women who "can take care of themselves"? You are both completely useless!

MANOLO: Pepang, I think we can discuss this without losing our tempers.

CANDIDA: There is no need to discuss it at all!

PAULA: We will never change our minds!

PEPANG: We have pampered the two of you long enough!

MANOLO: Pepang, will you let me do the talking!

PAULA: Oh, you can both go on talking forver—it will make no difference!

PEPANG: The most stubborn and stupid pair of old women!

CANDIDA: Paula, we may as well go to the kitchen.

MANOLO *(jumping up)*: You stay right here, both of you!

(The air raid siren begins to scream again. They pay no heed.)

PEPANG *(raising his voice)*: Oh, I know why they want to stay in this house! I know why they like it so much here! I know—and so does everybody! I have heard people whispering about it—behind my back!

MANOLO: Whispering about what?

PEPANG: And I'll bet all the people living on this street have been talking about nothing else!

MANOLO: About what? Talking about what?

PEPANG: About these two fine sisters of ours, Manolo! Oh, they have become quite a laughing stock—the talk of the town really—a regular scandal!

PAULA: Pepang, what are you saying! What have we done?

MANOLO: Just what is all this, Pepang! What the devil do you mean?

PEPANG: Surely you have the gossip?

MANOLO: I have more important things to do—thank God!

PEPANG: Oh, the shame I have suffered! Everybody knows, everybody is laughing at them!

MANOLO: WHY? WHY?

PEPANG: Because of this young man! This unspeakable young man! They have a young man living here—as a boarder! A man of loose morals—a vulgar vaudeville musician—and with the worst kind of reputation! A notorious character, in fact! But, according to what I hear, Candida and Paula are completely fascinated with him!

PAULA: PEPANG!

PEPANG: And he flirts with them! They allow him to flirt with them!

MANOLO: Pepang, that's enough!

PEPANG: At their age! To be fooled at their age—and by a man of the lowest type!

MANOLO: Pepang, I told you to shut up!

PEPANG: And that is why they refuse to leave this house! They cannot bear to leave this young man! They cannot bear to be separated from him—

(She turns away, trembling. They are tensely silent for a moment, not looking at each other. The siren stops screaming. Manolo grimly confronts his younger sisters.)

MANOLO: Now, do you see why you cannot remain in this house?

CANDIDA: Do you believe this evil talk?

MANOLO: Do you think me so stupid?

PAULA: Oh, there will be enough stupid people to believe it!

MANOLO: Exactly! And their tongues will go on wagging as long as you stay in this house!

CANDIDA: The wagging of all the evil tongues in the world cannot drive us away from here!

PAULA: They are not worth our contempt!

MANOLO: And how about the good name of our family? Is that worth nothing to you either? Is our name to go on furnishing entertainment for the malicious? And what about father? Have you considered how this would hurt him?

CANDIDA: Father knows nothing of this!

MANOLO: You deceive yourselves. Father always knows! Oh, I see now why he is ill!

CANDIDA: Father is not ill!

MANOLO: Yes, he is—and I know why!

CANDIDA: He is not ill—and you do not know, you do not know!

MANOLO: What is it I do not know?

PAULA: Oh, tell them, Candida—tell them! Let them know! Why should we hide it any longer?

MANOLO: Then, there is something!

PAULA: Yes! Yes!

MANOLO: What have you been hiding from us?

(A pause. Then Candida, gripping herself together, turns around to face her brother and sister.)

CANDIDA: Father wants to die. He tried to kill himself.

PEPANG *(sinking to a chair)*: Oh, my God.

MANOLO: To kill himself...When?

CANDIDA: When he had that accident. It was not an accident, Manolo. He did it on purpose.

PEPANG: But how do you know?

MANOLO: You said you did not see it happen.

CANDIDA: We did not see it happen—but we know he wanted to kill himself, we know he wanted to die.

MANOLO: Why should he want to die?

PAULA: Because of us! Because of us!

CANDIDA: I was to blame, Paula. You merely followed me!

PAULA: Oh no, no—we were in this together. We faced him together, we accused him together!

PEPANG: Accused him of what?

PAULA: Of having ruined our lives!

MANOLO: Paula! Candida!

PAULA: And we blamed him for our wasted youth, we blamed him for our poverty, we blamed him for the husbands we never had, and we blamed him for having squandered away mother's property!

PEPANG (*shutting her eyes tight*): Poor father! Poor, poor father!

CANDIDA: Yes, we flung it all in his face—all the humiliations we have suffered since childhood because we never had enough money. And we accused him of being heartless, of being selfish, of having lived his life only for himself and for his art. We told him to look at people like Don Perico, who are now rich and successful. We told him that he, too, could have become rich like Don Perico. Why not? He had the same talents, he had had the same opportunities. But he had wasted his talents, he had wasted his opportunities—he had been too cowardly, too selfish—so, now, he must pass his old age in poverty, he must depend on charity, while Paula and I—oh, we told him we could have made brilliant marriages if only we had been rich! We told him that it was his fault, his fault, that our youth had been wasted, that our lives had been ruined!

MANOLO: And what did he do when you had said all this?

CANDIDA: Nothing.

MANOLO: He should have slapped your faces!

PAULA: He asked us to excuse him.

(*A pause, during which they all slowly turn their faces towards PORTRAIT.*)

MANOLO: And did you ever ask him to forgive you?

CANDIDA: Oh, we tried, we tried—in the days that followed. What we had done, we had done in a fit of depression. We were ashamed of it at once. We wanted to know ourselves at his feet—to beg him to forgive us, and to forgive all the bitter things we had said. But he would not give us the chance. He kept away from us. He had begun to paint this picture; he was working on it night and day. And when it was finished, he called us to his room and showed us this picture. He said he had painted it very especially for us, that it was his final gift to us. We wanted to kneel down then and beg his forgiveness—but he pressed the picture on us, he waved us away. And when we were at the door he said: "Goodbye, Candida, Goodbye, Paula." And then that night...that very night he... he fell from the balcony...

(A pause, as she chokes back her tears. When she speaks again her voice is flatter and more desolate.)
Do you see now? Do you see now? It could have not been an accident...

MANOLO *(grimly)*: No, Candida—it was not an accident.

PAULA: And he will never, never forgive us!

PEPANG *(rising and swiftly approaching her sisters and putting an arm around each of them)*: Paula, Candida—do not say that! Of course he will forgive you! He is our father. You must go to him again—

PAULA: We have been trying and trying ever since.

CANDIDA: It is no use. He refuses to forgive us.

PAULA: When we kneel by his bed, he turns his face away.

CANDIDA: That is why we cannot part with this picture. It is our punishment. He painted it to punish us. We cannot look at it without suffering. We can never escape from this picture. It is our punishment.

MANOLO *(sobbing; sinking down to a chair)*: Oh Paula, Candida—how could you have done it! You were all he had—and you abandoned him too, you turned against him too!

(He buries his face in his hands.)

PEPANG: They were only doing, Manolo, what you and I had done.

MANOLO *(sobbing into his hands)*: Oh father! Oh, poor, poor father!

PEPANG: We all have to grow up, Manolo—we all have to grow up. Oh, how we worshipped him when we were children! We were so proud of him because he was a genius, because he was different from all other fathers. We always took his side against mother—remember? Poor mother, with her eternal worrying and her eternal complaints—poor mother did not understand him, of course. Only we, his children, understood him. And we defended him, we justified him, we were willing to be poor, to go without the things other children had, so that our father could go on being just an artist. Oh, we were happy enough, I know—though, even then, I promised myself that my children should never suffer what we had to suffer. And when we grew up, Manolo—then what did we do? When he could not give us the things the young people of our age all had—what did you and I do? Did we not face him also and accuse him of cowardice and selfishness? Did we not blame him also for the humiliations of our youth? Did we not berate him also for having squandered mother's property? And did we not also tell him that he could have been a rich man if he had only used his talents to advance himself in the world? Yes, we did, Manolo—you and I! We faced him and we accused him and we rejected him! And how can we blame Candida and Paula now?

MANOLO *(looking up)*: But I thought they were happy together. Candida, Paula—I thought you were contented to stay with father.

CANDIDA: Yes, we were—as long as we were sure of our life together. But you and Pepang had begun to complain about the cost of this house; you were talking of selling it. And we realized how little sure we were of the future.

PAULA: We were desperate.

CANDIDA: And whom could we blame but…but him?

MANOLO *(rising)*: Well, one thing is definitely settled now. You cannot go on living together, the three of you—not with all this hatred and bitterness among you. This house must be sold. Father must be placed in a hospital.

PAULA: You cannot take him away from us now!

CANDIDA: You must give us time—time to atone for what we did!

PAULA: We must go on working for our forgiveness!

MANOLO: I want no more arguments! Oh, I did not dare to sell this house as long as I thought that father wanted to stay here. But now I know he does not want to stay here, he does not want to stay with you! He will never get well until he has been completely separated from the two of you!

PAULA: Manolo!

CANDIDA: Oh, he has a right to be cruel. His conscience is clear!

MANOLO: I am glad I found out about this.

CANDIDA: Yes, you are glad—both of you—very glad! Oh, you are delighted to find Paula and I have proved unfaithful too—that we turned against father even as you did! And what a relief you must be feeling now, you and Pepang! Because, now, we are all alike, we are all the same, we have all destroyed our father.

PEPANG: Candida, control yourself. Manolo, you must give them time.

MANOLO: They can stay until this house has been sold—but they must dismiss this boarder of theirs at once—and I shall arrange to have father transferred to a hospital as soon as possible. I expect to have this disposed of before the end of this month. You will come to live with me, Candida. Paula must will live with Pepang. And listen, all of you—this is absolutely the last talk we shall ever have on this matter. Pepang, are you ready to go now?

PEPANG *(going for her bag)*: Yes, Manolo...

MANOLO: Wait a minute while I go in and see if father is awake. *(He exits.)*

PEPANG *(earnestly)*: Candida, Paula—have confidence; everything will turn out for the best. And father will be better off really in a hospital. You must not blame yourselves. Father will forgive you. In fact, he has already forgiven you. You say this picture is your punishment. I do not think father would be so cruel. He did not paint this picture to punish you; he painted it to release you, to free you! Do you not see? When you said all those bitter things to him, he was not angry; he understood your predicament; and he took pity on you. He could not give you any money, of course—but he could give you this picture, knowing that you could make money out of it—the money to release you, to set you free! Paula, Candida—your happiness is in your hands. You can have money of your own. You will feel secure and independent. You will not have to worry anymore about the future.

(Enter Manolo.)

MANOLO: Father is still asleep. Come on, Pepang.

PEPANG *(kissing her sister)*: Goodbye, Candida. Goodbye, Paula.

MANOLO: Now remember—you are to dismiss this boarder of yours immediately!

PAULA: Yes, Manolo.

MANOLO: Candida, did you hear me?

CANDIDA: Yes, Manolo.

MANOLO: And take away all those signs from the door

PAULA AND CANDIDA: Yes, Manolo.

MANOLO: Well, goodbye now. And do be more sensible, both of you!

PAULA AND CANDIDA: Goodbye, Manolo.

MANOLO: Tell father I shall be around again soon.

(*Exit Pepang and Manolo.*)

PAULA (*after a pause*): Candida, have you no news? Oh, tell me you have news—good news!

CANDIDA: We must go and do the cooking if we are to eat anything.

PAULA: Then, you did not go?

CANDIDA (*bitterly*): Yes, I did!

PAULA: To this Bureau of Health and Science?

CANDIDA (*shuddering*): Oh Paula, it was horrible!

PAULA: No place for you?

CANDIDA: They thought I was crazy!

PAULA: Oh Candida!

CANDIDA: They only made fun of me. They sent me from one department to another. Oh, I thought they were serious—and I tried to act very smart, like a woman of the world—I went into every office and told them that I wanted to catch rats, that I was an expert—and they listened very attentively—I thought they were really interested—but they were only laughing at me, they were only making fun of me. And then they began to be afraid of me—they thought I was dangerous. They became more and more nervous. They began running about excitedly and shouting and blowing whistles. A crowd began to gather.

They thought I was a criminal! I had to run away! They chased me down to the street! I had to run and run!

PAULA *(taking her sister's hands)*: Oh, Candida!

CANDIDA: Pepang is right. There is no place for us anywhere in the world. We are completely useless. We must separate. You go and live with Pepang. I will go and live with Manolo. I will take care of his children and keep an eye on his servants. You will look after Pepang's laundry, brush her hair, and answer her telephone.

PAULA: She will make me wear her old clothes and I must pretend to be grateful.

CANDIDA: And Manolo's wife will make me cut my hair and paint my face.

PAULA: Oh Candida, is there no escape for us?

CANDIDA *(turning her face towards PORTRAIT)*: Did you hear what Pepang said? She said this picture is our release, our freedom…

(As they stared wonderingly at PORTRAIT, a car is heard stopping down in the street. They glance quickly at each other. Candida shudders.)

Oh, I cannot talk to him now!

(She hurries to doorway and Paula follows. Tony Javier is heard running up the stairs and shouting: "Miss Candida! Miss Paula!" The sisters pause in the doorway. Tony appears on the landing, breathless.)

TONY: Oh, there you are! Come here, both of you! Come and sit down! Oh Miss Paula, Miss Candida—I bring wonderful news! This is your salvation!

CANDIDA: Our salvation?

TONY: If you want to be saved—and I know you do!

PAULA: Mr. Javier, what is all this?

TONY: Come here, ladies—and you shall know! Come and listen to me—please!

(Paula glances at Candida; Candida walks back into the room and Paula follows.)

CANDIDA: Well, what is it Mr. Javier?

TONY *(waving towards sofa):* Oh, sit down, sit down first! I don't want you to go running off before you have heard everything.

PAULA: Oh Candida, this is all nonsense!

TONY *(giving her his most appealing look):* Please, Miss Paula!

CANDIDA *(going to sofa):* Very well, Mr. Javier—but you must hurry. We still have our cooking to do.

(She and Paula sit down on sofa.)

TONY: Oh, you'll forget all about your cooking after you've heard what I have to tell you! And—oh, yes—I know you have forbidden me ever to mention this matter again—but I must disobey you.

PAULA: Is it about that picture again?

TONY: And about the American who has long been wanting to buy it.

PAULA *(rising):* Oh, Mr. Javier!

TONY: Sit down, Miss Paula—sit down and listen! *(Paula obeys.)* Now, about this American—he's going back to the States. All the Americans are being sent home—evacuated, you know—so they won't get caught here when the war breaks out. Well, this particular American is leaving in a week. He still wants this picture; he wants to take it back with him. Oh, he says he's crazy about it—and so, he's offering a crazy price for it. His last price. Take it or leave it. He simply doesn't want any more bargaining. And, ladies, do you know how much he's offering now for that picture of yours? *(A pause, while he looks at the sisters.)* He is offering ten thousand dollars!

CANDIDA *(after a stunned pause):* Ten thousand dollars!

TONY: And that's twenty thousand pesos.

PAULA: Twenty thousand pesos!

TONY: Oh, he wants it bad, and he wants it at once! He's leaving Friday *(The sisters are silent, staring at PORTRAIT.)*

Well, what do say know? But take your time, take your time! Don't let me hurry you! Think carefully, think very carefully! Oh, just think of it! Twenty Grand! Enough money to last you for years and years! Why, you'll be loaded!

You'll be sitting on the top of the world! And you can snap your fingers at this brother and sister of yours!

PAULA *(after a pause, rising)*: We... we are sorry, Mr. Javier. But we told you before that the picture is not for sale. Well... it is still... still not for sale.

TONY: WHAT?

PAULA: Come along, Candida.

(Candida remains seated, staring at PORTRAIT.)

TONY: Wait, wait, WAIT! Oh, my God! Think, ladies—think! This may never happen again! This is the chance of your lifetime!

PAULA *(with a slight smile)*: It seems to be rather the chance of your lifetime, Mr. Javier.

TONY: Mine? Why?

PAULA: You are so anxious to make the sale. Has this American offered you a very big reward?

TONY: Just think how much he's offering you!

PAULA: And how much is he offering you, Mr. Javier?

TONY: Why do you ask?

PAULA: A lot of money?

TONY: Sure! And I need it!

PAULA: We are very sorry you cannot earn your reward.

TONY: But think of yourselves, think of yourselves! Miss Candida, just think what you'll be throwing away!

PAULA: We know what we are doing. Candida, will you tell him he is only wasting his time?

TONY: Miss Candida, will you tell her what a chance you'll be wasting?

(Candida rises in silence and walks away. Paula, astonished, takes a step to follow her.)

TONY (*grabbing Paula's arm*): Oh, stay and listen! Listen to me—please!

CANDIDA (*walking slowly towards doorway*): I must go and do the cooking…

PAULA: Oh Candida, do not leave me alone!

CANDIDA (*whirling around; with sudden passion*): Why? Are you afraid?

PAULA (*startled*): Afraid? (*Tony releases her arm.*)

CANDIDA (*fiercely*): Yes, yes—afraid! Afraid to stay! Afraid to find out that it is true after all! Everything they are saying, everything they are whispering and laughing about!

PAULA: Candida! You know it is not true!

CANDIDA: Then why are you afraid to stay? Why do you always need me at your side? Are you a baby, am I your nurse?

PAULA (*grimly*): I am not afraid to stay. I shall stay, Candida. I do not need you.

CANDIDA: Why should you need me? Why should we need each other? Oh, it is time that each of us faced facts alone by herself! Alone, Paula! Not together, not always together!

PAULA (*with the shake of the head*): We are not together anymore, Candida. You have already made your decision.

(*They stare a moment at each other. Then Candida turns away quickly, towards doorway. Paula smiles mockingly.*)

And I know why you are running away, Candida! I know, I know!

CANDIDA (*turning around in doorway; defiant*): And you are right, Paula! You are absolutely right! Why should I go on suffering? And why you should go on suffering? But you must decide that for yourself, Paula—alone! Yes, I have already made my decision! Oh, you are right, Paula! We are not together anymore! We are not together anymore!

(*She covers her face with her hands and rushes out.*)

TONY (*after a pause*): I'm sorry, Miss Paula.

(*Paula is motionless, looking at doorway. Tony shrugs.*)

I suppose you know what you're doing...but twenty thousand bucks!

(He whistles.)

Saying no to twenty grand! Saying no to a chance like that! God, if it was me! If it was only me!

(He moves towards PORTRAIT and stands before it, staring bitterly.)

What I could do with twenty grand! That's all I need—just the money to start me off. Get away from this hick town, get away from vaudeville, get away from all those bums... oh, I could make something out of myself—they'd see that soon enough! Make a name for myself, make a big shot out of myself... all I need is a little money. Organize my own band and play all over the orient— Hong Kong, Shanghai, Java, India. I'd be making money fast enough. And then I'd go to Europe. Sure, why not? This war won't last forever. I'd go to Europe and really learn to play the piano...

(Paula, at the mention of Europe, turns her face towards him and listens intently. He has forgotten all about her.)

God knows I'm not just a piano player! I've got ambitions, I've got a lot of big dreams—I've got so much inside me! And I just go wasting what I've got on vaudeville! It's not fair! Why don't somebody come and offer to give me twenty grand—just like that? Oh baby, what I could do with twenty grand! Go to Paris, go to Vienna, go to New York...

(Paula comes and stands beside him. Absorbed in his dreams, he does not notice her.)

PAULA *(in a sort of trance herself)*: Paris...? Vienna...? New York...?

TONY *(not really noticing her)*: Yeah—and all those other glamorous places over there. Spain, Italy, South America... but I wouldn't be going there just to have fun—no, siree! This won't be a punk whoopee party like the last time. I'd really be serious this time. I'd really study, really get educated. And then we'll see if I'm wrong about what've got!

PAULA: I used to dream of traveling myself...

TONY *(looking at her now)*: Huh?

PAULA *(smiling dreamily at PORTRAIT)*: Europe... I've always wanted to go to Europe. Spain and France and Italy...

(Slightly horrified, Tony steps back, away from her side. She does not notice.)

I've always wanted to go to all those places where my father lived when he was a young man...

(Tony now looks up at PORTRAIT. Suddenly, he smiles.)

Do you think it would be possible to go there now?

(She turns her face towards him and notice his grin.)

Why are you smiling?

TONY *(grinning at PORTRAIT)*: Because your father is going to get it!

PAULA: Get what?

TONY: What was coming to him!

PAULA: What do you mean?

TONY *(turning his grin towards her and stepping forward beside her)*: So, you want to travel, too—eh?

PAULA *(smiling again)*: When I was a girl.

TONY: How about now?

PAULA: And they were just dreams—just the foolish dreams of a young girl...

TONY: You could make your dreams come true.

PAULA *(with a sigh)*: Ah, it is too late now!

TONY *(moving closer)*: Paula—

PAULA (stiffening): It is too late now!

TONY *(softly, tenderly)*: Paula... too late?

PAULA *(beginning to shiver)*: Yes!

TONY: But why, Paula—why?

PAULA: I am not a young girl anymore!

TONY *(moving still closer)*: Paula, listen to me—

PAULA *(shivering; rooted to the floor; but keeping herself rigidly averted from his approaching face):* No, no! it is too late now! I am not young anymore, I am not young anymore!

TONY: Paula, you do like me a little, don't you?

(She is tensely silent, her face averted.)

Won't you say you like me a little, Paula?

PAULA: Oh, you must not talk like that! What would people say?

TONY: Who cares what people say? Are you afraid of their big mouths?

PAULA *(with sudden spirit):* I despise them!

TONY: Then show it! Show your contempt! Do what you like—and to hell with what people say!

PAULA *(her face hardening):* Yes, you are right!

TONY: And what can they do to you anyway?

PAULA: I am not afraid!

TONY: You can leave them to their nasty talk! Pack up whenever you please, and go wherever you want!

PAULA: Far away?

TONY: Yes, Paula—as far as you like. You can make your dreams come true.

PAULA *(faltering):* My dreams are dead.

TONY: Dreams don't die.

PAULA: Mine did. A long time ago.

TONY: But suppose somebody came along and said the right words, do you think they would come alive again?

PAULA: I stopped waiting—a long time ago...

TONY: Paula, look at me. *(She keeps face averted.)* Look at me, Paula—please!

(She begins to turn her face; but catching sight of PORTRAIT she freezes, her eyes widening with horror. He looks at her and the at PORTRAIT and he begins to back off.)

Turn your back on him, Paula! Turn your back on him!

PAULA *(agonized; unable to move; eyes fixed on PORTRAIT)*: I cannot do it! I cannot do it!

TONY *(sternly)*: Yes, you can! Yes, you can! Turn around, Paula! If he wants to rot here, then let him! Why should you rot with him? Turn around, Paula—turn around!

PAULA *(struggling to move her body)*: I cannot do it!

TONY: Try, Paula—try! Here I am, Paula—here I am behind you! Come to me, Paula.

(With a supreme effort, she twists around until she is facing him, her back to the audience. He utters a great groan of relief and breaks into a gay smile.)

There! You did it! Oh Paula, you're not afraid anymore! You have turned your back on him! You have won! Oh, come—come Paula!

(Holding out his arms, he begins to step backward slowly, towards stairway, talking steadily. Tranced, she steps forward slowly, following him.)

Come on, girl—keep moving! You've smashed your shell! No, don't look back, don't stop—just keep moving! That's right! That's the spirit! Atta, girl, Paula! Hooray for you! Oh, you'll join the navy and see the world! Hell, you won't either—you don't have to! You're loaded—you lucky girl! And think of it! All those places you've dreamed about—Spain and France and Italy! You'll see them now! You're still young, Paula! You've got a right to be happy! And you'll be happy, Paula! Your dreams aren't dead yet! They'll come alive again! They'll come true at last!

(He has reached the balustrade, and stops. She stops too. He moves towards her, his arms extended. She suddenly shudders away from his touch.)

PAULA: No, no! Do not touch me! You must not touch me! Not—*(glancing round the room)* —not here…

TONY *(with knowing smile)*: Okay, Paula—not here. *(He goes to stair landing.)* Come, Paula.

(He waits, smiling. After a while, she walks to his side, her head bowed. He smiles down at her; she looks up at him, her face grave. Looking thus into each other's eyes, they descend the stairs. After a moment, his car is heard starting. Simultaneously, Candida begins to shout "Paula! Paula!" inside.)

CANDIDA (appearing in doorway): Paula!

(The car is heard moving away. She runs to balcony where she stands, looking up the street. Then she turns around, a hand pressed to her throat.)

CANDIDA (in shocked whisper): Paula!

Then, resolutely, she strides towards stairway. But she catches sight of PORTRAIT and, with a terrified gasp, she cowers away. She stands shuddering, her eyes fixed on PORTRAIT, her breath coming faster and faster as

THE CURTAIN FALLS

THE THIRD SCENE

As in preceding Scene, curtains open on the "Intramuros Curtain", with Bitoy Camacho standing at far left, in light.

BITOY: The next time I went to the Marasigan house was on a cold cloudy afternoon—the afternoon of the second Sunday of October. A typhoon wind was blowing; the skies above were dark—as dark as the weather in our hearts—for the rumors of war were thickening fast; panic was in the air. But that afternoon, Intramuros was in a holiday mood. As though knowing that is was about to die, about to be obliterated forever, this old city was celebrating— celebrating for the last time. The streets were decorated, and filled with hurrying people. The bells rang out high and clear. It was the feast of La Naval de Manila.

(A faint faraway sound of bells and band music.)

As I walked down the street, I could hear my footsteps reverberating against the cobblestones; when I talked and laughed, my voice seemed to echo on and on. Aware of the doom hanging overhead, I looked about me with keener eyes; and everything I saw—even the slum tenements—seemed suddenly very beautiful and very precious—because I might be seeing them for the last time.

(The lights go on inside the stage; through the curtain, the sala becomes visible.)

I was seeing them for the last time. Two months later, the bombs began to fall. There is nothing left of it now—of the old Manila. It is dead, obliterated forever—except in my memory—where it lives: still young, still great, still the Noble and Ever Loyal City. And whenever I remember it, the skies about are dark; a typhoon wind is blowing; it is October; it is the feast of the Naval.

(The "Intramuros Curtain" begins to open, revealing the sala. It is late in the afternoon and the room is rather dim. The doorway at right and the balconies have been decorated with festive curtains, which are blowing steadily in the wild wind.)

In October, a breath of the North stirs Manila, blowing summer's dust and doves from the tile roofs, freshening the moss of old walls, as the city festoons itself with arches and paper lanterns for its great votive feast to the Virgin.

(Candida comes slowly up the stairs, carrying prayer book, rosary and umbrella. She goes to the stand to deposit her umbrella.)

Women hurrying into their finery upstairs, be whiskered men tapping canes downstairs, children teeming in the doorways, coachmen holding impatient ponies in the streets, glancing up anxiously, fearing the wind's chill: would it rain this year?

(Candida pauses in front of balcony and puts out a hand to feel the wind.)

But the eyes that long ago had gazed up anxiously, invoking the Virgin, had feared a grimmer rain—of fire and metal—for pirate craft crowded the horizon.

(Candida goes to the table at enter where she lays down her prayer book and rosary. She takes off her veil and begins to fold it. She pauses, hearing a sound of distant bells and band music.)

The bells begin to peal again and sound like silver coins showering in the fine air; at the rumor of drums and trumpets as bands march smartly down the cobblestones a pang of childhood happiness smites every heart. October in Manila!

(Candida stands still, listening. The veil drops from her hands onto table. Candida is wearing her best dress—an archaic blue frock—and her jewels.)

But the emotion, so special to one's childhood, seems no longer purely one's own; seems to have traveled ahead, deep into Time, since one first felt its pang—growing ever more poignant, more complex: a child's rhyme swelling epical; a clan treasure one bequeaths at the very moment of inheritance, having added one's gem to it.

(Candida goes to the other balcony, on one side of which she stands, her face lifted, her eyes closed, the wind blowing her hair.)

And Time creates unexpected destinations; history raises figs from thistles: yesterday's pirates become today's roast pork and paper lanterns, a tapping of impatient canes, a clamor of trumpets...

(Candida bows her head and covers her face with her hands. The distant rumor of bells and music fades out. Bitoy steps into the room and places himself at stair landing.)

Hello, Candida.

(She whirls around, nervously.)

CANDIDA *(with relief):* Oh, it is you, Bitoy.

BITOY *(walking in):* Boy, are you all dressed up!

CANDIDA *(coming forward):* The fiesta, you know.

BITOY: I saw you and Paula in church.

CANDIDA: Yes, I came home ahead. There was such a crowd. I felt dizzy. Sit down, Bitoy. Paula will be coming in a moment.

BITOY *(remaining standing):* And how is your father?

CANDIDA: Oh, just the same as usual. Do you want to see him? But he will—

CANDIDA AND BITOY *(together):* —be having a nap just now.

BITOY *(laughing):* I knew you would say that!

(Candida smiles. Sound of bells pealing again. They listen, glancing towards the balconies.)

CANDIDA: Have you come for the procession?

BITOY: October again, Candida!

CANDIDA: Yes... oh Bitoy, the Octobers of our childhood! The dear, dear Octobers of our childhood!

BITOY: Remember how my family used to come here to watch the Naval procession from your balconies?

CANDIDA: And so did the families of all our friends.

BITOY: Year after year—

CANDIDA: And year after our house stood open to all comers on this day, the feast of the Naval. It was always the biggest fiesta in this house.

BITOY: Lechon and relleno in the dining room—

CANDIDA: And ice cream and turrones here in the sala—

BITOY: And the chandeliers all lighted up—

CANDIDA: And all our windows and balconies simply crowded with visitors—

BITOY: The procession passing below and all the children shouting continually: "Who is that one, mama?" and "Who is that other one now, mama?"

CANDIDA *(in pious maternal tones):* that, my son, is the good San Vicente Ferrer—and he is wearing wings because he was as eloquent as an angel.

BITOY *(wide-eyed and craning his neck):* And who is that one coming now, mama?

CANDIDA: That, my son, is the noble San Pedro Martir.

BITOY: Oh look, look—he has a bolo in his head! Why has he got a bolo in his head?

CANDIDA: Because a wicked man killed him with a bolo.

BITOY: And who is that one now carrying a flag?

CANDIDA *(laughing):* Oh, shut your big mouth, my son! You are a pest and a nuisance!

BITOY: And then you knock me on the head—

CANDIDA: And one more nuisance carried off howling—

BITOY: To be silenced with ice cream and turron—

CANDIDA: Or dragged off to the small room—

BITOY: And the bells ringing, the bands playing, the crowds clamoring in the street—

CANDIDA: And the rain suddenly falling!

BITOY: Alas!

CANDIDA: Remember?

BITOY: If I forget there, o, Jerusalem—

CANDIDA: Oh, smell that wind, Bitoy! It is the smell of the holiday, the smell of the old Manila—the Manila of our affections!

BITOY *(throwing back his head and singing):*
"Adios, Reina del cielo!
Madre, madre del Salvador…"

CANDIDA *(suddenly pressing a hand to her eyes):* Oh, stop it, Bitoy!

BITOY *(laughing):* Gosh, do I sing that bad?

CANDIDA *(trying to smile):* Much, much worse!

BITOY: You should have knocked me on the head!

CANDIDA: Shall I?

BITOY *(offering his head):* Sure. Go ahead. Right here.

(Candida disconsolately turns away. Bitoy straightens up.)

I'm sorry, Candida. Is anything wrong?

CANDIDA *(bitterly):* Yes! Everything!

BITOY: What?

CANDIDA: This is our last October here—in this house—where we were born, where we grew up!

BITOY: The last October?

CANDIDA: We are leaving this house.

BITOY: Why?

CANDIDA: Because to save one's life is to lose it!

BITOY: Oh Candida, you would have had to leave this house anyway, sooner or later. It is too old—

CANDIDA: It is our youth.

BITOY: And when the war breaks out it will become very unsafe—

CANDIDA: There is no safety for us anymore, anywhere.

BITOY: And you must think of your father, you must think of this painting—

(He looks towards the site of the PORTRAIT and, suddenly, his eyes pop out, he gasps and steps forward, staring in amazement.)

Candida, the painting! It is gone!

CANDIDA *(not looking around):* Yes.

BITOY: Where is it?

CANDIDA: I do not know.

BITOY: Has it been sold?

CANDIDA: No, no!

BITOY: Then, where is it!

CANDIDA: I tell you I don't know!

BITOY: Oh Candida, what have you done with it!

CANDIDA: Paula took it down and put it away. She did not tell me where.

BITOY: But why did she take it down?

CANDIDA: She did not tell me that either.

BITOY: But how could you allow—

CANDIDA: Oh, stop asking, Bitoy! I know nothing, I know nothing at all!

(Sound of rapid knocking downstairs. Candida starts nervously again, and presses a hand to her forehead.)

Oh God, God! Bitoy, please see who that is. And remember: whoever it is, I am not at home, Paula is not at home, nobody is at home!

(She turns around quickly to leave the room but Susan and Violet have already appeared on the landing.)

SUSAN: Oh yes—you are at home all right!

(Susan and Violet advance into the room. They are sober this time, and look extremely determined. They have hurried right over from the Sunday matinee, and are still wearing their stage make-up and costumes: very brief gaudy ballet skirts.)

VIOLET: Excuse us for coming right up.

SUSAN: And don't tell us to go away because we won't go away!

VIOLET: Not till we found out what we want to find out!

SUSAN *(earnestly)*: Look, we'll behave ourselves—honest!

VIOLET: You remember us, don't you? We're from the Parisian Theater. We were here about a week ago.

SUSAN: And I'm sorry about how I acted that time—and about the things I said.

CANDIDA: What can I do for you?

SUSAN: We want to see Tony.

VIOLET: What's the matter with him?

SUSAN: Is he sick?

VIOLET: He hasn't shown up at the theater for the last two days. And if he still doesn't show up tonight, the manager is going to fire him.

SUSAN: He'll lose his job!

VIOLET: We came right over from the shoe to tell him. It's important!

SUSAN: Where is he?

CANDIDA: I do not know. Mr. Javier hasn't come back here either for the last two days.

SUSAN: Oh, where did he go!

VIOLET: Did he take his clothes with him?

CANDIDA: No; his clothes and all his things are still here. Tell me—are you very good friends of his?

VIOLET: Yes, we are!

CANDIDA: Then will you do me a favor? I have put his clothes and all his things together. They are downstairs.

VIOLET: In those two suitcases?

CANDIDA: Yes. Will you take them with you and give them to Mr. Javier when you find him?

SUSAN: So you're throwing him out!

VIOLET: Couldn't he pay his rent?

CANDIDA: And please tell Mr. Javier that I beg him never, never to show himself here again!

SUSAN: What did he do?

BITOY: Now look girls—that's strictly between Tony and Miss Marasigan. It's none of our business. You go and take his clothes with you. He's bound to show up sooner or later.

SUSAN: We won't go away until I find out what's happened to him!

BITOY: Nothing's happened to him. He's probably just out on a binge!

SUSAN: Are you throwing him out because of what I said the last time?

CANDIDA: That had nothing to do with it.

SUSAN: Oh, he's not bad, he's not bad! But you make him feel cheap! You make him run wild!

BITOY: I thought you said you were going to behave!

(Sound of people coming up the stairs.)

CANDIDA: Oh God, who are those now!

(They all look towards stairway. Enter Doña Loleng, Elsa and Charlie. Elsa is wearing a terrific Carmen Miranda costume with a towering head-dress. Charlie is in the costume of a Cuban rhumba dancer. Doña Loleng is in a swanky terno. She hurries forward and gasps at Candida's hands.)

LOLENG: Candida my dear—do forgive us for dropping in like this! But I have been so worried about you, my dear—so very worried! I have been hearing the most fantastic rumors!

CANDIDA: What rumors, Doña Loleng?

LOLENG *(looking around)*: Where is Paula?

CANDIDA *(trying to draw away)*: Won't you sit down? Paula will be coming in a moment. She has gone to church.

LOLENG *(astonished; keeping firm hold of Candida)*: Then nothing has happened to her?

CANDIDA *(lightly)*: Why, what have you been hearing?

LOLENG: That she had eloped with somebody—or that she had been kidnapped!

(Susan and Violet, who are listening alertly, glance at each other.)

CANDIDA *(with a careless laugh)*: Oh, but what nonsense!

LOLENG *(incredulous)*: Nothing has happened?

CANDIDA: Paula has not eloped—and she certainly has not been kidnaped.

LOLENG: Oh, thank God, thank God! I have been so worried, my dear.

CANDIDA: We are grateful for your very kind interest, Doña Loleng.

LOLENG *(avidly studying Candida's face)*: And everything is all right with you and Paula? You are quite sure, my dear?

CANDIDA: One hears nothing but wild rumors nowadays.

LOLENG *(disappointed; releasing Candida's hands)*: Well...

CANDIDA: Are you going?

LOLENG: Yes, we must be running off again.

CANDIDA: Do stay a moment and have a drink.

LOLENG: How we wish we could—but duty, Candida, duty! Oh, there are serious days for all of us! And so much good work to be done. I hardly have time to sit down anymore. Tonight we are giving a dance for the American servicemen. These poor boys, Candida—so far away from home and so lonely. We are doing all we can to console them. Elsa here is doing a jungle conga.

(Sound of knocking downstairs.)

CANDIDA: Bitoy, will you please see who that is?

LOLENG: Well, goodbye, Candida—and remember: the senator is your godfather and your mother was one of my dearest friends; so, if you and Paula have any troubles, I want you to come and tell me all about them. I shall only be too happy to listen.

CANDIDA: Thank you, Doña Loleng.

BITOY *(at stair landing):* Candida, it's the people from the newspapers. Do you want to see them?

CANDIDA *(with a gay laugh):* Now what on earth can they want with me! Yes, Bitoy—tell them to come up.

LOLENG: On second thought... I believe we could stay a moment, Candida.

CANDIDA *(hollowly):* Oh, how nice.

LOLENG *(moving to the sofa):* And we are all so exhausted from running around that we would all be grateful for a drink, my dear—if you still care to offer us any.

CANDIDA: Of course, Doña Loleng. Excuse me just a moment. Bitoy, will you tell those people to wait?

(Exit Candida, Enter Pete, Eddie and Cora. Pete is in white shorts and polo shirt, and carries a tennis racket. Eddie is in a dinner jacket. Cora is wearing a smart evening gown, and carries her camera.)

BITOY *(as the newcomers come up)*: Well, what do you people want now!

PETE *(excitedly)*: Bitoy, is it true?

BITOY: What's true?

PETE *(pushing past him into the room)*: Oh Christ—it's true! The painting has disappeared!

LOLENG *(rising)*: Why, so it has!

(They are all staring towards site of PORTRAIT.*)*

EDDIE: What do they say, Bitoy? Have they sold it?

BITOY: No.

PETE: Well, where is it then?

BITOY: They have only hidden it—for safekeeping, I suppose.

CORA: Ho-hum. Another wild goose—that laid an egg.

PETE: Are they here, the sisters?

BITOY: Candida is here.

EDDIE: Then the other one is still missing?

ELSA *(rising)*: You see! What did I tell you, Loleng!

BITOY: Paula is not missing. I saw her at the Dominican church just a while ago.

EDDIE: She was reported missing the day before yesterday.

ELSA: And that was when we saw her with this fellow. They were in his car.

SUSAN: Excuse me—but which fellow was she with?

CORA: Your boyfriend, girls—but, oh, don't worry. He was only teaching her how to drive.

ELSA: A fine time to teach her! It was almost midnight. Charlie, what time exactly did we see them?

CHARLIE: Quarter past eleven.

ELSA: P.M.

CHARLIE *(coming forward):* Hello, Violet. Hi Susan.

SUSAN: Charlie, did you really see her with Tony?

CHARLIE: Is Tony the guy who plays the piano at your show?

VIOLET: That's him.

CHARLIE: Then, that was Tony with her all right. They were having a nice long ride in the moonlight.

SUSAN: Tony hasn't come back since then.

PETE: You know what I think? They eloped—and took the picture with them!

BITOY: I tell you—I saw Paula with my own eyes this afternoon!

EDDIE: Then he doublecrossed her! He pretended he was eloping with her—but he just ran off with the picture and left her flat!

CORA: I wish I had your imagination!

PETE: What we have is a nose for news.

LOLENG: And my nose was not wrong either when it led me all the way here.

VIOLET: We smelled something rotten ourselves!

CORA *(aside to Bitoy):* What's this—a gathering of the vultures?

ELSA: There's nothing so dangerous as an old maid! Oh, I studied all about it in New York. Sex frustration, you know.

LOLENG: And I'm so glad I found out all this! Oh, this house, this house! Well, it has begun to smell after all!

ELSA: Come on, Loleng—let's go!

CHARLIE: She can hardly wait to spread the good news!

LOLENG: No—I must talk to Candida.

CHARLIE: And learn all the details!

(Unnoticed, the Watchman and Detective have crept stealthily up the stairs. The detective whips out his gun, his hand wobbling.)

LOLENG: I simply must know what really has happened to the painting. Charlie, will you—MADRE MIA!

(She has seen the two newcomers and the gun. The others look around and freeze.)

THE DICK: Hands up, everybody! Nobody moves!

(They all put up their hands. The Dick and the Watchman advance into the room. The Watchman is a small nervous old man; the Dick is a tall nervous young man.)

WATCHMAN: Where is she? Where is she?

BITOY: Who?

WATCHMAN: That old woman!

LOLENG *(indignant):* There is no old woman here!

WATCHMAN: Oh yes, there is! I saw her come in here a while ago!

THE DICK: You should have followed her inside!

WATCHMAN: Are you crazy! I was unarmed, I had to call you up first! She must be carrying a time bomb!

ELSA: A time bomb!

THE DICK: She is a spy—a fifth-columnist!

PETE: And you saw her come in here?

LOLENG: Why, she may be hiding somewhere below!

(Susan and Violet begin to screech.)

ELSA: We may all be just about to be blown out!

VIOLET *(whimpering)*: Oh Susan, why did we ever come!

SUSAN: Why don't you go and search the house!

LOLENG: Call the police, you boons! Call the police!

ELSA: Oh Loleng, let's get out of here at once!

THE DICK: Silence! Nobody moves!

EDDIE: Suppose you tell us just who you are.

THE DICK *(flashing his badge)*: I'm a detective!

WATCHMAN: And I'm the watchman at the Bureau of Health and Science!

CORA: Then look—you can put that gun away. We're not spies or fifth-columnist.

VIOLET *(crying)*: We're innocent!

SUSAN: We're peaceful law-abiding tax-payers!

LOLENG *(fuming)*: Will somebody tell them just who I am!

CHARLIE *(to watchman)*: Hey, you—come over here!

> *(Watchman approaches; Charlie whispers in his ears. The watchman glances towards Doña Loleng and his eyes pop out. He hurries to the Dick, and whispers in his ear. The Dick's eyes pop out; he immediately puts away his gun.)*

LOLENG *(sinking down to the sofa)*: Idiots! *(The other limply put down their hands.)*

THE DICK: We are very sorry, señora!

WATCHMAN: We are very, very, sorry señora; please forgive us!

THE DICK: We are only doing our duty, señora!

WATCHMAN: We were trying to catch this old woman—

PETE: What does she look like?

WATCHMAN: She looks suspicious!

THE DICK: We've been on her track for the last two days. She is a member of The RATS!

CHARLIE: What rats?

THE DICK: The RATS, The R.A.T.S. The Rope and Trigger Society!

EDDIE: Oh God, Pete—that's the band of terrorists!

THE DICK: Exactly! They go around the government offices trying to start a Reign of Terror! This old woman was last seen at the Bureau of Health and Science—and she was openly declaring her connection with the rats!

(Enter Candida with a tray containing glasses and bottles. On seeing her, the watchman staggers backward so suddenly he bumps against the other people, almost falling down.)

WATCHMAN *(pointing and screaming; terrified):* AND THERE SHE IS! THAT'S HER! THAT'S THE WOMAN!

THE DICK *(whipping out his gun and pointing it at Candida):* You're... you're under arrest!

CANDIDA *(pausing; startled):* What!

CHARLIE: Oh, rats!

LOLENG: Will you idiots get out of here before I break your necks!

EDDIE: Miss Candida, you had better offer these two fellows a drink. They need it.

THE DICK *(looking about uncertainly; lowering his gun):* Do... do you all know this woman?

CHARLIE: Yes!

THE DICK: She is not a gangster?

CORA: If she's a gangster, so's your grandmother!

WATCHMAN: But she's the woman I saw! She's dangerous! She came to the—

LOLENG: Shut up!

WATCHMAN: I am sorry, señora.

LOLENG: I answer for this woman, do you hear!

WATCHMAN AND DICK: Yes, señora.

CANDIDA *(placing tray on table):* What has happened?

LOLENG: Let them tell you. Go on, idiots! What did you say she was?

ELSA: They suspect you for being a spy!

CANDIDA *(laughing):* I—a spy! But how exciting! Yes, do tell me all about it! Oh, I feel like a character in a romantic novel! Doña Loleng, do you think I might be just the right—

(She stops short as two policemen appear on the stairway. A silence, while the policemen fetch out their notebooks and glance around the room. Then, as nobody says anything, they move forward. One of them has a black eye.)

1ST COP: We want to speak to Miss Marasigan.

CANDIDA *(faintly):* I am Miss Marasigan.

2ND COP *(glancing at his notebook):* Miss Candida Marasigan?

CANDIDA: What can I do for you?

2ND COP: Miss Marasigan, the day before yesterday, at around noontime, you telephoned us and reported that your sister had been abducted—

1ST COP: We have been unable to locate your sister but we have found the man who—

CANDIDA *(quickly interrupting):* Please forgive me—but it was all, all a mistake!

1ST COP: What was a mistake?

CANDIDA: My telephoning you. Nothing had happened, really.

2ND COP: Your sister was not abducted?

CANDIDA: No.

1ST COP: And she is not missing?

CANDIDA: I only thought she was.

(*The cops glance wearily at each other and shrug.*)

1ST COP: Then why did you not call again to tell us?

CANDIDA: I am sorry. I forgot.

2ND COP: You are withdrawing your charges?

CANDIDA: It was all a mistake.

2ND COP (*pocketing his notebook*): Miss Marasigan, you see this black eye? I got this because of your mistake. Be more careful next time, will you?

1ST COP: Could we use your telephone?

CANDIDA: We have no telephone.

1ST COP (*to his companion*): You go down and call up the station. Tell them to release this fellow.

PETE (*as 2nd Cop exits*): Which fellow, officer?

THE COP: The fellow she said had run away with her sister. We picked him up this morning.

SUSAN (*approaching*): Is his name Tony Javier?

THE COP: That's right.

VIOLET: Where did you find him?

THE COP: In a bar—trying to break all the furniture.

PETE: Drunk?

THE COP: And violent. He gave my companion the black eye.

SUSAN: But they're going to release him now?

THE COP: Oh, sure—after he pays a fine.

SUSAN *(turning on Candida):* You see! Now I hope you and that sister of yours are satisfied!

THE COP: Just what actually happened, Miss Marasigan?

CANDIDA: Nothing at all, really. My sister simply went off for a drive—and forgot to tell me she was going.

THE COP: And this was at around twelve o'clock noon, the day before yesterday?

CANDIDA *(desperately):* But she came back right away!

SUSAN: Oh no—she didn't!

BITOY: Will you shut up!

SUSAN: She did not come back right away, Miss Marasigan! You think nobody knows? Oh, we all know, Miss Marasigan! Everybody knows! That sister of yours was still out driving with him at midnight, the day before yesterday!

THE COP: What time did she come back, Miss Marasigan?

BITOY: Officer, since no charges are being made, I see no point in all these questions.

SUSAN: Well, I do! I want this dirty business dragged out into the open!

VIOLET: Why should they get off free? They started this trouble, they ought to pay for it!

LOLENG: Oh, my poor, Candida!

SUSAN: Poor Candida—hell! They get poor Tony in jail, they make him lose his job—and then they laugh and say: "Oh, excuse us please! It was all a mistake!" And then they try to get everybody to hush up! Oh, they got what they wanted from Tony—they've been wanting that a long time—and now they think they can get away with it, just like that! Oh, they think they can keep it all safe and quiet, do they? Well, you don't, Miss Marasigan! I'll take care of that!

VIOLET: We'll shout your name all over town!

SUSAN: We'll see everybody knows about this fine ride your sister had in the moonlight!

VIOLET: So, she came back right away, did she?

CANDIDA (*going to pieces*): NO! No, she did not come back right away! I lied, I was lying, I speak nothing now but lies and les! No, she did not come back right away; she came back at three o'clock in the morning. I was standing right here. I was waiting for her. No, she did not come back right away... I was lying...

LOLENG: CANDIDA!

CANDIDA: I was lying, I tell you! I was lying! No, she did not come back right away; she came back at three o'clock in the morning. I know. I was waiting. I was standing right here, waiting for her to come back. And I was going to throw her out. Oh, I felt righteous! I was horrified with what she had done. And I knew just what I was going to say to her—all the bitter, bitter words I was going to fling in her face! I felt justified—I was the virtuous one. And then she came... It was three o'clock in the morning. I was standing right here. And she came slowly up those stairs... And the she stood there, not saying anything... And her face, her face! How can I ever forget her face!

LOLENG: Candida, stop it!

CANDIDA: How can I ever, ever forget her face! And I knew then who was the guilty one! I knew who was the evil one! Oh, pray for me! Pray for me! I have destroyed my sister!

(*She bows down, rocking her head from side to side.*)

CORA: Bitoy, make her go in!

ELSA: Who are those two creatures anyway?

VIOLET (*bristling*): Listen, do you mean us?

PETE: Yes, now shut up!

EDDIE: Oh, why? They have been a great help. We all came to find out, didn't we?

CANDIDA (*looking up, with a faint smile*): Yes, didn't you?

BITOY: Candida, why not go in and lie down?

CANDIDA *(smiling):* You all wanted to know, didn't you? You all came to find out, didn't you? Well, now you know! Now you have found out!

CORA: Oh Bitoy, take her away!

CHARLIE: Why don't we all just go away!

CANDIDA *(wildly):* Wait, wait! You know where she was, you know what she did, you know what happened to her—but, listen: I am the guilty one, I have committed a greater sin, I have committed a terrible crime against my sister! It was I who let her go—who made her go! I knew it was going to happen—and I let it happen—I wanted it to happen! And do you know why? Because of ten thousand dollars! Oh, I was thinking of my own future safety, my own future security! And no more poverty, no more bickering over money, no more haggling at the market, and no more hiding here in the darkness, the light cut off, the water stopped, the bill collectors pounding and pounding at the door!

BITOY *(grasping her by the arms):* Candida!

CANDIDA: Oh, I was thinking of ten thousand dollars in the bank! And so I let her go! And so I let her perish! I have destroyed my father—and now I have destroyed my sister! I am evil, evil, evil—

BITOY *(shaking her):* Candida! Candida!

CANDIDA *(subsiding):* And now you all know... Now you have found out...

(She turns away from Bitoy's grasp and passes a hand over her brow.)

And now you must excuse me... I... I do not feel well...

(Charlie instantly claps on his hat and exits. Doña Loleng, after a glance at the motionless Candida, goes off too, followed by Elsa. The Cop shrugs, pockets his notebook and, looking embarrassed, departs, followed by the Dick and the Watchman. Pete takes Susan and Violet by the arm and walks them off, followed by Cora and Eddie. Only Bitoy is left. He approaches Candida.)

BITOY: Candida—

CANDIDA *(dully):* Go to her, Bitoy. Please go to her.

BITOY: To Paula?

CANDIDA: She is in the church. Go and look for her. Tell her to hurry home. I must speak to her. Oh Bitoy, we have not spoken to each other since she came back! There has been only silence, silence between us. But now I can break the silence. Now, I can look in her face and speak. I know my sin, I recognize it.

BITOY: Candida, you must not blame yourself.

CANDIDA: Don't you see, Bitoy? I lost faith, I lost valor. I turned cowardly. Father brought us up to be heroes—but I refused his heroism. I wanted only to be safe, to be secure. My crime is prudence.

BITOY: It is not a crime, Candida. Everybody wants to be safe and secure.

CANDIDA: And that is why we are all destroying each other—

BITOY: We have to kill—

CANDIDA: And being destroyed by each other.

BITOY: Or be killed.

CANDIDA: Will you go to Paula?

BITOY: What shall I tell her?

CANDIDA: Tell her... tell her that we are together again!

BITOY: Only that?

CANDIDA: She has been waiting and waiting to hear me say that!

BITOY: Very well, Candida.

(Exit Bitoy. Candida stands still a moment; then she turns away, towards table. The bells peal out again; she pauses and listens, gazing wistfully at the blowing curtains. Then she goes to table, intending to take out the untouched tray of drinks. She takes hold of the tray but does not lift it, remaining thus: stooped over the table, her back to the stairway. Tony Javier comes up the stairs and pauses on the landing. He is hatless, uncombed, unshaved, untidy, and unsteady. He sports a black'eye, and looks physically and—yes!—spiritually ravaged. He is still wearing the same clothes as in preceding scene; the clothes being very soiled and rumpled now, the loosening tie still dangling around the unbuttoned shirt's collar.

From this point, Twilight starts and the stage dims very gradually.)

TONY *(at stairway; curtly)*: Where is she?

(Candida straightens up but does not look around nor reply. Tony raises his voice.)

Where is she?

CANDIDA *(still not looking around)*: She is not here.

(Tony has turned his face towards site of PORTRAIT; his eyes ablaze.)

TONY: And where is it? Where is the picture?

CANDIDA *(moving away; wearily)*: I do not know.

(Tony grabs her by the arm and whirls her around.)

TONY: I said—WHERE IS THE PICTURE!

CANDIDA *(moaning)*: Go away... Please, please go away...

TONY: Oh, I'll go away—don't you worry. I'll go as far away from here as I can get! But not till you give me that picture!

CANDIDA *(with a toss of the head)*: I will never give it to you!

TONY *(sneering)*: Well! You have changed your mind, haven't you? Oh I could see you were willing enough to sell the last time, Candida!

CANDIDA: And you were right!

TONY *(with a leer)*: And you were willing to let me persuade your sister to tell, too!

CANDIDA: Oh yes—yes indeed!

TONY: You were even willing to let me take her out and convince her! You didn't care how I did it—as long as it was effective!

CANDIDA *(mockingly)*: And was it?

TONY: You bet it was! I chose the most effective way in the world to convince her!

CANDIDA *(smiling contemptuously)*: Ah—but did you?

TONY (*flushing furiously and giving her a shake*): You know I did! You know I did!

CANDIDA: All I know is that she came back alone! All I know is that she got away from you!

TONY: Well, she can't back out now! And you can't either! I've got the both of you in my hands! Oh, don't worry—I won't double cross you! You'll get your ten grand; all I want is my commission.

CANDIDA (*jerking her arm loose*): Your commission! And that is all you ever wanted, wasn't it?

TONY: Sure! Why? Did you think I wanted you? Did you think I wanted your sister?

CANDIDA: How could you have the nerve to touch her!

TONY: Remember, Candida—I had your permission! When you walked out of this room that day, you left her completely in my hands!

CANDIDA (*trembling; her fists clenched*): Please go! I beg you to go at once!

(*Unnoticed, Paula has come up the stairs, carrying prayer book, rosary and umbrella; her church veil draped around her shoulders. She pauses and glances towards the two people in the dim room. Paula, too, is wearing her best dress—an archaic blue frock—and her jewels; and she looks very young, happy and tranquil. She has fought, she has conquered: now she comes back radiant—merciless as a child; ruthless as innocence; terrible as an army with banners.*)

TONY: I'm waiting for that picture. The American is waiting for that picture. Give it to me and we'll get what we want. He gets his picture, you get your ten grand, I get my commission. Yes, Candida—that was all I ever really wanted! Just a little money to start me off—to get me away from here! But I wouldn't take you or your sister with me if both of you had a million dollars! What do you take me for—a nut? I can get younger women, Candida—women to my taste! Not a pair of skinny, screwy, dried up old hags!

(*Paula goes to set her umbrella in stand.*)

CANDIDA: Will you go—or shall I call the police?

TONY: Will you give me that picture—or shall I go in and tell your father?

PAULA: My father knows, Tony.

TONY *(whirling around)*: PAULA!

PAULA *(moving calmly forward)*: My father always knows.

TONY *(hurrying to meet her; organized)*: Why did you run away, Paula? Why did you leave me.

PAULA *(passing him by as she goes to table and lays down her prayer book and rosary)*: Because there was something I had to do. Something very important.

TONY *(in anguish)*: Oh Paula, I could kill myself! I could kill myself for having touched you!

PAULA *(smiling at him)*: How vain you are!

TONY *(approaching)*: Do you know what I did when I found you gone? I went out and got drunk! I got roaring drunk! I wanted to kill myself! I wanted to kill everybody!

PAULA: Poor Tony! And all he wanted was his commission!

TONY: To hell with it! I don't want it anymore! All I want is. . . that you forgive me.

PAULA: You will never forgive me, Tony, for what I have done to you.

TONY: Oh Paula, don't hate me!

PAULA: Why should I?

TONY: Then listen to me! Believe me!

PAULA: I listened to you before, Tony, and I believed you—remember?

TONY: I was lying, then I was only fooling you! Oh, you know what kind of a beast I am! I'm always out for what I can get! You were there for the taking—so, I took you!

PAULA: And besides, you were thinking of your commission.

TONY: Yes, I was thinking of the money, too! I needed the money!

PAULA: And you also wanted to hurt my father.

TONY: Yes, yes—that, also! I wanted to hurt him, to spite him, and to spite this house! I've been wanting to do that for a long time! Oh, I did it for spite, and I did it for the money, and I did it for a lot of other reasons you wouldn't understand because you haven't lived my kind of life! I'm all twisted inside, Paula! Paula, don't hate me for what I did! Try to understand me! Oh, we started all wrong, you and I—but we could start all over again. We could make it right. I want to make it right, Paula; I want to make up for what I did to you. Oh, say you believe me!

PAULA: I believe you.

TONY: I deceived you that time, Paula, but now I speak to you from the heart! I'm on the level now—as I've never been in all my life!

PAULA: I believe you.

TONY: Then, where is the picture, Paula? Give it to me. It is not your salvation alone anymore: it is my salvation too. It is our salvation—yours and mine! We'll go away, Paula—just like we said. We'll go away together. Spain, France, Italy. We'll start a new life. And I'll make you happy, Paula—I promise! I will learn to be good, you will learn to be free!

PAULA *(with a laugh)*: To be free!

TONY *(horrified)*: Oh Paula, don't laugh, don't laugh!

PAULA: You were laughing the last time, Tony. Now, it is my turn.

TONY *(staring at her)*: Don't you believe me?

PAULA *(gravely)*: Do you... love me?

TONY: I will learn to love you, Paula—I promise! All we need is to get away from here. All we need is the money so we can run away and be free. Where is the picture, Paula? The American is waiting.

PAULA: Then you must go and tell him to stop waiting.

(She turns her face toward the site of the PORTRAIT.) The picture is no more.

TONY *(his eyes widening)*: What have you done with it?

PAULA: I have destroyed it.

(A pause, while Tony and Candida stare at her. She is gazing down at her hands.)

TONY *(stunned):* OH NO! OH NO! NO!

PAULA *(turning towards candida):* Did you hear what I said, Candida?

TONY *(feverishly):* Say it's not true, Paula! Say it's not true!

PAULA: I have destroyed our picture, Candida.

TONY: No! No! It's not true! It's not true.

PAULA *(exultant):* I slashed it up and I smashed it up and I tore it up and then I burned it! There is nothing left of it now! Nothing, nothing, nothing at all!

TONY *(bursting into sobs):* Oh, you are mad, mad!

PAULA: Are you angry, Candida?

CANDIDA *(approaching):* No, Paula.

(She embraces her sister. Tony has sunk, sobbing, to his knees.)

PAULA: Candida, are you crying?

CANDIDA: Oh no—look at me!

PAULA: *(looking round the dim room):* But someone is crying. I hear someone crying.

CANDIDA *(indicating Tony):* Only Mr. Javier.

PAULA *(approaching the sobbing Tony):* Oh yes... Poor Tony! He has found his tears. He has learned to cry.

TONY: Oh, why did you do it, Paula? Why did you do it!

PAULA: Because I do not want to run away, Tony, like you do.

TONY: I could have made you happy! I could have made you free!

PAULA *(laughing):* But I am free! I am free again. Tony! Oh, there is no Freedom in your world. Only nervous people huddled together, distrusting each other, trying to run away all the time. Only frightened slaves trying to buy their way out! But you cannot buy the freedom I have for a million dollars! Oh, I was mad—mad for a moment—infected with your fear, desiring your slavery! When I burned that picture I set myself free again!

TONY *(rising savagely)*: Yourself, yourself! And that was all you were thinking of, wasn't it? Yourself! How about me? Do you know what you did to me when you burned that picture?

PAULA: Now you know who is the victim!

TONY *(staring at her)*: And you've got no pity! You don't feel any pity!

PAULA: I told you, didn't I, that you would never forgive me for what I had done to you.

TONY: You could have saved me—

PAULA: But I have saved you, Tony. Oh, you do not know now—

TONY: You could have save me but you didn't want to! Okay, now I'm going to the devil.

(He begins to move backward, towards stairway.)

I'm through with struggling and trying to be good! I'm going back to where I came from—back to the gutter! Back to the life you could have saved me from!

PAULA: You will not go back, Tony. You cannot go back anymore. You will never be the same again. It is the price you pay. And you will not go back.

TONY *(sobbing again; moving backwards)*: Yes, I will! Yes, I will I'm going back—back to the gutter! I'm through with fighting! I just want to rot! You could have saved me but you didn't want to! And I could have saved you, Paula. Well, now you're damned! And I'm glad—yes, I'm glad! Oh, I've done just what I wanted to do: I've damned you and I've damned your father and I've damned this house! Oh, you dug your own grave, Paula, when you burned that picture! You nailed your own coffin! I could have set you free! Well, now you're going to rot here! You're all going to rot in this house, the three of you, and be afraid to look in each other's faces! You're all going to sit here hating each other and rotting away till you die! That's what I've done to you! And I'm glad, I'm glad. I'm glad! *(He is already at stairway and stops, overcome with sobs. He peevishly brushes his nose with his fist, fighting to control himself.)* Oh, I'll be rotting myself—but I'll be happy to rot! Yeah—happy! I want to rot, I want to go to the devil! I'll enjoy it, I'll have the time of my life, I'll simply love—Oh, damn you, damn you!

(He stops again, choked by sobs. Furiously he draws himself up to his full height and makes a final attempt at bravado.)

So you think I've got to pay, do you? So you think I won't ever be the same again, do you? You flatter yourself, Paula! Oh, you never touched me! Look at me! I'm still Tony! I'm still the same old Tony! And believe me girls, I'm going to—

(It's no use. He breaks down completely; he doubles over, sobbing hoarsely; his face in his hands.)

Oh, why did you do it, Paula? Why did you do it? Why did you do it!

(He staggers down the stairs.)

PAULA: The poor victim of our little sacrifice!

CANDIDA *(approaching; timidly)*: Was it... our sacrifice, Paula?

PAULA *(turning around; gaily)*: Oh Candida, I merely wielded the knife! It was you who laid the wood on the altar, it was you who lighted the fire!

CANDIDA *(sinking down to her knees)*: Oh Paula, forgive me!

PAULA *(sinking down beside her)*: Candida, tell me you have no regrets!

CANDIDA: About the picture?

PAULA: What would you have done?

CANDIDA *(spiritedly)*: Just what you did! I would have destroyed it!

PAULA: Be careful, Candida! Have you considered to what we commit ourselves?

CANDIDA: To the darkness and the bill collectors and the wagging tongues!

PAULA: And now they will say we have lost our senses. Remember: we have destroyed a piece of property worth ten thousand dollars. That is something they will never understand. They will say we are mad they will say we are dangerous! And Candida—they may be right after all—eventually...

CANDIDA: I am willing to take the risk.

PAULA: Listen! They are talking about us now... They are gathering, they are coming!

CANDIDA *(with a smile)*: Ours is a very special talent, Paula.

PAULA: Alas, yes! We can only catch rats and speak Babylonian. What place is there for us in the world?

CANDIDA: Why should we want a label or a number?

PAULA: And you are not afraid, Candida?

CANDIDA: Of being... a Babylonian?

PAULA: And of being exterminated.

CANDIDA: May God forgive me for ever having desired the safeness of mediocrity!

PAULA *(rising and drawing her sister up):* Then stand up, Candida—stand up! We are free again! We are together again—you and I and father. Yes—and father too! Don't you see, Candida? This is the sign he has been waiting for—ever since he gave us that picture, ever since he offered us our release—the sign that we had found our faith again, that we had found our courage again! Oh, he was waiting for us to take this step, to make this gesture—this final, absolute, magnificent, unmistakable gesture!

CANDIDA: And now we have done it!

PAULA: We have recognized our true vocation!

CANDIDA: We have taken our final vows!

PAULA: And we have placed ourselves irrevocably on his side!

CANDIDA: Does he know?

PAULA: Oh yes, yes!

CANDIDA: Have you told him?

PAULA: But what need is there to tell him?

CANDIDA *(rapturously):* Oh Paula!

PAULA: He knows, he knows!

CANDIDA: And he has forgiven us at last! He has forgiven us, Paula!

PAULA: And we will stand with him?

CANDIDA: *Contra mundum!*

PAULA: Oh Candida, let us drink to it!

CANDIDA *(as Paula pours the drinks):* But now we stand with him as persons; we stand with him of our own free will, knowing what we do and why we do it. Oh, we did not know before, Paula. We loved him only because he was our father and because we were his daughters. But now we are no longer his daughters—no... and how I shiver with terror! We cannot resume the past, Paula; we must work out a new relationship—the three of us. Something has happened to the three of us—and to father most of all. Paula, do you realize that we do not know him anymore? He is no longer the charming artist of our childhood; and he is no longer that bitter broken old man who jumped out of the window. Something has been happening to him all this year. He has come to terms with life; he has made his own peace; he has found a solution. We will be facing a man risen from the grave... Oh Paula, how I shiver! And yet I can hardly wait! I can hardly wait to face him, to show him these new creatures he has made of us! We are no longer his daughters; we are his friends, his disciples, his priestesses! We have been born again—not of his flesh but of his spirit!

PAULA *(offering glass):* Then, come! Let us drink to our birthday!

CANDIDA *(taking glass):* And nothing can divide us now! They can drive us away from this house and separate us—but we will still be together, you and I and father. And as long as we stand together, the world cannot be wholly lost or doomed or destroyed!

PAULA *(raising her glass):* We stand against the world only to save it!

CANDIDA *(raising her glass):* And to save it, we must stand against the world!

(They touch glasses.)

PAULA: Happy Birthday, Candida!

CANDIDA: Happy Birthday, Paula!

(They drink; then burst into laughter. The bells peal out again, and continue pealing to end the scene. From the distance comes a rumor of drums.)

PAULA: Candida, the procession!

CANDIDA: And why are we standing in darkness!

PAULA: Let us turn on the chandelier!

CANDIDA: Let us turn on all the lights!

PAULA: It is a Holiday!

CANDIDA: It is the birthday of our lives!

(They fly apart—Paula to the left; Candida to the right—and turn on all the lights as Bitoy appears on the stair landing.)

PAULA: Halt! Who goes there!

BITOY *(blinking)*: Why, Paula!

PAULA: Are you friend or foe?

BITOY: Friend!

PAULA: Advance, friend, and be recognized!

BITOY *(walking in)*: I have been looking for you everywhere.

CANDIDA: I sent him to look for you, Paula.

PAULA *(clasping her hands to her breast)*: My hero! And at last you have found me—in this enchanted castle!

BITOY *(laughing)*: What on earth has happened?

PAULA *(whispering)*: The evil spell has been broken!

CANDIDA: The enchantment has dissolved!

PAULA: The princesses will now return to their kingdoms—

CANDIDA: And live happily ever after!

BITOY: Don't I get half of the kingdom?

PAULA: Beware, Bitoy! Our kingdom is a barren land; and the king, our father, an old man.

CANDIDA: Are you willing to carry him on your back?

BITOY: With all his ancestral gods!

PAULA: Candida, our first novice!

CANDIDA: Bitoy Camacho, I am delighted with you!

BITOY: And everything is all right now?

CANDIDA *(her expression quickly changing):* No! No, not yet!

PAULA: Oh Candida, they are gathering now! They are coming!

BITOY: Who?

CANDIDA *(giggling):* Oh, what shall we do, Paula? Where shall we hide!

BITOY: What is all this!

PAULA: Shh! Listen!

(They listen, looking towards stairway. Enter Don Alvaro and Doña Upeng.)

ALVARO: A holy and good evening to everyone in this house!

PAULA AND CANDIDA *(hurrying to meet visitors; finger on lips):* Shhh! Shhh!

ALVARO: Is your papa sick?

PAULA: Oh no, no, Don Alvaro!

CANDIDA: He is in the best of health!

PAULA *(hurrying visitors into the room):* Come over here, Doña Upeng! Come over here, Don Alvaro! Oh, we are so glad you have come! Candida, some brandy for our guests!

CANDIDA: And of course you remember Bitoy Camacho. He was a regular member of our old tertulias. Bitoy, say good evening to your old friends.

BITOY: Good evening, Doña Upeng. Good evening, Don Alvaro.

PAULA: He, too, has come to celebrate the Naval with us!

ALVARO: You do well, my boy, to honor an old tradition before it disappears.

CANDIDA *(as she offers glasses)*: Disappear?

ALVARO: Yes—there is all this talk of war, war, war!

UPENG: And that is why we have come tonight. We wanted to salute the Virgin again from your balconies—as we used to do in the old days. Oh Paula, Candida—this may be the last time!

(Enter Don Pepe.)

PEPE: Yes, Upeng—this may well be the last time!

UPENG: Pepe! Pepe, you old carabao—where have you come from?

PEPE: Practically from the graveyard, Upeng. But I felt I had to come tonight—

PAULA *(hurrying to meet him)*: Shhh! Come over here, Don Pepe!

PEPE *(as he is hurried into the room)*: My dear Paula, what is happening?

ALVARO: Yes—just what is wrong, girls?

PAULA: Listen—we are in trouble—Candida and I.

CANDIDA: We need your help!

PEPE: Candida, Paula, we will do anything for you!

CANDIDA: Oh! Thank God, you have come tonight!

PAULA: We need our old friends tonight!

PEPE: Well, here we are! *(He glances towards stairway.)* And here come some more of us!

(He goes to stairway as Don Miguel and Doña Irene come up; greeting them with finger on lips.)

Shhh! Come over here, you two! Candida and Paula are in danger!

IRENE *(kissing the sisters)*: My dear Paula! And dearest Candida!

MIGUEL: What is it, girls? Can we help?

PAULA: Don Miguel, you have already helped us!

CANDIDA: Simply by coming tonight!

IRENE: Oh, we simply had to come tonight!

MIGUEL: They say a war is coming—a big war!

IRENE: Nothing will be left of what we have loved so much!

UPENG *(taking the other woman's hand):* Aie, Irene—not much is left—even now!

IRENE: No, Upeng. Not much is left even now...

PEPE: The wind is left anyway. Look at it blowing! It is the same wind, the good old wind of October! Oh, feel it, smell it—all of you! It is blowing from the old Manila—*la Manila de nuestros amores!*

MIGUEL: And here we are—gathered again—relics of the old dispensation...

(A pause, while they watch the blowing curtains of the balconies and listen to the sound of bells and approaching drums. The visitors are all very old, very frail and very faded—but still talk and carry themselves with an air of grandeur, being impoverished gentlefolk. They are poorly but neatly dressed—canes and the "Americana Cerrada" for the men; fans and the starchy "saya" with train for the women; old shawls draped under their pañuelos.)

ALVARO: And what memories, eh? Personal memories, ancestral memories... That wind, those bells, this feast... La Naval de Manila! How the words ache in one's hearth!

MIGUEL: Ah, but you speak only for ourselves, Alvaro.

ALVARO: Yes. In this, we are the last of the generations.

MIGUEL: Already, for our children, these things awaken no special emotion, no memories, no filial pieties...

IRENE: The old traditions are dying...

PEPE: There is no need for a war to kill them.

(Enter Don Aristeo.)

ARISTEO: Alas, no! And there is no need for a war to kill us either!

VISITORS: Aristeo!

ARISTEO: Caramba, you are all here!

VISITORS: Shhh!

ARISTEO: Huh?

PAULA *(approaching; whispering)*: Welcome again to our house, Noble Soldier!

ARISTEO *(in booming voice)*: Paula, I have dragged my dying bones up here to salute the Virgin for the last time!

VISITORS: Shhh!

ARISTEO: But what is the matter with all of you!

UPENG: Stop your shouting, Aristeo! Paula and Candida are in great peril!

IRENE: Their lives are threatened!

ARISTEO: Girls, is this true?

CANDIDA *(smiling)*: Will you defend us?

ARISTEO: Oh, I should have brought my pistol!

PAULA: We need only your presence, Noble Soldier! Candida, some brandy for our champion!

ARISTEO *(taking her hands)*: Wait a minute, Paula—let me look at you. Caramba, your hands are cold!

PAULA: Oh, truly?

ARISTEO *(looking her in the eye)*: Paula, all this is not… just a joke?

PAULA: Oh no, no!

ARISTEO: You are actually in grave danger?

PAULA *(bending her face towards him)*: Surely you can feel the floor trembling beneath us?

ARISTEO: I can feel your hands trembling, yes.

(She withdraws her hands, still smiling.)

What is it, girl?

PAULA *(with a shrug)*: Oh, this may be the last time, the last night, we shall stand here—Candida and I—in our own house.

ARISTEO: I see.

CANDIDA *(offering him a glass)*: But of course we mean to be stubborn!

PAULA: And listen—I am not afraid.

ARISTEO: Why you should you be? Am I not here?

UPENG: And we will all stand with you, Paula and Candida!

ALVARO: You must remain in this house!

IRENE: We need you here in this house!

PEPE: To continue us—

UPENG: And preserve us—

ALVARO: And as a symbol of permanence!

PEPE: This house is our assurance that life will go on!

MIGUEL: Exactly! Why, just look at us now.
Terrified by rumors of destruction, we have all come here as to a rock! Even so, for those great warriors of Thermopylae—

ARISTEO: My dear Miguel!

MIGUEL: My dear Aristeo!

ARISTEO: We are in no mood for orations! Candida, pass the brandy! *Animo, Amigos! Sursum Corda!* We all have no money in our pockets—but we are not dead yet! We can still drink!

CANDIDA *(laughing)*: Don Aristeo is always right! Come on, everybody—more brandy!

PAULA: Yes, let us all drink and be merry!

IRENE: And to whom shall we drink?

CANDIDA: To the Virgin! To the Virgin, of course!

ARISTEO: Amigos, let us drink to the Virgin. We are gathered here in her honor.

ALVARO: And this is our feast—

PEPE: And the feast of our fathers!

ARISTEO: And they're still alive—our fathers. Something of them is left; something of them survives, and will survive, as long as we live and remember—we who have known and loved and cherished these things...

MIGUEL: And we will live for a long time yet!

PEPE: We will live to be a hundred!

UPENG: Oh, what old fools we were—to be so timorous, to be so terrified!

IRENE: And tonight is not the last night!

ALVARO: We will live to be a hundred!

MIGUEL: We will live forever!

EVERYBODY: Viva!

PAULA: And listen, everybody—tertulia on Friday! Tertulia again on Friday!

CANDIDA: Yes, yes! Our house shall be open again as usual—next Friday—and every Friday! We must continue, we must preserve!

EVERYBODY: VIVA! VIVA!

PAULA *(raising her glass):* Don Aristeo?

ARISTEO: *Amigos y paisanos!*

   (He raises his glass.)

   A la gran señora de Filipinas en la gloriosa fiesta de su Naval!

EVERYBODY: *VIVA LA VIRGEN!*

(They drink. Enter Pepang and Manolo, and advance grimly into the room. Paula and Candida are standing side by side at center. The visitors are grouped solidly behind them. Bitoy is standing a little apart at left, a worried on looker.)

PAULA *(gaily)*: Pepang! Manolo!

CANDIDA: Have you also come to salute the Virgin?

MANOLO *(grimly)*: You know very well why we have come!

PAULA: Have you come to confess at last?

PEPANG: To confess!

MANOLO: Are you crazy? Is it who—

PAULA: Confess, Manolo! Confess Pepang! Oh, you will feel so happy afterwards! You will be free! Look at us!

MANOLO: Yes, look at yourselves! Just look at yourselves! What a fine public spectacle you have made of yourselves!

PEPANG: Oh, this shameful, shameful scandal!

MANOLO: Go and get some clothes! You are both leaving this house at once!

CANDIDA: Where are your manners, Manolo? Do you not see we have visitors?

PEPANG: How can you have the nerve? You should be hiding your face—if you have any shame left!

MANOLO: Tell these people to go away!

(The procession is now approaching; and the drums rumble ever closer, ever louder.)

ARISTEO *(coming forward)*: Caramba, it is Manolito! I hardly recognized you, my boy—you have grown so fat!

MANOLO: Don Aristeo, I am sorry but I must ask you to leave. My sisters and I have family matters to discuss.

ARISTEO: And this is Pepita?

MANOLO: Don Aristeo, did you hear what I said!

ARISTEO: Aie, Pepita—what an exquisite child you were: so tender, so affectionate! And how you loved to ride on my back, round and round this room—remember?

PEPANG: Don Aristeo, we have no time—

ARISTEO: No time, no time! Always no time, always in a hurry! Relax, both of you! Here, sit down—have a drink—and let us talk about the old days!

MANOLO: Candida, will you send these people away!

ARISTEO: The, teh! And you used to be such a quiet boy—very thin, very dreamy—

MANOLO: Don Aristeo—

ARISTEO: Upeng, do you remember how you used to scold him for being so bashful?

UPENG *(laughing)*: Oh, he was always blushing—especially in the presence of the fair sex!

IRENE: And you blushed very charmingly, Manolito, when you were a boy!

MANOLO: I ask you politely—all of you—for the last time—

ALVARO: And always reading, always off in a corner with a book—

PEPE: Or playing his violin down there in the patio—

MIGUEL: Or directing a zarzuela, Pepita here as the primadonna—

MANOLO *(shouting)*: Will you let me speak!

ARISTEO: Oh, they were the most intellectual children I have ever known!

MANOLO: Don Aristeo, I beg you—

PEPANG: Oh, why do you waste your time, Manolo! It is useless to talk to them!

IRENE: And, Pepita, I will never forget how you used to recite the "Ultimo Adios" when you were hardly seven!

PEPE: It was I who taught you to dance, Manolo, on the night of your fifteenth birthday—remember? Right in this very room!

ALVARO: What gay memories this house holds for all of us!

MIGUEL: And how Manolo and Pepang must love this old scene of their childhood!

PAULA: Alas, no!

MIGUEL: They do not love it?

CANDIDA: They want it sold!

THE VISITORS: SOLD!

UPENG: *Que horror!*

IRENE: But why?

PAULA: That is something they refuse to confess, even to themselves!

ARISTEO: But perhaps they cannot afford this house any longer.

PAULA: Oh, it is not the expense!

CANDIDA: Although that is the reason they give!

PAULA: But they deceive themselves!

PEPANG: Paula! Paula!

PAULA: It is not the expense. Why, they throw money away right and left, night and day, at the gambling tables, and think nothing about it!

PEPANG: Manolo, are you going to stand there and let these—

PAULA: No, it is not the expense! They simply cannot stand this house—they cannot bear it!

CANDIDA: It haunts them, it spoils their fun!

PAULA: It is always rising before their eyes at the most inconvenient moments—

CANDIDA: When they are gossiping with their friends—

PAULA: Or playing mahjong—

CANDIDA: Or having a nice time at the races at the Jai-Alai—

PAULA: Or when they cannot sleep—

CANDIDA: Suddenly—*cataplum!*—the shadow of this house falls upon them!

PAULA: And then their hands falter—

CANDIDA: Their blood turns cold!

ARISTEO: You mean, they are afraid of this house?

CANDIDA: And they want it destroyed!

ALVARO: But why?

PAULA: Because it is their conscience!

MANOLO AND PEPANG: PAULA!

(The drums are now rumbling right under balconies.)

PAULA *(advancing slowly)*: Yes, Manolo! Yes, Pepang! This house is your conscience—and that is why you hate it, that is why you fear it, that is why you have been craving so long and so desperately to destroy it! No, you cannot afford it! You cannot afford to have a conscience! Because you know you will have no—

MANOLO *(stepping back)*: SHUT UP! SHUT UP!

PAULA *(standing still)*: You know you will have no peace as long as this house stands here to rebuke you!

MANOLO *(raising his fists)*: SHUT UP—or, by God, I'm going to—

(The balconies light up dazzlingly as the procession passes below.)

PAULA: And you will not rest—no—you will never rest until you have laid waste this house; until you have stripped it naked, and torn down its walls, and uprooted its very foundations!

PEPANG: Manolo, this is beyond endurance!

CANDIDA: Confess, Pepang! Confess, Manolo!

MANOLO: They have gone mad!

PAULA: Confess, confess—and be free!

PEPANG: Are you going to let them frighten you?

MANOLO: They are leaving this house this very moment!

PEPE: Oh no, Manolito—nobody can leave now!

UPENG *(waving towards balconies)*: Look! The procession!

ALVARO: The streets are closed!

IRENE: The Holy Virgin herself has come to save them!

MANOLO *(advancing)*: They are leaving this house right now if I have to throw them down the stairs!

ARISTEO: Then you will first have to throw me down those stairs, Manolito!

PEPE *(stepping forward)*: And me!

UPENG *(stepping forward)*: And me!

IRENE *(stepping forward)*: And me!

MIGUEL: You will first throw all of us down those stairs, Manolito!

(Manolo stands still, staring.)

ARISTEO: Well, my boy—what do you say now?

CANDIDA: And that is not all, Manolo. There is father as well. Are you prepared to throw him also down those stairs?

PEPANG: Father hates you!

PAULA: Father stands with us!

CANDIDA: And we stand with father!

BITOY *(Suddenly shouting; with astonished gesture towards doorway)*: AND HERE HE COMES! HERE HE COMES!

PEPANG *(staring; gripping Manolo's arm)*: Manolo, look! It's father!

(Chorus of "Lorenzo!" and "Here comes Lorenzo!" and "Hola, Lorenzo!" from the visitors as they all gaze, amazed, towards doorway. Candida and Paula, who have their backs to the doorway, turn around slowly and fearfully. But, suddenly, their faces light up and lift up; they gasp, they smile; they claps their hands to their breasts.)

PAULA AND CANDIDA *(in ringing, rising, radiant exultation)*: OH PAPA! PAPA! PAPA!

(From the street comes a flourish of trumpets as the band breaks into the strains of the Gavotta Marcha Procesional; and as Bitoy Camacho steps forward to his usual place at left front of stage, the "Intramuros Curtain" closes in on the sala scene, everybody inside remaining frozen.)

BITOY *(speaking exultantly through the sound of bells and music):* October in Manila! The month when, in full typhoon seasons, the city broke out into its biggest celebrations! The month that started the display of hams and cheeses among its grocers, and of turrones among its sweet shops; when her markets overflowed with apples, grapes, oranges, pomelos—and her sidewlks with chestnuts and lanzones! The month when, back in our childhood, the very air turned festive and the Circus came to town and the season opened at the old Opera House!

(The lights die out inside the stage; the sound of bells and music fades off. The ruins stand out distinctly.)

Well, that was the last October the old city was ever to celebrate. And that was my last time to see it still alive—the old Manila; my last time to see the Naval procession advancing down this street, and to salute the Virgin from the balconies of the old Marasigan house.

It is gone now—that house of Don Lorenzo el Magnifico. This piece of wall, this heap of stones, are all that's left of it. It finally took a global war to destroy this house and the three people who fought for it. Though they were destroyed, they were never conquered. They were still fighting—right to the very end— fighting against the jungle.

They are dead now—Don Lorenzo, Candida, Paula—they are all dead now—a horrible death—by sword and fire… They died with their house and they died with their city—maybe it's just as well they did. They could never have survived the death of old Manila.

And yet—listen!—it is not dead; it has not perished! Listen Paula! Listen Candida! Your city—my city—the city of our fathers—still lives! Something of it is left; something of it survives, and will survive, as long as I live and remember—I who have known and loved and cherished these things!

(He stoops down on one knee and makes a gesture of scooping earth.)

Oh Paula, Candida—listen to me! By your dust, and by the dust of all the generations, I promise to continue, I promise to preserve! The jungle may advance, the bombs may fall again—but while I live, you live—and this dear city of our affections shall rise again—if only in my song! To remember and sing: that is my vocation…

(The light dies out on Bitoy. All you can see now are the stark ruins, gleaming in the silent moonlight.)

FINAL CURTAIN

Ang Larawan, The Musical

Based on Nick Joaquin's
A Portrait of the Artist as Filipino

Music by Ryan Cayabyab

Libretto by Rolando S. Tinio

Production Design by Salvador Bernal
National Artist for Theater and Design

**Stage Direction by Rolando Tinio
and Antonio Mabesa**

LAST CONVERSATION WITH A MASTER DIRECTOR
by Edmund L. Sicam

*Reprinted with permission from the *Philippine Daily Inquirer* and Edmund L. Sicam
12 July 1997

Photos from the musical Ang Larawan *staged at the Cultural Center of the Philippines*

It was going to be his comeback vehicle as a stage director. Musical Theater Philippines was mounting *Ang Larawan*, a musical version of Nick Joaquin's *A Portrait of the Artist as Filipino*, and Joaquin gave his approval on condition that Rolando Tinio wrote the libretto and directed the play.

Tinio accepted the assignment and by July 1, he has started blocking the play after the cast had mastered the music of Ryan Cayabyab. By Sunday last week, he had already blocked the entire musical.

However, Fate intervened. Ten days before the premiere of *Larawan* at the CCP (on July 17), Tinio passed away at the age of 60.

In the Late June, we sat down for a talk with Tinio a few days before he would start rehearsing the cast. The interview was held at a rehearsal booth at Ryan Cayabyab's music studio on Bohol ave., while the cast was rehearsing the music in another studio.

Here are the excerpts from the interview:

How faithful is your translation of Nick Joaquin's work?

It is a translation and compression. The text is 90 percent Nick Joaquin. *Meron lang silang songs na pinagawa* that contain ideas developed from the play. I want to be as faithful to Nick Joaquin as possible.

What's the difference between doing *Larawan* as a straight play and doing it as a musical?

The musical is essentially a musical comedy. The play is an elegy. In fact if you look at the story, aside from the fact that the house at Intramuros was bombed, it has comedy in that sense. I'd like to describe it as a poignant musical comedy.

There's also this to consider, which I hope Nick will agree with: The audience, now, unlike the audiences of the Barangay Theatre Productions of the '50s are so far removed from Intramuros and the Intramuros experience–the pre-war experience, the life of graciousness, art and beauty represented by the Marasigans.

Today's audiences can't possibly relate to that. You can't expect the audience of today to respond to that kind of nostalgia. They don't have any nostalgia. Even your generation, even my generation cannot really relate to that era. So that has to be considered.

The music helps in making the characters accessible to the modern audience without losing their strangeness. I'd like to think that Ryan succeeded in capturing the look and feel of the era and not think that they are from the moon or Babylon, as Candida and Paula call themselves.

Pero may problema 'yan. If I were doing this as a straight play, the problem would be the same. I think it is wrong to do this play as some have done in the past, demanding that the audience feel nostalgic about life that doesn't mean anything to them.

So how do you plan to handle your version of *Larawan*?

Present the play as it is, but with that consideration *na* you are telling them, "You may not be able to relate to this but there was a time when Filipinos were like this." It is a glance at history. Like, let's take the Revolution…you don't feel nostalgic about the Katipunan, you are interested in it as a historical event. *Wala 'yong* nostalgia.

You can relate it to the EDSA revolution… *Sa evaluation 'yan*, e. What's the problem with Candida and Paula? They're impractical women. They don't believe in careers. How will a modern Filipina girl look at them? They will look at them the way Tony Javier and Pepang and Manolo look at them. More people will look at them as out of place.

Para sa akin, I have to emphasize the fact that they are not at all that different. They are not old maids. They are in their late 20s. They are not in their 40s.

Based on today's standards, they are not old maids.

Sinabi nga nila, "We are not old maids." The only difference is that they are homebodies. They're anti-feminist, in other words, "We belong to the home with our father." We can still relate to them but in a more complex way than the people in the '50s did.

When Barangay did *Portrait*, it was in English. Theater was an affair of the cultural elite. *Ngayon mas na-*democratize *ang* theater. *Magkaiba na ang social class ng nanonood.* Even *Larawan* as a straight play. *Mas maraming audience ngayon* who will tend to laugh at Candida and Paula. *Samantalang noon, makaka-*relate *pa ang mga* audiences.

How would you approach the cast *na karamihan ay bata pa*?

Bata, by choice. You must remember *na noong panahon na 'yon mababa* pa ang life expectancy. When you turned 60, you were really old. So *sila* Candida and Paula, who were in their late 20s, would not be considered old maids now. So the cast is just the right age.

May nagsasabi nga noon na napakatanda na ng cast ng Barangay Theater Guild. But then you forget, they had been doing *Portrait* for 30 years. They were the correct ages when they started.

Did Nick ask for final approval of the libretto?

I hate to be the one to tell you this myself but when they asked for approval, don't quote me, Nick gave it only on the condition that I do the adaptation and that I direct it. *Kasi noon pa niya ako hinahabol.* Really, I felt *na hubung buhay si* Ms. Avellana, I couldn't ask Ella to do Candida. E, *namatay na si* Ella, *buhay pa si* Ms. Avellana.

How many productions of *Larawan* have you seen?

I've only seen the Barangay version and the first PETA production with Rita Gomez, Lolita Rodriguez and Dante Rivero.

I understand the cast first had to learn the music before you blocked them.

Kailangan memorized *na nila* when I stage it. *Tamang tama naman ang timpla ng* music. Even the length. *Kasi ayokong sabihin nila na maganda pero mahaba.*

So your blocking will be dictated by the music?

Exactly, I intend to block it and then I have Edna Vida as choreographer. Much of the conversation is danced theatrically. Ang idea ko, I don't know how to work it out with Edna, but *nag-uusap tayo ng ganyan, tapos* without our knowing *nagsasayaw na tayo. Pag hindi ko ginagawang ganoon,* the audience will find it uncomfortable. It's the music I'm directing, not the play.

May dance numbers doon, *di ba*?

May dalawang dance numbers. *'Yon ang talagang* dance numbers. But the rest... more will be danced than that. In fact, I would guess *siguro* 70 percent of it. I don't mean dance in the strictest sense of the word. For instance, *ang* conversation ni Bitoy at Tony. *Nagta-*tap dance while they are talking. I feel now, because of the music, imperative *'yan*. You cannot just have them singing their lines and remaining still. It's danced through, almost.

What about the costume design? I know you're particular about costume design...

I trust Badong (Bernal) completely. He has designed so many productions. *Hindi naman mahirap ang* costumes *dito*.

This is a star-studded production. Do you foresee any difficulties dealing with the cast?

No, Certainly, Celeste has been my actress. Armida, *ako nag*-introduce... It was I who transformed Armida from an opera singer to an actress.

She was in Barangay Theater's production of Bernarda Alba in 1966 or 1967. I directed her in a play produced by her mother, *Ibong Mandaragit*, the adaptation of "Little Foxes."

What about Zsa Zsa?

I've never worked with her. I don't expect any problems. They are too professional. *Mga* amateurs *lang naman ang may* ego, e.

What about Ricky Davao, who's not really a singer?

Tony Javier had to be the perfect physical type.

So musicality was secondary...

Besides *hindi naman kailangang* beautiful singing *lahat. Kailangan,* character singing. In fact, my fear is *masyadong magaganda* ang singing *ng* entire cast. *Sa akin, ang dapat na beautiful singing, sina* Candida, Paula, Don Perico and the old people. *Kasi* they represent the world of beauty. The rest shouldn't. Even *sila... kailangan medyo* strident *ang boses*.

Ricky Davao has been singing with Pilita in concerts abroad. He hasn't been singing extensively but he certainly has been singing. *Tama lang yon na hindi na masyadong magaling*. He will not sound like... Martin Nievera. *Hindi dapat ganoon ang boses*.

What was the process in the creation of the musical? You started with the translation?

Translation and adaptation. Then I gave it to Ryan to put the music.

Then Ryan went back to you...

No. Then Ryan went to the cast and started rehearsing.

I thought they asked for additional songs.

This was before Ryan started writing the music. Well, we talked about it a little. It's a musical comedy...

What kind of Tagalog did you use in the translation?

Very colloquial... with some period quality.

You used the term *"tente butente"* in the script. *Saan galing 'yon?*

Sa mother *ko*. It means hunky dory. I used the word *lamyerda,* which is very now. I'm never *naman* a purist *sa* language. Whatever captures the moment. *Merong mga* very colloquial. Most are very lyrical. Very flexible *ako*.

Do you think this material will appeal to a wide audience?

It is something that will be enjoyable. It's not going to be a tedious homage to a classic. It will be something very entertaining, very enjoyable, I hope.

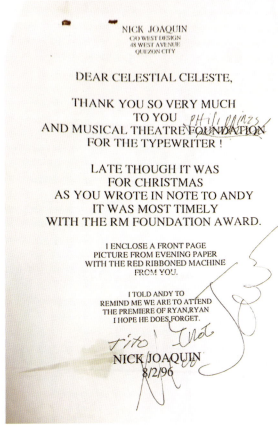

A note of thanks from Nick Joaquin to *Ang Larawan* producer and star, Celeste Legaspi.

The producers of the stage musical *Ang Larawan*: Celeste Legaspi, Girlie Rodis and Rachel Alejandro with Nick Joaquin.

Actress and film producer Armida Siguion Reyna (who played Doña Upeng) and Zsa Zsa Padilla (who played Paula).

Zsa Zsa Padilla with Hajji Alejandro who played Don Perico.

The performers who played the society people of *Ang Larawan*: Raul Ramirez (as Charlie Dacanay), Dawn Zulueta (as Elsa Montes), Carla Martinez (as Doña Loleng), and Mikee Cojuangco (as Patsy).

Dawn Zulueta leading the hilarious conga dance, a part that librettist-director Rolando Tinio described as "the struggle between the vulgar and the sublime."

Cris Villonco (rightmost), who also played Patsy in the 1998 musical, rehearsing onstage at the Cultural Center of the Philippines.

THE MUSICAL

Publicity photo of the cast of the first staging of *Ang Larawan*. Seated, left to right: Roeder Camañag, Carla Martinez, Dawn Zulueta and Zsa Zsa Padilla. Standing, left to right: Eugene Villaluz, Celeste Legaspi, Hajji Alejandro, Ricky Davao, and Louie Reyes.

The 1998 cast of *Ang Larawan* musical.

Ang Larawan was restaged at the Cultural Center of the Philippines in 1998 with Celeste Legaspi and Ricky Davao reprising their roles of Candida and Tony Javier respectively; Rachel Alejandro joined them to play Paula.

Celeste and Rachel with Roeder who played Bitoy Camacho in both the first staging and the repeat of *Ang Larawan*.

Two faces of passion: Rachel as Paula and Ricky as Tony in the seduction scene (top), and in Paula's triumph after she breaks from the "ghosts" haunting her.

The rousing finale

ANG LARAWAN, the Musical
Libretto by Rolando Tinio, National Artist
based on an original three-act play by
Nick Joaquin, National Artist
Music by Ryan Cayabyab
Produced by Musicat, Inc.

MGA TAUHAN

CANDIDA at PAULA, mga anak na dalaga ni Don Lorenzo Marasigan
MANOLO, panganay ni Don Lorenzo; may asawa
PEPANG, kasunod na anak ni Don Lorenzo; may asawa
BITOY CAMACHO, kaibigan ng mga Marasigan
TONY JAVIER, nangangasera sa bahay ng mga Marasigan
PETE, patnugot ng magasin
EDDIE, manunulat ng pahayagan
CORA, potograpo sa pahayagan
SUSAN at VIOLET, mga bodabilista
DON PERICO, isang senador
DONYA LOLENG, maybahay ni Don Perico
PATSY, anak ni Don Perico at Donya Loleng
ELSA MONTES at CHARLIE DACANAY, mga kaibigan
ni Donya Loleng
DON ALVARO at DONYA UPENG
DON MIGUEL at DONYA IRENE
DON ARISTEO, mga kaibigan ng mga Marasigan
DALAWANG PULIS
ISANG DETEKTIB

TAGPUAN

Unang Yugto
Sala ng bahay ng mga Marasigan sa Intramuros. Isang
hapon bandang umpisa ng Oktubre, 1941.

Ikalawang Yugto
Ganoon din. Pagkaraan ng isang linggo. Mga alas diyes ng umaga.

Ikatlong Yugto
Ganoon din. Pagkaraan ng dalawang araw. Hapon ng ikalawang linggo
ng Oktubre, pista ng La Naval de Manila.

PROLOGO

    Koro
    [sa mga manonood]
    Intramuros

Ang Maynila nung araw.
Intramuros—
Ang Maynila nung araw.
Siyudad ng kasaysayan:
Mga kalyeng tinatawid
Ng biseroy at arsobispo,
Martir na Kristiyano,
Madre't haliparot,
Eleganteng markesa,
Piratang Ingles,
Mandaring Intsik,
Traydor na Portuges,
Espiyang Olandes,
Sultan ng mga Moro
At pilotong Amerikano.
Tatlong dantaong
Parang Babilonya
Sa dami ng paninda;
Parang Herusalem
Linis ng Kaluluwa.
Matagal nang dumaan
Ang dakilang parada.
Laos na'ng Intramuros
Bago pa magkagera.
Noong bata pa man kami,
Bulok na'ng mga bahay;
Siksikan sa kuwarto
Ang mga pamilya;
Sa patyo sa bukana
Nagtambak ang basura;
Sa lundo nang balkonahe
Nagsampay ang labada.
Ang siyudad ng imperyal
Ng ating mga ama,
Parang gubat na ngayon
Na panay barong-barong.

BITOY
May nag-iisang bahay
Sa gubat na marusing
Na ayaw pang palulon
Sa lupit ng panahon. Pagpasok mo
Sa antigong puwerta,
Nababalik ka

Sa mundo ng ganda,
At ng seremonya.

UNANG YUGTO
*[Papasok si BITOY sa sala;
papasok si CANDIDA na may dalang bandehang may tsokolatera
na ipapasok sa kuwarto ng kanilang ama.]*

BITOY
Candida, kumusta, kumusta?

CANDIDA
Bitoy! Si Bitoy Camacho ka!

BITOY
[Kukunin ang bandeha at ipapatong ito sa isang tabi.]
Akin na 'yan.

CANDIDA
Ang tanda mo na?

BITOY
Beynte singko na ako.

CANDIDA
Naaalala ko.
Nung nakakorto ka pa't.
Nakabulsa-marino.

BITOY
Hindi ka nagbago!

CANDIDA
Anong hindi, anong hindi?
Nang huli mo 'kong makita, Marangya pa akong senyorita:
Mataas ang pangarap— Siguradong darating at tatangay sa akin
Prinsipe ng Asturias.

BITOY
Dumating ba
Ang Prinsipe ng Asturias?

CANDIDA
Walang dumating. Wala nang dumarating na kahit sino pa.

BITOY
Kahit Biyernes ng gabi—

CANDIDA
Wala nang tertulya. Nangamamatay na
Ang mga matanda.

[Tatawagin si PAULA.]

Naku, Paula, Paula. Nandito si Bitoy!

BITOY
Ang mga tertulya—

*[Papasok si PAULA na
may dalang platera ng mga biskuwit.]*

PAULA
Natatandaan mo pa?

BITOY
Kasama 'kong lagi ng Papa…

PAULA
Ang liit mo pa noon!

BITOY
Pag Sabado sa Binondo,
Sa bahay ng mga Monson; Pag Lunes sa Quiapo,
Sa Botica ni Doktor Moreta;
Miyerkoles sa Carriedo
Sa tindahan ng mga libro
Ni Don Aristeo.
At pag Biyernes, sa bahay ng mga Marasigan!

PAULA
Brandi pa, Don Pepe! Brandi pa, Don Isidro! Mapresko sa may bintana,
Do'n tayo, Donya Upeng! Ano 'ka mo, Don Alvaro—
Hindi mo pa nabasa
Bagong tula ni Dario? Aba'y nasa huling labas Ng "Blanco y Negro"! Donya Irene,
ang tula ng Dakilang si Ruben

Ang pinaguusapan: "Tuvo razon tu abuela con su cabello cano, muy mas que tu con rizas n que se enrosca el dia…"

CANDIDA
Sa banda rito, Don Aristeo! Brandi, Paula, ang gusto ni Don Aristeo!

PAULA
[Mag-aabot kunwari ng baso ng brandi.]
Puwera ang politika sa usapan dito!

CANDIDA
Oo, Donya Irene, ang dalas naming nanood sa kompanya ng sarsuwelang 'yon.

PAULA
Ituloy Don Alvaro, ang kwento mo tungkol kay Heneral Aguinaldo.

BITOY
[Sa tinig ng 10 anyos.]
Tita Paula,
Tita Paula,
Chichichi ako!

PAULA
Manahimik, salbahe, tingnan mo'ng uhog mo.

CANDIDA
Ilang beses ka naming pinagsabihan: Ma-Tita-Tita!

CANDIDA/PAULA—DUWETO
Hindi pa kami matandang dalaga.
Tawagin mo kami ng Candida't Paula.
Bata pa kami't marilag pa raw.
Basta't may bayle riyan, handang sumayaw.
Kami'y pagmasdan pag kami'y nag-balse.
Sa bisig ng Papa pag aming konsorte.
Sabi ng lahat—pinakasikat,
Umikot-ikot man buong magdamag.
Akala ng iba, dinaanan kami ng panahon.
Ang buhay raw namin ay parang de-kahon.
Hindi nila alam na lalong gumaganda ang lahat.
Pag may seremonya ang bawat iglap.
Bilis ng mundo'y hindi para sa amin;
Karerang daga'y hindi kakayanin.
Hawak-hawak ma'y pulos lang barya.
Sa buhay lang na ito kami masaya.

[Tapos na ang laro; nagwakas na ang pagkukunwari. Mananatili silang tahimik, nakatitig sa bandang itaas nang mapanglaw—dalawang gusgusing matandang dalaga sa isang gusgusing lumang bahay.]

[Itataas ni BITOY ang kaniyang paningin at makikita niya ang LARAWAN sa unang pagkakataon.]

BITOY
'Yan ba?

CANDIDA
Oo.

BITOY
Kailan 'pininta ng inyong Papa?

PAULA
May isang taon na.

BITOY
Kagilagilalas!

CANDIDA
Ang tawag niya—"Retrato del artista como Filipino."

PAULA
"Larawan ng Pintor bilang Filipino."

BITOY
Ngunit bakit?
Hindi Filipino ang eksenang 'yan.
Ano'ng ibig niyang ipakahulugan?
Matandang nakababa sa bata pang isa;
sa likod ng dalawa, nasusunog na lungsod.

PAULA
Si Papa ang matanda.

CANDIDA
Si Papa rin naman ang batang nariyan—
Si Papa sa panahon
Ng kaniyang kabataan.

BITOY
Oo nga, oo nga!

PAULA
At ang lungsod na nag-aapoy—

BITOY
Ang lungsod ng Troya, Hindi ba, hindi ba?

PAULA
Alam mo pala
Ang lamang istorya.

BITOY
Bitbit ni Eneas
Si Angkises na ama
Paglikas sa Troya;
Pininta ng Papa n'yo
Ang sarili niya
Sa papel ni Eneas
At ni Angkises pa.

CANDIDA
Ang sarili ngayon
At ang sarili niya
Nung nagdaang panahon.

BITOY
Kagimbal-gimbal
Ang dating sa akin.

CANDIDA
Ang epekto pala sa iyo'y gano'n din.

BITOY
Parang nagdodoble
Ang aking paningin.

CANDIDA
Kung minsan, isip ko—
Isa 'yang halimaw:
Nag-iisang tao
Na dalawa ang ulo!

BITOY
Kagilagilalas na halimaw
Ang sinumang alagad ng sining...

BITOY
Alam n'yo bang
May Pranses na turistang
Sumulat ng artikulo—
Panay ang pagpuri
Sa larawan ninyo?

CANDIDA
Noon pang tagahanga
Ng Papa ang mama.
Nagkilala sila
Sa Madrid at Barcelona.

[Maglalabas si BITOY ng kuwaderno at itatala nito ang sinasabi sa kaniya.]

CANDIDA
Sabihin mo, Bitoy,
Reporter ka ba
Sa isang peryodiko?

BITOY
A, oo... oo...

CANDIDA
Kaya ka lang pala napadalaw sa amin.

PAULA
Lahat ng maparito
Hindi kami ang sadya kundi ang ritrato.

BITOY
Dapat kayong matuwa, dapat kayong magmarangal.
Maraming nag-akalang patay na'ng inyong Papa.
Ngayon, pagkaraan ng maraming taon, siya'ng pinag-uusapan ng lahat kahit saan.
Nabulabog ang bayan—Si Don Lorenzo Marasigan,
Ang dakilang pintor na kaibiga't karibal ng dakilang si Juan Luna'y nakalikha pa
man ng isang obra maestro sa kaniyang katandaan!

PAULA
Ginawa ng Papa ang larawang 'yan
Para sa 'min ni Candida.

Isang taong tahimik na nakasabit diyan.
Nang dumating ang Pranses at sumulat siya.
Hindi na kami natahimik, hindi na.
Walang araw na nagdaan na wala ni isang
Reporter sa diyaryo o potograpo
O estudyanteng napaparito.
At kami—
Ayaw namin ng gano'n.
Ayaw namin, Bitoy.

[Ipamumulsa ni BITOY ang kuwaderno.]

BITOY
Patawarin n'yo ako. Candida at Paula.

[Patuloy na iaayos ni PAULA ang bandeha. Patuloy na babatihin ni CANDIDA ang tsokolate.]

BITOY
Bueno, kailangan kong
Lumakad na.

CANDIDA
Huwag, Bitoy!
Magmeryenda ka.
'Sang tasa pa, Paula!

BITOY
May naghihintay sa 'kin.

PAULA
Maupo ka, Bitoy.

BITOY *[Mauupo.]*
Talaga bang kayo'y Ginagambala ng tao?

CANDIDA
At may mga tao isang araw.
Mga miyembro ng kung anong
asosasyon—
Nahindik nang malamang
'Sang taon nang nasa amin ang
larawan.
"Binibining Marasigan,
Ipakukumpiska ko

Ang Larawan ng Gobyerno.
Hindi karapat-dapat
Kayong magkapatid
Na maghawak ng gan'yang
Obra maestro!"

BITOY
Nakikita ko na
Kung ano ang problema.
[Papasok si PAULA na may dalang isa pang tasa.]

CANDIDA
Naku, hindi kami ang problema.
Ang Papa ang aming inaalala.

[Kukunin ang tasa at iaabot ang bandeha ng meryenda ni Don Lorenzo kay PAULA.]

Eto, Paula,
At sabihin sa Papang
Dinadalaw siya
Ng anak ng kaibigan niyang
Si Camacho.

[Lalabas si PAULA.]

BITOY
Kumusta siya, ang inyong Papa,
Si Don Lorenzo el Magnifico?

CANDIDA
Mabuti naman.

BITOY
Hindi na ba kayang
Lumabas ng kuwarto?

CANDIDA
Naaksidente siya.

BITOY
Kailan?

CANDIDA
Nung isang taon pa.

BITOY
Nang kaniyang ipinta ang retrato?

CANDIDA
Nang matapos ang obra.

BITOY
Ano ang nangyari?

CANDIDA
Hindi namin nakita,
Nangyari sa gabi.
Naglakad siguro sa pagtulog
At nahulog...
Mula sa balkon ng kuwarto...
Nahulog sa patyo.

BITOY
Diyos ko, nabalian ba?

CANDIDA
Salamat sa Diyos,
Hindi naman.

BITOY
Ano'ng lagay ngayon?

CANDIDA
Bitoy, alam mo ba,
Isang taon na ngayong hindi lumalabas
Sa kuwarto niya.
Naku, sinisisi namin
Ang aming sarili
Sa nangyari.

BITOY
Ngunit bakit? Aksidente 'ka mo ang nangyari.

CANDIDA
Aksidente...

[Lilitaw si PAULA sa pintuan.]

PAULA
Halika, Bitoy!

Tuwang-tuwa ang Papa,
Puntahan daw siya!

BITOY
Salamat, Paula.

CANDIDA
Bitoy...
Hindi ka reporter.
Isa kang kaibigan.
Hindi ka naparito
para mag-interbyu
O kumuha ng ritrato.
Naparito ka lang
Para bumisita.

BITOY
Oo, Candida.

[Lalabas sina PAULA at BITOY. Muling uupo si CANDIDA at bubuksan niya ang mga sulat na natanggap. Babalik si PAULA.]

PAULA
Masiglang nag-uusap
Nang iwanan ko sila. Bumubuti na yata
Ang lagay ng Papa! Mga utang natin?

CANDIDA
Sa gas, sa tubig, sa doctor, at ito—Sa kuryente.
Pakinggan mo...
"Muli namin kayong pinagsasabihan
Na pag hindi nabayaran agad ang inyong mga utang,
Mapipilitan kaming
Putulan kayo ng serbisyo."
Pangatlong babala na ito.

PAULA
Nagsabi ka ba kay Manolo?

CANDIDA
Tinawagan ko siya. Tinawagan ko si Pepang.
Ang sabi nila, Oo. Magpapadala ng pera
Isang buwan nang nagsasabi, wala naming padala.

PAULA
Ang mga mahal nating kapatid!

CANDIDA
Ang gusto ng dalawa, iwanan na natin ang bahay na ito.

PAULA
Hindi nila tayo mapipilit. Basta't dito tayong dalawa.

CANDIDA
Dito tayo ipinanganak, dito tayo mamamatay.

PAULA
Pa'no kung umayaw na silang magsustento pa sa atin?

CANDIDA
Tingnan mo, May bagong ideya ako.
[Titindig at lilinga sa paligid.] Nasaan ang diyaryo?
[Mahahanap ang pahayagan.] Aba, eto… Ang sabi rito…

[Lilitaw si TONY JAVIER mula sa hagdanan.]

TONY
Magandang hapon, mga binibini! Aba, meryenda!

CANDIDA
Gusto mo ng tsokolate, Mister Javier?

TONY
Tsk, tsk… Masama 'yan sa negosyo. Kuwarto lang ang arkilado ko!

CANDIDA
Paula, isang tasa pa.

TONY
Naku, para ano?

[Aabutin ang tasa ni Paula.] Puwede na ang tasang ito.

CANDIDA
Mister Javier. Iniuutos kong ibaba mo
Ang tasang 'yan ngayon din!

TONY
[Hindi papansinin si CANDIDA.]
Salamat, Miss Paula.
[Ipagtatagay ang tasa.]
Sa masamang negosyo!

[Hihigupin ni TONY ang tsokolate mula sa tasa ni PAULA.]

CANDIDA
Mister Javier, Kalunos-lunos—

TONY
[Aabot at magsusubo ng biskuwit.]
Masarap nga!

CANDIDA
Walang kuwentang tratuhin ka nang disente!

TONY
[Palayo sa mesa.]
Pahintulutan n'yong ilayo ko sa inyong paningin
Ang malaswa kong pagkatao.
O… at salamat
Sa meryenda.

CANDIDA
Mister Javier. May sasabihin kami sa 'yo.

TONY
Ano 'yon?

PAULA
[Biglang daramputin ang tsokolatera.]

Kailangang ilabas ito sa kusina.

CANDIDA
Dumito ka, Paula.

TONY
Ano ba'ng gusto n'yo?
Gusto kong humiga
Bago umalis uli.
Pagod na pagod ako;
Kulang ako sa tulog.

Nag-aaral sa araw, trabaho sa gabi.
May ambisyon kasi.
Tingnan n'yo ko, isang tagapiyano sa bulok na bodabil.
Hindi ako piyanista.
Alam n'yo ba'ng diperensiya ng piyanista at tagapiyano?
Sasabihin ko…

TONY—SOLO
Ang piyanista, aral sa konserbatoryo
at nagkokonsiyerto sa alta sosyedad.
May kultura ang piyanista
Samantala… Ang tagapiyanong tulad ko,
Walang naging titser, nag-aral nang sarili
At alam na alam kong walang kuwenta ang tugtog ko.
Tumitipa ng piyano sa bulok na bodabil.
Tatlong tugtog sa isang araw sa bulok na sinehan.
Dinuduraan sa batok ng mga manonood.
Parang lata ang tunog ng piyano mong bulok.
At hindi mo alam kung hanggang kailan ang trabaho mo.

CANDIDA
Mister Javier!
Nang pumayag kaming
Rumenta ka sa amin
May isang kondisyon—
Hindi ka magdadala
Ng sugal o alak
O babae sa kuwarto.

TONY
E 'no ngayon?

CANDIDA
Nilabag mo
Ang aming reglamento.

TONY
Hindi ako nagsusugal.

CANDIDA
Hindi sugal ang tinutukoy ko.

TONY
Bueno, sige,
Nagseserbesa 'kong minsan.

CANDIDA
O ang pag-inom mo.

TONY
Ang ibig mong sabihin—
[Nakangising imumuwestra ang hugis ng babae.]

CANDIDA
'Yon mismo!

TONY
Kailan?

CANDIDA/PAULA/TONY—TRIYO
CANDIDA
Narinig ka namin kagabi may kasama kang babae

TONY
Gising pa kayo nang umuwi ako?

CANDIDA
Sabi ko kay Paula, Tingnan mo.
Nakita ba
Kung sino?

TONY
Miss Paula, ano ang nasilip mo?

PAULA
Babae siguro…

CANDIDA
Hindi lang siguro…

PAULA
Puting kung ano…

CANDIDA
Puti bang bestido?

PAULA
Baka kamisadentro…

TONY
'Yon nga! Kamisadentro—

Ni K'wan... 'yong tambolero
Ng banda naming—
Sumama sa'kin...
Kinuha lang ang p'yesang
Nasa k'warto ko.

CANDIDA
Hindi ako naniniwala—

PAULA
[kay CANDIDA]
Maling-mali ang iyong hinala.

TONY
Hindi na bale. Ako naman
Kung iisipin
Basura lang.

CANDIDA
Hinihingi ko ang patawad
Kung ang bintang sa 'yo'y di dapat.

PAULA
Mister Javier, huwag nang magalit
Kung nagsuspetsa nga ng pangit.

TONY
Isang basahang Dinuduran,
Nangangamoy—
Kasi'y pambrawn.

CANDIDA
Mister Javier,
Hindi na'yan
Katawa-tawa.

TONY
Sino ba'ng
Nagpapatawa?

[Lalabas si PAULA patungong kusina. Lilitaw si Bitoy na may alang bandeha.]
Aba kaibigan, Nandiyan ka pala!

BITOY
Tony, kumusta!

CANDIDA
Magkakilala kayo?

BITOY
Nagkasama kami sa trabaho.

TONY
Sa piyer.

BITOY
Ano'ng ginagawa mo rito?

TONY
Dito ako nakatira.

BITOY
Bola!

CANDIDA
Nagpapaupa kami Ng ilang mga kuwarto.
Si Mister Javier pa lang—

PAULA
[Mula sa kusina.] CANDIDA! CANDIDA!

CANDIDA
Bakit Paula?

PAULA
May daga, may daga sa ating kusina!

CANDIDA
Naku Paula, Paula…

PAULA
Kasinlaki ng pusa!

CANDIDA
Tingnan natin! *[Lalabas ang magkapatid.]*

TONY
Mga sira ulo!

BITOY
Mga matandang
Kaibigan ng aking pamilya.

TONY
Puwes, huwag kang masyadong
Dumikit sa kanila. Gutom na gutom sila sa lalaki.

BITOY
Bakit? Sinubukan ka bang kainin?

TONY
Parehong sira. Nangangatal
Pag nasa harap ko.
Pag kinausap ko,
Nilalagnat. At pag hinipo ko—

BITOY
Niligawan mo ba?

TONY
Niligawan sila?
[Dudura.]
Ligawan ko na lang ang Jones Bridge!
Sila ang baliw,
Hindi ako!

BITOY
Pobreng-pobre kasi.

TONY
Puwede silang yumaman kung—

BITOY
Kung ano?

TONY
Nakikita mo Ang Larawang 'yan?
May Amerikano akong
Handang bilihin 'yan
Nang dos mil dolyares.
Dolyares, ha!

BITOY
Ayaw nila?

TONY
Ang tagal ko nang pinipilit.

BITOY
Ikaw?

TONY
Kinuha akong tagapamagitan.

BITOY
Walang mangyari?

TONY
Mga sira ang ulo!

BITOY
Mahal na mahal siguro ang larawan ng ama.

TONY
Kinamumuhian nga.

BITOY
Pa'no mong nalaman?

TONY
Kinamumuhian ko rin!

BITOY
Ba't naman?

TONY—SOLO
Palaging nakatitig.
Minamaliit ako, iniismiran
Pagpasok ko sa bahay,
Pag-akyat sa hagdan.
Kahit sa loob ng aking kuwarto,
Lumulusot sa dahoon ng pintuan
Ngiti niyang nagmamayabang.

BITOY
Ang larawan ba'ng tinutukoy mo o ang matandang baldado?

TONY
Kagagaling mo sa kuwarto
Ni Don Lorenzo El Magnifico.

Walang kuwarta sa bulsa, Panay hangin ang nasa ulo.
Ilan buwan na ko rito,
Ni minsan hindi pa'ko inimbita
Sa kuwartong pinagkukulungan.

BITOY
Pero hindi ka niya kilala.

TONY
Pinasok ko siya minsan
Nang sapilitan.

BITOY
Pinalayas ka?

TONY
Naku, hindi.
Mapitagang-mapitagan siya.
Nang sabihin kong may Amerikanong
Gustong bumili ng kaniyang obra,
Nakangiting humingi ng paumanhin.
"Sa mga anak kong dalaga 'yon;
Hindi sa akin.
Kung may interesado ro'n,
Sila ang kausapin."
Saka nagsabing
Magsisiyesta siya. Walang kaanu-ano,
Napaiskram ako. Naku, magbabayad siya.
At alam ko kung paano
Ko siya pagbabayarin.

BITOY
Ba't ba masugid kang
Maibenta ang retrato?

TONY
Dahil sa 'king porsiyentong
'Pinangako ng Amerikano.

[Papasok sina CANDIDA at PAULA.]

Aba, mga binibini, Nahuli n'yo'ng daga?

PAULA
Siyempre naman Mister Javier, walang nakakaligtas kay Candida.

TONY
Kampeon sa pagpatay ng daga!

CANDIDA
Masasabing eksperto.

BITOY
Pa'no ba ginagawa mo?

CANDIDA
Kailangan siyempre ng talento!

TONY
Talentong ekstraordinaryo!

CANDIDA
At pinaplano kong pagkakitaan
Ang aking kaalaman.

[May kakatok sa ibaba.]

CANDIDA
May mga bisita?

BITOY
Pihadong alam ko kung sino.

CANDIDA
Mga kaibigan mo?

BITOY
Paalisin ko!

PAULA
Aba, huwag.

CANDIDA
Tuloy ka' mo.

[Lalabas si BITOY sa hagdanan. Papasok sina
SUSAN at VIOLET, medyo lasing.]

VIOLET/SUSAN
Yuhuuuu!

TONY
Demontres!

PAULA
Sino kayo?

SUSAN
Ako si Susan.

VIOLET
Ako si Violet.

SUSAN/VIOLET
Mga artista sa Teatro Parisian! Mga istar sa entablado!
Mga hiyas ng bodabil!

TONY
Ano'ng ginagawa n'yo rito?

SUSAN/VIOLET
Gusto naming makita
Kung sa'n ka nakatira!

TONY
Nakita n'yo na;
Layas na!

SUSAN/VIOLET
Huwag kang magsalita
Nang ganyan. Titigil kami rito. Hanggang kahit kailan.

TONY
Susan, lasing ka. Umuwi ka muna.
Sa loob ng 'sang oras Magpapalabas na.

[Aakayin si SUSAN nang palabas.]

SUSAN
Bitiwan mo ako! Uuwi ako
Kung kailan ko gusto!

TONY
Ano ba'ng problema mo't
Gumagawa ka ng gulo?

SUSAN
Ano'ng keber mo?

TONY
May ginawa ba ako?

SUSAN
Saan ka naroon kagabi? Saan ka nagpunta
Pagbaba ng kurtina?

TONY
Sumakit ang ulo ko; umuwi ako rito.

SUSAN
Wala kang sinabi sa 'kin.
Kinalimutan mong
May date pa tayo.

TONY
Violet, puwede ba? Iuwi mo si Susan
Nang mabanyusan mo.

VIOLET
Ayoko. Gusto naming mag-ensayo.

TONY
Ng ano?

VIOLET
Ng number namin mam'ya.

SUSAN
[kay TONY]

Kung hindi ka umalis,
Kagabi pa naming napraktis.

TONY
[Tutugtog sa piyano.]
O sige, bilis!

SUSAN/VIOLET
"A-tithket, a-tathket, Ipathok mot ha bathket.
Then put it in your pocket,
Don't athk na lang kung baket."

[Eensayuhin nina SUSAN at VIOLET ang kanilang dance number.]

CANDIDA
Huwag kayong maingay,
Natutulog ang Papa!

TONY
Umuwi na nga naman!

SUSAN
Ayoko pa!

TONY
Uwi na!

VIOLET

Bakit? Sino sila?

SUSAN
Sila ba'ng may-ari ng casa?

VIOLET
Alam ko kung anong klase sila!

SUSAN
[Kay TONY.]
Kitang-kita kita. Isinama mo rito
Yaong Intsik beha!

TONY
Sharap na!

VIOLET
[Kina CANDIDA at PAULA.]
Alam na alam ko ang sistema ninyo!

TONY
[Kina SUSAN at VIOLET.]
Layas na, layas na!

BITOY
Sige na, pakiusap lang!

[Aalis sina SUSAN at VIOLET nang tangay-tangay si TONY.]

Kina CANDIDA at PAULA.]

Lalakad na rin ako.
Pupuntahan ko na
Ang mga kaibigan ko.
Sasabihin kong
Tulog ang Papa n'yo.

CANDIDA/PAULA
Babalik ka?

BITOY
Aba, siyempre naman!

[Lalabas si BITOY. Mauupo sina CANDIDA at PAULA]

PAULA
Nakatatawa si Mr. Javier, hindi ba?

CANDIDA
Maniniwala ka ba naman
Sa pagtestigo ng lasengga?

PAULA
Bukod sa ro'n, kailangan natin
Ng 'binabayad niyang pera.

CANDIDA
Alam ko'ng gagawin natin.

[Ipakikita ang pahayagan.]

Tingnan mo:
"Singkuwenta sentimos
Para sa bawat dagang mahuli." Pupunta 'ko sa—sa'n ba naro'n Ang Oficina de
Sanidad y Ciencia? Kuruin mo, babayaran ako
Para gawin ang gustong-gusto kong ginagawa. Ikaw naman, magbibigay ng leksiyon
Sa pagpipiyano at pag-eespanyol. Maglalagay tayo ng karatula sa harap.

PAULA
Leksiyon para kanino?

CANDIDA
Mga babae sa pagpipiyano,
Mga lalaki sa pag-eespanyol

PAULA
Pagtatawanan ako!

CANDIDA
Kapag binastos ka ng mga lalaki,
Tumawag ka lang ng pulis!
Malaki ang kikitain natin. Hindi na nila tayo mapipilit umalis,
Makikita nina Pepang at Manolong
Kaya nating sustentuhan ang bahay na ito.

PAULA
Hindi na natin kailangang mangamba. Hindi na natin kailangang mangamba.

CANDIDA/PAULA
Mananatili tayo rito
Hanggang mamatay tayo—
Ikaw, ako at ang Papa! Gagaling siya,
Lalabas siya sa kuwarto,
Liligaya uli tayo,
Magkakasama tayong tatlo.

CANDIDA/PAULA DUWETO

CANDIDA
Kay sarap ng buhay nung araw.
Maayos ang bihis ng lahat.
Parang haplos pag-ihip ng hangin
Pag may mga Ideal.

PAULA
Poesya ang ating agahan.
May awit na kalong kung gabi.
Sining ang lagi nang kapitbahay.
Pag may mga Ideal.

CANDIDA/PAULA
Kagandahan, Katotohanan
Ang panlaban ko sa mundo.
Wala akong takot,
Walang panlulumo
Bumaha man o bumagyo.

CANDIDA
Maibabalik ba natin
Ang mga araw na 'yon?

CANDIDA/PAULA
Kagandahan, Katotohanan
Ang panlaban ko sa mundo.
Wala akong takot,
Walang panlulumo
Bumaha man o bumagyo.

PAULA
Ang saya natin noon!
Bakit natin sinira
Ang ating kaligayahan?
Bakit naaksidente ang Papa?
Bakit niya 'pininta ang larawang 'yon?

[Aabutin ni PAULA ang switch ng ilaw:]

CANDIDA
Lilipas ang lahat. Patatawarin tayo ng Papa. Tayong tatlo'y magsasaya uli!

PAULA
Candida, walang ilaw!

CANDIDA
Subukan mo uli!

PAULA
Ilang beses ko nang sinubukan nang sinubukan!

CANDIDA
Subukan mo sa ibaba ng hagdanan. Susubukan ko sa pasilyo.

[Bababa si PAULA sa hagdanan. Papasok si CANDIDA sa pasilyo.]

Wala ring ilaw sa hagdanan?

PAULA
Wala! May ilaw ba sa pasilyo?

CANDIDA
Wala. At wala ring ilaw
Sa kuwarto ng Papa!

PAULA
Naku, Candida,
Pinutulan tayo ng kuryente!

Tawagan mo sina Manolo't Pepang!
Tawagan mo ang kompanya ng ilaw!

CANDIDA
Huwag kang maingay!
Gusto mong makitawag ako sa kanto?
Alam na ng lahat sa kalye nating
Pinutulan tayo ng kuryente
Dahil hindi tayo nakabayad!

PAULA
Naku, Candida! Naku, Candida!

CANDIDA
Sarhan mo'ng mga bintana!

PAULA
Makikita ako ng mga kapitbahay!

CANDIDA
Alam ko na'ng tsismisan nila!
Tingnan mo'ng dalawang nagrereyna-reyna,
Ni hindi makabayad sa kuryente nila!

PAULA
Paano pa natin maihaharap
Mga mukha natin sa labas?

CANDIDA
Sarhan mo'ng mga bintana!

PAULA
Makikita nila tayo.

CANDIDA
Baka wala pang nakakapansing
Madilim ang ating bahay!

[Dahan-dahang lalapit sa bintana.]

Walang ilaw kahit saan!

PAULA
Walang ilaw?

CANDIDA
Madilim lahat ng bahay!

PAULA
Madilim?

CANDIDA
Madilim ang buong lansangan!

PAULA
Ano'ng nangyari?

CANDIDA
Napakagaga natin!

PAULA
Ano ba ang nagyari?

CANDIDA
Walang ngang nangyari!

PAULA
Ano'ng wala?

CANDIDA
Nasa diyaryo nga pala!
Hindi kasi tayo nagbabasa!

PAULA
Ano'ng sabi sa diyaryo?

CANDIDA
[Tumatawa.]
May black out ngayon.
Nagpapraktis ng black out!
Naghahanda para sa gera.
At akala natin…
Natatakot tayong
Magsara ng bintana!
Natatakot tayong
Matanaw ng kapitbahay!
Di ba ilang pares tayong
Tonta at kalahati!
Isang pares na tonta!
Naku, Paula,

> Nakatatawa,
> Nakatatawa,
> Nakatatawa!

[Patuloy na tatawa hanggang sa mapahagulgol. Lalapitan siya ni PAULA at yayakapin ito.]

> PAULA
> Candida, Candida…

> CANDIDA
> Hindi ko na kaya. Hindi ko na kaya.

IKALAWANG YUGTO
[Pagkaraan ng isang linggo. Mga alas diyes ng umaga. Pinagmamasdan nina MANOLO at PEPANG ang LARAWAN.]

> PEPANG
> Ang idolo ng ating kabataan, Manolo

> MANOLO
> Higit pa sa idolo ang Papa!

> PEPANG
> Ang ating Diyos Ama!

> MANOLO
> Ang mundo at langit---

> PEPANG
> Buwan at araw at mga bituin!

> MANOLO
> Ang buong uniberso!

> PEPANG
> Ang sarap magkaro'n ng amang isang henyo!

> MANOLO
> Ang lupit, sabihin mo!

> PEPANG
> Masakit ding talikuran
> Ang idolo ng nakaraan!

MANOLO
Tingnan mo si Don Eneas—
Karga-karga ang sariling ama!

PEPANG
'Yon ba ang ibig
Ipahiwatig ng Papa?
Na iniwanan natin siyang
Nagkakarga sa sarili niya?

MANOLO
Magtigil Ka! Hindi natin siya pinababayaan.
Nandiyan sina Paula at Candida.

PEPANG
Namalengkeng pihado ang dalawa.

MANALO
Lalo nang nagiging loka-loka!

PEPANG
Kailangang kausapin natin.
Nangako kang magmamatigas na.
Nasa'n si Don Perico?

MANOLO
Nasa kuwarto pa ng Papa.
Nagdadaldalan pa ang dalawa.

PEPANG
Pakikinggan siya nina Candida.

MANOLO
Dahil senador siya?

PEPANG
Dahil poeta.

MANOLO
Nung araw pa, ano ka ba?

PEPANG
At dahil *ninong* nila. Kailangang makumbinse silang
Umalis na sa bahay na ito.

MANOLO/PEPANG DUWETO
MANOLO
May buyer na nga ako.

PEPANG
Sinabi ko na sa'yo—Ako ang may buyer na.

MANOLO
Huwag kang makialam. Ako ang panganay n'yo.

PEPANG
Wala akong kumpiyansang
May ulo para sa negosyo'ng
Mga lalaki ng pamilya.

MANOLO
Pa'no'ng mga muwebles?

PEPANG
Sa' kin na ang aranya,
Ang mesang marmol sa estudyo.
Sa'yo ang muwebles sa sala, puwera lang ang piyano.
Sa'kin din ang nasa komedor.
Paghatian natin
Mga kubyertos at plato.

MANOLO
Bakit pa? Kamkamin mo na ang lahat.

PEPANG
Di, salamat!

MANOLO
Sa'yo na pati ang suwelo, Sa'yo na ang hagdanan, Sa'yo ng mga dingding,
Pati bubong, sa'yong sa'yo!

PEPANG
Pag-aawayan ba natin
Ang ilang mesa at silya?

MANOLO
Ipagpaumanhin mo… Binigay mo na sa 'kin ang mga silya.
Kailangan pa bang makipag-away sa 'yo
Para 'yon ay makuha ko?

PEPANG
Alam mong ikakasal sa isang taon
Ang anak kong si Mila.
Kailangan niya ng muwebles.

MANOLO
Ikakasal ang aking si Roddie
Sa taong ito mismo.
At magkakamuwebles siya!
Sa akin ang nasa sala,
Ang nasa kumedor,
Ang nasa tatlong silid-tulugan,
Pati mga libro at aparador sa estudyo,
Ang malaking salamin sa ibaba,
Ang kama matrimonyal!

PEPANG
Kay Mila ko ang kama!

MANOLO
Subukan mong maglabas dito
Ng kahit na ano
Nang wala akong permiso!

PEPANG
At bakit ko kakailanganin
Ang permiso mo?
Sino ba'ng bayad nang bayad
Para sa bahay na ito
Sa loob ng nagdaang sampung taon?

MANOLO
Huwag mong sabihing
Hindi ako pumaparte
Sa mga pagbabayad.

PEPANG
Kung maalala mo.

MANOLO
Paminsan-minsan
Nakakalimutan ko.

PEPANG
Anong paminsan-minsan?
Kailangan kitang tawagan nang tawagan
Buwan-buwan
Pag oras na ng bayaran.
Ung binayaan kitang mag-isa,
Matagal nang namatay sa gutom ang Papa!
Hiyang-hiya na ko sa aking asawa
Tuwing itatanong niya
Kung bakit hindi ikaw
Ang nag-aasikaso
Sa mga kapatid at ama!
Palaging wala kang pera para sa kanila,
Pero ang dami mong pera
Para ipangkarera
At para sa 'yong mga kerida!

MANOLO
Aba, sabihin mo nga Sa magaling mong asawa—

PEPANG
Tama na! Nandiyan na sila!

[Papasok si PAULA na may dalang basket ng ipinamili, saka lalabas.]

MANOLO
Tama na nga tayo!

PEPANG
Ayan ka na naman, Manolo!

MANOLO
Pero kung gusto nilang
Dumito na lang sila.

PEPANG
Hindi na natin kaya
Ang magbigay ng sustento.

MANOLO
Talaga bang hindi na?

PEPANG
Ke kaya natin o hindi,
Hindi 'yon ang pinag uusapan.
Naiimbiyerna na ako sa lumang bahay na ito!

Naiimbiyerna na ako sa lumang bahay na ito!

MANOLO
Ako rin, aaminin ko.

PEPANG
Titira si Candida sa'yo. Titira sa 'kin si Paula.

MANOLO
Paano ang Papa?

PEPANG
Sa 'yo kung gusto mo.

MANOLO
Sa 'yo kung gusto niya.

PEPANG
Basta't sa 'yo si Candida,
Sa 'kin si Paula.

MANOLO
Para magkaalila kang
Mag-aasikaso sa bahay mo
Habang nagmamadyong ka
Kasama ng mga amiga!

PEPANG
At nang may maasahan ang asawa mong
Magbantay sa bahay n'yo
Habang nagsososyal siya
Sa mga klub at komiteng kung ano-ano!

MANOLO
Kawawang Candida!
Kawawang Paula!

PEPANG
Ang tagal naman nating
Sinustentuhan sila!

MANOLO
Kawawang Candida! Kawawang Paula!

[*Papasok si DON PERICO.*]

PERICO
Dumating na ba, Pepang,
Ang aking asawa?

PEPANG
Darating ba siya?

PERICO
Sunduin 'ka ko ako. Kailangan ako ng Pangulo
Sa Malacañang nang ala una.
May mga kagipitang
Kailangang pag-usapan.

PEPANG
Maupo ka muna, Don Perico. Nandiyan na sila Paula.
Manolo, Tawagin mo.

[Lalabas si MANOLO.]

Kumusta ang Papa?

PERICO
Umiidlip na. Pepang, ano ba
Ang nangyari sa kanya?
Naku, dapat na binisita ko na
Noon pa.

PEPANG
Malaki ba'ng 'pinagbago?

PERICO
Gaya pa rin ng dati
Ang liksi ng isip
Ang talas ng kombersasyon.
Ngunit may kulang,
May kung anong nawala.
Malubha ba ang kan'yang aksidente?

PEPANG
Malubha rin naman. Ngunit tiningnan siya
Ng pinakamahusay na mga doktor. Bumubuti na ngayon.

PERICO
Bakit parang nagtatago
Sa loob ng kuwarto?

PEPANG
Ano ba'ng napansin mo, Don Perico?

PERICO
Parang ayaw na niyang mabuhay...

[Papasok si PAULA.]

PAULA
Kumusta, *Ninong*? *[Magmamano.]*

PERICO
Ito ba si Paula? Caramba, ang liit mo pa
Nang huli ko kayong makita!

PAULA
Ang tagal na kasing
Hindi kayo bumibisita.

PERICO
Kaming nasa gobyerno
Wala nang oras
Para sa 'ming sarili.

PAULA
Binabati ko kayo
Sa pagkakapanalo
Sa huling eleksiyon.

PERICO
Matutulungan ko ngayon
Kayo ni Candida

PAULA
Salamat, *Ninong*. Hindi namin kailangan
Ng kahit anong tulong.

PEPANG
Makinig ka muna!

PERICO
Ayaw raw ng Papa n'yong
Humingi ng pensiyon.

PAULA
Hindi siya tatanggap
Kailanman ng pera.

PERICO
Bueno, kung ayaw niya,
Hindi siya maa'ring pilitin.
Ngunit, Paula,
Nakahanda ba kayong
Magsakripisyo para sa bayan?

PAULA
Anong klaseng sakripisyo?

PERICO
Ang larawan,
Ang huling obra ng inyong Papa...
Kung ihahandog n'yo yon sa bayan,
Magagawa ng gobyerno—
Bilang tanda ng pasasalamat—
Na magpresupuwesto ng pondong kayo ang magmamaneho
Para sa inyo ni Candida
At sa inyong Papa
Habang nabubuhay siya.
Hindi makatututol ang inyong Papa
Dahil hindi sa kanya
Kundi sa inyo
Ibinibigay ang perang
Tugon sa inyong handog.
Naku, Paula, malaking biyaya
Para sa 'ting bayang
Hindi nagkaro'n ng kahit isang obra
Ni Don Lorenzo el magnificong
Nagkalat ang mga obra Sa mga museo Sa Espanya at Italya.

PEPANG
Ano'ng masasabi mo, Paula?

MANOLO
Siyempre, Don Perico,
Kailangang pag-usapan 'yon
Nina Paula at Candida.

[Nakapasok na si CANDIDA nang hindi nila namalayan.]

CANDIDA
Wala kaming kailangang pag-usapan.

PEPANG/MANOLO
Candida!

PERICO
Ito ba si Candida? Kumusta, hija. Natatandaan mo pa ba ako?

CANDIDA
Natatandaan ko kayo. Ikinalulungkot kong
Nag-aaksaya kayo ng panahon.
Hindi namin ipamimigay
Ang larawan kahit kailan!

PEPANG
Manahimik ka at makinig!

CANDIDA
Narinig ko na
Ang lahat ng gusto kong marinig.
[Akmang aalis.]

PERICO
Sandali lang, Candida. Galit ka ba sa matanda mong *Ninong*?

CANDIDA
Kayo ang pinakahuling taong
Aakalain kong maghahangad
Na mailay sa amin
Ang larawan ng Papa.

PEPANG
Gusto lang makatulong ni Don Perico.

PERICO
Naiintindihan ko
Na 'pininta 'yon
Para sa inyo.
Ngunit kung may malasakit kayo
Sa inyong Papa,
Kapakanan niya ang isipin n'yo. May sakit siya.
Kailangan niya ng araw,

At masarap na hangin;
Kailangan niya ng doctor. Kailangang magpaospital;
Magastos siyempre 'yon.
Kung tatanggapin n'yo
Ang handog ng gobyerno,
Magagawa n'yong
Ibigay sa inyong Papa
Ang klase ng pag-aalagang
Kinakailangan niya.

CANDIDA
Wala siyang sakit! Hindi n'yo lang alam…

PAULA
Walang ospital
Na makagagamot sa kaniya.

PEPANG/MANOLO
Ano'ng ibig mong sabihin?

CANDIDA
Na hindi naming maa'rin tanggapin
Ang anumang iniaalay sa amin.

PAULA
Walang sakit ang Papa. Kailangan niyang dumito—

CANDIDA
Nang kasama namin.

MANOLO
Hindi ba ninyo alam,
Malapit nang magkagera? At ang Intramuros nga
Ang pinakapeligroso. Sabihin mo, Senador,
Sabihin mo sa kanila.

CANDIDA
[Lalapit kay Don Perico.]
Sige, sabihin n'yo… Talikdan ba naming
Ang bahay na ito
Tulad ng pagtalikod n'yo
Sa inyong poesiya?
Sige na *Ninong*,
Pagsabihan n'yo kami.

PAULA
Susundin naming
Ang anumang ipayo n'yo.

CANDIDA
Pero mag-isip kayong mabuti. Nasa kamay n'yo ang buhay namin.
Ngunit bakit kailangan pang
Mag-isip uli kayo?
Tinalikuran n'yo na ang bahay na ito,
Nang talikuran n'yo ang pagkamakata,
Nang tinalikuran n'yo ang kawawang mundo
Ng mga nakalipas! Pinagsisisihan n'yo na ba
Ang inyong desisyon?
Naku, gagang tanong! Kailangan lang tingnan
Ang itsura n'yo ngayon.
Mayaman na kayo,
Sinasanto ng marami,
Pinakikinggan
Pati ng Presidente!

PEPANG/MANOLO
Candida, manahimik ka!

CANDIDA
Bakit hindi makasagot
Ang bunying Senador?

PERICO
Candida, Paula,
Wala akong karapatang
Pagpayuhan kayo.

CANDIDA
Bakit wala?

PAULA
Nakinig kami noon
Sa inyong mga tula. Makikinig kami uli
Sa inyong salita.

CANDIDA
Siguro naman, mas matimbang
Ang salita ng Senador
Kaysa sa salita ng makata lamang.

PERICO
Kailangang tingnan n'yo
Ang katotohanan.

PAULA
Hindi ba totoo ang mga tula?

PERICO
Hindi kayo ililigtas sa bomba
Ng kahit anong poesiya.

PAULA
Tanging politika
Ang makapagliligtas sa 'min,
Gano'n ba?

PERICO
Candida, Paula,
Mahal sa akin ang bahay na ito.
Ngunit kapag nagkagera't
Naiwan kayo rito,
Ano'ng mangyayari sa inyo?
Ano'ng mangyayari sa inyong Papa?

PAULA
Kakargahin naming siya tulad ni Eneas
Na nagkarga sa kanyang ama.

PERICO
Nasa kalooban n'yo'ng
Dedikasyon ni Eneas,
Dedikasyong maganda sa Sining
Ngunit katawa-tawa
Sa tunay na buhay.

CANDIDA
Palaging katawa-tawa sa mundo
Ang anumang dakila, Senador.

PERICO
At tama ang mundo.

CANDIDA
Hindi ganiyan ang sabi n'yo noon.
Ang ganda ng mga tula n'yong
Lumilibak sa mundo noon.

PERICO
Kahibangan ng kabataan ang panunula ko noon.
Laruan lamang ng bata.

PAULA
Itinatabi ang laruan,
Pag ang bata'y tumanda.

PERICO
Walang taong may karapatang
Kumalaban sa mundo.

CANDIDA
Kaya't ang payo'y n'yo'y,
Sumukong gaya n'yo?

PERICO
Ano'ng gusto mong
Sana'y ginawa ko?
Nagpatuloy sumulat ng tula
Habang nagugutom ang pamilya ko?
Ibinaon ang sarili ko
Tulad ng Papa ninyong
Nagbaon sa sarili nang buhay? Ano'ng maipakikita niyang
Bunga ng mga taong nakaraan?
Isang larawan, isang obra maestra?
Sapat na ba 'yon
Para ipangatwiran ang ginawa niya
Sa inyo ni Paula?
Hindi ako ang dahilan
Ng galit ninyong magkapatid.
Ano ba'ng nagawa ko sa inyo?

CANDIDA
Wala, Senador. Ngunit ano
Ang ginawa mo sa sarili mo?

PERICO
Naku, Candida,
May mga pumipilit sa ating mga desisyon—
Ang mundong ginagalawan natin,
Ang taong minamahal natin,
Ang mga pangyayari sa ating panahon.
Akala ko, inaakay ko ang aking buhay Ayon sa mga pinsipyo ng aking kabataan.
'Yon pala, may mga kamay
Na umaakay sa'kin nang di ko namamalayan.

PERICO—SOLO
Hindi simple ang buhay
Katulad ng sining.
May puwersang humuhubog,
Sa ating landasin.
Hindi tayo'ng may hawak
Sa kinabukasan. Nagmimiron ka lamang
Sa 'yong kapalaran. Hindi ko sinabi kailanman
Ayoko na ngang maging makata.
Hindi ko naging ambisyon
Ang politika nung ako'y bata.
Mga ideal ang hanap ko.
Hindi ko inisip ang yumaman.
Hindi kailanman hinangad
Na maghawak ng kapangyarihan.
Ngunit… Hindi simple ang buhay
Katulad ng sining.
May puwersang humuhubog
Sa ating landasin.
Hindi tayo'ng may hawak
Sa kinabukasan.
Nagmimiron ka lamang
Sa 'yong kapalaran.
Nagmimiron ka lamang
Sa 'yong kapalaran.

CANDIDA
[lalapit kay PERICO.] Patawarin mo ako, *Ninong*.

PERICO
Ako ang patawarin mo.
Alalahanin mo na lang;
Hindi ko pinatay
Ang makata sa dibdib ko.

Namatay siya nang kusa
dahil natatadhana ang kanyang pagkamatay.

[Papasok sina DONYA LOLENG, PATSY, ELSA MONTES at CHARLIE DACANAY.]

LOLENG
Sino'ng namatay? Hola, Manolo! Hola, Pepang!
Kung alam ko lang
Na nandito kayo,
Kanina pa sana ako.
Aba, ito ba
Sina Candida at Paula? Kaibigang-kaibigan ko ang nasira n'yong ina. Natatandaan
n'yo ba 'ko?

PAULA/CANDIDA
Oo, Donya Loleng.

LOLENG
Ito'ng bunso kong si Patsy. At ito si Elsa Montes,
la Elsa Montes! Ang nagdala ng conga sa Maynila!
At ito si Charlie Dacanay
Na walang ginagawa sa buhay
Kundi sumunod-sunod sa amin. Kumusta'ng inyong Papa?

MANOLO/PEPANG/CANDIDA/PAULA
Umiidlip sandali, Donya Loleng.

LOLENG
Kumusta n'yo 'ko sa kaniya. *[Lalapit at titingin sa LARAWAN.]*
At ito ba ang retratong
Pinag-uusapan ng lahat?
[Kina PATSY, ELSA at CHARLIE.] Halikayo't pag-aralan n'yo!

PEPANG
Kailangang marinig namin
Ang iyong opinyon,
Miss Elsa. Laki ka sa New York Pihadong batikan ka
Sa pagtingin at pagtaya
Sa sining ng pagpipinta!

[Sandaling pag-aaralan ni ELSA ang LARAWAN.]

ELSA
Aba'y... aba'y... Binibigyan ako
Ng kay gandang inspirasyon!

CANDIDA/PAULA/MANOLO/PEPANG/PERICO/LOLENG/PATSY/CHARLIE
Inspirasyon?

ELSA/PATSY/LOLENG/CHARLIE/MANOLO/PEPANG/PERICO—KUWINTETO

ELSA
Disenyong pang-evening gown
Ang bihis ng mamang 'yan.
Ganiyan ang cut at bagsak, pati ang
Kulay, ganyan.
Pati ang sinepa niya,
Kailangang makopya rin.
Sinepa nga'y pag ginto
Istrombotiko ang dating.

PATSY
Pati sinturon,
At mga nakasabit.
Gagayahin lahat
Ng makitang burloloy

ELSA
Isusuot ko,
Pag ako ay nag kongga.

PATSY
Para sa tela kaya,
Ano'ng dapat gamitin?

ELSA
Chiffon o satin? Pelus ba o tafetta?

LOLENG
Paisip na lang
Sa inyong kosturera.

CHARLIE
Sino ba ang dal'wang nariyan?

MANOLO
Si Eneas ang nagkakarga.

CHARLIE
At iyang matandang karga n'ya?

MANOLO
Si Angkises na kaniyang ama.

PEPANG
At sino Sila?

PERICO
Ang Artista,
At ang kanyang Kunsiyensiya.

[Biglang maririnig ang nakatutulig na paghugong ng sirena.]

PAULA
Ano 'yon?

MANOLO
Practice air raid lang 'yan.

CANDIDA
Tumigil ang lahat sa daan.
Mga tao't mga sasakyan.

CHARLIE
Practice blackout, practice air raid,
Pinapraktis pati pag-eebakweyt! Pagod na 'ko sa kapapraktis.
Ba't di pa magkagera nang totohanan?

PATSY—SOLO
Anong magkagera?
Aba, hindi puwede!
May bago na 'kong traheng
Isusuot sa bayle
Sa Bagong Taon!
Kapag nagbombahan,
Manila Otel ba'y
Magsasarang biglaan?
Papa, huwag mong payagang
Manggera'ng Hapon!
Ano't hindi na lamang
Mag-party't magsayawan,
Saka magposturahan?
Much better than digmaan!
Much better than, much better than
Much better than digmaan!

LOLENG
Kailangang pumunta sa bayle
Ke me gera o wala!

PATSY
Papa, bukas ba ang Manila Hotel
Kung sakaling—

PERICO
Bukas 'yon anuman ang mangyari
Walang gerang iistorbo sa inyo!

LOLENG
Ano? Ano'ng ibig mong sabihin?

PERICO
Kahit pa man lumindol, Hindi matitigil Ang inyong pagmamadyong. Mababasag lang siguro
Ang isang munting tasa,
Mababali ang paa ng pinagmamadyongang mesa.
Maaatraso nang kaunti
Ang inyong kosturera. Pag tapos na ang lindol,
Bibili ng bagong tasa,
Bibili ng bagong mesa,
Darating ang kosturera—
Tuloy ang ligaya!

LOLENG
Pepang, ano ba'ng ginawa n'yo sa kanya?

PERICO
Querida mia, ano'ng magagawa nila
Sa isang malamig na bangkay na?

PATSY
Sino'ng bangkay, Papa?

PERICO
Kadidiskubre ko lang:
Tatlumpung taon na palang
Ako'y patay na!

LOLENG
Perico!

PATSY
Papa!

LOLENG
Patsy! Ang sombrero ng iyong Papa!
Kailangan lumakad na.
Nagkakasakit si Perico
Tuwing papasok sa bahay na ito!

[Kukunin ni Patsy ang sombrero ng ama.]

CANDIDA/PAULA/MANOLO/PEPANG
May sakit ang Senador?

ELSA/CHARLIE
May sakit si Don Perico?

LOLENG
Inaatake ng poesiya!

MANOLO/PEPANG
Madre de Dios!

PERICO
Candida, Paula! Manatili kayo
Sa tabi ng inyong Papa! Kampihan n'yo si Lorenzo
Kalaban man ang buong mundo!

LOLENG
Huwag kayong mabahala! Ilang tabletas ng aspirina,
Kaunting sopas, kaunting siyesta—
Mamaya lang, magaling na.

PERICO
Adios, mga kaibigan. Walang laban ang poesia Sa bisa ng Cafiaspirina! *Contra mundum*, Paula! *Contra mundum*, Candida!

[Lalabas sina DON PERICO, DONYA LOLENG, PATSY, ELSA at CHARLIE.]

PEPANG
Dinobol-kros tayo
Ng pahamak na matanda!

CANDIDA/PAULA
Narinig n'yo
Ang bilin sa 'min.

Nangako kaming
Susunod sa kaniyang
Sasabihin. Didito kami habang-buhay
Sa piling ng Papa
Contra mundum.
"Contra mundum,"
Ang sabi kanina.

MANOLO
Candida, Paula,
Buo na ang isip ko.
Dadalhin sa ospital ang Papa!

CANDIDA/PAULA
Hindi maa'ring kunin
Ang Papa sa amin.
Didito kami anuman ang mangyari.

PEPANG
Paano kayong mabubuhay?

CANDIDA/PAULA
Bahala kami sa aming sarili.
Hindi kami aalis dito.

PEPANG
Espera, espera,
Totoo ba ang tsismis?

MANOLO
Anong tsismis, Pepang?

PEPANG
Na nahuhumaling ang dalawang ito
Sa binatang nangangasera?

MANOLO
Ano 'ka mo?

PEPANG
Isang patay-gutom,
Walang pinag-aralan,
Isang bodabilista,
Isang pambrawn!

MANOLO
Hindi na ninyo isinaalang-alang
Ang pangalan ng ating angkan?
Paano kung umabot ang tsismis sa Papa? Naku, alam ko na kung bakit
Nagkakasakit ang matanda!

CANDIDA
Walang sakit ang Papa.

MANOLO/PEPANG
Anong wala?

CANDIDA
Wala siyang sakit.
Hindi n'yo lang alam.

MANOLO/PEPANG
Ano'ng hindi namin alam?
Ano'ng inililihim n'yo sa amin?

CANDIDA
Gusto na niyang mamatay.

PAULA
Sinubukan niyang
Magpatiwakal.

MANOLO/PEPANG
Aksidente 'ka n'yo—

CANDIDA
Hindi aksidente.

PAULA
Tumalon siya sa balkonahe.

MANOLO/PEPANG
Pero bakit, Dios mio?

CANDIDA/PAULA
Kasi'y hinarap namin siya,
Sinisi sa paghihirap namin.
Sayang lang ang galing niya, sabi namin. Ba't hindi siya gumaya kay Don Perico?
Sana'y nakapag-asawa kami nang mahusay
At gumanda ang takbo ng aming buhay.

MANOLO
Ano'ng sabi niya?

CANDIDA
Wala.

PEPANG
Ano'ng ginawa?

PAULA
'Pininta ang larawan.

CANDIDA
'Binigay sa 'min nang matapos.

PEPANG
Para maibenta n'yo
Nang magkapera kayo.

PAULA
Regalo raw niya.

PEPANG
Ang larawang 'yon Ang inyong pag-asa.

CANDIDA
Nang paalis kami, ang sabi—

PAULA
"Paalam, Candida,
Paalam, Paula."

MANOLO
Puwes, lalong mahalagang
Mahiwalay kayo sa kaniya.

CANDIDA/PAULA
Kailangan naming manatili rito
Para mahingi ang kaniyang patawad.

MANOLO
Hindi siya gagaling
Hanggang hindi nalalayo sa inyo.
Dadalhin siya sa ospital. Titira kayo sa amin ni Pepang.

CANDIDA/PAULA
Tinalikuran namin siya
Tulad ng pagtalikod n'yo sa kaniya.
Ihihingi namin ng tawad
Tayong apat.

MANOLO
Basta ya! Tayo na Pepang.

[Paalis na sina MANOLO at PEPANG. Kina CANDIDA at PAULA]

At tanggalin n'yo 'ng
Mga karatula sa labas!
Dispatsahin ninyo
Ang inyong kasero.

[Maiiwanan sina CANDIDA at PAULA.]

PAULA
Ano'ng nangyari sa lakad mo kanina?

CANDIDA
Pinagtawanan ako.

PAULA
Ayaw maniwalang mahusay kang
manghuli ng daga?

CANDIDA
Ang trato sa akin, parang loka-loka.

PAULA
Naku, Candida!

CANDIDA
Tama si Pepang: Isang pares tayong
Parehong inutil.
Kailangan nating
Magkahiwalay.

PAULA
Naku, Candida!

CANDIDA
Aalagaan ko'ng
Mga anak ni Manolo. Pangangasiwaan ko'ng
Kanilang kusina.

PAULA
Aasikasuhin ko'ng
Labada ni Pepang.
Ako'y magugupo
Sa kaniyang buhok

CANDIDA
Ipapasuot sa yo'ng
Mga luma niyang damit.

PAULA
'Papaputol ng asawa ni Manolo'ng buhok mo.
Talaga ba, Candidang
Wala na tayong magagawa?

[Lalapit si CANDIDA sa LARAWAN at titingin dito.]

CANDIDA
Narinig mo
Ang sabi ni Pepang? Ang larawang iyan
Ang ating pag-asa.

PAULA
Pag ating 'binenta? Naku, Candida!'

[Papasok si TONY mula sa labas.]

TONY
Miss Candida, Miss Paula!

CANDIDA
Buwisit! Ayoko siyang makita.

TONY
Ito na'ng solusyon
Sa inyong mga prublema!

CANDIDA/PAULA
Ano'ng ibig mong sabihin?

TONY
Maupo kayo't makinig.

CANDIDA
Bilisan mo't magluluto pa kami.

PAULA
Ano 'yon, Mister Javier?

TONY
Yung Kanong sabi ko sa inyo,
Babalik na sa States.
Pinauuwi na'ng lahat ng Kano Para huwag abutan dito ng gera.
Puwes, 'yong may interes sa retrato,
Gusto niyang maiuwi ang retrato. Ang in'aalok na presyo—
Ihanda n'yo ang tenga n'yo—
Ten thousand dollars,
Sampung libo!

CANDIDA
Sampung libong dolyares?

TONY
Dalawampung libong piso! Gustong-gusto kasi ang retrato.

PAULA
Pag-iisipan namin.

TONY
Huwag n'yo nang pag-isipan.
Aalis na siya sa Biyernes.

CANDIDA
Samakalawa?

TONY
Kuruin n'yo lang... Pag may dal'wampung libo kayo
Tente-bunete na kayo sa darating na panahon.
Wala na kayong aalalahanin.
Maiingusin na ninyo
Ang dalawang kapatid n'yo.

PAULA
Ikinalulungkot namin, Mister Javier. Gaya ng sabi namin sa 'yo noon,
Hindi 'binebenta ang retrato ng Papa.

TONY
Ano? Naloloka ba kayo? Ito na'ng oportunidad
Na pinakahihintay ninyo!

PAULA
Ang ibig mong sabihin,
Ito na'ng oportunidad
Na pinakahihintay mo!

TONY
Ako?

PAULA
Magkano'ng in'aalok sa 'yo?

TONY
Sa akin?

PAULA
Na komisyon!

TONY
Bueno… aaminin ko: Malaki rin.

PAULA
Ikinalulunkot naming
Magiging bato
Ang sana'y kuwarta mo.

TONY
Miss Candida,
Sabihin mo kay Miss Paulang
Nasisiraan siya ng ulo.

CANDIDA
Kailangan ko nang magluto.
Siya ang kausapin mo.

[Akmang paalis si CANDIDA.]

PAULA
Huwag mo 'kong iwanang mag-isa!

CANDIDA
Bakit? Natatakot ka ba?

PAULA
Natatakot?

CANDIDA
Na masabing totoo pala
Ang itsinitsismis nila.

PAULA
Candida! Alam mong
Walang katotohanan 'yon!

CANDIDA
'Yon pala!
Bakit takot kang maiwanan?
Bakit palaging kailangang
Kumabit ka sa aking pundiya?
Batang munti ka bang
Nangangailangan ng yaya?

PAULA
Hindi ako natatakot,
Hindi kita kailangan.

CANDIDA
Hindi natin kailangan ang isa't isa.
Kailangang harapin nang nagsosolo
Ang kinabukasan ko at kinabukasan mo!

PAULA
Alam ko kung bakit ka umiiwas ngayon.
Nakapagdesisyon ka na.

CANDIDA–SOLO
Tama ka, Paula.
Bakit ko kailangang
Magpakahirap pa?
Bakit mo kailangang magtiis pa nang magtiis?
Oo, nagdesisyon na ako. At totoo
Na hindi na tayo magkasama.

[Aalis si CANDIDA. Maiiwan si PAULA
na matagal ding walang-mik.]

TONY
Ikinalulungkot ko, Miss Paula.
Alam mo siguro ang ginagawa mo.

Pero beynte mil pesos.
Diyos ko!
Kung ako'ng magkaro'n ng gano'ng halaga.
Magtatayo ako ng sarili kong banda.
Magliliwaliw ako
Sa Hong Kong sa Shanghai, Sa Java, sa India. Pupunta 'ko sa Europa
Para mag-aral magpiyano. Pupunta 'ko sa Paris,
Sa Vienna, sa New york.

PAULA
Paris... Vienna... New York...?

TONY
Sa Espanya, Italya, America del Sur...
Hindi lang ako maggagaranatsa—Mag-aaral ako,
Sisinghot ng kultura.

PAULA TONY—DUWETO
PAULA
Noon ko pa pinapangarap
Ang maglakbay sa buong mundo.

TONY
Pangarap mo'y magiging tunay.
Magagawang totoo'ng lahat.

PAULA
Ayoko nang umasa-asa.
Masyado nang matanda ako.

TONY
Magsama tayo sa Europa. Lahat ng ibig, matutupad.

PAULA
Maa'ri pa kaya?
Hindi ba't huli na?

TONY
May oras pa ngayon.
Huwag lang mababakla.

PAULA
Kung bata lamang ako,
Di "oo" na'ng sagot ko.

TONY
Tapangan ang loob mo,
Ako'ng bahala sa'yo.

PAULA
Hindi pa huli? Matanda na ako.

TONY
Miss Paula,
May gusto ka ba sa 'kin
Kahit na kaunti?

PAULA
Huwag kang magsalita nang ganiyan!
Ano'ng sasabihin ng mga tao?

TONY
Ano'ng pakialam mo sa sasabihin nila?

PAULA
Kinamumuhian ko sila!

TONY
Ipakita mo nga ang pagkamuhi sa kanila!
Sampilingin mo ang kanilang mga mukha!

PAULA
Tama ka siguro.

TONY
Ano ba ang magagawa nila sa'yo
Para matakot ka sa kanila?

PAULA
Hindi ako natatakot!

TONY
Puwede kang mag-impake ngayon mismo,
At pumunta kahit saan mo gusto!

PAULA
Patay na'ng mga pangarap ko.

TONY
Puwedeng may bumuhay pa
Sa pangarap mo noon!

PAULA
Puwede pa kaya?

TONY
Kung sakaling may dumating,
At masabi niya ang salitang
Makabubuhay uli
Sa pangarap mong naunsyami?

PAULA
Napagod na akong maghintay.

TONY
Miss Paula…
Tingnan mo ako…
[Dahan-dahang lilingunin niya si TONY ngunit madaraanan ng kaniyang paningin ang LARAWAN sa dingding.]

Huwag, Miss Paula! Kalimutan mo na siya.
Talikuran mo na siya,
Iwanan mo na siya!

[Lalayo si PAULA kay TONY.]

PAULA
Huwag dito, huwag dito!
Huwag sa bahay na ito!

IKATLONG YUGTO

[Hapon ng Oktubre, Pista ng "La Naval," Malapit nang gumabi.
Dahan-dahang aakyat si CANDIDA sa hagdanan, may dalang dasalan, rosaryo at payong. Ibababa niya ang payong sa lalagyan.
Lapapit si CANDIDA sa mesa sa gitna at ipapatong niya sa ibabaw nito ang kanyang dasalan at rosaryo. Saka niya aalisin ang kanyang belo at titiklupin ito.

Pupunta si CANDIDA sa balkonahe at manunungaw sadali. Papasok si BITOY mula sa labas.]

BITOY
Candida.

CANDIDA
Ikaw pala.

BITOY
Nakita ko kayo ni Paula sa simbahan.

CANDIDA
Nauna 'kong umuwi. Nahilo ako
Sa dami ng tao.

BITOY
Kumusta'ng inyong Papa?

CANDIDA
Gano'n pa rin. Manonood ka ba
Ng prusisyon?

BITOY
Gaya nung araw. Natatandaan mo pa?

CANDIDA
Peste kang talaga! Panay ang tanong mo:
Sinong santo 'yong may pakpak?
Sino 'yong may itak sa ulo?

BITOY
Panay ang teng-teng ng kampana,
Ang tugtog ng mga banda,
Ang ingay ng mga tao sa kalsada.

CANDIDA
Amuyin mo ang hangin, Bitoy!
Ang amoy ng piyesta, amoy ng Intramuros, siyudad ng ating mga pagmamahal!

[Biglang malulungkot si CANDIDA at iiwas.]

BITOY
Bakit, Candida?

CANDIDA—SOLO
Ito'ng huling Oktubre

Sa bahay na ito.
Lubusang maglalaho
Ang lahat ng ito
Paalam nang tuluyan
Sa bawat gunita
Ng dati nating buhay
Na ano't nawala?
Kailangan daw magbago
Ang ikot ng mundo.
Nang ma'ligtas ang buhay
Kailangang mamatay.
Paalam nang tuluyan
Sa bawat gunita
Ng dati nating buhay
Na ano't nawala?
Maibabalik ba natin
Ang mga araw na 'yon?

BITOY
Kailangang madala
Sa ligtas na lugar
Ang inyong Papa.
Ang obra mestra niya.

[Lilingon sa LARAWAN.]
Candida! Sa'n napunta'ng larawan?

CANDIDA
Ewan ko.

BITOY
'Pinagbili n'yo na?

CANDIDA
Hindi.

BITOY
Ninakaw?

CANDIDA
Hindi.

BITOY
Ano'ng nangyari?

CANDIDA
Ewan ko, sabi.

BITOY
Naku, Candida.
Ano'ng ginawa n'yo
Sa Larawan?

CANDIDA
Ibinaba ni Paula.
Itinabi kung saan.

BITOY
Saan niya dinala?

CANDIDA
Hindi sinabi sa 'kin.

BITOY
Pero pa'no mong—

CANDIDA
Tama na'ng tanong-tanong.
Wala akong alam, Bitoy!

[May kakatok sa ibaba.]

Wala ako kung
May maghanap sa 'kin.

[Biglang susulpot sina SUSAN at VIOLET.]

SUSAN
Naku, nandiyan ka.

VIOLET
At hindi kami aalis—

SUSAN/VIOLET
Hanggang hindi namin nakikita ang hinahanap namin.

CANDIDA
Ano'ng kailangan n'yo?

SUSAN
Gusto naming makita si Tony.

VIOLET
May sakit ba siya?

SUSAN
Dal'wang araw nang
Hindi sumisipot sa teatro.

VIOLET
Masisisante na.

SUSAN
Kailangang malaman niya.

SUSAN/VIOLET
Nasa'n si Tony?

CANDIDA
Ewan ko. Dal'wang araw na ring
Hindi umuuwi rito.

SUSAN
Dala ba'ng mga damit niya?

CANDIDA
Nand'yan pa'ng mga damit niya.
Mga kaibigan ba kayo?

SUSAN/VIOLET
Oo.

CANDIDA
Nasa maleta na'ng
Lahat ng damit niya.
Ibibigay ko sa 'yo;
Ihatid mo sa kaniya.

SUSAN/VIOLET
Hindi siya nakabayad ng renta?

CANDIDA
'Pakisabing ayoko nang makita
Ang kaniyang pagmumukha!

[Akmang lalabas si CANDIDA patungo sa kuwarto ni Tony.
Papasok sina DONYA LOLENG, PATSY, ELSA at CHARLIE nang nakabihis pansayawan.
Mala-Carmen Miranda ang gayak ni ELSA; mala-Xavier Cugat ang kay CHARLIE.]

LOLENG
Ipagpaumanhin mo, napasugod kami.
Kung ano-ano'ng naririnig namin.

CANDIDA
Ano'ng naririnig n'yo, Donya Loleng?

LOLENG
Nasa'n si Paula?

CANDIDA
Pauwi na si Paula
Galing sa simbahan.
Maupo muna kayo.

LOLENG
Wala palang nangyari, kung gano'n?

CANDIDA
Ano naman ang mangyayari? Ano ba ang narinig n'yo?

LOLENG
Nagtanan daw si Paula. Dinukot daw.

CANDIDA
Hindi 'yan totoo, Donya Loleng.

LOLENG
Salamat sa Diyos!

[Kina ELSA at Charlie]
Kung gan'on, tara na.

[Kina CANDIDA at BITOY.]
Magpapabayle kami mam'yang gabi Para sa mga sundalong Amerikano.
Magrurumba si Charlie. Magkokongga si Elsa.

[May maririnig na katok sa ibaba.]

CANDIDA
Bitoy, tingnan mo nga.

[Bababa si BITOY.]

LOLENG
[Kina PATSY, ELSA at CHARLIE.]
Sige, dito muna tayo. Nahapo ako sa kaiikot.

*[Lalabas si CANDIDA patungo sa kuwarto ni TONY.
Papasok sina PETE, EDDIE at CORA, kasunod si BITOY.]*

BITOY
Ano bang sadya n'yo rito?

[Tuloy-tuloy sina PETE, EDDIE at CORA sa may dingding.]

PETE/EDDIE/CORA
Wala na nga pala!

LOLENG/ELSA/CHARLIE
Wala na ang larawan?

BITOY
Itinago nila.

PETE/EDDIE/CORA
Gano'n lang?

BITOY
Baka magkagera, hindi ba?

EDDIE
Pero wala si Paula...

ELSA
Tama ako, Donya Loleng:
Nawawala si Paula.

BITOY
Hindi nawawala si Paula.
Nakita ko kanina lang sa simbahan.

EDDIE
Nawawala raw kahapon.

ELSA
Nakita naman namin sa isang kotse,
Kasama ang kung sinong lalaki.

SUSAN
Excuse me lang... Sino'ng lalaki'ng—

CORA
Ang boy friend n'yo.
Pero huwag kayong mag-alala.
Tinuturuan lang magmaneho si Paula.

ELSA
Sa hatinggabi?

BITOY
Sinabi ko na nakita ko mismo si Paula ngayong hapon lang.

EDDIE
Kung gano'n, dinobol-kros siya. Itatanan kunwari,
Tapos tinangay ang retrato, at iniwan siya.

LOLENG
Kailangang makausap si Candida!

*[Papasok si CANDIDA, dala ang maleta ni TONY.
Maririnig ang katok sa ibaba.]*

CANDIDA
Naku, sino na naman?
[Papasok ang DALAWANG PULIS. May black eye ang isa sa kanila.]

PULIS 1
Gusto naming makausap si Miss Marasigan.

CANDIDA
Ako si Miss Marasigan.

PULIS 2
Miss Candida Marasigan?

CANDIDA
Ako nga.

PULIS 1
Noong makalawa,
Tumelepono ka sa 'min,
Halos tanghaling tapat…
Kinidnap 'ka mo
Ang iyong kapatid na babae.

PULIS 2
Hindi pa namin nahahanap
Ang inyong kapatid,
Ngunit nahuli naming
Ang lalaking—

CANDIDA
Ipagpaumanhin n'yo.
Nagkamali ako.
Hindi nawawala
Ang aking kapatid.

PULIS 1
Bakit di n'yo kami
Tinawagan uli?

PULIS 2
In'uurong n'yo na
Ang inyong reklamo?

CANDIDA
Ikinalulungkot ko.

PULIS 2
Nakikita n'yo
Ang black eye ko?
Maa'ri bang sa susunod,
Maghinay-hinay muna
Bago kayo sumugod?

PULIS 1
Maa'ri bang gamitin
Ang inyong telepono?

CANDIDA
Wala kaming telepono.

PULIS 1
Tumelepono ka sa kanto. Pakawalan na 'ka mo
Ang lalaking hinuli ko.
[Lalabas ang PULIS 2.]

PETE
[sa maiiwanang PULIS] Sino'ng lalaki, Tsip?

PULIS
Yung kumidnap daw Kay Miss Paula Marasigan.

SUSAN
Tony Javier ba ang pangalan?

PULIS
Tony Javier nga.

VIOLET
Saan n'yo nahanap?

PULIS
Sa isang bar. Sinisira lahat Ng muwebles!

PETE
Lasing?

PULIS
At biyolente. Nakita n'yo'ng black-eye Ng kumpare ko?

SUSAN
Pero pakakawalan na siya?

PULIS
Pagkatapos niyang Magbayad ng multa.

SUSAN
[kay CANDIDA] 'Ta mo na! Masyado kayong magkapatid!

PULIS
[kay CANDIDA] Miss Marasigan, Ano ba talaga'ng nangyari?

CANDIDA
Wala naming talaga. Namasyal sa kotse. Ang aking kapatid. Nakalimutan nga lang
Magpaalam sa akin.

PULIS
Alas dose ng tanghali. Nung 'sang araw pa.

CANDIDA
At nagbalik kaagad.

SUSAN
Hindi nagbalik. Hatinggabi na, Namamasyal pa rin Ang iyong kapatid, Nung 'sang araw pa.

BITOY
Senyor Pulis, Wala rin lang namang naghahabla, Maa'ri bang kalimutan mo na?

SUSAN
Aba, hindi! Kailangang bulatlatin ang lahat!

VIOLET
Sila'ng gumawa ng gulo, Sila ang magpena.

LOLENG
Kawawang Candida, Kawawang Paula!

SUSAN
Si Tony ang kawawa, Nabilibid nang di oras, Nawalan pa ng trabaho. Ngayon, Miss Marasigan, Gusto mo pang maitago Ang baho n'yong magkapatid!

VIOLET
Itsitsismis ko sa lahat!

SUSAN
Ikakalat ko ang baho n'yo!

VIOLET
Mababalitaan ng lahat Ang paglalamiyerda Ng iyong kapatid Nang buong magdamag!

SUSAN
Ano'ng sinasabi mong Nagbalik kaagad?

CANDIDA
Hindi nagbalik kaagad! Nagsinungaling ako! Alas tres na ng umaga Nang umuwi si Paula.

LOLENG
Candida!

CANDIDA
Hinintay ko siya. Nakatayo ako rito. Tangka ko talagang Murahin siya. Ngunit nang dumating, Dahan-dahang umakyat sa hagdanan, Tumindig lang diyan... Hindi nagsalita... At ang itsura niya... Hindi ko malilimutan!

LOLENG
Tama na, Candida!

CANDIDA
Pa'no kong malilimutan ang itsura ng mukha niya?

LOLENG
Tama na sabi!

CANDIDA
At natalos ko noong ako ang may sala, ako ang masama, ako ang sumira sa buhay ni Paula!

CORA
Bitoy, ipasok mo siya sa loob.

BITOY
[kay CANDIDA] Halika na sa loob.

CANDIDA
Sandali! Gusto n'yong malaman kung sa'n siya nanggaling, sa'n siya nagpunta, Ano'ng ginawa niya?

BITOY
Tama na, Candida!

CANDIDA
Ako'ng nagkamali. Ako'ng nagkasala sa aking kapatid. Ako'ng nagtulak sa kaniyang lumakad. Ako'ng may gustong mangyari ang nangyari! Alam n'yo kung bakit? Dahil sa diyes mil dolares! Inisip ko kasi ang aking kinabukasan. Inisip kong hindi ko na kaya'ng kahirapan. Ayoko nang makipagtawaran sa palengke, magtago sa kubrador, maputulan ng tubig at ilaw! At para do'n lang—para sa beynte mil pesos, isinubo ko'ng kapatid ko, itinulak ko sa malaking kahihiyan!

BITOY
Candida! Candida!

CANDIDA
At ngayong alam n'yo na, ipagpaumanhin n'yo, masama ang aking pakiramdam.

[*Mag-aalisan ang PULIS, SUSAN, VIOLET, ELSA, CHARLIE at DONYA LOLENG. Si BITOY lamang ang maiiwanan.*]

BITOY
Candida!

CANDIDA
Hanapin mo siya, Bitoy. Nasa simbahan pa siguro. Sabihin mong umuwi na. Mahaharap ko na siya.

BITOY
Huwag mong masyadong sisihin ang sarili mo.

CANDIDA
Sabihin mo sa kanyang magkasama kaming muli, magkakapit, magkakampi.

BITOY
Sige, Candida.

[*Aalis si BITOY. Lalapit si CANDIDA sa dingding at titingin sa dating kinalalagyan ng LARAWAN*]

[*Papasok si TONY na walang sombrero, hindi nasuklay ang buhok, gasak ang damit, may black eye sa mukha at parang natalo sa labanan.*]

TONY
Nasa'n siya? Nasa'n si Paula?

CANDIDA
Wala rito.

TONY
At nasa'n ang litrato? Saan napunta?

CANDIDA
Ewan ko.

[*Lalapitan ni TONY si CANDIDA at susunggaban ang mga braso nito.*]

TONY
Nas'an 'ka ko ang litrato?

CANDIDA
Iwanan mo ako. Lumayo ka rito.

TONY
Iiwanan kita, huwag kang mag-alala.
Lalayo ako pero hindi bago ko makuha ang litrato!

CANDIDA
Hindi ko 'yon kailanman ibibigay sa 'yo!

TONY
Nagbago ka ng tono! Handa kang magbenta noon.

CANDIDA
Tama ka.

TONY
Handa kang ipagbili pati ang iyong kapatid!

CANDIDA
Tama ka.

TONY
Payag kang gawin ko ang kahit ano. Pumayag lamang siyang ipagbili 'ng litrato.

CANDIDA
At pumayag ba?

TONY
Aba, siyempre!

CANDIDA
Ang alam ko, mag-isa siyang umuwi. Nakawala siya sa 'yo.

TONY
Pero hindi na siya puwedeng umatras. Hawak ko na kayong dalawa.
At huwag kayong matakot, hindi ko kayo dadayain.
Makukuha n'yo ang beynte mil ninyo,
Makuha ko lang ang aking porsiyento.

CANDIDA
Ang iyong porsiyento, ang iyong porsiyento. 'Yon lang talaga ang habol mo.

TONY
E ano pa nga?

[Nakaakyat na si PAULA nang hindi namamalayan ng dalawa.]

PAULA
Ikinalulungkot ko, Tony. Huwag mo nang asahan ang porsiyento mo.

TONY
Paula! Bakit mo 'ko tinakbuhan?

PAULA
Dahil may kailangan akong gawin—Bagay na napakahalaga.

TONY
Naku, Paula, alam mo ba'ng ginawa ko
Nang matalos kong wala ka na?
Naglasing ako,
Gusto kong patayin ang sarili ko,
Gusto kong patayin ang lahat ng tao.

PAULA
Kawawang Tony, Para lang sa kaniyang komisyon!

TONY
Demonyong komisyon! Ang habol ko lang ngayon—mapatawad mo ako.

PAULA
Hindi mo 'ko mapapatawad sa ginawa ko sa iyo.

TONY
Naku, Paula, huwag mo 'kong kamuhian. Aaminin kong masama ang intensiyon ko noon. Galit kasi ako sa inyong Papa. Gusto ko siyang gantihan. Pero ngayon Intindihin mo ako, gusto kong maiayos ang lahat sa atin, gusto kong mapaligaya ka. Gusto kong matupad ang mga pangarap mo.

PAULA
Gano'n ba?

TONY
Maniwala ka sa 'kin.

PAULA
Naniniwala ako sa 'yo.

TONY
Nasa'n ang litrato, kung gan'on? 'Yon ang ating kaligtasan.
Maglalayag tayong magkasama—sa Espanya, Pransiya, At Italya.
Magbabagong-buhay tayo.
Magiging disente ako,

Magiging malaya ka.

PAULA
Malaya! *[Tatawa.]*

TONY
Huwag kang tumawa.

PAULA
Sige, hindi na.

TONY
Naniniwala ka ba sa 'kin?

PAULA
Iniibig mo ba ako? Magsabi ka ng totoo.

TONY
Matututuhan kitang ibigin. Kailangan lang nating makalayo. Nasa'n ang litrato? Naghihintay ang Amerikano.

PAULA
Kung gano'n, sabihin mo sa kanyang huwag na 'ka mong maghintay. Wala na ang litrato.

TONY
Ano'ng ginawa mo?

PAULA
Sinira-sira ko.

TONY
Anoooo??? Ano'ng ginawa mo?

[Hahagulgol si TONY.]

PAULA
Sinira ko, Candida, ang ating ritrato. Ginutay-gutay ko, at sinunog-sunog. Wala na ngayon. Wala nang talaga. Nagagalit ka ba?

CANDIDA
Hindi, Paula.

PAULA
Umiiyak ka ba?

CANDIDA
Hindi.

PAULA
Sino'ng naririnig ko?

CANDIDA
Si Tony Javier yata.

PAULA
Aba, oo, nahanap na niya'ng kanyang luha. Natuto na siyang umiyak.

TONY
Paula, Paula,
Bakit mo 'yon ginawa?

PAULA
Ayokong tumakas na gaya mo.

TONY
Paliligayahin sana kita. Palalayain kita.

PAULA—SOLO
Malaya na ako ngayon
Malaya na akong muli.
Sinunog ko na'ng diyaskeng litrato,
Saka ako umuwi.
Wala na ang mga multo.
Wala na ang mga pangamba.
Ang sumiping sa aking maligno,
Yumayakap na sa iba.
Matayog na ako ngayon.
Sa ulap na akong muli.
Ang pugad kong nasa panginorin,
Ngayo'y maa'ri uling liparin!
Ang pugad kong nasa panginorin,
Ngayo'y maa'ri uling liparin.

TONY
Ililigtas sana kita.

PAULA
Ikaw ang aking iniligtas.

TONY
Itinapon mo akong muli sa imbornal at pusali.

PAULA
Hindi ka na babalik do'n. Nagbago ka na. 'Yan ang napala mo.

TONY
Hindi ako nagbabago. Gano'n pa rin ang buhay ko!
Ikinait mo sa akin ang nag-iisang pag-asang mapabuti ako!
Pa'no mo nagawa 'yon? Bakit mo 'ko niloko?

[*Aalis si TONY nang pasuray-suray sa sama ng loob.*]

PAULA
[*Tutukuyin si TONY.*] Ang biktima ng ating pag-aalay!

CANDIDA
Ng ating pag-aalay?

PAULA
Ako lang ang humawak sa kutsilyo. Ikaw ang naghanda ng panggatong sa altar,
Ikaw ang nagparikit ng apoy.

CANDIDA
[*Luluhod.*] Paula, patawarin mo ako.

PAULA
[*Luluhod din.*] Hindi mo ba pinagsisisihan—

CANDIDA
Ang tungkol sa litrato?

PAULA
Ano'ng ginawa mo, kung ikaw?

CANDIDA
'Yon mismong ginawa mo.

PAULA
Pero, Candida, alam mo ba'ng haharapin natin?

CANDIDA
Araw-gabing walang kuryente, naghahabol na kubrador,
tsismis na hindi magkamayaw.

PAULA
Sasabihin nilang sira talaga'ng ating ulo. Kuruin mo, Diyes mil dolyares ang ating pinakawalan. Sasabihin nilang sampares tayong lukaret. Sasabihin nilang peligroso tayo.

CANDIDA
Sabihin nila'ng gusto nilang sabihin.

PAULA
Manghuhuli lang tayo ng daga.

CANDIDA
At mag-uusap sa salita ng mga taga-Babilonya.

PAULA
Hindi ka ba natatakot—

CANDIDA
Sa mundo ng Babilonya?

PAULA
Na pa'lisin, parang daga?

CANDIDA
Patawarin ako ng Diyos dahil hinangad kong maging kasing karaniwan ng iba.

PAULA
Tumindig, kung gano'n. Malaya tayong muli, Ikaw, ako at ang Papa! Hindi mo ba nakikita? Ito'ng palatandaang hinihintay ng Papa magmula nang ihandog sa atin ang litrato! Ito ang hakbang na nagpapatunay na buhay pa sa atin. Ang ating pananalig, na hindi pa rin natin itinatatwa ang pagiging mga anak ni Lorenzo el magnifico!

CANDIDA
Ngayon, makahaharap tayo sa kaniya. Hindi lamang bilang mga anak kundi bilang kapanalig at kasangga.

PAULA
Hindi na siya idolo lamang ng kahapon—

CANDIDA
Kaagapay na sa pagharap sa darating.

PAULA
Naku, Candida, binigyan tayo ng bagong buhay. Tayo ngayo'y—

CANDIDA
Kaniyang mga kaibigan—

PAULA
Kaniyang mga disipulo—

CANDIDA
Kaniyang mga babaylan!

PAULA
Halika, uminom tayo! *[Magtatagay.]* Ipagtagay natin ang bagong pagsilang!

CANDIDA
[Magtatagay.] Kakalabanin natin ang mundo upang mailigtas ito!

PAULA
Tayong tatlo ng Papa, contra mundum!

CANDIDA/PAULA—DUWETO
Bakit natin hinangad na litrato'y maibenta
Para magkapera't makasali Ssa mundo ng walang kuwenta?
Bakit tayo naiinggit sa mundo ng ordinaryo?
Bakit ba naloka't naisipang buhay natin ay kalbaryo?
Kung ang tao sa ngayon, nasa isip puro pera
At hindi na uso'ng poesi, 'di na baleng magkagera!

CANDIDA
Buksan natin lahat ng ilaw!!

[*Bubuksan nina CANDIDA at PAULA ang lahat ng ilaw sa sala. Papasok si Bitoy, kasunod sina DON ALVARO at DONYA UPENG.*]

BITOY
Paula! Nandito ka na!

ALVARO/UPENG
At nandito kami!

CANDIDA/PAULA
Don Alvaro, Donya Upeng!

UPENG
Kumusta'ng Papa n'yo?

CANDIDA/PAULA
Magaling na, magaling na!

PAULA
Candida, brandi para kay Don Alvaro, brandi para kay Donya Upeng, brandi para kay Bitoy. *[Aabutan ni CANDIDA ng brandi sina DON ALVARO, DONYA UPENG at BITOY.]*

ALVARO/UPENG
Ito ba si Bitoy Camacho?

BITOY
Ito nga. Narito para ipagdiwang ang pista ng La Naval.

ALVARO
Mabuti nga't sumasali ka sa tradisyong baka mawala na.

CANDIDA
Mawala na?

ALVARO
Pag nagkagera!

UPENG
Kaya't naririto kami upang batiin ang Birhen mula sa mga balkonahe n'yo gaya nung araw. Naku, Candida at Paula, baka sa huling pagkakataon na!

ALVARO
Baka nga, baka nga!

UPENG
Naku, mga bata, kay laking kalamidad ang baka suungin natin!

PAULA
Halikayo rito, Don Alvaro!

UPENG
Bakit, hija? May problema?

ALVARO
Ano'ng problema, mga hija?

CANDIDA/PAULA
Kailangan namin kayo.

ALVARO
Kaya kami nandito.

UPENG
At narito pa ang ibang tutulong sa inyo.

[Papasok sina DON MIGUEL at DONYA IRENE.]

IRENE
Naku, Paula at Candida!

MIGUEL
Anong tulong ang kailangan n'yo?

CANDIDA/PAULA
Natulungan n'yo na kami sa inyong pagparito.

UPENG/IRENE
Hindi maa'ring hindi makipag-La Naval sa inyo.

MIGUEL
Malapit na raw magkagera.

UPENG
Mawawala na ang lahat ng mahal na mahal sa atin

IRENE
Kung may natitira pa.

ALVARO/MIGUEL
Nariyan pa ang hangin, ang hangin ng Oktubre. Umiihip pa mula sa nagdaan, Mula sa ating kabataan. Umiihip mula sa Maynilang antigo, la Manila de nuestros amores!

ALVARO
Ang mga alaala ng lumipas! "La Naval de Manila"—
Kay sarap, kay saklap sambitin.

MIGUEL
Ngunit tayo lang ang tinutukoy natin, tayong nakabon sa ating henerasyon.

IRENE
Namamatay na nga, ang mga tradisyon.

UPENG
Di kailangan ng gera, para mamatay yo'n.

[Papasok si DON ARISTEO.]

ALVARO/MIGUEL/UPENG/IRENE
Aristeo!

ARISTEO
Caramba! Nandito tayong lahat!

CANDIDA
Tuloy sa aming bahay, magiting na sundalo!

ARISTEO
Hinila ko'ng katawan ko para magpugay sa La Naval.

UPENG
Sandali, Aristeo! Namimiligro raw ang buhay nina Candida at Paula.

ARISTEO
Namimilgro?

CANDIDA/PAULA
Ipagtatanggol n'yo ba kami?

ARISTEO
Dapat palang dinala ko ang aking armas!

CANDIDA/PAULA
Tama na ang naririto kayo.

PAULA
Brandi, Candida, para sa 'ting tagapagtanggol.

[Lalabas si CANDIDA para kumuha ng karagdagang brandi.]

ARISTEO
[Aabutin ang kamay ni PAULA.] Bakit, hija? Ang lamig ng kamay mo...

PAULA
Walang kuwenta 'yon.

ARISTEO
Anong peligro'ng lumalapit sa inyo?

PAULA
Pinaaalis kami sa bahay na ito. Kailangan naming maging matatag sa pananatili rito.

UPENG
Sasamahan namin kayo, kailangang naririto kayo—

ALVARO
Para huwag mawala—

IRENE
Para huwag mamatay—

ALVARO
Ang sagisag na nagsasabing—

MIGUEL/IRENE
Magpapatuloy ang buhay!

[*Lalabas si CANDIDA na may dalang bandeha ng mga kopita ng brandi. Aabot ng kopita sina DON MIGUEL, DONYA IRENE, DON ARISTEO, CANDIDA at PAULA.*]

CANDIDA
Tama kayo. Mag-inuman tayo.

PAULA
Sa Birhen ng La Naval!

ALVARO
Sa pista ng ating mga ninuno!

MIGUEL
May maiiwanan sa anumang Binubuhay sa alaala!

ARISTEO
Amigos y paisanos! A la gran senora de Filipinas en la gloriosa fiesta de su Naval!

LAHAT
VIVA LA VIRGEN!

[*Mag-iinuman sila. Nasa gitna ng sala sina CANDIDA at PAULA. Nakapaligid sa likod nila ang MGA MATANDA samantalang nasa isang tabi si BITOY na nagmamasid lamang.*

Papasok sina MANOLO at PEPANG na magmumukhang pikang-pika.]

PAULA
Pepang! Manolo!

CANDIDA
Nagpunta kayo rito para umilaw sa La Naval?

MANOLO
Alam n'yo'ng sadya namin.

PAULA
Handa na ba kayong umamin?

PEPANG
Anong "umamin?"

PAULA
Umamin na kayo, Pepang, Manolo! Gagaan ang loob n'yo, Makakalaya kayo!

PEPANG
Nababaliw kayong dalawa!

MANOLO
Tingnan n'yo'ng sarili n'yo! Gumagawa kayo ng eskandalo!

PEPANG
Nakakahiya, nakakahiya!

MANOLO
Kunin ninyong mga damit n'yo. Sasama kayo sa amin ngayon din.

PEPANG
Palisin n'yo sila.

ARISTEO
Caramba! Ito ba si Manolito? Hindi kita halos nakilala. Ang laki mo na, bata ka!

MANOLO
Don Aristeo, ikinalulungkot ko. Kailangan n'yo nang magsilakad.
May pag-uusapan kaming makakapatid.

UPENG
At ito ba si Pepita?

PEPANG
Narinig n'yo'ng sabi ni Manolo?

ALVARO
Pepita, ang ganda mo nung bata ka!

MIGUEL
Ang hilig mong mangabayo sa likod ko.

PEPANG
Don Miguel, wala nang oras—

IRENE
Wala nang oras, wala nang oras, palagi na lang nagmamadali!

MANOLO
Candida, paalisin mo sila!

UPENG
Naku Manilito, tahimik na tahimik ka nung araw.

MIGUEL
Naalala mo, Upeng, madalas mo siyang kagalitan dahil torpeng-torpe pa?

MANOLO
Nakikiusap ako nang mapitagan—

ALVARO
Nagbabasa kang lagi sa 'sang sulok

IRENE
O Nagbiyobiyolin sa patyo—

ARISTEO
O nagdidrihe ng sarsuwela, si Pepang ang babaeng bida.

PEPANG
Makinig kayo sa amin!

MIGUEL
Sila'ng pinakamatalas ang ulo, sa lahat ng batang nakilala ko!

IRENE
Naku, Pepita, hindi ko malilimutan ang iyong pagbigkas ng "Ultimo Adios" ni Don Jose nung siyete anyos ka pa lang.

MIGUEL
Ako'ng nagturo sa kaniya.

UPENG
Ako'ng nagturo sa 'yong magsayaw, Manolo, nung kinse anyos ka sa salas na ito mismo.

ALVARO
Anong ganda ng mga alaalang naninirahan sa bahay na ito!

MIGUEL
Ang laki siguro ng amor nina Pepang at Manolo sa bahay ng kanilang kabataan!

PAULA
Naku, hindi nga!

MIGUEL
Hindi ito mahal sa kanila?

PAULA
Gusto nilang ipagbili.

ALVARO/UPENG/MIGUEL/IRENE/ARISTEO
Ipagbili?

UPENG
Que horror!

IRENE
Ngunit bakit?

PAULA
'Yon ang ayaw nilang aminin.

ARISTEO
Baka masyado nang magastos.

PAULA
Hindi pera ang problema.

CANDIDA
Bagaman 'yon ang sabi nila.

PAULA
Nagtatapon sila ng pera sa madyong, sa karera.

CANDIDA/PAULA
Ikinakaila nila ang totoo kahit sa kanilang sarili.

PEPANG
Candida! Paula!

CANDIDA/PAULA
Sinusumbatan sila ng bahay na ito, nasisira'ng kanilang pagsasaya—

CANDIDA
Habang nakikipagtsismisan—

PAULA
Habang nakikipagsugal—

CANDIDA
Habang nasa karerahan o Jai Alai—

PAULA
O habang hindi sila makatulog—

CANDIDA/PAULA
Cataplum! Bumabagsak ang anino ng bahay ni Lorenzo el magnifico!

CANDIDA
Nanginginig sila—

PAULA
Lumalamig ang dugo!

ALVARO/UPENG/MIGUEL/IRENE/ARISTEO
Ang ibig n'yong sabihin, takot sila sa bahay na ito?

CANDIDA
Takot sila!

ALVARO/UPENG/MIGUEL/IRENE/ARISTEO
Ngunit bakit?

PAULA
Dahil ito ang kanilang kunsiyensiya!

MANOLO/PEPANG
Paula!

PAULA
Oo, Manolo, Oo Pepang. Ito ang inyong konsiyensiya kaya muhing-muhi kayo. Gusto n'yong gibain, Gusto n'yong lansagin nang hindi kayo usigin.

MANOLO/PEPANG
Manahimik kayo!

BITOY
Manahimik na! Dumarating ang Birhen!

IRENE
Ang Birhen ang magliligtas sa atin!

MANOLO
Candida, Paula! Halina kayo! Ubos na ang pasensiya ko!

PEPE
Naku, Manolo, wala nang makaaalis. Sarado na'ng daanan. Nandito na ang La Naval!

MANOLO
Lalayas sila rito kung kailangan ko silang itulak sa hagdanan!

ARISTEO
Kung gayo'y kailangang itulak pati ako sa hagdan!

ALVARO
At ako!

MIGUEL
At ako!

UPENG/IRENE
At kami!

CANDIDA
At ang Papa, Manolo! Magagawa mo bang itulak din siya sa hagdanan?

PEPANG
Kinamumuhian kayo ng Papa!

PAULA
Nasa panig namin ang Papa!

BITOY
[Makikita si Don Lorenzong lumalabas sa kuwarto.] At nandito na siya!

CANDIDA/PAULA
Ang Papa!

PEPANG
Manolo, ang Papa!

[Haharap ang LAHAT sa pintuan ng kuwartong nilalabasan ni Don Lorenzo.]

ALVARO/UPENG/PEPE/MIGUEL/IRENE/ARISTEO
Hola, Lorenzo! Hola, 'panero!

[Magfi-freeze ang LAHAT

Mangingibabaw ang martsa ng prusisyon ng La Naval at ang kalembang ng kampana ng iba't-ibang simbahan.
Magdidilim

Ipahihiwatig sa pamamagitan ng sound effects, usok at ilaw ang pagkakabomba sa at pagkasunog ng Intramuros.]

EPILOGO

KORO *[sa mga manonood]*
Oktubre sa Maynila, buwang kahit bumagyo,
Hindi mapigil ang pagpip'yesta.
Itinatanghal sa mga tindahan,
Hamon at keso at turones;
Nag-uumapaw sa palengke,
Mansanas, ubas, dalandan, at suha,
At sa mga bangketa, lansones at kastanyas!
Dumarating ang Karnabal,
Nagbubukas ang Opera House!
Puwes, 'yon na ang huling Oktubreng
'Pinagdiwang ng siyudad;
'Yon ang huling pagkakataong
Nanood sila ng La Naval sa dating Maynila
At nagpugay sa Birhen
Mula sa mga balkonahe ng mga Marasigan.
Nagpugay sa Birhen

Mula sa mga balkonahe ng mga Marasigan.
Wala na ang bahay na 'yon,
Ang bahay ni Don Lorenzo el Magnifico.
Kapirasong pader, santumpok na bato—
'Yon ang natira. Kinailangan ng gera mundial
Para masugpo ang diwa ng tatlong nanirahan doon.
Paalam, Candida! Paalam, Paula!
Lamunin man ng gubat
Ang inyong istorya, naririto kami't
Pinagdiriwang kayo sa 'ming pagkanta!
Paalam, Candida! Paalam, Paula!
Lamunin man ng gubat ang inyong istorya,
Naririto kami't pinagdiriwang kayo
Sa 'ming pagkanta!
WAKAS

Ang Larawan, The Movie

Based on Nick Joaquin's
A Portrait of the Artist as Filipino

Libretto by Rolando S. Tinio

Music by Ryan Cayabyab

Production Design by Gino Gonzales

Direction by Loy Arcenas

AFTERWORD

Our foray into producing musicals began in 1988. My father Cesar Legaspi, National Artist for Visual Arts, encouraged me to pursue original works. Accepting his challenge, we, Girlie Rodis and I, spearheaded the production of the original Filipino musical *Katy!* which is based on the life of Filipina jazz singer Katy dela Cruz. In the years that followed, we made more: *Kenkoy Loves Rosing* in 1991, *Alikabok* in 1995, *Sino Ka Ba Jose Rizal?* in 1996.

In 1997, we embarked on our biggest project yet: *Ang Larawan*, a Filipino musical based on Nick Joaquin's play *A Portrait of the Filipino as an Artist*, considered as one of the most important Filipino plays in English and one of the pioneers of realism in Philippine theater.

We were fans of the material. Nick, National Artist for Literature, granted us the permission to adapt his play under one condition: that Rolando Tinio, National Artist for Theater and Literature, must do the Filipino translation.

We got Rolando to write the translation and even direct the musical. Ryan Cayabayab created the enthralling music to go with Rolando's beautiful libretto.

To our great delight, Nick was pleased with the outcome. He would later write in the playbill, "... for the first time, my play is set to music. It gives me great pleasure to endorse 'Ang Larawan, The Musical.'... It is significant for our people to look back and remember our culture and heritage as we look forward to the future."

Everyone—from the production team, to the cast and the crew—were thrilled to be part of something created by two National Artists (Nick and Rolando) and a musical genius (Ryan). We prepared for the staging at the Cultural Center of the Philippines in high spirits.

Our only pain was the passing of Rolando a mere ten days before opening night. Rolando would have been so heartened with how the audience responded. How the people always broke into thunderous applause during the curtain call. Up until the last performance, we were in awe.

Due to insistent public demand, we restaged *Ang Larawan* in 1998. Even for those who had watched it the year before, there was something magical about it. The musical deserves to be relived.

After *Ang Larawan*, we would produce two more musicals, *Fire Water Woman* (based on Nick Joaquin's short story "Summer Solstice") in 1999 and *Saranggola ni Pepe* in 2000.

Among our seven original musicals, *Ang Larawan* is our favorite because of the many geniuses involved in the project and because of what it stands for—the battle between materialism and art.... as Rolando Tinio put it... "this is the struggle of the vulgar and the sublime."

Some time ago, we observed there was a dearth of Filipino films to offer schools. There must be a need for the creation of relevant and educational viewing for students.

Together with Rachel Alejandro, who had joined us in our producing endeavor, we were already thinking of bringing *Ang Larawan* to the big screen. We felt this musical can be an alternative to the mainstream romantic comedies, horror movies and similar flicks.

We feel the current audience is going to enjoy *Ang Larawan*. Most of all, we are hopeful that they are going to be provoked by it, especially now that we live in a materialistic society.

Turning *Ang Larawan* into a movie is our response to the need for films with educational and cultural value. It is also our effort to preserve the great works of our Filipino artists so that the youth can learn, be challenged and cherish our Filipino history and culture.

After reading the play and watching the film, we want today's kids to be involved in a discussion: about why Paula did what she did to the thing that could have changed their lives; about how Filipinos used to live and behave; about how much we may have lost; about how our history evolved and brought us to today.

Celeste Legaspi
with
Girlie Rodis and
Rachel Alejandro
Executive Producers
Ang Larawan

DIRECTOR'S NOTES

Music is deeply ingrained in the Filipino consciousness, but that has seldom been fully explored in the realm of film. And as a nation, we, Filipinos, have the tendency to deny and forget our own history in pursuit of the now and the here. That tendency has brought us to the messy crossroads that the nation faces right now. I took on *Ang Larawan* because I felt it touches on these two seemingly opposing facets: music and our nation's history. Hopefully, the film will help open up a clearer understanding of why we, Filipinos, are what we are at the moment, both to ourselves and to the rest of the world...

Loy Arcenas

ABOUT THE DIRECTOR

Loy Arcenas is an award-winning production designer and director in the US and the Philippines.

Some of the Broadway productions he designed were *Once On This Island, Prelude To A Kiss, Love! Valour! Compassion* and *Chita Rivera: The Dancer's Life*. He also created sets for off-Broadway and major American regional theater companies, and collaborated with distinguished American playwrights and directors such as Joe Mantella, George C. Wolfe, Anne Bogart, Robert Falls, Terrence McNally, Craig Lucas, and Paul Vogel.

His exemplary work was recognized with an Obie for Sustained Excellence of Scenic Design, Drama Desk Award, Bay Area Critics Circle Award, Jefferson Award, L.A. Drama Critics Circle Award, and Michael Merritt Award for Design Collaboration.

In 2011, Arcenas returned to the Philippines to make his first full-length feature film, *Niño*, a story about the decline of an affluent Filipino family. *Niño* won a Special Jury Prize at the 2011 Cinemalaya Film Festival and was co-winner of Best Film at the 2011 Busan International Film Festival's New Currents Section. It also received Special Mention and Emile Guimet Awards at the 2012 Vesoul International Film Festival of Asian Cinema.

His second feature, *Requieme*, a comedy about how two deaths affect an estranged mother and gay son, received a Special Jury Prize at the 2012 Cinemalaya Film Festival.

Ang Larawan is his third full-length feature film.

Heartthrob Paulo Avelino portrays Tony Javier in *Ang Larawan, The Movie*.

Rachel Alejandro was too young when she first played Paula in the stage musical. Twenty years later, she was the right age to portray Paula in the movie.

Ang Larawan is the first full-length feature film of Westend star and international recording artist Joanna Ampil.

Joanna Ampil (*left*) and Rachel Alejandro (*right*) take on the roles of the Marasigan sisters Candida and Paula.

Sandino Martin (*center*) as reporter Bitoy Camacho examining the painting of Don Lorenzo Marasigan.

Stage stalwarts Menchu Lauchengco-Yulo and Nonie Buencamino are the Marasigan siblings Pepang and Manolo.

Veteran actor Robert Arevalo as Don Perico with young jazz singer Cara Manglapus as Patsy and Celeste Legaspi as Doña Loleng.

Singers Aicelle Santos (as Violet), Ogie Alcasid (as Pulis Tinio) and Cris Villonco (as Susan) make special appearances in the movie.

Zsa Zsa Padilla plays Elsa Montes, the Filipina socialite from New York.

Rayver Cruz as Charlie Dacanay

The finale scene with veteran stars Nanette Inventor as Donya Irene, Noel Trinidad as Don Miguel, Jaime Fabregas as Don Aristeo, Dulce as Donya Upeng, Bernardo Bernardo as Don Alvaro.

THE MOVIE

Rachel Alejandro as Paula praying in San Agustin Church in Intramuros.

Joanna Ampil as Candida joining the throng of churchgoers.

The actual image of the Virgin of La Naval borrowed from the Sto. Domingo Parish.

Over 700 people participated in the La Naval procession scene filmed in Intramuros, Manila.

ANG LARAWAN

Dulang Pampelikula ni Rolando Tinio,
National Artist for Theater and Literature

Hango sa dulang musikal na *ANG LARAWAN*
Libretto ni Rolando Tinio na hango sa dulang may tatlong yugto na
A PORTRAIT OF THE ARTIST AS FILIPINO
ni Nick Joaquin, National Artist for Literature

Musika ni Ryan Cayabyab
Produksiyon ng Culturtain Musicat Productions
Direktor: Loy Arcenas
Script Editor: Waya Gallardo

MGA NAGSIGANAP

Joanna Ampil bilang Candida
Rachel Alejandro bilang Paula
Paulo Avelino bilang Tony Javier
Nonie Buencamino bilang Manolo
Menchu Lauchengco-Yulo bilang Pepang
Robert Arevalo bilang Senador Perico
Celeste Legaspi bilang Donya Loleng
Sandino Martin bilang Bitoy
Cris Villonco bilang Susan
Aicelle Santos bilang Violet

Espesyal na partisipasyon nina
Ogie Alcasid bilang Pulis Tinio
at
Zsa Zsa Padilla bilang Elsa Montes

at
Bernardo Bernardo bilang Don Alvaro
Jaime Fabregas bilang Don Aristeo
Noel Trinidad bilang Don Miguel
Dulce bilang Donya Upeng
Nanette Inventor bilang Donya Irene
Rayver Cruz bilang Charlie Dacanay
Cara Manglapus bilang Patsy
Jojit Lorenzo bilang Pulis Bernal
Leo Rialp bilang Don Lorenzo Marasigan

*PAALALA: Lahat ng bahaging naka-**bold** ay inaawit.*

1. INT/EXT. INTRAMUROS. ARAW.
PROLOGO. *Habang tumutugtog ang isang lumang awitin, makikita ang iba't ibang mga eksena at sitwasyon sa Intramuros noong dekada '40 na pawang archival footage na black-and-white tulad ng mga babaeng nagsisimba, mga babaeng nagtitinda, bandera ng Amerikano at Pilipinas na sabay na nagwawagayway, mga sundalong nagmamartsa, at iba pa. Ang susunod na awitin ay maririning na waring awit na nagmumula sa makalumang radyo.*

BABAENG MANG-AAWIT

Intramuros, masdan ang nakalipas. Kagandahan, unti nang kumukupas. Intramuros, ang Maynilang lumipas, ang alahas ng Kastilang Pilipinas. Nagbagong lahat, pati na watawat. Galak nakayakap. Makabagong aklat. Intramuros, ang siyudad na iniwan. Iniwanan makalumang lipunan.

Fade in title credit: ANG LARAWAN

2. EXT. KALYE NG INTRAMUROS. ARAW.
Mula sa black-and-white footage ng prologo, unti-unting magkakakulay ang eksena at makikita ang isang lalaking nagbibisikleta sa loob ng Intramuros. Ito ang Intramuros noong Oktubre 1941, bago magsimula ang Ikalawang Digmaang Pandaigdig. Ang lalaking nagbibisikleta ay si BITOY CAMACHO, nasa edad na 25, isang baguhang peryodista.

Patuloy ang babaeng boses na kumakanta.

> BABAENG MANG-AAWIT
> **Intramuros, ang Maynilang lumipas.**
> **Intramuros, limot na kasaysayan!**

Titigil si BITOY sa tapat ng isang bahay kung saan naghihintay ang ilan sa kanyang mga kasama sa trabaho: DALAWANG REPORTER—isang babae at isang lalaki—at isang POTOGRAPO na may dalang kamera.

Kakausapin sila ni BITOY.

> BITOY
> Akin na ang kamera.

> BABAENG REPORTER
> Ano?

> BITOY
> Ako na papasok.

> LALAKING REPORTER
> *(Tatango. Ibibigay ang kamera kay Bitoy at kukunin ang bisikleta ni Bitoy.)*
> Ako na ang bahala rito.

Tatanggalin ni BITOY ang kaniyang amerikana at aabutin ang kamera. Magmamadali si Bitoy na pumasok sa bahay. Titigil si Bitoy sa harap ng pinto ng bahay at titingnan nang makahulugan ang mga kasama. Papasok si Bitoy sa bahay.

3. INT. BAHAY NG MGA MARASIGAN (SILONG). ARAW.
Pagpasok ni BITOY sa silong ng bahay, sari-saring lumang gamit ang babati sa kanyang paningin: mga laruan, muwebles, mga larawan at iba pa. Ang lahat ng mga ito ay tinatakpan ng telang maalikabok. Ginawang bodega ang silong, tambakan ng mga alaala. Pagmamasdan ni BITOY ang mga nasa paligid at hahawakan ang ilan sa mga gamit. Mabagal na maglalakad at aakyat sa hagdan.

Boses ng matandang si BITOY ang maririnig.

       MATANDANG BITOY
  (voice-over)
  May nag-iisang bahay
  Sa gubat na marusing
  Na ayaw pang palulon
  Sa lupit ng panahon.
  Pagpasok mo sa antigong puwerta
  Nababalik ka sa mundo ng ganda
  At ng seremonya.

4. INT. RECIBIDOR. ARAW.
Madaratnan ni Bitoy si CANDIDA MARASIGAN, mga nasa edad na 41, na nag-aayos ng lamesa.

       BITOY
      Candida...

Titigil si CANDIDA sa kaniyang ginagawa at lalapit sa bagong dating.

       CANDIDA
      Bitoy?

Tatango si BITOY.

       CANDIDA
  Ang tanda mo na!

       BITOY
  Beynte singko na ako...Hindi ka nagbago!

       CANDIDA
  Anong hindi? Nang huli mo 'kong makita, marangya pa akong senyorita. Mataas ang pangarap—siguradong darating at tatangay sa akin ang Prinsipe ng Asturias.

Matatawa nang bahagya si BITOY.

       BITOY
  Dumating ba ang Prinsipe ng Asturias?

CANDIDA
Walang dumating. Wala nang dumarating na kahit sino pa.

BITOY
Kahit Biyernes ng gabi—

CANDIDA
Wala nang tertulya. Nangamamatay na ang mga matanda.

Tatawagin ni CANDIDA ang kapatid na si PAULANG nasa sala.

CANDIDA
Paula. Nandito si Bitoy!

Lalabas si PAULA MARASIGAN, edad na 40, mula sa sala.

PAULA
Bi-Bitoy?

BITOY
Ang mga tertulya—

PAULA
Bitoy, natatandaan mo pa?

BITOY
Kasama 'kong lagi ng Papa…

PAULA
Ang liit mo pa noon!

BITOY
'Pag Sabado sa Binondo, sa bahay ng mga Monson. 'Pag Lunes sa Quiapo, sa Botica ni Doktor Moreta. Miyerkoles sa Carriedo, sa tindahan ng mga libro ni Don Aristeo. **At 'pag Biyernes, sa bahay ng mga Marasigan!**

5.   INT. SALA. GABI.
PAGBABALIK-TANAW. *Ipipikit ni PAULA ang kanyang mga mata, sinasariwa sa alaala ang mga tertulyang ginanap sa kanilang tahanan. May tertulya na naman sa bahay ng mga Marasigan. Maraming bisita. Lahat sila'y nakasuot ng magarbong kasuotan. Bubuksan ni PAULA ang kanyang mga mata at magsasalita na parang kaharap niya ang mga donya at don na bumibisita sa kanilang bahay noon.*

PAULA
Brandy pa, Don Pepe... Brandy pa, Don Isidro. Mapresko sa may
bintana. Do'n tayo, Donya Upeng.

*Suot pa rin nina Candida at Paula ang luma nilang damit pambahay habang
nakikisalamuha sa mga magagarang bisita na suot ang kanilang mga traje de boda at
amerikana. Maingay at masayang kumakain at nag-uusap ang mga tao. Sa eksenang ito
patuloy na maririnig ang pagkanta.*

PAULA
**Donya Irene, ang tula ng dakilang si Ruben ang pinag-uusapan:
"Tuvo razon tu abuela con su cabello cano...**

PAULA AT CANDIDA
...muy mas que tu con rizas...

PAULA
...en que se enrosca el dia..."

CANDIDA
**Sa banda rito, Don Aristeo! Brandy, Paula, ang gusto ni Don
Aristeo!**

PAULA
(Mag-aabot kunwari ng baso ng brandi.) **Puwera ang politika sa
usapan dito!**

CANDIDA
**Oo, Donya Irene. Ang dalas naming nanood sa kompanya ng
sarsuwelang 'yon.**

PAULA
**Ituloy, Don Alvaro ang kuwento mo tungkol kay Heneral
Aguinaldo.**

6. INT. SALA. ARAW.
*Matatapos ang pagbabalik-alaala. May ngiti sa mga labi nina CANDIDA at PAULA.
Lalapit si BITOY patungo sa kung saan nakasabit sa dingding ang larawang ipininta ni
Don Lorenzo Marasigan, ama nina Candida at Paula.*

BITOY
Iyan ba?

CANDIDA
Oo.

BITOY
Kailan pininta ng inyong Papa?

PAULA
May isang taon na.

BITOY
Kagilagilalas!

CANDIDA
Ang tawag niya—"Retrato del Artista Como Filipino."

PAULA
"Larawan ng Pintor Bilang Pilipino."

BITOY
Ngunit bakit? Hindi Pilipino ang eksenang 'yan. Ano'ng ibig niyang ipakahulugan? Matandang nakababa sa bata pang isa; sa likod ng dalawa, nasusunog na lungsod.

PAULA
Si Papa ang matanda.

CANDIDA
Si Papa rin naman ang batang nariyan—si Papa sa panahon ng kanyang kabataan.

BITOY
Oo nga, oo nga!

PAULA
At ang lungsod na nag-aapoy—

BITOY
Ang lungsod ng Troya, Hindi ba, hindi ba?

PAULA
Alam mo pala ang lamang istorya.

BITOY
Bitbit ni Eneas si Angkises na ama paglikas sa Troya; pininta ng Papa n'yo ang sarili niya sa papel ni Eneas at ni Angkises pa.

CANDIDA
Ang sarili ngayon at ang sarili niya no'ng nagdaang panahon.

BITOY
Kagimbal-gimbal ang dating sa akin.

CANDIDA
Ang epekto pala sa iyo'y gano'n din.

BITOY
Parang nagdodoble ang aking paningin.

CANDIDA
Kung minsan, isip ko—sa 'yang halimaw! Nag-iisang tao na dalawa ang ulo!

BITOY
Alam n'yo bang may Pranses na turistang sumulat ng artikulo. Panay ang pagpuri sa larawan ninyo?

PAULA
Noon pang tagahanga ng Papa ang mama. Nagkilala sila sa Madrid at Barcelona.

Maglalabas si Bitoy ng kamera at magsisimulang kunan ng retrato ang larawang pininta ni Don Lorenzo.

CANDIDA
Sabihin mo, Bitoy, reporter ka ba sa isang peryodiko?

BITOY
A, oo... oo...

CANDIDA
Kaya ka lang pala napadalaw sa amin.

PAULA
Lahat ng maparito hindi kami ang sadya, kundi ang retrato.

BITOY
Dapat kayong matuwa. Dapat kayong magmarangal. Maraming nag-akalang patay na'ng inyong Papa. Ngayong pagkaraan ng maraming taon, siya'ng pinag-uusapan ng lahat kahit saan. Nabulabog ang bayan—si Don Lorenzo Marasigan, ang dakilang

pintor na kaibiga't karibal ng dakilang si Juan Luna'y hindi lang pala buhay, nakalikha pa man ng isa pang obra maestra sa kaniyang katandaan!

PAULA
Ginawa ng Papa ang larawang 'yan para sa 'min ni Candida. Isang taong tahimik na nakasabit diyan. Nang dumating ang Pranses at sumulat siya, hindi na kami natahimik, hindi na. Araw-araw na lang may reporter sa diyaryo o potograpo o estudyanteng napaparito. At kami—ayaw namin ng gano'n. Ayaw namin. Ayaw namin, Bitoy.

Mahihiya si BITOY sa kaniyang ginawa. Itatabi niya ang kaniyang kamera.

BITOY
Patawarin n'yo ako, Candida at Paula. Bueno, kailangan kong lumakad na.

CANDIDA
Huwag, Bitoy! Magmeryenda ka. 'Sang tasa pa, Paula!

BITOY
May naghihintay sa 'kin.

PAULA
Maupo ka, Bitoy.

CANDIDA
Eto, Paula. *(Iaabot kay PAULA ang tasa.)* At sabihin sa Papang dinadalaw siya ng anak ng kaibigan niyang si Camacho.

Tatango si PAULA at aalis patungong kuwarto ni Don Lorenzo, dala ang tasa ng tsokolate para ibigay sa kanilang ama. Maiiwan sina CANDIDA at BITOY sa sala.

BITOY
Kumusta siya, ang inyong Papa, Si Don Lorenzo el magnifico?

CANDIDA
Mabuti naman.

BITOY
Hindi na ba kayang lumabas ng kuwarto?

CANDIDA
Naaksidente siya.

BITOY
Kailan?

CANDIDA
No'ng isang taon pa.

BITOY
Nang kaniyang ipininta ang retrato?

CANDIDA
Nang matapos ang obra, hindi namin nakita. **Nangyari sa gabi. Naglakad siguro sa pagtulog at nahulog… Mula sa balkon ng kuwarto… Nahulog sa patyo.**

BITOY
Diyos ko! Nabalian ba?

CANDIDA
Salamat sa Diyos, hindi naman.

BITOY
Ano'ng lagay ngayon?

CANDIDA
Bitoy, alam mo ba, isang taon na ngayong hindi lumalabas sa kuwarto niya? Naku, sinisisi namin ang aming sarili sa nangyari.

BITOY
Ngunit bakit? Aksidente 'ka mo ang nangyari.

CANDIDA
Aksidente ang…

Darating si PAULA.

PAULA
Halika, Bitoy! Tuwang-tuwa ang Papa, puntahan daw siya!

BITOY
Salamat, Paula.

CANDIDA
Bitoy... hindi ka reporter. Isa kang kaibigan. Hindi ka naparito para kumuha ng retrato o mag-interbyu. Naparito ka lang para bumisita.

BITOY
Oo, Candida.

Sasamahan ni Paula si Bitoy sa kuwarto ni Don Lorenzo.

Pag-aaralan ni CANDIDA ang mga papel na nasa mesa. Babalik si Paula sa sala.

PAULA
Masigla silang nag-uusap. Bumubuti na yata ang lagay ng Papa!

Maghahanda si Paula ng tsokolate para sa sarili. Patuloy na titingnan ni CANDIDA ang mga papel na parang hindi narinig ang sinabi ni Paula. Iiling si CANDIDA, iritable.

PAULA
Mga utang natin?

Isa-isang ipakikita ni CANDIDA ang mga papel na listahan ng mga bayarin.

CANDIDA
Sa gas, sa tubig, sa doktor, at ito—sa kuryente. "Muli namin kayong pinagsasabihan na pag hindi nabayaran agad ang inyong mga utang, mapipilitan kaming putulan kayo ng serbisyo." Pangatlong babala na ito.

PAULA
Nagsabi ka ba kay Manolo?

CANDIDA
Tinawagan ko siya. Tinawagan ko si Pepang. Ang sabi nila, oo, magpapadala ng pera. Isang buwan nang nagsasabi, wala namang padala.

PAULA
Ang mga mahal nating kapatid!

CANDIDA
Ang gusto ng dalawa, iwanan na natin ang bahay na ito.

                              PAULA
                     Hindi nila tayo mapipilit!

                             CANDIDA
                Dito tayo ipinanganak, dito tayo mamamatay.

                              PAULA
              Pa'no kung umayaw na silang magsustento pa sa atin?

                             CANDIDA
                        May bago akong idea.

7.   INT. SALA. PAGPAPATULOY.
Darating si TONY JAVIER, nasa edad na mga 29, tagapiyano at arogante. Mapuputol ang usapan ng magkapatid.

                               TONY
                 Magandang hapon, mga binibini! Aba, meryenda!

                             CANDIDA
                    Gusto mo ng tsokolate, Mister Javier?

                               TONY
             Tsk, tsk... Masama 'yan sa negosyo. Kuwarto lang ang arkilado ko!

Hindi papansinin ni CANDIDA ang pang-aasar ni TONY.

                             CANDIDA
                         Paula, isang tasa pa.

Kukunin ni TONY ang tasa ng tsokolate na ininuman ni PAULA. Iinumin ni TONY ang natirang tsokolate sa tasa habang inaakit niya si PAULA sa kaniyang tingin.

                               TONY
                  Naku, para ano? Puwede na ang tasang ito.

                             CANDIDA
              Mister Javier! Inuutos kong ibaba mo ang tasang 'yan ngayon din!

                               TONY
                         Salamat, Miss Paula.

Mauubos ni TONY ang tsokolate sa tasa. Iaangat ni TONY ang tasa na kunwari ay nagpupugay siya kay CANDIDA.

TONY
Sa masamang negosyo!

CANDIDA
Mister Javier, kalunos-lunos—

TONY
Masarap nga!

Didilaan ni TONY ang kaniyang mga labi.

CANDIDA
Walang kuwentang tratuhin ka nang disente!

TONY
Pahintulutan n'yong ilayo ko sa inyong paningin ang malaswa kong pagkatao. O... at salamat sa tsokolate.

CANDIDA
Mister Javier, may sasabihin kami sa 'yo.

TONY
Ano 'yon?

Biglang daramputin ni PAULA ang tsokolatera.

PAULA
Kailangang ilabas ito sa kusina.

Magtatangka si PAULA na umalis. Pipigilan siya ni CANDIDA.

CANDIDA
Dumito ka, Paula.

Mananatili si PAULA kung saan siya nakatayo.

TONY
Ano ba'ng gusto n'yo? Gusto kong humiga bago umalis uli. Pagod na pagod ako. Kulang ako sa tulog. Nag-aaral sa araw, trabaho sa gabi. May ambisyon kasi.

Tingnan n'yo ko, isang tagapiyano sa bulok na bodabil. Hindi ako piyanista. Alam n'yo ba'ng diperensiya ng piyanista at tagapiyano? Sasabihin ko…

Tutugtugin ni TONY ang piyano.

TONY
Ang piyanista, aral sa konserbatoryo at nagkokonsiyerto sa alta sosyedad. May kultura ang piyanista. Samantala… ang tagapiyanong tulad ko, walang naging titser. Nag-aral nang sarili at alam na alam kong walang kuwenta ang tugtog ko.

Tumitipa ng piyano sa bulok na bodabil. Tatlong tugtog sa isang araw sa bulok na sinehan. Dinuduraan sa batok ng mga manonood. Parang lata ang tunog ng piyano mong bulok. At hindi mo alam kung hanggang kailan ang trabaho mo.

CANDIDA
Mister Javier! Nang pumayag kaming rumenta ka sa amin, may isang kondisyon—hindi ka magdadala ng sugal o alak o babae sa kuwarto.

TONY
E 'no ngayon?

CANDIDA
Nilabag mo ang aming reglamento.

TONY
Hindi ako nagsusugal.

CANDIDA
Hindi sugal ang tinutukoy ko.

TONY
Bueno, sige, nagseserbesa 'kong minsan.

CANDIDA
O ang pag-inom mo.

TONY
Ang ibig mong sabihin—

Tatanggalin ni TONY ang kaniyang sombrero. Aasarin niya si CANDIDA. Ilalagay ni TONY sa harap ng kaniyang pundiya at iaangat ang sombrero.

CANDIDA
Mismo!

Matatawa si TONY. Mananatiling nakasimangot si CANDIDA.

May mga tapak na maririnig paakyat ng hagdanan. Darating ang mga nagsisihagikgik na sina SUSAN at VIOLET, mga mananayaw sa bodabil.

SUSAN AT VIOLET
Yuhuuuu!

CANDIDA
Sino kayo?

SUSAN
Ako si Susan.

VIOLET
Ako si Violet.

Iaabot ni VIOLET ang kanyang kamay kay CANDIDA pero tatalikuran siya ni CANDIDA. Hindi matitinag si VIOLET, maging si SUSAN. Patuloy silang mambubulabog sa tahanan ng mga Marasigan.

SUSAN
Mga artista sa Teatro Parisian!

VIOLET
Mga istar sa entablado!

SUSAN
Mga hiyas ng bodabil!

TONY
Ano'ng ginagawa n'yo rito?

SUSAN/VIOLET
Gusto naming makita kung sa'n ka nakatira!

TONY
Nakita n'yo na. Layas na!

SUSAN
Huwag kang magsalita nang ganyan. Titigil kami rito, hanggang kahit kailan.

TONY
Susan, lasing ka. Umuwi ka muna. Sa loob ng 'sang oras magpapalabas na.

SUSAN
Bitiwan mo ako! Uuwi ako kung kailan ko gusto!

TONY
Ano ba'ng problema mo't gumagawa ka ng gulo?

May galit sa tono ng boses ni TONY kaya't sesenyas si VIOLET kay SUSAN, yayayain ang kaibigan na umuwi. Hindi aalis si SUSAN.

SUSAN
Ano'ng keber mo?

TONY
May nagawa ba ako?

Biglang maglalambing si SUSAN kay TONY.

SUSAN
Saan ka naroon kagabi? Saan ka nagpunta pagbaba ng kurtina?

TONY
Sumakit ang ulo ko. Umuwi ako rito.

Babalik si BITOY sa sala. Mapapatingin sa kaniya si TONY.

TONY
Aba, kaibigan! Nandiyan ka pala!

BITOY
Tony, kumusta?

Gulat si CANDIDA na magkakilala pala ang dalawang lalaki.

CANDIDA
Magkakilala kayo?

BITOY
Nagkasama kami sa trabaho sa piyer. *(Kay Tony.)* Ano'ng ginagawa mo rito?

TONY
Dito ako nakatira.

BITOY
(Hindi makapaniwala.)
Bola!

CANDIDA
Nagpapaupa kami ng ilang mga kuwarto. Si Mister Javier pa lang—

Tumatakbong darating si PAULA galing sa kusina.

PAULA
Candida! Candida! May daga, may daga sa ating kusina! Kasinlaki ng pusa!

Lalabas ang magkapatid. Susunod sina SUSAN and VIOLET na parehong tumatawa.

TONY
(Iiling.)
Mga sira ang ulo!

BITOY
Mga matandang kaibigan ng aking pamilya.

TONY
Puwes, huwag kang masyadong dumikit sa kanila. Gutom na gutom sila sa lalaki.

BITOY
Bakit, sinubukan ka bang kainin?

TONY
Parehong sira. Nangangatal pag nasa harap ko. Pag kinausap ko, nilalagnat. At pag hinipo ko—

BITOY
Niligawan mo ba?

TONY
Niligawan sila? Pwe! *(Dudura.)* Ligawan ko na lang ang Jones Bridge! Sila ang baliw, hindi ako!

BITOY
Pobreng-pobre kasi.

TONY
Nakikita mo ang larawang 'yan? May Amerikano akong handang bilhin 'yan ng dos mil dolyares. Dolyares, ha! Ang tagal ko nang pinipilit.

BITOY
Ikaw?

TONY
Kinuha akong tagapamagitan.

BITOY
Walang nangyari? Mahal na mahal siguro ang larawan ng ama.

TONY
Kinamumuhian nga.

BITOY
Pa'no mong nalaman?

TONY
Kinamumuhian ko rin!

TONY
Palaging nakatitig, minamaliit ako, iniismiran. Kahit sa loob ng aking kuwarto, lumulusot sa kuwarto ko ang ngiti niyang nagmamayabang.

BITOY
Ang larawan ba'ng tinutukoy mo o ang matandang baldado?

TONY
Kagagaling mo sa kuwarto ni Don Lorenzo el magnifico. Ilan buwan na 'ko rito, ni minsan hindi pa 'ko inimbita sa kuwartong pinagkukulungan. Pinasok ko siyang minsan nang sapilitan.

BITOY
Pinalayas ka?

TONY
Naku, hindi. Mapitagang-mapitagan siya. Nang sabihin kong may Amerikanong gustong bumili ng kaniyang obra, nakangiting humingi ng paumanhin. "Sa mga anak kong dalaga 'yan; hindi na akin. Kung may interesado ro'n, sila ang kausapin." Saka nagsabing magsisiyesta siya. At walang kaano-ano, napaiskram ako… Naku, magbabayad siya. Magbabayad siya. At alam ko kung paano ko siya pagbabayarin!

BITOY
Ba't ba masugid kang maibenta ang retrato?

TONY
Dahi sa porsiyentong pinangako ng Amerikano.

Darating sina CANDIDA at PAULA kasunod sina SUSAN at VIOLET.

TONY
Aba, mga binibini, nahuli n'yong daga?

PAULA
Siyempre naman, Mister Javier, walang nakaliligtas kay Candida.

TONY
Kampeon sa pagpaptay ng daga!

CANDIDA
Masasabing eksperto.

BITOY
Pa'no ba'ng ginagawa mo?

CANDIDA
Kailangan siyempre ng talento!

TONY
Talentong ekstraordinaryo!

CANDIDA
At pinaplano kong pagkakitaan ang aking kaalaman.

Tatawa muli sina SUSAN at VIOLET. Titingnan sila nang masama ni BITOY.

TONY
Violet, puwede ba? Iuwi mo si Susan nang mabanyusan mo.

VIOLET
Ayoko. Gusto naming mag-ensayo.

TONY
Ng ano?

VIOLET
Ng number namin mam'ya.

SUSAN
(Kay TONY.) Kung hindi ka umalis, kagabi pa namin napraktis.

TONY
(Tutugtog sa piyano.) O sige na, bilis!

SUSAN/VIOLET
"A-tithket, a-tathket, ipathok mo tha bathket. Then put it in your pocket. Don't athk na lang kung baket."

Eensayuhin nina SUSAN at VIOLET ang kanilang dance number habang tumutugtog si TONY ng piyano.

CANDIDA
Huwag kayong maingay, natutulog ang Papa!

TONY
Uwi na nga naman!

SUSAN
Ayoko pa!

TONY
Uwi na!

VIOLET
Bakit? Sino sila?

SUSAN
Sila ba'ng may-ari ng casa?

VIOLET
Alam ko kung anong klase sila!

SUSAN
(Kay TONY.) **Kitang-kita kita. Isinama mo rito yaong Intsik beha!**

TONY
Sharap na!

VIOLET / SUSAN
(Kina CANDIDA at PAULA.) **Alam na alam ko ang sistema ninyo!**

TONY
(Kina SUSAN at VIOLET.) Layas na, layas na!

BITOY
Sige na, pakiusap lang!

Aalis sina SUSAN at VIOLET nang tangay-tangay si TONY. Kakausapin ni BITOY sina PAULA at CANDIDA.

BITOY
Lalakad na rin ako. Pupuntahan ko na ang mga kaibigan ko.
Sasabihin kong tulog ang Papa n'yo.

CANDIDA
Babalik ka?

BITOY
Aba, siyempre naman!

Lalabas si BITOY.

8. INT. SALA. PAGPAPATULOY.
Tahimik na panonoorin nina CANDIDA at PAULA na lumabas si BITOY ng pinto ng bahay. Nang nakaalis na si BITOY, kakausapin ni PAULA si CANDIDA.

PAULA
Nakatatawa si Mr. Javier, hindi ba?

CANDIDA
Maniniwala ka ba naman sa pagtestigo ng lasengga?

PAULA
Bukod sa ro'n, kailangan natin ng 'binabayad niyang pera.

CANDIDA
Alam ko'ng gagawin natin.

Ipakikita ni CANDIDA ang pahayagan kay PAULA.

CANDIDA
Tingnan mo: "Singkuwenta sentimos para sa bawat dagang mahuli." Pupunta 'ko sa— sa'n ba naro'n ang Oficina de Sanidad y Ciencia? Kuruin mo, babayaran ako para gawin ang gustong-gusto kong ginagawa. Ikaw naman, magbibigay ng leksiyon sa pagpipiyano at pag-e-Espanyol. Maglalagay tayo ng karatula sa harap.

PAULA
Leksiyon para kanino?

CANDIDA
Mga babae sa pagpipiyano, mga lalaki sa pag-e-Espanyol.

PAULA
Pagtatawanan ako.

CANDIDA
Kapag binastos ka ng mga lalaki, tumawag ka lang ng pulis! Malaki ang kikitain natin. Hindi na nila tayo mapipilit umalis. Makikita nina Pepang at Manolong kaya nating sustentuhan ang bahay na ito.

PAULA
Hindi na natin kailangang mangamba. Hindi na natin kailangang mangamba.

CANDIDA/PAULA
Mananatili tayo rito hanggang mamatay tayo—ikaw, ako at ang Papa! Gagaling siya, lalabas siya sa kuwarto. Liligaya uli tayo. Magkakasama tayong tatlo.

CANDIDA
Kay sarap ng buhay no'ng araw. Maayos ang bihis ng lahat. Parang haplos pag-ihip ng hangin pag may mga ideal.

PAULA
Poesiya ang ating agahan. May awit na kalong kung gabi. Sining ang lagi nang kapitbahay. Pag may mga ideal.

CANDIDA/PAULA
Kagandahan, katotohanan ang panlaban ko sa mundo. Wala akong takot, walang panlulumo, bumaha man o bumagyo.

CANDIDA
Maibabalik ba natin ang mga araw na 'yon?

Maaalala nila CANDIDA at PAULA ang kanilang kabataan...nag-uusap, nagbibiruan, nagtatawanan sila sa sala.

CANDIDA/PAULA
Kagandahan, katotohanan ang panlaban ko sa mundo. Wala akong takot, walang panlulumo, bumaha man o bumagyo.

Pagmamasdan nina PAULA at CANDIDA ang mga retrato ng pamilya na nakasabit sa dingding ng sala.

PAULA
Ang saya natin noon! Bakit natin sinira ang ating kaligayahan? Bakit naaksidente ang Papa? Bakit niya pininta ang larawang 'yon?

9. INT/EXT. MONTAGE. SA IBA'T IBANG BAHAGI NG BAHAY. TAKIPSILIM.

9A. EXT. KALYE NG INTRAMUROS.
May kotse at mga taong nagdaraan sa kalye. Pauwi na ang mga tao sa kani-kanilang mga tahanan.

9B. INT. KUSINA.
Nagluluto si CANDIDA ng hapunan.

9C. EXT. BAHAY NG MGA MARASIGAN (SA LABAHAN).
Nagsisilong si PAULA, tinatanggal niya ang mga tuyong damit mula sa sampayan. Makikita ni PAULA ang butas sa damit at mapapabuntonghininga.

END OF MONTAGE.

cut to:

10. INT. SALA. GABI.
Gabi na. Isasara ni CANDIDA ang bintanang capiz sa sala habang sinasara ni PAULA ang mga bintana sa ibang bahagi ng bahay. Papasok si PAULA sa sala.

PAULA
Candida, walang ilaw!

CANDIDA
Subukan mo uli!

PAULA
Ilang beses ko nang sinubukan nang sinubukan!

CANDIDA
Subukan mo sa ibaba ng hagdanan. Susubukan ko sa pasilyo.

Bababa si PAULA sa hagdanan. Papasok si CANDIDA sa pasilyo.

CANDIDA
Wala ring ilaw sa hagdanan?

PAULA
Wala! May ilaw ba sa pasilyo?

CANDIDA
Wala. At wala ring ilaw sa kuwarto ng Papa!

PAULA
Naku, Candida, pinutulan tayo ng kuryente! Tawagan mo sina Manolo't Pepang! Tawagan mo ang kompanya ng ilaw!

CANDIDA
Huwag kang maingay! Gusto mong makitawag ako sa kanto? Alam na ng lahat sa kalye nating pinutulan tayo ng kuryente dahil hindi tayo nakabayad!

PAULA
Naku, Candida! Naku, Candida!

CANDIDA
Sarhan mo'ng mga bintana!

PAULA
Makikita ako ng mga kapitbahay!

CANDIDA
Alam ko na'ng tsismisan nila! Tingnan mo'ng dalawang nagrereyna-reyna, ni hindi makabayad sa kuryente nila!

PAULA
Paano pa natin maihaharap mga mukha natin sa labas?

Itutulak ni CANDIDA si PAULA.

CANDIDA
Sarhan mo'ng mga bintana!

PAULA
Makikita nila tayo.

CANDIDA
Baka wala pang nakapapansing madilim ang ating bahay!

Dahan-dahang lalapit si CANDIDA sa bintana at dudungaw sa labas.

CANDIDA
Walang ilaw kahit saan!

PAULA
Walang ilaw?

CANDIDA
Madilim lahat ng bahay!

PAULA
Madilim?

CANDIDA
Madilim ang buong lansangan!

PAULA
Ano'ng nangyari?

Matatawa nang malakas si CANDIDA.

CANDIDA
Napakagaga natin!

PAULA
Ano ba ang nangyari?

CANDIDA
Walang ngang nangyari!

PAULA
Ano'ng wala?

CANDIDA
Nasa diyaryo nga pala! Hindi kasi tayo nagbabasa!

PAULA
Ano'ng sabi sa diyaryo?

CANDIDA
(Patuloy na tatawa.) May blackout ngayon. Nagpapraktis ng blackout! Naghahanda para sa giyera. At akala natin… Natatakot tayong magsara ng bintana! Natatakot tayong matanaw ng kapitbahay! Di ba isang pares tayong tonta at kalahati?! Isang pares na tonta! Naku, Paula! Nakatatawa! Nakatatawa! Nakatatawa!

Patuloy na tatawa si CANDIDA hanggang sa mapahagulgol. Lalapitan siya ni PAULA at yayakapin ito.

PAULA
Candida, Candida...

CANDIDA
Hindi ko na kaya! Hindi ko na kaya!

Mapapasalampak si Candida sa sahig dahil sa panlulumo.

11. INT. SALA. ARAW.
Pagkaraan ng isang linggo. Mga alas diyes ng umaga, nasa bahay ng mga Marasigan sina MANOLO AT PEPANG, ang mga nakatatandang kapatid nina CANDIDA at PAULA. Pinagmamasdan nina MANOLO at PEPANG ang LARAWAN.

PEPANG
Ang idolo ng ating kabataan, Manolo.

MANOLO
Higit pa sa idolo ang Papa!

PEPANG
Ang ating Diyos Ama!

MANOLO
Ang mundo at langit—

PEPANG
Buwan at araw at mga bituin!

MANOLO
Ang buong uniberso!

PEPANG
Ang sarap magkaro'n ng amang isang henyo!

MANOLO
Ang lupit, sabihin mo!

PEPANG
Masakit ding talikuran ang idolo ng nakaraan!

MANOLO
Tingnan mo si Don Eneas— karga-karga ang sariling ama!

PEPANG
'Yon ba ang ibig ipahiwatig ng Papa? Na iniwanan natin siyang nagkakarga sa sarili niya?

MANOLO
Magtigil ka! Hindi natin siya pinababayaan! Nandiyan sina Paula at Candida.

PEPANG
Namalengkeng pihado ang dalawa.

MANOLO
Lalo nang nagiging loka-loka!

PEPANG
Kailangang kausapin natin. Nangako kang magmamatigas na. Nasa'n si Don Perico?

MANOLO
Nasa kuwarto pa ng Papa. Nagdadaldalan pa ang dalawa.

PEPANG
Pakikinggan siya nina Candida.

MANOLO
Dahil senador siya?

PEPANG
Dahil poeta.

MANOLO
No'ng araw pa, ano ka ba?

PEPANG
At dahil ninong nila, kailangang makumbinse silang umalis na sa bahay na ito.

MANOLO
(bubulong kay PEPANG.)
May buyer na nga ako.

PEPANG
Sinabi ko na sa 'yo, ako ang may buyer na.

MANOLO
Huwag kang makialam. Ako ang panganay n'yo.

PEPANG
Wala akong kumpiyansang may ulo para sa negosyo'ng mga lalaki ng pamilya.

MANOLO
Pa'no'ng mga muwebles?

PEPANG
Sa 'kin na ang aranya, ang mesang marmol sa estudyo. Sa 'yo ang muwebles sa sala, puwera lang ang piyano. Sa 'kin din ang nasa komedor. Paghatian natin ang mga kubyertos at plato.

MANOLO
Bakit pa? Kamkamin mo na ang lahat!

PEPANG
Di salamat!

MANOLO
Sa 'yo na pati ang suwelo, sa 'yo na ang hagdanan, sa 'yo'ng mga dingding! Pati bubong, sa 'yong sa 'yo!

PEPANG
Pag-aawayan ba natin ang ilang mesa at silya?

MANOLO
Ipagpaumanhin mo…Binigay mo na sa 'kin ang mga silya. Kailangan pa bang makipag-away sa 'yo para 'yon ay makuha ko?

PEPANG
Alam mong ikakasal sa isang taon ang anak kong si Mila. Kailangan niya ng muwebles.

MANOLO
Ikakasal ang aking si Roddie sa taong ito mismo. At makakamuwebles siya! Sa akin ang nasa sala, ang nasa komedor, ang nasa tatlong silid-tulugan. Pati mga libro at aparador sa estudyo, ang malaking salamin sa ibaba, ang kama matrimonyal!

PEPANG
Kay Mila ko ang kama!

MANOLO
Subukan mong maglabas dito ng kahit na ano nang wala akong permiso!

PEPANG
At bakit ko kakailanganin ang permiso mo? Sino ba'ng bayad nang bayad para sa bahay na ito sa loob ng nagdaang sampung taon?

MANOLO
Huwag mong sabihing hindi ako pumaparte sa mga pagbabayad.

PEPANG
Kung maalala mo.

MANOLO
Paminsan-minsan nakakalimutan ko.

PEPANG
Anong paminsan-minsan? Kailangan kitang tawagan nang tawagan buwan-buwan pag oras na ng bayaran. Kung binayaan kitang mag-isa, matagal nang namatay sa gutom ang Papa! Hiyang-hiya na ako sa aking asawa tuwing itatanong niya kung bakit hindi ikaw ang nag-aasikaso sa mga kapatid natin at ama! Palaging wala kang pera para sa kanila. Pero ang dami mong pera para ipangkarera at para sa 'yong mga kerida!

MANOLO
Aba, sabihin mo nga sa magaling mong asawa—

PEPANG
Tama na! Nandiyan na sila!

Papasok si PAULA na may dalang basket ng ipinamili. Kakaway si PAULA kina MANOLO at PEPANG. Kakaway rin sina MANOLO at PEPANG kay PAULA. Pupunta si PAULA sa kusina.

MANOLO
Tama na nga tayo!

PEPANG
Ayan ka na naman, Manolo!

MANOLO
Pero kung gusto nilang dumito na lang sila. . .

PEPANG
Hindi na natin kaya ang magbigay ng sustento.

MANOLO
Talaga bang hindi na?

PEPANG
Ke kaya natin o hindi, hindi 'yon ang pinag-uusapan. Naiimbiyerna na ako sa lumang bahay na ito!

MANOLO
Ako rin, aaminin ko.

PEPANG
Titira si Candida sa 'yo. Titira sa 'kin si Paula.

MANOLO
Paano ang Papa?

PEPANG
Sa 'yo kung gusto mo.

MANOLO
Sa 'yo kung gusto niya.

PEPANG
Basta't sa 'yo si Candida, sa 'kin si Paula.

MANOLO
Para magkaalila kang mag-aasikaso sa bahay mo habang nagmamadyong ka kasama ng mga amiga!

PEPANG
At nang may maasahan ang asawa mong magbantay sa bahay n'yo habang nagsososyal siya sa mga klub at komiteng kung anu-ano!

MANOLO
Kawawang Candida! Kawawang Paula!

PEPANG
Ang tagal naman nating sinustentuhan sila!

MANOLO
Kawawang Candida! Kawawang Paula!

Papasok si DON PERICO, edad 60, senador ng Pilipinas.

PERICO
Dumating na ba, Pepang, ang aking asawa?

PEPANG
Darating ba siya?

PERICO
Sunduin 'ka ko ako. Kailangan ako ng Pangulo sa Malacañan nang ala-una. May mga kagipitang kailangang pag-usapan.

PEPANG
Maupo ka muna, Don Perico. Nandiyan na si Paula. Manolo, tawagin mo

Lalabas si MANOLO para tawagin si PAULA. Maiiwan sina PEPANG at DON PERICO sa sala.

PEPANG
Kumusta ang Papa?

PERICO
Umiidlip na. Pepang, ano ba ang nangyari sa kaniya? Naku, dapat na binisita ko na noon pa.

PEPANG
Malaki ba'ng pinagbago?

PERICO
Gaya pa rin ng dati ang liksi ng isip, ang talas ng kumbersasyon. Ngunit may kulang, may kung ano'ng nawala. Malubha ba ang kaniyang aksidente?

PEPANG
Malubha rin naman. Ngunit tiningnan siya ng pinakamahusay na mga doktor. Bumubuti na ngayon. Ano ba'ng napansin mo, Don Perico?

PERICO
Parang ayaw na niyang mabuhay…

Papasok si MANOLO kasama si PAULA. Magmamano si PAULA kay DON PERICO.

PAULA
Kumusta, *Ninong*?

PERICO
Ito ba si Paula? Caramba, ang liit mo pa nang huli kitang makita!

PAULA
Ang tagal na kasing hindi kayo bumibisita.

PERICO
Kaming nasa gobyerno, wala nang oras para sa 'ming sarili.

PAULA
Binabati ko kayo sa pagkakapanalo sa huling eleksiyon.

PERICO
Matutulungan ko kayo ngayon ni Candida.

PAULA
Salamat, *Ninong*. Hindi namin kailangan ng kahit anong tulong.

PEPANG
Makinig ka muna!

PERICO
Paula, nakahanda ba kayong magsakripisyo para sa bayan?

PAULA
Anong klaseng sakripisyo?

PERICO
Ang larawan… ang huling obra ng inyong Papa… Kung ihahandog n'yo 'yon sa bayan, magagawa ng gobyerno, bilang tanda ng pasasalamat, na magpresupuwesto ng pondong kayo ang magmamaneho para sa inyo ni Candida at sa inyong Papa, habang nabubuhay siya.

Hindi makatututol ang inyong Papa dahil hindi sa kaniya kundi sa inyo ibinibigay ang perang tugon sa inyong handog. Naku, Paula, malaking biyaya para sa 'ting bayang hindi nagkaro'n ng kahit isang obra ni Don Lorenzo el Manigficong nagkalat ang mga obra sa mga museo sa Espanya at Italya.

Makikita si CANDIDANG umaakyat sa hagdan. Maririnig niya ang usapan.

MANOLO
Siyempre, Don Perico, kailangang pag-usapan 'yon nina Paula at Candida.

Nakapasok si CANDIDA sa sala nang hindi namalayan nina DON PERICO, PAULA, MANOLO at PEPANG.

CANDIDA
Wala kaming kailangang pag-usapan.

PEPANG/MANOLO
Candida!

PERICO
Ito ba si Candida? Kumusta, hija. Natatandaan mo pa ba ako?

CANDIDA
Natatandaan ko kayo. Ikinalulungkot kong nag-aaksaya kayo ng panahon. Hindi namin ipamimigay ang larawan kahit kailan.

PEPANG
Manahimik ka at makinig!

PERICO
Sandali lang, Candida. Galit ka ba sa matanda mong *Ninong*? Naiintindihan ko na pininta 'yon para sa inyo. Ngunit kung may malasakit kayo sa inyong Papa, kapakanan niya ang isipin n'yo. May sakit siya. Kailangan niya ng araw at masarap na hangin. Kailangan niya ng doktor. Kailangang magpaospital. Magastos siyempre 'yon. Kung tatanggapin n'yo ang handog ng gobyerno, magagawa n'yong ibigay sa inyong Papa ang klase ng pag-aalagang kinakailangan niya.

CANDIDA
Wala siyang sakit! Hindi n'yo lang alam...

PAULA
Walang ospital na makagagamot sa kaniya.

PEPANG/MANOLO
Ano'ng ibig mong sabihin?

MANOLO
Hindi ba ninyo alam, malapit nang magkagiyera? At ang Intramuros nga ang pinakapeligroso. Sabihin mo, Senador, sabihin mo sa kanila.

CANDIDA
(Lalapit kay Don Perico.) Sige, sabihin n'yo... talikdan ba namin ang bahay na ito tulad ng pagtalikod n'yo sa inyong poesiya? Sige na *Ninong*, pagsabihan n'yo kami.

PAULA
Susundin namin ang anumang ipayo n'yo.

CANDIDA
Pero mag-isip kayong mabuti. Nasa kamay n'yo ang buhay namin. Ngunit bakit kailangan pang mag-isip uli kayo? Tinalikuran n'yo na ang bahay na ito nang talikuran n'yo ang pagmamakata, nang talikuran n'yo ang kawawang mundo ng mga nakalipas! Pinagsisihan n'yo ba ang inyong desisyon? Naku, gagang tanong! Kailangan lang tingnan ang itsura n'yo ngayon. Mayaman na kayo, sinasanto ng marami, pinakikinggan pati ng Presidente!

CANDIDA
Bakit hindi makasagot ang bunying Senador?

PERICO
Candida, Paula, wala akong karapatang pagpayuhan kayo.

CANDIDA
Bakit wala?

PAULA
Nakinig kami noon sa inyong mga tula. Makikinig kami uli sa inyong salita.

CANDIDA
Siguro naman, mas matimbang ang salita ng Senador kaysa sa salita ng makata lamang.

PERICO
Ano'ng gusto mong sana'y ginawa ko? Nagpatuloy sumulat ng tula habang nagugutom ang pamilya ko? Ibinaon ang sarili ko tulad ng Papa ninyong nagbaon sa sarili nang buhay? Ano'ng maipakikita niyang bunga ng mga taong nakaraan? Isang larawan, isang obra maestra? Sapat na ba 'yon para ipangatwiran ang ginawa niya sa inyo ni Paula? Hindi ako ang dahilan ng galit ninyong magkapatid. Ano ba'ng nagawa ko sa inyo?

CANDIDA
Wala, Senador. Ngunit ano ang ginawa mo sa sarili mo?

PERICO
Hindi simple ang buhay
Katulad ng sining.
May puwersang humuhubog
Sa ating landasin.
Hindi tayo'ng may hawak
Sa kinabukasan.
Nagmimiron ka lamang
Sa 'yong kapalaran.
Hindi ko sinabi kailanman
"Ayoko na ngang maging makata."
Hindi ko naging ambisyon
Ang politika no'ng ako'y bata.
Mga ideal ang hanap ko.
Hindi ko inisip ang yumaman.
Hindi kailanman hinangad
Na maghawak ng kapangyarihan.
Nagmimiron ka lamang
Sa 'yong kapalaran.
Hindi simple ang buhay
Katulad ng sining.
May puwersang humuhubog
Sa ating landasin.
Hindi tayo'ng may hawak
Sa kinabukasan.
Nagmimiron ka lamang
Sa 'yong kapalaran.

CANDIDA
Patawarin mo ako, *Ninong*.

PERICO
Ako ang patawarin mo. Alalahanin mo na lang, hindi ko pinatay ang makata sa dibdib ko. Namatay siya nang kusa dahil natatadhana ang kaniyang pagkamatay.

12. INT. SALA. CONTINUATION.
Darating sina DONYA LOLENG, asawa ni DON PERICO; PATSY, dalagitang anak ni Don Perico; ELSA MONTES, isang Pilipinang socialite mula sa New York, at CHARLIE DACANAY, kaibigan ni Elsa. Lahat sila'y posturang-postura ang suot.

LOLENG
Sino'ng namatay?

Biglang mapapatingin sina MANOLO, PEPANG, DON PERICO, CANDIDA at PAULA sa kinatatayuan ni DONYA LOLENG.

LOLENG
Hola, Manolo! Hola, Pepang!

Magmamano sina MANOLO at PEPANG kay DONYA LOLENG.

LOLENG
Kung alam ko lang na nandito kayo, kanina pa sana ako. Aba, ito ba sina Candida at Paula? Kaibigang-kaibigan ko ang nasira n'yong ina. Natatandaan n'yo pa ba ako?

PAULA/CANDIDA
Opo, Donya Loleng.

Isa-isang ipakikilala ni DONYA LOLENG ang kaniyang mga kasama.

LOLENG
Ito'ng bunso kong si Patsy. At ito si Elsa Montes, la Elsa Montes! Ang nagdala ng conga sa Maynila! At ito si Charlie Dacanay na walang ginagawa sa buhay kundi sumunod-sunod sa amin. Kumusta ang inyong Papa?

MANOLO/PEPANG/CANDIDA/PAULA
Umiidlip sandali, Donya Loleng.

LOLENG
Kumusta n'yo 'ko sa kanya.

MANOLO/PEPANG/CANDIDA/PAULA
Opo, Donya Loleng.

Lalapit si DONYA LOLENG at titingin sa LARAWANG nakasabit sa dingding.

LOLENG
At ito ba ang retratong pinag-uusapan ng lahat? *(Kina PATSY, ELSA at CHARLIE.)* Halikayo, halikayo't pag-aralan n'yo!

PEPANG
Kailangang marinig namin ang iyong opinion, Miss Elsa. Laki ka sa New York. Pihadong batikan ka sa pagtingin at pagtaya sa sining ng pagpipinta!

Sandaling pag-aaralan ni ELSA ang LARAWAN.

ELSA
Aba'y… aba'y… binibigyan ako ng kay gandang inspirasyon!

LAHAT
Inspirasyon?

ELSA
Disenyong pang-evening gown ang bihis ng mamang 'yan. Ganiyan ang cut at bagsak, pati ang kulay, ganiyan. Pati ang sinepa niya, kailangang makopya rin. Sinepa nga'y pag ginto, istrombotiko ang dating.

PATSY
Pati sinturon at mga nakasabit, gagayahin lahat nang makita ang burloloy.

ELSA
Isusuot ko, 'pag ako ay nagkokongga.

PATSY
Para sa tela kaya, ano'ng dapat gamitin?

ELSA
Chiffon o satin? Pelus ba o tafetta?

LOLENG
Paisip na lang sa inyong kosturera.

Magsisimulang magsayaw ng conga si ELSA. Makikisayaw na rin sina CHARLIE, PATSY, DONYA LOLENG, at maging sina PEPANG at MANOLO, hanggang magkaroon ng "Conga Line" na iikot sa sala ng bahay. Masaya ang mga nagkokonga. Panonoorin lamang sila nina DON PERICO, CANDIDA at PAULA. Hihinto si CHARLIE sa harap ng LARAWAN.

CHARLIE
Sino ba ang dal'wang nariyan?

MANOLO
Si Eneas ang nagkakarga.

CHARLIE
At iyang matandang karga n'ya?

MANOLO
Si Angkises na kaniyang ama.

LOLENG
At sino sila?

PERICO
Ang Artista at ang kaniyang Konsiyensiya.

Biglang maririnig ang nakatutulig na paghugong ng sirena.

PAULA
Ano 'yon?

MANOLO
Practice air raid lang 'yan.

Dudungaw si CANDIDA sa bintana. Makikita niyang biglang hihinto ang mga taong nagsisilakad.

CANDIDA
Tumigil ang lahat sa daan. Mga tao't mga sasakyan.

CHARLIE
Practice blackout, practice air raid, pinapraktis pati pag-eebakweyt! Pagod na 'ko sa kapapraktis. Ba't di pa magkagiyera nang totohanan?

PATSY
Anong magkagiyera? Aba, hindi puwede! May bago na 'kong traheng isusuot sa bayle sa Bagong Taon!

Lalapit si PATSY kung saan nakaupo si DON PERICO at tatabihan ito.

PATSY
Papa, huwag mong payagang manggiyera'ng Hapon! Ano't hindi na lamang mag-party't magsayawan, **much better than digmaan! Much better than, much better than, much better than digmaan!**

LOLENG
Kailangang pumunta sa bayle ke me giyera o wala!

PATSY
Papa, bukas ba ang Manila Hotel kung sakaling—

PERICO
Bukas 'yon anuman ang mangyari. Walang giyerang iistorbo sa inyo!

LOLENG
Ano? Ano'ng ibig mong sabihin?

PERICO
Kahit pa man lumindol, hindi matitigil ang inyong pagma-madyong. Mababasag lang siguro ang isang munting tasa, mababali ang paa ng pinagma-madyongang mesa. 'Pag tapos na ang lindol, bibili ng bagong tasa, bibili ng bagong mesa, tuloy ang ligaya!

LOLENG
Pepang, ano ba'ng ginawa n'yo sa kaniya?

PERICO
Querida mia, ano'ng magagawa nila sa isang malamig na bangkay na?

PATSY
Sino'ng bangkay, Papa?

PERICO
Kadidiskubre ko lang: tatlumpung taon na palang ako'y patay na!

LOLENG
Perico!

PATSY
Papa!

LOLENG
Patsy! Ang sombrero ng iyong Papa! Kailangan lumakad na. Nagkakasakit si Perico tuwing papasok sa bahay na ito!

Kukunin ni Patsy ang sombrero ng ama.

MANOLO/PEPANG
May sakit ang Senador?

ELSA/CHARLIE
May sakit si Don Perico?

LOLENG
Inaatake ng poesiya!

MANOLO/PEPANG
Madre de Dios!

PERICO
Candida, Paula! **Manatili kayo sa tabi ng inyong Papa! Kampihan n'yo si Lorenzo, kalaban man ang buong mundo!**

LOLENG
Huwag kayong mabahala! Ilang tabletas ng aspirina, kaunting sopas, kaunting siyesta— mamaya lang, magaling na.

PERICO
Adios, mga kaibigan. Walang laban ang poesiya sa bisa ng Cafiaspirina! Contra mundum, Paula! Contra mundum, Candida!

Lalabas sina DON PERICO, DONYA LOLENG, PATSY, ELSA at CHARLIE.

13. INT. SALA. PAGPAPATULOY.
Pagkaalis ng grupo, maglalabas ng galit sina MANOLO at PEPANG.

PEPANG
Dinobol-kros tayo ng pahamak na matanda!

CANDIDA/PAULA
Narinig n'yo ang bilin sa 'min. Nangako kaming susunod sa kaniyang sasabihin. Dirito kami habang-buhay, sa piling ng Papa. Contra mundum. "Contra mundum," ang sabi kanina.

PEPANG
Espera, espera, totoo ba ang tsismis? Na nahuhumaling ang dalawang ito sa binatang nangangasera?

MANOLO
Ano 'ka mo?

PEPANG
Isang patay-gutom, walang pinag-aralan, isang bodabilista, isang pambrawn!

MANOLO
Hindi na ninyo isinaalang-alang ang pangalan ng ating angkan? Paano kung umabot ang tsismis sa Papa? Naku, alam ko na kung bakit nagkakasakit ang matanda!

CANDIDA
Wala siyang sakit, hindi n'yo lang alam.

MANOLO/PEPANG
Ano'ng hindi namin alam? Ano'ng inililihim n'yo sa amin?

CANDIDA
Gusto na niyang mamatay!

PAULA
Sinubukan niyang magpatiwakal.

MANOLO/PEPANG
Aksidente 'ka n'yo—

PAULA
Tumalon siya sa balkonahe.

MANOLO/PEPANG
Pero bakit, Dios mio?

CANDIDA
Kasi'y hinarap namin siya.

PAULA
Sinisi sa paghihirap namin.

CANDIDA
Sayang lang ang galing niya, sabi namin.

PAULA
Ba't hindi siya gumaya kay Don Perico?

CANDIDA
Sana'y nakapag-asawa kami nang mahusay at gumanda ang takbo ng aming buhay.

MANOLO
Ano'ng sabi niya?

CANDIDA
Wala.

PEPANG
Ano'ng ginawa?

PAULA
Pininta ang larawan.

CANDIDA
Binigay sa 'min nang matapos.

PEPANG
Para maibenta nang magkapera kayo. Ang larawang 'yon ang inyong pag-asa.

CANDIDA
Nang paalis kami, ang sabi—

PAULA
"Paalam, Candida, paalam, Paula."

MANOLO
Puwes, lalong mahalagang mahiwalay kayo sa kanya. Hindi siya gagaling hanggang hindi nalalayo sa inyo. Dadalhin siya sa ospital. Titira kayo sa amin ni Pepang!

CANDIDA
Tinalikuran namin siya tulad ng pagtalikod n'yo sa kanya!

PAULA
Ihihingi namin ng tawad tayong apat!

MANOLO
Basta ya! Tayo na Pepang. (*Paalis na sina MANOLO at PEPANG. Kina CANDIDA at PAULA.*) **At tanggalin n'yo'ng mga karatula sa labas! Dispatsahin ninyo ang inyong kasero.**

14.   INT. SALA. PAGPAPATULOY.
Makikita ang patuloy na pagtakbo ng buhay sa labas ng bahay ng mga Marasigan. Mga taong naglalakad, naglalako ng bilihin, may awtong dumaraan habang naririnig ang tugtog ng piano.

Sa loob ng bahay, makikitang walang ganang nagpipiyano si PAULA. Nakaharap si CANDIDA sa nakabukas na bintana, nakatingin sa kawalan. Titigil si PAULA sa pagpipiyano.

PAULA
Ano'ng nangyari sa lakad mo kanina?

CANDIDA
Pinagtawanan ako.

PAULA
Ayaw maniwalang mahusay kang manghuli ng daga?

CANDIDA
Ang trato sa akin, parang loka-loka.

PAULA
Naku, Candida.

CANDIDA
Tama si Pepang: isang pares tayong parehong inutil. Kailangan nating magkahiwalay.

PAULA
Naku, Candida!

CANDIDA
Aalagaan ko'ng mga anak ni Manolo, pangangasiwaan ko'ng kanilang kusina.

PAULA
Aasikasuhin ko'ng labada nina Pepang. Ako'ng maggugugo sa kaniyang buhok.

CANDIDA
Ipasusuot sa 'yo'ng mga luma niyang damit.

PAULA
Papuputol ng asawa ni Manolo'ng buhok mo. Talaga ba, Candidang wala na tayong magagawa?

Lalapit si CANDIDA sa LARAWAN at titingin dito.

CANDIDA
Narinig mo ang sabi ni Pepang? Ang larawang iyan ang ating pag-asa.

PAULA
Pag ating binenta? Naku, Candida!

15. INT. SALA. TAKIPSILIM.
Papasok si TONY mula sa labas.

TONY
Miss Candida, Miss Paula!

CANDIDA
Buwisit! **Ayoko siyang makita.**

TONY
Ito na'ng solusyon sa inyong mga problema!

CANDIDA/PAULA
Ano'ng ibig mong sabihin?

TONY
Maupo kayo't makinig.

CANDIDA
Bilisan mo't magluluto pa kami.

PAULA
Ano 'yon, Mister Javier?

TONY
'Yong Kanong sabi ko sa inyo, babalik na sa States. Pinauuwi na'ng lahat ng Kano para huwag abutan dito ng giyera. Puwes, 'yong may interes sa retrato, gusto niyang maiuwi ang retrato. Ang inaalok na presyo—ihanda n'yo ang tenga n'yo—ten thousand dollars, sampung libo!

CANDIDA
Sampung libong dolyares?

TONY
Dalawampung libong piso! Gustong-gusto kasi ang retrato.

PAULA
Pag-iisipan namin.

TONY
Huwag n'yo nang pag-isipan. Aalis na siya sa Biyernes.

CANDIDA
Sa makalawa?

PAULA
Ikinalulungkot namin, Mister Javier. Gaya ng sabi namin sa 'yo noon, hindi binebenta ang retrato ng Papa.

TONY
Ano? Naloloka ba kayo? Ito na'ng pagkakataong pinakahihintay n'yo!

PAULA
Ang ibig mong sabihin, ito na'ng pagkakataong pinakahihintay mo!

TONY
Ako?

PAULA
Magkano'ng inaalok sa 'yo?

TONY
Bueno, aaminin ko, malaki rin.

PAULA
Ikinalulunkot naming magiging bato ang sana'y kuwarta mo.

TONY
Miss Candida, sabihin mo kay Miss Paulang nasisiraan siya ng ulo.

CANDIDA
Kailangan ko nang magluto. Siya ang kausapin mo.

Akmang paalis si CANDIDA.

Matatakot si PAULANG maiwang mag-isa kay TONY. Magmamakaawa si PAULA kay CANDIDA.

PAULA
Huwag mo 'kong iwanang mag-isa!

CANDIDA
Bakit? Natatakot ka ba?

PAULA
Natatakot?

CANDIDA
Na masabing totoo pala ang itsinitsismis nila.

PAULA
Candida! Alam mong walang katotohanan 'yon!

CANDIDA
'Yon pala! Bakit takot kang maiwanan? Bakit palaging kailangang nakakabit ka sa aking pundiya?

PAULA
Hindi ako natatakot. Hindi kita kailangan.

CANDIDA
Hindi natin kailangan ang isa't isa.

Aalis si CANDIDA.

PAULA
(sa kaniyang sarili)
Nakapagdesisyon ka na.

Maiiwanan si PAULA na matagal ding walang-imik. May tensiyon sa pagitan nina TONY at PAULA.

TONY
Ikinalulungkot ko, Miss Paula. Alam mo siguro ang ginagawa mo. Pero beynte mil pesos. Diyos ko! Kung ako'ng magkaro'n ng gano'ng halaga, magtatayo ako ng sarili kong banda. **Magliliwaliw ako sa Hong Kong, sa Shanghai, sa Java, sa India. Pupunta 'ko sa Europa para mag-aral magpiyano. Pupunta 'ko sa Paris, sa Vienna, sa New York.**

Pakikinggang mabuti ni PAULA ang mga sinasabi ni TONY. Unti-unting tumatalab sa dalaga ang sinasabi ng binata.

PAULA
Paris... Vienna... New York...?

TONY
Sa Espanya, Italya, America del Sur... Hindi lang ako maggagaranatsa, mag-aaral ako... Sisinghot ng kultura.

PAULA
Noon ko pa pinapangarap ang maglakbay sa buong mundo.

TONY
Pangarap mo'y magiging tunay. Magagawang totoo'ng lahat.

PAULA
Ayoko nang umasa-asa. Masyado nang matanda ako.

TONY
Magsama tayo sa Europa. Lahat ng ibig, matutupad.

PAULA
Maa'ri pa kaya? Hindi ba't huli na?

Lalapitan ni TONY si PAULA.

TONY
Miss Paula, may gusto ka ba sa 'kin kahit na kaunti?

PAULA
Huwag kang magsalita nang ganiyan! Ano'ng sasabihin ng mga tao?

TONY
Ano'ng pakialam mo sa sasabihin nila?

PAULA
Kinamumuhian ko sila!

TONY
Ipakita mo nga ang pagkamuhi sa kanila! Sampilingin mo ang kanilang mga mukha! Puwede kang mag-impake ngayon mismo at pumunta kahit saan mo gusto

PAULA
Patay na'ng mga pangarap ko.

TONY
Puwedeng may bumuhay pa sa pangarap mo noon!

PAULA
Puwede pa kaya?

Hahawakan ni TONY ang balikat ni PAULA at hahaplusin ang buong braso ng dalaga. Pagkatapos, hahawakan nang mahigpit ang kamay ni PAULA.

                          TONY
Kung sakaling may dumating at masabi niya ang salitang makabubuhay uli sa pangarap mong naunsiyami?

Bagaman pipilitin ni PAULA na umiwas kay TONY, makikita sa mga mata ni PAULA na bumibigay na siya sa pang-aakit ni TONY.

                          PAULA
             Napagod na akong maghintay.

                          TONY
             Miss Paula... tingnan mo ako...

Dahan-dahang lilingunin ni PAULA si TONY na akmang hahalikan ang dalaga.

                          TONY
Huwag, Miss Paula! Kalimutan mo na siya. Talikuran mo na siya, Iwanan mo na siya!

Ngunit madaraanan ng paningin ni PAULA ang LARAWAN sa dingding. Lalayo si PAULA kay TONY.

                          PAULA
             Huwag dito, huwag dito! **Huwag sa bahay na ito!**

16. INT. SALA. HATINGGABI.
Mag-isa si CANDIDA na nakaupo sa sala. Hindi siya mapakali. Tatayo siya at maglalakad-lakad. Halatang may bumabagabag sa kaniya. Mapapatingin si CANDIDA sa dingding at mapapatigil dahil sa gulat.

17. EXT. SIMBAHAN. UMAGA.
Nagdarasal si CANDIDA sa loob ng simbahan nang makita niya si PAULA. Lalapit si CANDIDA kay PAULA. Makikita ni PAULA si CANDIDA pero iiwas ito. Hindi magpupumilit si CANDIDA. Sa kalaunan, lalabas si CANDIDA sa simbahan nang mag-isa.

18. EXT. KALYE NG INTRAMUROS. ARAW.
Habang naglalakad pauwi si CANDIDA, makikita siya ni BITOY at tatawagin.

BITOY
Candida!

CANDIDA
Ikaw pala!

BITOY
Nakita ko kayo ni Paula sa simbahan.

CANDIDA
Nauna akong umuwi. Nahilo ako sa dami ng tao.

May kotseng daraaan, hihilahin ni BITOY si CANDIDA nang bahagya para umilag dito.

BITOY
Ingat.

Tatabi ang dalawa habang patuloy na naglalakad papunta sa bahay ng mga Marasigan.

CANDIDA
Manonood ka ba ng prusisyon?

BITOY
Gaya noong araw. Natatandaan mo pa ba?

CANDIDA
Peste kang talaga. Panay ang tanong mo! "Sinong santo iyong may pakpak?" "Sino iyong may itak sa ulo?"

19. INT. RECIBIDOR. ARAW.
Papasok sina CANDIDA at BITOY sa bahay ng mga Marasigan. Bubuksan nila ang mga bintana. Dudungaw sa bintana sina CANDIDA at BITOY.

BITOY
Panay ang teng-teng ng kampana, ang tugtog ng mga banda, ang ingay ng mga tao sa kalsada.

CANDIDA
Amuyin mo ang hangin, Bitoy! Ang amoy ng piyesta, amoy ng Intramuros, siyudad ng ating mga pagmamahal!

Biglang malulungkot si CANDIDA at titingin sa kawalan.

BITOY
Bakit, Candida?

CANDIDA
Ito'ng huling Oktubre
Sa bahay na ito.
Lubusang maglalaho
Ang lahat ng ito,
Paalam nang tuluyan
Sa bawat gunita
Ng dati nating buhay
Na ano't nawala?
Kailangan daw magbago
Ang ikot ng mundo.
Nang maligtas ang buhay,
Kailangang mamatay.
Paalam nang tuluyan
Sa bawat gunita
Ng dati nating buhay
Na ano't nawala?

Magbabalik sa alaala ni CANDIDA ang kabataan nila ni PAULA. Naglalaro silang dalawa sa bahay na puno ng karangyaan at kasiyahan noong dating panahon.

CANDIDA
Maibabalik ba natin
Ang mga araw na 'yon?

BITOY
Kailangang madala sa ligtas na lugar ang inyong Papa at ang obra maestra niya.

Bubuksan ni BITOY ang pinto papuntang sala. Magugulat si BITOY na wala na ang LARAWAN sa dingding.

BITOY
Candida! Sa'n napunta'ng larawan?

Hindi makatingin si CANDIDA kay BITOY.

CANDIDA
Ewan ko.

BITOY
Pinagbili n'yo na?

CANDIDA
Hindi.

BITOY
Ninakaw?

CANDIDA
Hindi.

BITOY
Ano'ng nangyari?

CANDIDA
Ewan ko, sabi.

BITOY
Naku, Candida. Ano'ng ginawa n'yo sa Larawan?

CANDIDA
Ibinaba ni Paula. Itinabi kung saan.

BITOY
Saan niya dinala?

CANDIDA
Hindi sinabi sa 'kin.

BITOY
Pero pa'no mong nalaman—

CANDIDA
Tama na'ng tanong-tanong. Wala akong alam, Bitoy!

May kakatok sa ibaba.

CANDIDA
Wala ako kung may maghanap sa 'kin.

Biglang susulpot sina SUSAN at VIOLET.

CANDIDA
Ano'ng kailangan ninyo?

SUSAN
Gusto naming makita si Tony.

VIOLET
May sakit ba siya?

SUSAN
Dal'wang araw nang hindi sumisipot sa teatro.

VIOLET
Masisisante siya.

SUSAN
Kailangang malaman niya.

SUSAN/VIOLET
Nasa'n si Tony?

CANDIDA
Ewan ko. Dal'wang araw na ring hindi umuuwi rito.

SUSAN
Dala ba'ng mga damit niya?

CANDIDA
Nand'yan pa'ng mga damit niya. Mga kaibigan ba kayo?

SUSAN/VIOLET
Oo.

CANDIDA
Nasa maleta na'ng lahat ng damit niya.
Ibibigay ko sa 'yo, ihatid mo sa kaniya.

SUSAN/VIOLET
Hindi siya nakabayad ng renta?

CANDIDA
Paki sabing ayoko nang makita ang kaniyang pagmumukha!

Akmang lalabas si CANDIDA patungo sa kuwarto ni Tony.

Papasok sina DONYA LOLENG, PATSY, ELSA at CHARLIE nang nakabihis pansayawan. Mala-Carmen Miranda ang gayak ni ELSA, mala-Xavier Cugat ang kay CHARLIE.

LOLENG
Nasa'n si Paula?

CANDIDA
Pauwi na si Paula galing sa simbahan. Maupo muna kayo.

LOLENG
Wala palang nangyari, kung gano'n?

CANDIDA
Ano naman ang mangyayari? Ano ba ang narinig n'yo?

LOLENG
Nagtanan daw si Paula. Dinukot daw.

CANDIDA
Hindi 'yan totoo, Donya Loleng.

LOLENG
Salamat sa Diyos! *(Kina ELSA at Charlie.)* Kung gan'on, tara na.

(Kina CANDIDA at BITOY.) **Magpapabayle kami mam'yang gabi para sa mga sundalong Amerikano. Magrurumba si Charlie. Magkokongga si Elsa.**

May maririnig na katok sa ibaba.

CANDIDA
Bitoy, tingnan mo nga.

Bababa si BITOY.

LOLENG
(Kina PATSY, ELSA at CHARLIE.) Sige, dito muna tayo. Nahapo ako sa kaiikot.

20. INT. SALA. ARAW.
Papasok ang DALAWANG PULIS. May black eye ang isa sa kanila. Kakabahan si CANDIDA.

PULIS 1
Gusto naming makausap si Miss Marasigan.

CANDIDA
Ako si Miss Marasigan.

PULIS 1
Miss Marasigan, **noong makalawa, tumelepono ka sa 'min, halos tanghaling tapat. Kinidnap 'ka mo ang iyong kapatid na babae.**

PULIS 2
Hindi pa namin nahahanap ang inyong kapatid, ngunit nahuli namin ang lalaking—

CANDIDA
Ipagpaumanhin n'yo. Nagkamali ako. Hindi nawawala ang aking kapatid.

PULIS 1
Bakit hindi n'yo kami tinawagan muli? Inurong na ang inyong reklamo?

CANDIDA
Ikinalulungkot ko.

PULIS 2
Nakikita n'yo ang black eye ko? Maa'ri bang sa susunod maghinay-hinay muna bago kayo sumugod?

PULIS 1
Maa'ri bang magamit ang inyong telepono?

CANDIDA
Wala kaming telepono.

PULIS 1
(*Sa PULIS 2.*) **Tumelepono ka sa kanto. Pakawalan na 'ka mo ang lalaking hinuli ko.**

Lalabas ang PULIS 2.

Lalapit si CHARLIE kay PULIS 1.

CHARLIE
Sino'ng lalaki, tsip?

PULIS 1
'Yong kumidnap daw kay Miss Paula Marasigan.

SUSAN
Tony Javier ba ang pangalan?

PULIS 1
Tony Javier nga.

VIOLET
Saan n'yo nahanap?

PULIS 1
Sa isang bar, sinisira lahat ng muwebles!

CHARLIE
Lasing?

SUSAN
Pero pakakawalan na siya?

PULIS
Pagkatapos niyang magbayad ng multa.

SUSAN
(Kay CANDIDA.) **'Ta mo na! Masyado kayong magkapatid!**

PULIS
(Kay CANDIDA.) Miss Marasigan, ano ba talaga'ng nangyari?

CANDIDA
Wala naman talaga. **Namasyal sa kotse ang aking kapatid. Nakalimutan nga lang magpaalam sa akin.**

PULIS
Alas dose ng tanghali no'ng 'sang araw pa.

CANDIDA
At nagbalik kaagad.

Lalapit si BITOY kay PULIS 1 at makikiusap dito.

BITOY
Senyor Pulis, wala rin lang namang naghahabla, maa'ri bang kalimutan mo na?

Mapilit sina Violet at Susan.

> VIOLET
> **Aba, hindi! Kailangang bulatlatin ang lahat!**

> VIOLET/SUSAN
> **Sila'ng gumawa ng gulo! Sila ang magpena!**

> LOLENG
> Kawawang Candida, kawawang Paula!

> SUSAN
> **Si Tony ang kawawa, nabilibid nang di oras. Nawalan pa ng trabaho. Ngayon, Miss Marasigan, gusto mo pang maitago ang baho n'yong magkapatid?**

> VIOLET
> **Itsitsismis ko sa lahat!**

> SUSAN
> **Ikakalat ko ang baho n'yo!**

> VIOLET
> **Mababalitaan ng lahat ang paglalamiyerda ng iyong kapatid nang buong magdamag!**

> SUSAN
> **Ano'ng sinasabi mong nagbalik kaagad?**

Mapipilitan si CANDIDA na ilabas ang katotohan dahil sa pagdiriin nina VIOLET at SUSAN.

> CANDIDA
> **Hindi nagbalik kaagad! Nagsinungaling ako! Alas tres na ng umaga nang umuwi si Paula.**

> LOLENG
> Candida!

Tatalikod si CANDIDA pero patuloy pa rin siya sa kaniyang "pangungumpisal."

CANDIDA
Hinintay ko siya. Nakatayo ako rito. Tangka ko talagang murahin siya. Nguni't nang dumating, dahan-dahang umakyat sa hagdanan, tumindig lang diyan... hindi nagsalita... at ang itsura niya... ang itsura niya...hindi ko malilimutan!

Mapapaiyak si CANDIDA.

LOLENG
Tama na, Candida!

CANDIDA
Pa'no kong malilimutan ang itsura ng mukha niya?

LOLENG
Tama na sabi!

CANDIDA
At natalos ko noong ako ang may sala, ako ang masama, ako ang sumira sa buhay ni Paula!

Hahagulgol si CANDIDA.

LOLENG
Bitoy, ipasok mo siya sa loob.

Sasamahan ni BITOY ang umiiyak na si CANDIDA papuntang kuwarto. Biglang haharapin ni CANDIDA ang lahat at buong tapang na magpapatuloy sa kanyang kuwento.

CANDIDA
Sandali... gusto ninyong malaman kung saan siya nagpunta. Ano'ng ginawa niya...

BITOY
Tama na, Candida!

CANDIDA
Ako'ng nagkamali. Ako'ng nagkasala sa aking kapatid. Ako'ng nagtulak sa kaniyang lumakad. Ako'ng may gustong mangyari ang nangyari! Alam n'yo kung bakit? Dahil sa diyes mil dolyares! Inisip ko kasi ang aking kinabukasan. Inisip kong hindi ko na kaya'ng kahirapan. Ayoko nang makipagtawaran sa

palengke, magtago sa kubrador, maputulan ng tubig at ilaw! At para ro'n lang— Para sa beynte mil pesos, isinubo ko'ng kapatid ko! Itinulak ko sa malaking kahihiyan!

Todo hagulgol na si CANDIDA dahil sa pag-usig ng kaniyang konsensiya.

BITOY
Candida! Candida!

CANDIDA
At ngayong alam n'yo na, ipagpaumanhin n'yo, masama ang aking pakiramdam.

Magsisialisan ang PULIS, sina SUSAN, VIOLET, ELSA, CHARLIE at DONYA LOLENG. Si BITOY lamang ang maiiwanan.

Nang makaalis na ang lahat, kakausapin ni CANDIDA si BITOY.

CANDIDA
Hanapin mo siya, Bitoy. Nasa simbahan pa siguro. Sabihin mong umuwi na. Mahaharap ko na siya. **Sabihin mo sa kanyang magkasama kaming muli, magkakapit, magkakampi.**

BITOY
Sige, Candida.

Aalis si BITOY. Makikita ang harap ng bahay. Lahat ng mga bintana ay nakapinid.

21. INT. SALA. PAREHONG ARAW.
Nakaupo si CANDIDA sa silyang tumba-tumba, nakatitig sa dingding kung saan naroon dati ang LARAWAN.

Papasok si TONY na walang sombrero, hindi nasuklay ang buhok, gasak ang damit, may black eye sa mukha at parang natalo sa labanan. Galit si TONY.

TONY
Nasa'n siya? Nasa'n si Paula?

CANDIDA
Wala rito.

TONY
At nasa'n ang retrato? Saan napunta?

CANDIDA
Ewan ko.

Lalapitan ni TONY si CANDIDA at susunggaban ang mga braso nito.

TONY
Nas'an 'ka ko ang retrato?

CANDIDA
Iwanan mo ako. Lumayo ka rito.

TONY
Iiwanan kita, huwag kang mag-alala. Lalayo ako pero hindi bago ko makuha ang ritrato!

CANDIDA
Hindi ko 'yon kailanman ibibigay sa 'yo!

TONY
Nagbago ka ng tono! Handa kang magbenta noon.

CANDIDA
Tama ka.

TONY
Handa kang ipagbili pati ang iyong kapatid!

CANDIDA
Tama ka.

TONY
Payag kang gawin ko ang kahit ano pumayag lamang siyang ipagbili'ng retrato.

CANDIDA
At pumayag ba?

TONY
Aba, siyempre!

CANDIDA
Ang alam ko, mag-isa siyang umuwi. Nakawala siya sa 'yo.

Darating si PAULA nang di namalayan nina CANDIDA at TONY. Makikita niya sina CANDIDA at TONY at maririnig ang kanilang usapan.

TONY
Pero hindi na siya puwedeng umatras. Hawak ko na kayong dalawa. At huwag kayong matakot, hindi ko kayo dadayain. Ibibigay ko ang beynte mil ninyo, makuha ko lang ang aking porsiyento.

CANDIDA
Ang iyong porsiyento!

TONY
Ano pa nga?

Malungkot na lalapit si PAULA kina TONY at CANDIDA.

PAULA
Ikinalulungkot ko, Tony, huwag mo nang asahan ang porsiyento mo.

TONY
Paula! Bakit mo 'ko tinakbuhan?

PAULA
Dahil may kailangan akong gawin… bagay na napakahalaga. Hindi mo 'ko mapapatawad sa ginawa ko sa iyo.

TONY
Naku, Paula, huwag mo 'kong kamuhian. Aaminin kong masama ang intensiyon ko noon. Galit kasi ako… intindihin mo ako. Gusto kong maiayos ang lahat sa atin.

PAULA
Gano'n ba?

TONY
Maniwala ka sa 'kin.

PAULA
Naniniwala ako sa 'yo.

Yayakapin ni TONY si PAULA. Pero walang bisa ang yakap ni TONY kay PAULA.

TONY
Nasa'n ang retrato, kung gan'on? 'Yon ang ating kaligtasan. Magbabagong-buhay tayo. Magiging disente ako. Magiging malaya ka.

PAULA
Malaya! *(Tatawa.)*

TONY
Huwag kang tumawa.

PAULA
Iniibig mo ba ako? Magsabi ka ng totoo.

Matitigilan si TONY, parang hindi alam kung ano ang isasagot. Haharapin ni TONY si PAULA.

TONY
Matututuhan kitang ibigin. Kailangan lang nating makalayo. Nasa'n ang retrato? Naghihintay ang Amerikano.

PAULA
Wala na ang retrato.

TONY
Ano'ng ginawa mo?

PAULA
Sinira-sira ko.

TONY
Ano?! Ano'ng ginawa mo?

Parang hindi narinig ni PAULA ang tanong ni TONY. Kaysa kausapin ni PAULA si TONY, kinausap nito si CANDIDA.

PAULA
Sinira ko, Candida, ang ating retrato. Ginutay-gutay ko at sinunog-sunog. Nagagalit ka ba?

CANDIDA
Hindi.

Mapapahagulgol si TONY.

PAULA
Umiiyak ka ba?

CANDIDA
Si Tony Javier yata.

PAULA
Nahanap na niya'ng kaniyang luha. Natuto na siyang umiyak.

TONY
Bakit mo 'yon ginawa?

PAULA
Ayokong tumakas na gaya mo.

TONY
Ikinait mo sa akin ang nag-iisang pag-asa para mapabuti ako. Paano mo nagawa 'yon? Bakit mo ako niloko? Paliligayahin sana kita. Palalayain kita.

PAULA
Malaya na ako ngayon.
Malaya na akong muli.
Sinunog ko na'ng diyaskeng ritrato,
Saka ako umuwi.

Aalis si TONY nang pasuray-suray sa sama-ng-loob.

PAULA
Wala na ang mga multo.
Wala na ang mga pangamba.
Ang sumiping sa aking maligno,
Yumayakap na sa iba.
Matayog na ako ngayon.
Sa ulap na akong muli.
Ang pugad kong nasa panginorin,
Ngayo'y maa'ri uling liparin!
Ngayo'y maa'ri uling liparin!

PAULA
(Tutukuyin si TONY.) Ang biktima ng ating pag-aalay!

CANDIDA
Ng ating pag-aalay?

PAULA
Ako lang ang humawak sa kutsilyo. Ikaw ang naghanda ng panggatong sa altar. Ikaw ang nagparikit ng apoy.

CANDIDA
Paula, patawarin mo ako.

PAULA
Hindi mo ba pinagsisisihan—

CANDIDA
Ang tungkol sa retrato?

PAULA
Ano'ng ginawa mo, kung ikaw?

CANDIDA
'Yon mismong ginawa mo.

PAULA
Pero, Candida, alam mo ba'ng haharapin natin?

CANDIDA
Araw-gabing walang kuryente, naghahabol na kubrador, tsismis na hindi magkamayaw.

Bubuksan nina PAULA at CANDIDA ang mga bintana.

PAULA
Sasabihin nilang sira talaga'ng ating ulo. Kuruin mo, diyes mil dolyares ang ating pinakawalan.

PAULA/CANDIDA
Sasabihin nilang sampares tayong lokaret. Sasabihin nilang peligroso tayo.

Dudungaw sina PAULA at CANDIDA sa bintana. Ngayon, may ngiti sa kanilang mga labi at taas-noo silang nakatingin sa labas.

CANDIDA
Sabihin nila'ng gusto nilang sabihin.

PAULA
Manghuhuli lang tayo ng daga.

CANDIDA
At mag-uusap sa salita ng mga taga-Babilonya.

PAULA
Hindi ka ba natatakot—

CANDIDA
Sa mundo ng Babilonya?

PAULA
Na pa'lisin, parang daga?

CANDIDA
Patawarin ako ng Diyos dahil hinangad kong maging kasingkaraniwan ng iba.

PAULA
Tumindig, kung gano'n. Malaya tayong muli, ikaw, ako at ang Papa! Magmula nang ihandog sa atin ang retrato, ito ang hakbang na nagpapatunay na buhay pa sa atin ang ating pananalig, na hindi pa rin natin itinatatwa.

CANDIDA/PAULA
(sabay)
...ang pagiging mga anak ni Lorenzo el magnifico!

22. INT. SALA. GABI.
Gabi ng piyesta ng La Naval. Marami nang tao sa labas ng bahay. Naghahanda sina CANDIDA at PAULA para sa piyesta at sa prusisyon na gaganapin sa gabing iyon. Inilabas ang pinakamagandang mga plato, baso at kubiyertos. May masaganang handa sa mesa. Bubuksan nina CANDIDA at PAULA ang lahat ng ilaw sa sala.

CANDIDA
(off-screen)
Buksan natin lahat ng ilaw!

Nakatayo si PAULA sa may bintana. Makikita si BITOY sa gitna ng mga taong nagtitipon upang ilawan ang prusisyon ng La Naval. Kakawayan niya ito.

Papasok si BITOY sa bahay, kasunod sina DON ALVARO at DONYA UPENG, mga nasa edad 60. Nakabihis ng amerikana sina DON ALVARO at BITOY. Nakabihis ng terno si DONYA UPENG.

BITOY
Nandito ka na!

ALVARO/UPENG
At nandito kami!

CANDIDA/PAULA
Don Alvaro, Donya Upeng!

UPENG
Kumusta'ng Papa n'yo?

CANDIDA/PAULA
Magaling na, magaling na!

PAULA
Candida, brandi para kay Don Alvaro! Brandi para kay Donya Upeng! Brandi para kay Bitoy.

ALVARO/UPENG
Ito ba si Bitoy Camacho?

BITOY
Ito nga. Narito para ipagdiwang ang pista ng La Naval.

ALVARO
Mabuti nga't sumasali ka sa tradisyong baka mawala na.

CANDIDA
Mawala na?

ALVARO
Pag nagkagiyera!

UPENG
Kaya't naririto kami upang batiin ang Birhen mula sa mga balkonahe n'yo gaya no'ng araw. Naku, Candida at Paula, baka sa huling pagkakataon na!

Darating sina DON MIGUEL at DONYA IRENE, mga kasing-edad din nina DON ALVARO at DONYA UPENG. Magarbo rin ang kanilang kasuotan.

DON MIGUEL
Baka nga! Baka nga!

Bubulong si DONYA IRENE kay DON MIGUEL, pagagalitan.

DONYA IRENE
Saan ka na naman galing matandang kalabaw ka?

PAULA
Halikayo rito.

DONYA IRENE
Bakit, hija? May problema?

CANDIDA/PAULA
Kailangan namin kayo!

DON ALVARO
Kaya kami naririto.

DONYA UPENG
At narito pa ang ibang tutulong sa inyo.

CANDIDA/PAULA
Natulungan n'yo na kami sa inyong pagparito.

May katok na maririnig. Dumating na si DON ARISTEO.

ALVARO/MIGUEL/UPENG/IRENE
Aristeo!

ARISTEO
Caramba! Nandito tayong lahat!

CANDIDA
Tuloy sa aming bahay, magiting na sundalo!

ARISTEO
Hinila ko'ng katawan ko para magpugay sa La Naval.

UPENG
Sandali, Aristeo! Namimiligro raw ang buhay nina Candida at Paula.

ARISTEO
Namimiligro? Dapat palang dinala ko ang aking armas!

Maghahalakhakan ang lahat.

PAULA
Brandi, Candida, para sa 'ting tagapagtanggol.

ARISTEO
(Aabutin ang kamay ni PAULA.) **Bakit, hija? Ang lamig ng kamay mo. Ano'ng peligro'ng lumalapit sa inyo?**

PAULA
Pinaaalis kami sa bahay na ito. Kailangan namin maging matatag sa pananatili rito.

UPENG
Sasamahan namin kayo. Kailangang naririto kayo—

ALVARO
Para huwag mawala—

IRENE
Para huwag mamatay—

ALVARO
Ang sagisag na nagsasabing—

MIGUEL/IRENE
Magpapatuloy ang buhay!

Aabutan ni CANDIDA ng mga kopita sina DON MIGUEL, DONYA IRENE, DON ARISTEO, CANDIDA at PAULA.

CANDIDA
Tama kayo. Mag-inuman tayo.

PAULA
Sa Birhen ng La Naval!

LAHAT
Viva La Virgen! Viva La Virgen! Viva La Virgen!

Darating sina MANOLO at PEPANG na magmumukhang pikang-pika.

PAULA
Pepang! Manolo!

CANDIDA
Nagpunta kayo rito para umilaw sa La Naval?

MANOLO
Alam n'yo'ng sadya namin.

PAULA
Handa na ba kayong umamin?

PEPANG
"Umamin?"

PAULA
Umamin na kayo, Pepang, Manolo! Gagaan ang loob n'yo. Makakalaya kayo!

MANOLO
Tingnan n'yo'ng sarili n'yo! Gumagawa kayo ng eskandalo!

PEPANG
Nakakahiya, nakakahiya!

Mapapansin ng matatanda na may alitan ang magkakapatid na Marasigan. Lalapit sila kung saan naroon sina MANOLO, PEPANG, CANDIDA at PAULA.

MANOLO
Kunin ninyong mga damit n'yo. Sasama kayo sa amin ngayon din.

PEPANG
Pa'lisin n'yo sila.

ARISTEO
Caramba! Ito ba si Manolito? Hindi kita halos nakilala.

Mapipilitang magmano si MANOLO kay DON ARISTEO.

ARISTEO
Ang laki mo na, bata ka!

MANOLO
Don Aristeo, ikinalulungkot ko, kailangan n'yo nang magsilakad.
May pag-uusapan kaming magkakapatid.

UPENG
At ito ba si Pepita?

ALVARO
Pepita, ang ganda mo no'ng bata ka!

IRENE
Naku, Pepita, hindi ko malilimutan ang iyong pagbigkas ng "Ultimo Adios" ni Don Jose no'ng siyete anyos ka pa lang.

MIGUEL
Ako'ng nagturo sa kaniya.

UPENG
Ako'ng nagturo sa 'yong magsayaw, Manolo, no'ng kinse anyos ka sa salas na ito mismo.

MIGUEL
Ang laki siguro ng amor nina Pepang at Manolo sa bahay ng kanilang kabataan!

PAULA
Naku, hindi nga!

MIGUEL
Hindi ito mahal sa kanila?

PAULA
Gusto nilang ipagbili.

ALVARO/UPENG/MIGUEL/IRENE/ARISTEO
Ipagbili?

UPENG
Que horror!

IRENE
Ngunit bakit?

PAULA
'Yon ang ayaw nilang aminin.

ARISTEO
Baka masyado nang magastos?

PAULA
Hindi pera ang problema.

CANDIDA
Bagaman 'yon ang sabi nila.

PAULA
Nagtatapon sila ng pera sa madyong, sa karera.

CANDIDA/PAULA
Ikinakaila nila ang totoo kahit sa kanilang sarili.

PEPANG
Candida! Paula!

CANDIDA/PAULA
Sinusumbatan sila ng bahay na ito. Nasisira'ng kanilang pagsasaya—

CANDIDA
Habang nakikipagtsismisan—

PAULA
Habang nakikipagsugal—

CANDIDA
Habang nasa karerahan o jai alai—

PAULA
O habang hindi sila makatulog—

CANDIDA/PAULA
Cataplum! Bumabagsak ang anino ng bahay ni Lorenzo el magnifico!

CANDIDA
Nanginginig sila—

PAULA
Lumalamig ang dugo!

ALVARO/UPENG/MIGUEL/IRENE/ARISTEO
Ang ibig n'yong sabihin, takot sila sa bahay na ito?

CANDIDA
Takot sila!

ALVARO/UPENG/MIGUEL/IRENE/ARISTEO
Ngunit bakit?

PAULA
Dahil ito ang kanilang kunsiyensiya! Oo, Manolo, Oo Pepang. Ito ang inyong konsiyensiya kaya muhing-muhi kayo. Gusto n'yong gibain! Gusto n'yong lansagin nang hindi kayo usigin!

MANOLO/PEPANG
Manahimik kayo!

Dudungaw si BITOY sa labas ng bintana. Makikita niya na paparating na ang imahen ng Birhen ng La Naval.

BITOY
Manahimik na! Dumarating ang Birhen!

IRENE
Ang Birhen ang magliligtas sa atin!

Akmang kakaladkarin ni MANOLO sina CANDIDA at PAULA.

MANOLO
Candida, Paula! Halina kayo! Ubos na ang pasensiya ko!

MIGUEL
Naku, Manolo, wala nang makaaalis. Sarado na'ng daanan. Nandito na ang La Naval!

MANOLO
Lalayas sila rito kung kailangan ko silang itulak sa hagdanan!

Haharangin ni DON ARISTEO si MANOLO.

ARISTEO
Kung gayo'y kailangang itulak pati ako sa hagdan!

Paliligiran ng matatanda si MANOLO.

ALVARO
At ako!

MIGUEL
At ako!

UPENG/IRENE
At kami!

CANDIDA
At ang Papa, Manolo? Magagawa mo bang itulak din siya sa hagdanan?

PEPANG
Kinamumuhian kayo ng Papa!

PAULA
Nasa panig namin ang Papa!

Palabas ng kuwarto si DON LORENZO.

BITOY
At nandito na siya!

CANDIDA/PAULA
Ang Papa!

PEPANG
Manolo, ang Papa!

Haharap ang LAHAT sa pintuan ng kuwartong pinanggagalingan ni DON LORENZO. Bagaman mukhang maysakit, may ngiti sa kaniyang mga labi. Yayakapin ni DON LORENZO sina PAULA at CANDIDA.

Cut to:

23.   EXT. IKALAWANG DIGMAANG PANDAIGDIG. IBA-IBANG ARAW.
Mga piling eksena ng Ikalawang Digmaang Pandaigdig. Mga eksena ng paglusob ng mga Hapon sa Maynila, pagsira ng mga Amerikano sa lungsod ng Maynila, paglikas ng mga tao, pagbomba sa Maynila at Intramuros at ibang mga eksena noong Ikalawang Digmaang Pandaigdig.

Fade to Black.

24.   EXT. INTRAMUROS. GABI.
Fade in:

Prusisyon para sa Birhen ng La Naval. Punong-puno ang kalye ng Intramuros ng mga deboto ng Mahal na Birhen. Mula sa iba't ibang antas ng lipunan ang mga deboto: mga pari, mga sundalo, mga socialite na nakaterno, mga bata at tinedyer, mga karaniwang mayayamang nakasuot ng kanilang pinakamaaayos na damit. May hawak silang mga kandila at rosaryo, nagdarasal nang taimtim habang dumadaan ang prusisyon. Tila hindi batid ang nagbabadyang giyera.

Dissolve to:

25. INT. BAHAY NG MGA MARASIGAN. GABI.
Lalapit sa bintana ang lahat ng mga tao sa bahay ng gabing iyon. Dudungaw sila para pagmasdan ang pagdaan ng imahen ng Birhen ng La Naval. Ang imahen ng Birhen ang mananatili hanggang sa katapusan ng pelikula.

MATANDANG BITOY
(voice-over)

Kinailangan ng giyerang mundial para masugpo ang diwa ng tatlong nanirahan doon. Paalam, Candida! Paalam, Paula! Lamunin man ng gubat ang inyong 'storya, naririto kami, nagdiriwang ngayon sa aming pagkanta.

KORO

Paalam, Candida!
Paalam, Paula!
Lamunin man ng gubat
Ang inyong istorya,
Naririto kami't
'Pinagdiriwang kayo
Sa 'ming pagkanta!

POSTSCRIPT
"To remember and to sing: that is my vocation."
—Nick Joaquin

LEARNING GUIDE FOR *ANG LARAWAN, THE MOVIE*
by Chelo Banal Formoso

Subjects — *English/Filipino drama/musical*
Social-emotional learning — *Family in crisis, friendship*
Moral-ethical emphasis — *Filial devotion, caring, responsibility*

Description: This movie version of the stage musical adaptation of Nick Joaquin's well-loved play is about two unmarried sisters going through hard times as they take care of their ailing father in the days before World War II.

Benefits of the Movie: *Ang Larawan* will introduce students to a Manila facing the threat of war, the extinction of cherished traditions and the growing social evils of the time. It will acquaint students with a musical telling of a story.

Helpful Background: The film is not simply an audio-visual recording of the musical adaptation as it is being acted and sung on a theater stage. It is a genuine movie, shot on location, with actors interacting in front of film cameras instead of a live audience.

The story's setting is Manila in October 1941. Although WWII did not break in the Pacific until after Pearl Harbor was bombed in December 1941, war had been going on in Europe since 1939.

Candida and Paula Marasigan live in a big *bahay na bato* in the elite area of Intramuros, a sign of family wealth. Now struggling financially, the sisters are resisting the sale of both the house and their father's highly valued self-portrait. Their piano player boarder Tony knows a foreigner willing to buy the painting for $10,000. To give students an idea how big an amount that was in 1941, the average price of a car in the United States at the time was $800 to $1,000.

Discussion Questions:
1. The movie opens with footage of city scenes a few months before war breaks out. What are the ways in which the impending war affects the story? *Suggested response: The residents are subjected to air raid drills. There is a general feeling of unease. The American buyer for the painting is jittery and wants to leave soon for America.*

2. Why is the artist (Don Lorenzo) a major character even if he only appears at the very end of the film? *Suggested response: Don Lorenzo is a significant Filipino artist and the equal of Juan Luna no less. His latest work, a self-portrait, has received rave reviews, prompting the visits of family friends Bitoy, a reporter interested in taking photos of the painting, and Don Perico, a senator who offers Candida and Paula some funds if they donate the painting to the government. In short, Don Lorenzo is the creator of the conflict in the story.*

3. Why are the sisters clinging to the painting when they can use the money from its sale to keep their home and stay together? Explain the significance of the painting to the story as a whole. *Suggested response: Don Lorenzo created the painting as a gift to Candida and Paula. Considered a masterpiece, it is the sisters' insurance against poverty. As the story unfolds, it is revealed that the sisters had confronted their father and blamed him for their being unmarried, unemployed and dependent on their siblings Manolo and Pepang for their upkeep. The old man tried to kill himself after completing the painting. The sisters are holding on to the painting out of a mix of guilt and love.*

4. What trick does Tony Javier use to try and get his hands on the painting that he believes can help him escape his present sordid life? *Suggested response: He manipulates Paula. He seduces Paula, promises her a life together traveling the world. Because he lives in the Marasigan house, he has all the opportunity to steal the painting but instead he goes through the trouble of charming the younger sister. And when he finds out that Paula has burned the painting even after their intimate time together, he does not get violently angry although he stands to lose a huge amount of money. He ends up crying. It turns out Tony is not so evil after all.*

5. Candida leaves Paula alone with Tony at a very crucial time. What is her motivation for doing so? *Suggested response: Candida knows Tony has sensed that Paula has feelings for him. She leaves to give Tony a chance to seduce her sister. She gives Paula the leeway to make a choice about what to do with her life—and the painting. It is not a selfless act though, as she admits later.*

6. Between the sisters, whose actions lead to the resolution of the conflict in the film? Describe the actions and their effects on the resolution. *Suggested response: It is Paula who solves the sisters' dilemma about the painting. By getting rid of the painting, she ends the inner and external conflicts that she and Candida have had to face since its creation, stopping the public attention, getting rid of Tony Javier and soothing the hurt that has caused their father to be reclusive.*

7. Who are the characters that are transformed or changed over the course of the story? Describe how the transformation comes about. *Suggested response: Candida and Paula are both transformed. They have been put to a test by their father and they have passed it. They prove that their love for each other and their father is stronger than the lure of money. Paula emerges the stronger woman who can make life-and-death decisions. Candida reveals a softer side in accepting the return of her sister and the loss of the painting. Don Lorenzo himself ceases to be a recluse when he rejoins his family and friends on the night of the procession. Another character who has an epiphany is Don Perico. When Candida and Paula chide him for giving up poetry for politics, he becomes defensive. But by the time he says goodbye to the sisters, he seems to have recovered his heart for art.*

8. Analyze the use of music in the movie. How would you have used music to enhance this story? *Suggested activity: Ask the class to put a modern spin to this classic story. Encourage the students to tweak the songs into rap.*

9. What is the most powerful scene in the movie? Why? *Suggested response: Some learners will say it is the scene where all the wrong people show up at the Marasigan house and Candida admits that Paula has run away with Tony. Others will say it is the confrontation scene between Paula and Tony after the destruction of the painting. But it can also be the scene where the sisters, thinking the power company has cut off their electricity, are too ashamed to go near the windows because the neighbors may be talking about them and their unpaid light bill, only to find out that an air raid drill is going on.*

10. What are the possible reactions of women today to the characters of Candida and Paula? What advice might they give the sisters to ensure a better future for themselves instead of going off separately to live with Manolo or Pepang? *Suggested response: Modern day women may feel sorry for Candida and Paula because both are of a generation brought up to stay home and take care of family. Candida can cook and catch rats. Paula can do the laundry and play the piano. Other than those, they have no employable skills. Any advice should take into account the culture of the time.*

ACKNOWLEDGMENTS

Culturtain Musicat Productions wishes to thank the following:

First Pacific Leadership Academy — Mr. Roy Evalle
National Commission on Culture and Arts through the Negros Foundation
Quezon City Government and the Quezon City Film
    Development Commission
Mayor Herbert Bautista
Vice Mayor Joy Belmonte
Intramuros Administration — Atty. Marco Sardillo III & Atty. Guiller Asido
Senator Emmanuel Pacquiao and Mrs. Jinkee Pacquiao
Phinma Universities — Chito Salazar
Carlos M. Santamaria
Bench
Resorts World Philippine Cultural Heritage Foundation
Ricardo Mabanta
Mikee & Dodot Jaworski
Myrna & David Demauro
Jon & Loida Abraham
Heaven's Best
Regal Entertainment
Korina Sanchez Roxas
The Music School of Ryan Cayabyab
Cinerent
Hit Productions
Ernesto & Ria Villavicencio
Philippe Chambon
ABS-CBN Philharmonic Orchestra — Mickey Muñoz & Eric Bolante
Star Cinema
ABS-CBN
    who gave generous support for *Ang Larawan, The Movie*

Anvil Publishing
National Bookstore
The Book Team composed of art director Benjor Catindig, artist Micah Castañeda & coordinator Gay Ace Domingo
Boy Yñiguez, Girlie Rodis, Jojit Lorenzo, Pong Ignacio, Toma Cayabyab, Bill Barrinuevo for the *Ang Larawan, The Movie* photos